OLD FRIENDS, NEW FRIENDS

Eighteen-year-old Debbie Hargreaves is heading to college in Leeds, where she'll be sharing digs with three girls. Debbie soon becomes firm friends with shy Lisa, outspoken Karen and self-assured Fran. Over the coming months, the four flatmates will share tears and laughter and the drama of a new romance. At the same time, Debbie's birth mother, Fiona Norwood, is struggling to cope with four young children and her duties as a rector's wife. The arrival of a new childminder should be an answer to her prayers, but Glenda's open flirting with Fiona's husband soon gets tongues wagging. Is Fiona's marriage really under threat?

OLD FRIENDS, NEW FRIENDS

OLD FRIENDS, NEW FRIENDS

by

Margaret Thornton

Magna Large Print Books
Long Preston, North Yorkshire,
BD23 4ND, England.

British Library Cataloguing in Publication Data.

Thornton, Margaret
    Old friends, new friends.

    A catalogue record of this book is
    available from the British Library

    ISBN   978-0-7505-4074-2

First published in Great Britain in 2014 by
Severn House Publishers Ltd.

Copyright © 2014 by Margaret Thornton

Cover illustration © Jacqueline Moore by arrangement with
Arcangel Images

The moral right of the author has been asserted

Published in Large Print 2015 by arrangement with
Severn House Publishers Ltd.

Magna Large Print is an imprint of Library Magna Books Ltd.

Printed and bound in Great Britain by
T.J. (International) Ltd., Cornwall, PL28 8RW

One

Debbie looked anxiously along the track as she had been doing for the last ten minutes, to see if the train was on its way. Mum had insisted on getting to the station in good time, as she always did when they were going anywhere. But Debbie hated these goodbye scenes – she knew her mother did, too – and now she couldn't wait to start out on her journey.

'Now, you're sure you've got everything?' asked her mother, Vera, for the umpteenth time.

'You know I have, Mum,' said Debbie, smiling and shaking her head. 'You put the sandwiches in my bag yourself, and I've got a magazine to read ... and a clean hanky, too,' she added with a laugh. That was something her mum had always checked, ever since she was a little girl going to the Infant school. 'Well, a packet of tissues, actually.'

'And make sure you've got your ticket safe. You'll need it for each leg of the journey, so look after it. It's a nuisance having to change at both Newcastle and Darlington, but there it is. It's just one of those things.'

'Don't worry about me, Mum. I've done this journey often enough, haven't I? I'm quite used to it by now.'

'Yes, of course you are, pet. But it seems different this time, somehow. You won't be coming back ... well, not for a while, I mean. It'll be too

9

far to come home for the weekend, won't it?'

'Probably; it depends on whether there are lectures on Saturday morning. But there's the half-term break; that'll be at the beginning of November. And Christmas, of course. The weeks will soon pass, Mum, you'll see.'

'Yes, love; I'm sure they will,' said her mother, not sounding sure at all. 'Anyway, you'll be able to visit Fiona and Simon some weekends, won't you? That'll be nice for you.'

'Yes, I will,' agreed Debbie. 'But I won't go every weekend. Mum ... that wasn't the reason I chose to go to college in Yorkshire, you know, because of Fiona. It sounds a jolly good course at Stanborough; I'd heard glowing reports of it. I don't want you to think–'

'Debbie, I don't think anything like that,' said Vera. 'We got over that little problem ages ago, didn't we? And I'm glad we all get on so well together. It was very good of Simon to come and collect your luggage, wasn't it? I was worried about you having to travel with those heavy suit-cases. No; I don't mind about you being nearer to Fiona. Anyway, you'll be looking forward to seeing your little god-daughter again, won't you?'

'Yes, so I am; little Michelle. She's a real bobby-dazzler, Mum, as Dad would say! And the other three as well.'

'Fiona's got her hands full though now, hasn't she, with four children?' commented Vera. 'I'm sure I don't know how she copes.'

'She seems to manage,' said Debbie. 'Although she did say that Matthew was into everything, now that he's walking, and Mark copies him, of

10

course... Oh, here's the train, at last.' She put her arms round her mother, and Vera hugged her tightly then kissed her cheek as the train pulled up at the platform.

'Bye, Mum...' Debbie opened the door and climbed the steps. 'I'll write, and I'll phone. Don't worry about me. I'll be OK.'

'Yes, I'm sure you will, pet.' Vera blinked and dashed away a tear. 'Take care of yourself and enjoy your course. I know you've been looking forward to it.'

Debbie nodded. 'And you look after yourself, Mum ... and Dad.'

The train didn't halt long at the little station at Whitesands Bay. In a moment it was off again, and Debbie waved from the window until her mother was out of sight. She sat down in a seat by the window. It was a train that had groups of four seats around small tables. There was no one else sitting there at the moment, and Debbie was glad to be on her own for a while to collect her thoughts.

She had done this same journey – from Whitesands Bay in Northumberland, where she lived, to Northallerton, the nearest railway station to Aberthwaite in the North Yorkshire Dales – several times over the past two years. But, as her mother said, it was different this time as she would not be returning home again for quite some time. Several weeks at least, the longest time she had ever been away.

She was on her way, eventually, to Leeds, where she would be living in 'digs' with three more students. She would travel the short distance each

11

day to Stanborough College, which was situated in the Vale of York, midway between York and the city of Leeds. She was to embark on a course in Horticulture and Garden Design which would lead in time, she hoped, to a career as a landscape gardener.

The term was due to start on the following Tuesday, the 8th of September, 1970. This would give the students time to settle into their accommodation over the weekend before commencing their various courses. Debbie, though, would be spending the weekend at the home of the Reverend Simon Norwood and his wife, Fiona, at the rectory in Aberthwaite, where Simon was the rector of St Peter's Church. Debbie Hargreaves had known from being a tiny girl that she was an adopted child. Her mother, Vera, had told her many times that she was a special little girl because she had been chosen. She had grown up with the knowledge without ever worrying too much about it.

That was until she was in her early teens, when she had started to wonder about the person who had given birth to her. She had been born in the May of 1952, and she discovered that her birth had taken place in Burnside House, a home for unmarried mothers in the Northumbrian countryside, not far from where she lived with her parents, Vera and Stanley, in the pleasant coastal resort of Whitesands Bay.

It was more usual for the adopted children to be placed a good distance away, but Debbie's adoption was different. And so, as she grew up, becoming more and more inquisitive as time went on, she found out enough to go in search of her birth mother. This, of course, was unknown to Vera and Stanley who were, understandably, upset and hurt at first when they discovered what Debbie had done.

Everything, however, had ended happily. Debbie had turned up on the doorstep of the rectory almost exactly two years ago, She had found out that her mother was a young woman called Fiona who was now married to the rector of St Peter's Church in Aberthwaite. Simon and Fiona had lost no time in letting Debbie's parents know of her whereabouts, and she was speedily forgiven by her understanding mum and dad. Debbie had assured them that she loved them, and had had no thoughts in her mind about leaving home. It was just that her curiosity had got the better of her. Debbie reflected now on the time she had spent with Fiona and Simon over the past two years. The scenery from the train window – of factory chimneys and slag heaps in the industrial heartland of Northumberland and Durham, then the pleasant green hills and vales of North Yorkshire – had become more familiar to her with each journey. Just as her relationship with Fiona and Simon had strengthened and become more relaxed as she had got to know them better.

Fiona had always seemed more like a friend or an older sister than a mother. She had been only seventeen years old when she had given birth to the baby that she had been forced to give up for adoption. She had insisted straightaway that Debbie should call her by her Christian name, and this came quite naturally now. Debbie had always thought of Vera as 'Mum', even though she had been curious to find out about the circumstances of her birth.

When Debbie had first met her, Fiona had been six months pregnant. They already had a little girl, Stella, who was then almost two. Then, halfway through her pregnancy, Fiona had been told that she was expecting twins. She and Simon were delighted at the news, but had not been prepared for the eventual outcome. At the beginning of November, 1968, she had given birth, a month early, to triplets!

It had so happened that Debbie had been spending that weekend with them in Aberthwaite. It had not been an easy birth, followed by an anxious time for both Fiona and the three tiny babies, two boys and a girl. All was well, however. Fiona soon recovered from the trauma of the birth, and the babies thrived, putting on weight and developing normally.

At the baptism in the spring of the following year Debbie had been asked to act as godmother to the babies, but most especially to the little girl whom they called Michelle. She had been delighted and very touched that Fiona and Simon had included her in this way, drawing her into their lovely family, and not making any secret to their friends and members of the congregation about who she was. She had grown very fond of little Michelle over the past two years; she had already formed quite a bond with Stella, who was now nearly four years old.

Debbie had been in the sixth form at her school, Kelder Bank, at that time. And now she was on her way to Stanborough College to learn about all the different aspects of gardening in greater depth, the subject that had been her consuming interest ever since she was a little girl.

'Did our Debbie get off alright then?' asked Stanley, the moment he came through the door.

'Yes, of course she did,' said his wife. 'I tried to keep cheerful while I was with her, but I must admit I shed a few tears when I got back home. Oh dear! We'll miss her, won't we, Stanley? The house seems different already; sort of ... deserted, now she's gone.'

'She was out quite a lot though, here, there and everywhere, especially these last two years, so happen it won't seem all that bad, once we've got used to it. I know what you mean, though. We'll miss her, even though she gave us a few headaches. Eeh! She was a little madam at times, wasn't she?'

'She was that!' Vera nodded. 'She was better, though, after she met Fiona. It was as though she had to find out, then she settled down. It could have been difficult, Stanley, but Fiona's a lovely lass, and they've been so kind to us, haven't they, Fiona and Simon? Do you know, Debbie mentioned it just before the train came in. She said it wasn't because of Fiona that she had chosen to go to college in Yorkshire; she wanted me to be sure about that. It's because she thought it would be a good course. I think she wanted to reassure me, you see, just in case I was – well – jealous, I suppose... Anyway, sit yerself down, and I'll dish out our tea.'

It was, strictly speaking, a dinner; a hot meal such as Vera prepared every evening for when Stanley came home from work. Old habits died hard, though. In the north, folk tended to think of dinner as the meal that you had in the middle of the day. It was posh people who referred to the midday meal as lunch and the evening one as dinner. To Vera, as to many of her ilk, any meal eaten later in the day was 'tea'.

Stanley took off his working boots and put on his slippers, and after a quick swill of his hands at the kitchen sink he sat down at the table in the living room. The house was the one they had moved to in the early fifties after leaving the little cottage in the mining village where they had lived since their marriage, and previous to that as well. The house was a modest two-bedroomed one in the residential area of the popular seaside resort Whitesands Bay. It was to there that they had brought home their precious adopted daughter. They had called her Deborah Mary, always known as Debbie.

Vera took the casserole dish out of the oven – braised steak with potatoes, carrots and onions – and dished it out on to the plates. She took off her pinny and carried the steaming plates to the table.

'There you are, Stanley, your favourite ... and here's the pickled onions and beetroot.'

'By heck! You've done us proud tonight, pet,' said Stanley. 'Is this a special meal, like, to celebrate? No, I don't mean that, do I? We're not celebrating, 'cause our Debbie's left. I mean ... is it because you thought I might be a bit upset?'

16

'Well, something like that,' said Vera. 'There's just you and me now, Stanley. We'll have to get used to it again, although we're very lucky, aren't we? We haven't got bored with one another like some married couples do.'

'No, that's true. We enjoy our quiet little life, don't we? Happen we could get out a bit more, though, if you like. To the pictures, or out for a nice meal. Not that I'm complaining about your meals, though, Vera. I just thought it might make a change.'

'Yes, so it might,' said Vera. 'We'll think about it ... sometime.'

She watched Stanley tucking into his meal with relish. He was always hungry and did justice to his meal after a hard day's work. He was employed as a gardener by the local council, and was now in a senior position in charge of the flower beds along the promenade and at the roundabouts in the town, which added to the attraction of the family resort. Vera thought he had aged recently, more so than she had. He was fifty-five now and she was a year younger. She knew she had put on a little weight but her reddish brown hair had scarcely any grey in it. Stanley, though, was completely grey-haired and balding a little on the top. He was lean and wiry, and ruddy-complexioned with all the outdoor work. He was more tired than he used to be in the evenings, but he never seemed to ail much.

'I hope she'll be happy at that there college,' he said now. 'It's what she's always wanted to do ever since she was a little girl, isn't it?'

'That was your influence, Stanley. You encouraged her with her own little plot of garden; and helping you in the greenhouse.'

'Aye, so I did, and she took to it like a duck to water. Then her job at "Sunnyhill"; that was what got her interested in taking it further.'

Debbie had had a part-time job at a local garden centre for the last few years, working at weekends and during the school holidays. It was through her conversations with Mr Hill, the owner, that she had become interested in the idea of becoming a landscape gardener.

'It's a strange sort of job for a girl though, isn't it?' said Vera, as she had said many times before. 'I've always thought so, as you know, Stanley. And this idea of landscape gardening, or whatever you call it. I can't see Debbie carting great boulders around, or doing all that strenuous digging. She'll be doing herself an injury.'

'She might be more of a designer,' said Stanley. 'You know – making the plans for other folk to carry out. Although I must admit that it's usual to start on the bottom rung of the ladder and work up. But don't worry about it, love. You never know what this course might lead to. She's going to study all sorts of things about horticulture, as they call it; just a fancy name for gardening, in my book. We'll just have to wait and see. And she'll get a diploma at the end of it.'

'It's not like getting a degree, though, is it? She's such a clever girl; all her teachers said so. She could have gone to university as easy as winking. Or to college to be a teacher. I really thought that's what she might want to do.'

'You mean you hoped she would,' said Stanley,

giving a wry grin. 'That was always your idea, Vera love, not Debbie's.'

'I just thought how grand it would be, Stanley, to say that our daughter was a teacher. You and me, we never had the chances, did we?'

'No, happen we didn't. But we've done alright, haven't we? I suppose it's only natural for parents to want their children to do better than they did themselves. But I don't think we've lost out much, Vera. If you remember, my da wanted a lot better for me that what he had. He was determined I wasn't going down the mine like he did.'

Stanley's father had been a coal miner, like most of the men in the village where he had grown up. He had suffered badly with bronchitis and had died of emphysema in his early sixties. But Stanley had always had a feeling for the land, and he had been fortunate to find work on a farm on leaving school at fourteen. Then, after his service in the Second World War he had been employed as a municipal gardener.

Vera had not worked in a woollen mill, as had many of her contemporaries, but had always been employed as a shop assistant. She had worked in the general store in the village where they lived. And later, when Debbie was at school she had gone to work in a fancy goods store in Whitesands Bay, where she still worked on a part-time basis.

'I don't suppose you've any lasses working with you, though, have you?' asked Vera. 'Like I say, it's not a job that girls usually want to do.'

'As a matter of fact we have,' Stanley replied. 'A young girl started a few weeks ago; a school leaver. Not from a grammar school, though, like the one our Debbie went to. No, she was at the local secondary modern school. She's a grand lass, very willing and eager to please; Sadie, she's called. A darned sight more capable than some of the lazy louts of lads we've had in the past. I had a chat with her; told her my daughter was going to college to study gardening; she was quite impressed. She says she's going to night school herself to get a bit more "know how".'

'Well, so long as Debbie's happy and doing what she wants to do, then I'll have to be content,' said Vera.

'You can't push your kids into summat they don't want to do,' said Stanley. 'It's asking for trouble. Anyway, it wouldn't have worked with Debbie, would it? She's always had a mind of her own.'

'You can say that again!' smiled Vera.

'Now then, what's for pudding?' asked Stanley. 'It were fair champion, that braising steak. Just the way I like it.'

'I've done a rhubarb crumble, another of your favourites,' said Vera, as she went into the kitchen. She had never wanted more than to be a good wife to Stanley, and then loving mother to Debbie. Now there was just Stanley to look after. Life would certainly be a good deal more peaceful now, but she knew she would be counting the days until Debbie came home again.

Two

Simon was in the car park waiting for Debbie when she alighted from the train at Northallerton station. He got out of the car and gave her a hug. 'Good to see you again, Debbie. All set for college, are you?'

'I hope so, Simon,' she replied. 'I must admit I've got a few collywobbles. I didn't say so to Mum, though. She thinks I'm quite cool about it all. I'll be OK – I hope – when I've seen where I'm going to be living and I've met the other girls. That's what I'm mostly worried about. I'm looking forward to getting started on the course...

'I like the car, Simon,' she added, looking at the much larger vehicle than the one he had previously owned. It was a Triumph 2000 in dark blue; it had a spacious boot and there was plenty of room at the back. She had seen it only briefly when he had come to collect her luggage a few days before. 'Is it new?' she asked.

'Well, new to me,' he replied. 'It's a few years old. Clergymen like me can't afford a new one!' He smiled. 'It's a question of needs must, though, with such a large family. Four children all under four years of age! How about that, eh?'

'You wouldn't be without them though, would you?' said Debbie. But she thought Simon looked a little tired, as well he might,

'Of course not,' he replied, 'but it was rather

21

more than we bargained for. We thought it would be just Stella, and one more. We weren't really prepared for the multiple birth… Anyway, come along.' He opened the passenger door. 'Let's get moving, shall we?'

'How is Fiona?' asked Debbie, when Simon had manoeuvred out of the car park and was driving along the straight road. 'Busy, no doubt. I don't know how she copes.'

'She was coping very well until recently,' replied Simon. 'I'd like to say that she's fine but I'm afraid that she's not. I rather think she's suffering from a form of depression. She was OK after the babies were born; she had none of the post-natal depression that some women suffer from. But now … maybe it's happening belatedly.'

'Oh no!' exclaimed Debbie. 'Poor Fiona. I'm so sorry, Simon. You should have told me. I feel awful now, descending on you this weekend.'

'Not at all,' he replied. 'It was Fiona's idea that you should break your journey here. It will do her good to see you again. You know she always looks forward to your visits. We've always had some help with the babies, as you know. Fiona had a nurse looking after her and the triplets for the first few weeks. And then … you met Paula, didn't you?'

'Yes, is she still with you?' asked Debbie. She had been impressed with the competent sixteen-year-old girl whom they had employed to help with the children.

'No, unfortunately not,' said Simon. 'She's just gone off to college to train to be a nanny. She'll be a jolly good one. We're looking out for someone else now. Some of Fiona's friends from the Young Wives group come and help her, but we need somebody more permanent. Stella's at nursery school now, each morning, so that makes things a bit easier. Not that Stella's ever been any trouble; she's always been as good as gold, bless her! And she tries to help with the little ones.'

Debbie stole a sideways look at Simon. He would be very concerned about Fiona; he thought the world of his wife. They were a devoted couple and still so much in love. She knew from what Fiona had told her that Simon would be fifty next year, thirteen years older than his wife. They had been married for five years, and Fiona was his second wife. His first wife had died, and they had had no children. Debbie had guessed that it had not been a happy marriage, and that meeting Fiona had been a great joy to both of them. Simon was still a good-looking fellow. His light brown hair showed little sign of greying. He was fit and agile, and his smile had been as welcoming as ever. She was aware, though, that he was more troubled than he usually appeared to be.

It was about an hour's journey to the little market town of Aberthwaite, travelling through the delightful scenery of the North Yorkshire Dales. They passed by greystone cottages, their gardens gay with the bright flowers of early autumn, and hump-backed bridges, with now and then a glimpse of a rippling stream. Eventually Debbie saw again the ruined castle on the hill, a few miles distant, and she knew they were nearly there.

The Church of St Peter and the rectory were at the northern end of the town. From there a leafy lane led into the market square and the town centre. As it was Saturday the twice weekly market would be in full swing. Debbie had enjoyed her trips there whilst on her visits to see Fiona and Simon, but it was already mid-afternoon and the market would be drawing to a close quite soon.

'Here we are, safely home again,' said Simon as he swung the car in between the open gates, stopping beneath the spreading branches of the rowan tree, bright with red berries. He jumped out of the car and courteously opened the passenger door for Debbie. She walked up to the door of the old Victorian rectory. Every time she did so she remembered the first time she had made the journey there, feeling lost and insecure, wondering whether she had done the right thing and what sort of a reception she would get.

There was no doubt about her welcome now. Fiona must have heard them arrive because the door opened before Simon could get out his key. There was Fiona on the threshold with Stella at her side.

'Debbie!' cried the little girl, a beaming smile lighting up her little face.

'Hello, darling,' said Debbie, stooping to hug and kiss her before greeting Fiona.

'Hello, Debbie love,' said Fiona quietly. 'It's so good to see you again.'

'And you too,' replied Debbie, responding to her embrace.

Her immediate reaction was that Fiona looked

worn out. She smiled fondly at Debbie as she always did. It was a sincere smile that reached her eyes. It did so now, but her lovely blue eyes had lost a little of their sparkle and the grey shadows beneath them indicated how tired she was. Debbie didn't say that she looked tired. She knew that was a very tactless thing to say to any woman. It was tantamount to saying that she looked unattractive, especially to such a lovely looking lady as Fiona was. She was still lovely, of course, but she looked pale and strained and her golden blonde hair was not as lustrous as usual. She had lost a little weight as well, which was something that Debbie could safely remark upon. Fiona had complained about being a little plumper than she liked to be, but that was before she had burgeoned to elephantine proportions whilst she was pregnant with the triplets.

'You've lost a bit of weight, haven't you, Fiona?' said Debbie. 'It's hardly surprising, though, with all you have to do. You're keeping well, though, are you? And the babies; are they all OK?'

'Fighting fit,' smiled Fiona. 'But hardly babies any more. I thought it might be easier when they were walking and getting a bit more independent. But I was wrong! I just wish sometimes that they would keep still! Yes, I'm OK myself... Well, I've felt a bit under the weather lately, to be honest, but I'll be all the better for seeing you. Anyway, come on in. We'll go and put the kettle on, shall we, Stella, and make a nice pot of tea.'

'That sounds like a splendid idea,' said Simon. 'Your luggage is upstairs, Debbie, in the bedroom you usually have. You go and sort yourself out, although you won't need to unpack very much, will you, until you get to your digs in Leeds.'

'No, just my nightdress for tonight, and a few things I'll need for tomorrow. I imagine my clothes will be all crumpled and creased by the time I arrive, but there'll probably be an iron there.' The thought passed through her mind that her mum would not be there to see to her washing and ironing, but no doubt she would cope. She would have to learn to do so!

'Thanks for coming to collect my luggage, Simon,' she said. 'It's a great help. And for offering to take me to Leeds on Monday. I really appreciate it, and so do my mum and dad.'

'Don't mention it; we're glad to help,' said Simon. 'It'll be just me, though, taking you to Leeds. Fiona will have her hands full here.'

'She looks very tired,' whispered Debbie. Fiona was in the kitchen, and she and Simon were talking at the bottom of the stairs. 'You must be worried about her, Simon.'

'So I am,' he said, 'although she's trying to make light of it. She went to see the doctor, because I insisted, but the tablets he gave her don't seem to have done much good. I shall make sure she goes again after this weekend. As I said, though, it will buck her up no end, having you here.'

'I'll try to help as much as I can,' said Debbie, 'even though it's only for a couple of days. I'm dying to see the triplets again. Where are they?'

'Can't you hear?' smiled Simon. 'Come along; I'll show you.'

There were sounds coming from the room at the back of the house which was the dining cum living room; sounds of bumps and of childish laughter.

'Here they are, our three little terrors!' said Simon, pushing open the door. The children were in two large-sized playpens, two of them in one, and the third child in the other. 'We don't really like doing this,' he admitted. 'Fiona says they're like animals at the zoo, but really we had no choice. We only leave them in here for short periods, but it does mean that Fiona can get a bit of peace now and again.'

The three children stared at the newcomer, not quite sure who she was. They hadn't seen her for several weeks. Then, 'Deb!' shouted one of the boys, a smile creasing his face as he recognized her. 'Deb, Deb, Deb...'

'Hello, Matthew,' she replied. He was the biggest and sturdiest of the three children. The boys were identical, but there was, in fact, a slight difference between them. Matthew, the first one to be born, had hair of a slightly darker shade of brown than that of his brother, and he had a small birthmark, like an oversized freckle, on his forehead. Both of the boys, Matthew and Mark, resembled their father rather than their mother, whereas the little girl, Michelle, was the image of Fiona, and of her sister, Stella. They all had the same golden blonde hair and delicate features. Debbie knew that she, too, resembled her birth mother. Her features were rather bolder, though, and her hair was dark brown in colour.

''Ello, Deb,' said Matthew, still staring at her. 'Look ... I made a tower.' He had been playing with his building bricks, bright wooden blocks –

red, blue, green and yellow – in various shapes and sizes.

'Very good; you're a clever boy,' she responded.

He smiled at her, a roguish grin, then kicked at the tower. It fell down with a great clatter, and he clapped his hands and screamed with laughter.

Simon laughed too. 'He's better on his own sometimes,' he said. 'He's far more boisterous than the other two. He threw a block at Mark and it hit his head. Of course he screamed blue murder – Mark, I mean – and I think it gave Matthew quite a shock. We had to be quite stern with him, but I think he got the message. He needs more watching – and more discipline – than the other two.'

Mark and Michelle were quietly occupied in the other playpen with sorting boxes into which blocks of different shapes had to be inserted into the correct holes.

'Michelle mastered it almost straight away,' said Simon, 'but Mark still hasn't quite got the hang of it. He didn't start to walk as quickly as the other two, either. They're all quite different in all sorts of ways.'

Michelle looked up and smiled shyly at Debbie. ''Ello,' she said, then returned to her task. Mark continued to look at her in puzzlement.

Debbie laughed. 'They're delightful, aren't they?'

'In moderation!' said Simon. 'We'll leave them to it for a little while. There'll be a cup of tea for you in the sitting room when you're ready.'

Debbie looked out of the bedroom window at the

familiar view of the back garden of the rectory. Her keen eye for precision and detail told her, not for the first time, that it was not a well-planned nor, indeed, a very tidy garden. Just a family plot – quite a large one – where the children could play and their parents relax, if they ever had the time.

Simon admitted he was not much of a gardener. There were bedding plants, now nearing the end of their summer flowering, several rose bushes, and a lawn where daisies and dandelions sprouted. At the bottom end there was a sand pit and a swing, and the most recent acquisition, a slide, which Debbie hadn't seen before.

She feasted her eyes on the further view, as she had done the first time she had come there. Far distant hills where a few sheep were grazing and, in the nearer distance, trees just beginning to change to their autumn colours, and a glimpse of the stream that ran through the outskirts of Aberthwaite. Near to the rectory was the fifteenth-century Church of St Peter with its squat grey tower, surrounded by ancient lopsided gravestones in the somewhat unkempt graveyard. The verger did his best, but he was fighting a losing battle with the long grass and the weeds. At the front of the church, though, not visible from the window, there was a well-tended lawn and flower beds.

Debbie's two large suitcases were on the floor, along with her cassette recorder and her box of tapes. The recorder had been a present from her parents on her eighteenth birthday last May, replacing her now rather old-fashioned Dansette record player. She doubted that there would be a television in the digs unless one of the other girls brought one along.

She opened the larger case and took out her nightdress and sponge bag, also the clothes she wanted to wear the next day, so that they wouldn't be too creased: a shift dress that was not too short and the only smartish jacket that she possessed. She knew that she would be going to church with Fiona on Sunday morning, most likely to hear Simon preach. She hung up the clothes at the side of the wardrobe, and after a quick visit to the bathroom she went downstairs.

Fiona, Simon and Stella were in the large sitting room at the front of the house. She could hear that the triplets were still amusing themselves in the back room. Fiona smiled at her and patted the settee next to her. 'Come and sit down and tell me all your news. Looking forward to starting college, are you?'

'Yes ... I think so,' replied Debbie. 'Like I said to Simon, though, I'm a bit nervous about where I'll be living and who I'll be with. But I'm looking forward to starting the course.'

'Don't you know where you'll be staying?' asked Fiona.

'Well, I've got the address, of course. It's quite near to the city centre. A large flat – an apartment, they call it – that I'll be sharing with three other girls. The college arrange the accommodation because they haven't any halls of residence on the site. And there'll be somebody in the house next door to let us have the keys.'

'You'll be fine,' said Fiona. 'Simon will get you

there safely, and see to your luggage and everything.'

'Yes, I'm really grateful,' said Debbie. 'Mum says thank you, too, and she sends her love.'

Simon poured out the tea and handed the mugs to Debbie and Fiona and a beaker of orange juice to Stella. 'We're saving on washing up these days,' he grinned. 'Anything to make life a bit easier.'

'Yes, and we're having a bit of peace for half an hour or so,' said Fiona. 'Simon's shown you the playpens, hasn't he? I was very much against it at first, shutting them in like zoo animals, but it's been a real boon to me, I can tell you. It'll be teatime soon for the children, then it's baths and early bedtime before we have our evening meal. I'm on my own at the moment since Paula went off to college, but Simon helps me a lot.'

'And I help you too, don't I, Mummy,' said Stella.

'Yes, you do, darling. You're a great help to Mummy.' Fiona stroked the blonde hair of the little girl sitting so quietly next to her. 'I don't know how I'd manage without you.'

Debbie noticed that Stella had grown, not only in size, but in maturity as well since she last saw her. She was not a baby or a toddler now, but a very sensible and thoughtful little girl. She and Debbie had formed an attachment the first time they met, and this grew stronger every time they saw one another.

'The little ones are naughty sometimes, aren't they, Mummy?' she said now.

'I'm afraid they are,' agreed Fiona. 'Well, it's

Matthew really, and the other two try to copy him. He was the first one to start walking, and talking, too. Mark was the slowest, in fact he still doesn't talk much, only a few words.'

'They're not two yet,' said Simon. 'I think maybe you're expecting rather too much, darling. They're all different, you know.'

'Yes, I suppose I'm comparing them with Stella. She was very quick to walk and talk.'

'I go to school now,' said Stella. 'Nursery school, not proper school.'

'And she'll be starting there a year from now,' said Fiona. 'And by that time the little ones will be nearly three, ready to start at the nursery ... I hope!'

Simon smiled at his wife. 'Don't worry, darling. We'll get you some help again before very long. Now ... teatime for the toddlers, isn't it. Let's get started, shall we?'

'Oh, let me help,' offered Debbie.

'Me too,' added Stella.

'I never refuse any offers of help,' said Fiona. 'Come along then, Debbie. Are you ready for the fray?'

From then on, until the little ones were tucked up in bed, it was all go. The playpens were dismantled and put to one side, and the three children seated in high chairs, wearing large bibs featuring Disney characters over their clothes.

'The people at church were very good when they were born,' Fiona told Debbie. 'Two of the high chairs were given to us, and one was Stella's; but she sits up at the table now, don't you, darling? You couldn't believe how generous people were. We were inundated with gifts and offers of help. And it was in the local paper, you know, about the triplets at the rectory!'

'Yes, you sent me the cutting,' said Debbie. 'You were the talk of the town, weren't you?'

'Yes, for a while. And the Cow and Gate firm kept us supplied with milk for a year; a good advert for them, of course. And the same with the Johnson's baby products; I'm still using the talc and the cream. And a mountain of nappies! They were a real godsend. Matthew and Michelle are almost dry now, thank goodness, but Mark's taking a bit longer.'

That little boy was needing a little more help with his meal than his siblings. Fiona had made a large shepherd's pie and the triplets were having their first share of it. Mark seemed quite content to let Fiona feed him, opening his mouth wide for the next spoonful, although she kept encouraging him to try on his own. Debbie was helping the other two, who were coping much better, and Stella was on hand with a cloth to mop up the spills.

'How did you manage, wheeling the three of them out in a pram?' asked Debbie.

'Well, it was OK when they were babies,' said Fiona. 'Stella's pram was a large one, and I put two at one end and one at the other. And Stella walked and helped to push the pram, didn't you, sweetheart? Then, when the babies could sit up properly the church people got together and bought them a double push chair for their first birthday.'

'And one of them had my push chair, 'cause I

was a big girl then,' said Stella. 'And they took it in turns, didn't they, Mummy?'

'Yes, that's right, love; they did. But we found it was usually better to have Matthew on his own; he used to wriggle and push the other one and cause havoc. Of course I couldn't push both prams at the same time; but there was usually somebody to come with me. Paula was a great help, and I've a few friends from the Young Wives who sometimes take them out for an hour or so. We manage quite well, and no doubt we'll continue to do so.'

Then it was bath time. Fiona bathed the two boys, one at each end while Debbie helped to undress Michelle. She remarked that they didn't look dirty, but Fiona said it was a nightly ritual and one that they enjoyed. Matthew started at once slapping the water with his hands and splashing his brother, who joined in a little less exuberantly.

'We won't bother with hair tonight,' said Fiona. 'They don't enjoy that quite so much when the water gets in their eyes, though I do try to be careful.'

She lifted Mark out and wrapped him in a large fluffy towel. 'Here, Debbie, you hold him,' she said. 'He's easier to handle than Matthew. And when you've dried him you can have a try at putting on his nappy! You've done it before, haven't you?'

'He's a lot bigger now, though,' said Debbie, struggling with the large terry towelling square and the safety pins, hoping that she didn't stab him.

'That's very good; you're a dab hand at it!' Fiona grinned at her. 'You won't want to be starting with babies just yet though, will you?'

'Not flippin' likely!' said Debbie. They smiled at one another in perfect understanding.

Fiona had told Debbie about the circumstances of her birth and how she had been forced to give her up for adoption. It was, Debbie knew, partly a cautionary tale which she had tried to take on board. She knew what a traumatic time Fiona had gone through. And now the two of them, mother and daughter, who had been reunited after sixteen years, were the best of friends.

'There, that's two done and dusted,' said Fiona. 'Now it's Michelle's turn.'

'And then Mummy reads them a story,' said Stella, 'or sometimes Daddy does.'

'I think Debbie could do that tonight, if she would like to?' Fiona suggested.

'Yes, I would like to,' said Debbie. She had read stories to Stella and enjoyed it very much. She had thought, at one time, that she didn't like small children. She had been horrified at her mother's idea that she should train to be a teacher. That was until she met Stella, and then the triplets. She thought they were adorable, although she still wouldn't change her mind about teaching.

'They like the one about the gingerbread man,' Stella told her, 'and they join in with the "Run as fast as you can" bit. Well, Matthew does...'

'That was one of my favourite stories when I was a little girl,' said Debbie. And so, when Michelle, too, was bathed and ready for bed, she sat with Stella and the triplets and read the familiar story.

Michelle and Mark, who was getting more used to Debbie now, pointed at the pictures, while Matthew shouted at the top of his voice, 'Run, run, as fast as you can. You can't catch me! I'm the gingerbread man!'

Fiona had been listening from the next room, and she smiled to herself as she took over, tucking them each in their separate cots, kissing them and saying, 'Goodnight... God bless.'

'Now, teatime for us,' said Fiona. 'I expect you're ready for it, Debbie.'

'Mummy says I can have my tea with all of you tonight,' said Stella. 'I usually have it with the little ones, but it's special tonight, because you're here, Debbie.'

After she had eaten the shepherd's pie and the fruit jelly and custard the little girl was nodding with tiredness.

'Well past your bedtime,' said Fiona. 'We won't bother with a bath tonight; just a lick and a promise!'

Stella insisted, though, that Debbie must read her a story as well. And so her half-sister read to her of the exploits of *Milly Molly Mandy* until she could scarcely keep her eyes open.

'Goodnight, darling,' said Debbie, as the little girl snuggled beneath the bedclothes. 'Sleep tight ... and God bless.'

By the time Fiona went up to say goodnight she was fast asleep.

Three

'Peace at last!' Fiona collapsed on to the settee, her legs outstretched and her arms hanging limply at her sides, like a floppy rag doll. 'Whew! I feel as though I've been through a wringer when it gets to this time in the evening.' She laughed. 'Not that they use them any more; wringers, I mean. It's an expression I heard my mother use. I remember how she used to put clothes through the mangle to get the water out. You won't remember that, Debbie.'

'No ... I don't think so.' Debbie shook her head. 'I remember my mum having a twin-tub at one time. She's got a fully automatic washer now.'

'Same here,' said Fiona. 'We've had a Bendix since before Stella was born. It's been a real god-send with all these nappies, although I sometimes need to soak them first. I've read that there are disposable nappies coming on the market. I can't imagine it at all. What a lot of mess to dispose of! I don't think they'll catch on.'

Simon got up from his chair. 'Well, I'm going to leave you girls to have a natter while I finish my sermon, if you don't mind?'

'Of course not, darling,' said Fiona. 'But we're not going to talk about nappies and washing machines all night, I can assure you.'

'I should hope not!' Simon said with a laugh. 'I won't be long; I've just got to add the finishing

37

touches, then I'll be with you.'

'You're preaching tomorrow, are you?' asked Debbie.

'Yes, I'm afraid so. There's only me at the moment, you see. Fiona will tell you ... see you in a little while.'

'We've no curate just now,' said Fiona as he closed the door behind him. 'Josh – you remember Joshua? – he's moved on. He was with us for two years. There's another curate starting at the end of September after his ordination. He's an older man – well, older than Josh, I mean. Late forties, I believe, with a wife and family. He's not been in the church long, though; it will be his first placement. So his wife might be able to lend a hand in the parish, if she's that way inclined.'

'That will be a help for you, won't it?' said Debbie.

'Yes: I've not been able to pull my weight as much as I like to just lately. Although Simon insisted when we first got married that I hadn't to be regarded as an unpaid curate, like some clergy wives are. His first wife, for instance; she was heart and soul into the church work. I carried on with my job at the library until just before Stella was born. Now, I lead the Young Wives group, and that's about all. You don't mind going to church in the morning, do you, Debbie?'

'No, of course not. I shall look forward to hearing Simon preach. I go on Sunday mornings with Mum and Dad. Not every Sunday, though. I was sometimes working at the garden centre.'

'Are you still friendly with that young man who

works there?' asked Fiona. 'Kevin ... wasn't it?'

'Yes; Kevin Hill. He's the owner's son and his father's right-hand man now, actually. I started going out with him soon after I went to work there. I was only fifteen, and Mum and Dad didn't approve at the time, as you can imagine! Although he was always a very nice sort of lad; well brought up, of course, and quite steady. We fell out, though. He dumped me, to be honest! I think I was bit of a nuisance in those days – well, I know I was! Very wilful and wanting my own way, and I suppose he got fed up with me. I must have been a real trial to my parents.'

Fiona smiled. 'Yes ... maybe so. I've noticed a change in you since we got to know you. You've grown up, haven't you, love?'

'I think so. I knew I had to find out about you, you see. And then ... everything fell into place, and I started to settle down.'

'And we're so glad you came,' said Fiona. 'But you already know that, don't you? So – tell me – you made it up with Kevin, did you?'

'Yes; to my amazement he asked me out again. He said I'd changed, too. It's not a serious relationship. I don't want to get involved in that way, not just yet; although I thought I did, at one time. So we're not "going out" together now, because I'll be at college. It's only for a year, though.'

'A lot can happen in a year,' said Fiona. 'It's sensible not to commit yourself at your age. How old is Kevin?'

'He's twenty, two years older than me. As you say, a lot can happen in a year.'

'Be careful, won't you, love?' said Fiona.

'Yes; I know what you're saying. Being away from home and all that. But I intend to work hard and see where it leads. Mum still keeps saying it's a funny job for a girl, but it's what I want to do.'

'Well, that's the answer then, isn't it?' Fiona nodded, then Debbie noticed that she closed her eyes for a moment. She really must be dreadfully tired. But then she shook herself and came round again.

'Would you like to watch the television?' she asked. 'Or are you OK just chatting?'

'I'm enjoying talking and catching up on things,' replied Debbie. 'Unless there's something you want to watch?'

'No; it'll be the usual variety show tonight, I suppose. Nothing I don't mind missing, although there are certain things I like to watch; Simon as well when he has time. We watch the news at least once a day, and *Panorama*. And I must admit we like Alf Garnett – *Till Death Us Do Part*. It's rather irreverent at times, so we don't let on to the congregation about our dubious tastes! But as Simon says, you can watch things and have a laugh; you don't have to agree with them or let them influence you. And we never miss *Z-Cars* or *Coronation Street!*'

'Yes; my parents watch some of the soaps, and *Steptoe and Son*; and Mum loves the variety shows and quiz games. We've still got our old black and white set, but Dad says they're going to get a coloured one soon. They don't go out very much and I think they deserve it. Television has become such a way of life hasn't it?'

'Yes; whether it's for better or for worse, I'm not sure. It's the same with us; I think a coloured "telly" might be the next thing on the agenda. Stella watched *The Magic Roundabout* in colour at her friend's home and she's been on about it ever since. But we told her she can't have everything she wants straight away.'

'She's very good, though, isn't she? I can't imagine her ever having a tantrum, or being naughty at all.'

'She has her moments, like they all do. But I must admit she's been almost the perfect child. That's why it was such a rude awakening with the other three!'

'You wouldn't be without them, though?'

'No; of course not. But as Simon says, God is sometimes a little overgenerous with the gifts he bestows!'

Debbie laughed. Her eyes wandered round the room as she leaned back in the comfortable armchair. This was a lovely elegant room which Fiona had furnished, and Simon had decorated, according to their individual style. She had told Debbie how she had inherited a mishmash of styles when she first went to live at the rectory.

Simon had given her a free hand, more or less, with the decor, according to what they could afford. She had chosen furniture from the popular shop, Habitat, for the dining room; table and chairs in light wood, Scandinavian in design. The lounge was more traditional; modern furniture but in a style that would not date; a sage green settee and two matching armchairs and a self-coloured carpet in a tweedy oatmeal shade. The

41

subdued effect of the room was relieved by gold crushed-velvet curtains and scatter cushions in gold, orange and lime green. She had, tactfully, disposed of the embroidered cushion covers which she had guessed were the work of Millicent, Simon's first wife.

'This is such a comfortable room,' Debbie told her. 'I always feel at home here. Stylish – sort of posh, if you know what I mean – but homely as well. We hardly ever use our front room, except at Christmas or when we have visitors.'

'Yes, it's the room we try to keep for best,' said Fiona. 'The Young Wives meet here, and Simon sometimes has committee meetings, but we use it as well in the evenings. I try to keep it tidy and restrict the clutter to the living room and the kitchen. It's not as spick and span as it used to be, though. I can't stop the children from coming in; it's there home as much as ours, and I don't want to be a fussy house-proud sort of mum. The stereogram's new, though, and they know they haven't to fiddle with the knobs, nor the ones on the television.'

Debbie looked at the newest acquisition, a light oak radiogram with two speakers. She guessed it would play the more modern cassettes as well as conventional records. There were a few newspapers on the top, a James Bond paperback novel and two toy cars. On an armchair there was a doll, a copy of *Woman's Own*, a tartan holdall and what seemed to be Fiona's latest knitting project; a lacy garment in bright pink, possibly a cardigan for one of the little girls. Fiona seemed to notice it at the same time. She got up and shoved it into

42

the bag.

'I'm an untidy sort of housewife, aren't I?' She smiled. 'Never mind, though; you're family, aren't you? I was trying to do a bit more of this before you came. It's a jumper for Michelle, and I intended to make one for Stella as well. I started it ages ago, but they'll be lucky if they get them in time for Christmas!'

'I'm surprised you find time to knit at all,' said Debbie. 'Isn't it easier to buy the clothes ready-made? More expensive, though, I suppose?'

'There's not much in it, when you've bought the wool and buttons and everything. I find it relaxing to knit while I'm watching the TV; at least I used to, but I fall asleep now, more often than not.'

Simon appeared at that moment. 'Have you had a good old chinwag?' he asked.

'We have indeed,' replied Fiona. 'You haven't been long.'

'I think my sermon's as good as I can get it... Now, are you two girls ready for a drink? Hot chocolate? Is that OK for you, Debbie?'

'Lovely,' she answered. 'You're spoiling me.'

'Not at all,' Simon replied. 'It's what we usually have about this time.'

'Simon's really good, isn't he?' said Debbie as he went out again. 'Very helpful.'

'Yes, he's one in a million,' said Fiona, 'and don't think I don't realize it, because I do. Meeting Simon was the best thing that ever happened to me. And then having the children, of course. And finding you again, Debbie. That was an unexpected bonus. I know I'm a very lucky lady. But I do have to remind myself – more and more just lately – to count my blessings. What do I have to be depressed about? A happy home, wonderful husband, lovely children...'

Debbie did not tell her that Simon had mentioned this, and that he was worried about her. She did not want Fiona to know that they had been discussing her.

'I don't think that has very much to do with it,' she replied. 'If you're feeling depressed there doesn't have to be a definite reason for it, does there? It's a sort of illness. You can be ill in your mind, just as you can be in your body. I don't know a great deal about it, but my friend Shirley – her mum was feeling like that last year. And there was no apparent reason for it. She's over it now. She went to see the doctor and she was on a course of medication – tranquilizers, I suppose – for a while, and she seems to be OK again now.'

'I've been to the doctor,' said Fiona. 'He's a very understanding sort of man. He said more or less what you've just said; that I mustn't feel guilty about it. I've been taking some pills, which I don't like doing – I've never been keen on pills or medicine of any kind – but I don't feel that they've done me much good. I've cheered up no end, though, with you being here. It's done me a world of good seeing you again, Debbie; and I'm trying to get things into perspective.'

'A change of company is always good,' said Debbie.

'Especially yours...' Fiona smiled at her fondly.

'Well, I'm glad if I've cheered you up. It's great for me as well, to see you again. You must go back to the doctor, though, Fiona. There's nothing to be ashamed of in seeking help.'

'No, that's what Simon says, and my friend Joan.'

'It could be a belated reaction to what has happened to you in the past,' said Debbie. 'You recovered remarkably well after the triplets were born, didn't you? And that was a very traumatic time.'

'Yes, that's true. But I did get a lot of help with them for the first few months.'

'And you had problems before that, didn't you? With some of the people in the church...'

'Yes; when they found out that Stella was not my first child...' She nodded. 'That's all forgiven and forgotten now, I hope. But you're right; sometimes events cast a long shadow. The past is always there, a part of us, even though we may try to put it behind us... How come you're so wise, Debbie?'

'I don't think I am,' Debbie laughed. 'But I do know that I've grown up a lot over the last two years. I've started to consider other people more; not just thinking about myself. I was a selfish little madam, and awkward, too.'

'You're a spirited lass, I know that,' smiled Fiona. 'Don't ever lose your enthusiasm for life, Debbie ... Ah, here's Simon with our supper.'

He handed round the mugs of hot chocolate and a plate with a selection of biscuits. He sat on the settee next to his wife, unashamedly dunking his ginger biscuit in his drink.

'My dad does that,' laughed Debbie. 'But sometimes he leaves it in too long and makes a real mess, and Mum gets cross with him.'

45

'There's an art to it,' said Simon, seriously. 'Just a few seconds immersion and no more. Don't tell anyone about my childish habit, will you?'

'I think your devoted flock would forgive you anything,' said Fiona patting his hand.

'Maybe so,' he smiled. 'I don't think anything they hear about us can shock them any more, do you, darling?'

'I doubt it.' Fiona knew to what he was referring. Her train of thought led her to Greg and his brother, Graham.

'We saw Greg a couple of weeks ago,' she told Debbie. 'He came on a surprise visit and brought his fiancée. That certainly was a surprise, wasn't it, Simon?'

'Indeed it was,' replied Simon, 'although Greg is twenty-six now, so I suppose it is time he was thinking about settling down. We liked Marcia very much. She came to work in their office about six months ago, and they realized at once, apparently, that that was it!'

'Love at first sight,' commented Debbie. 'So it can happen?'

'Most certainly,' said Simon, nodding assuredly. He put his arm round his wife. 'Like it did with us.'

'Well ... almost,' said Fiona. 'I had to be very sure that you really wanted me. You were such an important person! The rector of St Peter's, no less!'

'Well, I knew at once,' he said. 'They're getting married next year, Greg and Marcia. It will be in Manchester, of course.'

'And he told us that Graham has found a post in Leeds,' said Fiona. 'So you may meet up with him again, Debbie.'

Debbie's ears pricked up then. It was quite a while since she had seen Graham Challinor, Greg's younger brother...

Greg was Simon's son from a previous relationship, a son of whom he had had no knowledge until the young man had turned up at the rectory one day in the spring of 1966.

Simon had served as a navigator in the RAF during the Second World War, an important member of a bomber crew. It was a time when life was lived at fever pitch. He had fallen in love with Yvonne, a WAAF girl who was stationed at the same camp near Lincoln. But circumstances had parted them and they had gone their separate ways. Gregory – Greg, as he was always called – had not known about Simon until the man he had always believed to be his father had died. It had not taken him long to trace his real father. It had been a tremendous shock to Simon, but the two of them had taken to one another straight away. They had become firm friends over the past few years, more like brothers than father and son. Just as, two years later, Fiona and Debbie had been reunited and had become very close to one another. It was little wonder, therefore, that Simon often remarked how nothing that the family at the rectory could do would come as a surprise to the congregation any more.

Debbie, inevitably, had met Greg and his half-brother, Graham. On that momentous day in early November 1968 when Fiona, a month early, gave birth to triplets, the three young people had all been staying at the rectory having attended a brass band concert the previous evening. They had shared in the trauma of the difficult birth, their concern for Fiona forming a bond between them. Consequently Simon and Fiona had asked the three of them to act as godparents to the three babies.

Debbie had found them both to be very personable young men. Greg was like a younger version of Simon, and Graham was attractive, too, in a different way. At that time Graham had been in his second year at Leeds University, studying architecture.

Fiona was now saying that he had found a post as a junior in a firm of architects in the city of Leeds. Debbie had not seen him since the christening. She had not really given much thought to him either as she had been busy studying for her A levels and had been working part-time at the garden centre.

'Yes, it would be good to see Graham again,' she said, trying not to sound overenthusiastic, although she had a certain interest stirring in her at the thought of seeing him again. 'He's living in Leeds, then?'

'Yes; he's got digs, like you have. In Headingley, Greg told us, but I'm not sure just where. We can ask Greg to let Graham know that you're in Leeds. It would be nice to meet up with someone you know. You'll make friends, of course, but it's sure to feel a little strange at first. You'll like Leeds, though. There are lots of lovely shops and arcades, and it's an interesting city.'

Debbie knew that Fiona had been born and brought up in Leeds, although her memories of

48

her early days were not all happy ones.

'And Greg's doing well, is he?' she asked. He was a partner in a firm of solicitors.

'Yes; he's well established in the firm now,' Simon answered. 'He deals mainly with the property cases. He says he's selling his own flat, and he and Marcia are going to buy a house. We got the impression that she doesn't want to wait long before they start a family.'

'So you would be a grandad, Simon,' remarked Debbie. 'You don't look old enough.'

'I feel it at times!' he replied. 'But I've got quite enough to cope with, being a father, at the moment. We've only been married five years and we've already got four children!'

'What do you mean, already?' asked Fiona, giving him an odd look. 'Don't tell me you want any more?'

'No,' he reassured her. 'Just a slip of the tongue. We've decided that our family is complete, haven't we, darling?' They looked at one another lovingly, and Debbie mused, as she had done before, that theirs was a very amorous relationship.

They all retired to bed soon afterwards. Tomorrow was Sunday, Simon's busiest day of the week. Debbie was looking forward to visiting St Peter's church again. She had been made welcome there and had felt at home. There was a warm and friendly ambience to the place, and she knew that that was due, in no small part, to the influence of the rector and his wife.

Four

The organ was playing softly when Debbie, Fiona and Stella walked into the church the following morning. Simon had gone earlier, and they had just left the three little ones in the crèche. The young women of the congregation took it in turns to look after the babies and toddlers in the church hall during the service. The older children stayed in church for a while, then went out when the sermon started, to their Sunday School classes in the rooms adjoining the hall.

This was an experiment that had been started some two years earlier, and it had been found to work well. Simon had realized that the church had to move with the times. More and more people were getting cars and wanted to go out as a family on a Sunday afternoon. The long established afternoon Sunday School was suffering as a result, hence the decision to change to the morning. There had been an added benefit in that several parents had started to attend the morning service along with their children.

Stella, at not quite four years of age, was really rather young for the infant class, but as she was so sensible and well behaved – and because her father was the rector! – she had been allowed to start a little earlier. She trotted off to the front of the church to join her friends and her Sunday School teacher.

St Peter's was an ancient church, parts of it dating from the fifteenth century. There was a faint musty smell, common to all churches of that era, comprised of the dust from old hymn books, polish, and the fragrance of the late summer roses on the altar and on the closed lid of the font at the entrance. There was no smell of incense, however. The worship at this parish church did not consist of 'bells and smells' as it did in some of the more high Anglican churches. Simon thought of himself as a 'middle of the road' sort of vicar, although he was able to see the points of view of other clergymen, and did not criticize or condemn, provided they were sincere in what they believed and preached.

Debbie sat down next to Fiona in the pew a few rows from the front and, following her lead, leaned forward, bowing her head to say a brief silent prayer. It was not customary here to kneel down, although some of the older members did so. The building did not feel cold despite the high roof and stone floor and the huge stone pillars. A gentle heat issued from the iron grilles along the centre aisle, and the sun streamed through the stained-glass windows. Debbie looked up at the east windows above the altar depicting the story of Jesus from birth to crucifixion, with Christ in glory in the centre. It evoked in her a feeling of peace and that all was right with the world, for that moment at least, away from all the cares and problems of daily life.

The woman in the pew behind leaned forward to whisper 'Hello.' Debbie recognized her as Joan Tweedale, Fiona's friend, who kept a handicraft shop on the High Street. 'Hello, Debbie,' she said. 'Nice to see you again. Off to college soon, aren't you? I wish you all the best, my dear...'

The conversation stopped as the organist – who was, in fact, Joan's husband – struck up with the chords of the opening hymn. The congregation stood as the choir, churchwardens and the rector processed round the church, from the vestry at the side then down the centre aisle.

When morning gilds the skies, my heart awakening cries,
May Jesus Christ be praised...

The choir of men, women and teenagers – both boys and girls – sang harmoniously and the people joined in with enthusiasm. Debbie thought, as she always did, how striking Simon looked in his clerical robes; the white surplice and simple blue stole; he rarely went in for a great deal of adornment except on special occasions.

The hymns were all ones that she knew, including one of her favourites, a more modern hymn, 'How Great Thou Art'. They used a more avant-garde sort of hymn book now as well as the old established 'Ancient and Modern', an innovation that Simon had introduced. Another new venture, which had not been popular at first with all the members of the congregation, was the guitar group. The group of older teenagers played and sang their own version of 'Go, Tell It On The Mountain'. Several of the people, though by no means all, clapped quite vigorously at the end. Applause was something which, at one time, had never been heard in a church service.

Simon's sermon was about God being there in times of trouble, not only in the great tragedies of life but when you might be feeling a little bit down and dispirited, and finding that life was a struggle. She wondered if he had Fiona in mind; probably not just his wife, though. You could not tell what troubles other people might have, things deeply hidden, maybe, that they felt they could not discuss with anyone. Debbie's chief worry now was tomorrow and what might be in store for her in Leeds. What would her digs be like, and her flatmates? Would she get on with them? Would she take to the course? Maybe a quick prayer would help, but she knew that she had to take her courage in both hands and help herself as well.

After the service a few people recognized Debbie and came to speak to her.

'So you're off to college? Jolly good! I hope you enjoy it...'

'I thought college was tremendous fun...'

'So you're going to study gardening? Would you like to come and have a go with mine? I'm fighting a losing battle with the weeds...'

She had heard this sort of remark many times from people who heard of her unusual choice of career. If what they said was true she would not be short of work in the future!

'Hello, my dear. It's Debbie, isn't it?' She recognized this lady as Mrs Ethel Bayliss, the wife of the churchwarden and, she knew, a one-time adversary of Fiona. One of the 'old brigade' who did not like change of any kind. But apparently the woman herself had changed over the years and was now much more amenable.

'Yes, I'm Debbie,' she replied. 'Hello, Mrs Bayliss. How are you? You are looking well, I must say.'

The rather plump lady was smartly dressed as always in a tweed suit of pale green, with a frilly blouse showing at the neck and a large straw hat with an artificial flower at the side.

'Mustn't grumble, my dear. I'm very fit ... considering that I'll be seventy-two next birthday!' she whispered coyly.

'Well, fancy that! You don't look it,' replied Debbie, although the lady did, in fact, look every day of it.

'And good morning to you too, Fiona, my dear,' the woman said. 'You're doing a grand job with all those babies. I take my hat off to you; I do really...' She glided away like a ship in full sail to shake hands with Simon at the door.

Fiona chuckled. 'She acts like she's my bosom friend now, but I'm still rather wary of her. And you're quite a diplomat, aren't you? You'd make a good vicar's wife!'

'Now, you will write, won't you, and let us know how you're getting on. Or ring us; there'll be a phone in your digs, I expect?' Fiona sounded more concerned about the start of Debbie's college course than she was herself.

'I don't know till I get there,' she replied. 'I should think there'll be a phone. But there are phone boxes, and I'll certainly write. It isn't as if I shall be a million miles away, though.'

'No, but it's a new experience for you, isn't it,

living away from home for the first time? Now ... take care of yourself, love, and have a good time. I'm sure you will once you settle down there. You're going to study for your career; that's the main thing, but I'm sure there'll be lots of other interesting things to do as well.'

It seemed as though Fiona could not stop talking, trying to hold on to the last few minutes before Debbie set off on the journey to Leeds. They were both a little tearful. As Debbie said, it was not a million miles away, only forty miles or so from Aberthwaite to Leeds. Debbie had already had one parting from her parents in Whitesands Bay, but this one for some reason seemed even more poignant.

The two young women, Fiona and her first-born child, Debbie, had become very close. There was a bond between them, one of blood when all was said and done, and they felt responsible for one another. Vera, up in Northumberland, was still 'Mum' to Debbie. The woman who had loved and cared for her and brought her up had never felt like anything else, and Debbie had made sure that Vera knew how she felt about her, and her father, as well. Fortunately there had never been any animosity or jealousy between Fiona and Vera.

'Come along now; let's get on our way,' said Simon. He opened the boot and put in Debbie's two large suitcases, her cassette player, and a box of tapes, books and odds and ends. There was another cardboard box, too, containing tinned food – salmon, ham, corned beef and fruit – and a home-made fruitcake and packets of biscuits.

55

Both Vera and Fiona had contributed to this, knowing that girls at college and living in digs would find the contents very useful. 'I want to get back by early afternoon if I can,' he added.

'I'll save you some lunch,' said Fiona. 'There's some of the chicken left from the sandwiches I've made for Debbie.' Fiona had insisted that she should take a packed lunch to eat when she arrived at her new home.

'Don't worry; I'll see to myself when I get back,' said Simon. 'Now don't forget what I said, darling. You must ring the doctor this afternoon and make another appointment... Now, you get in the front seat, Debbie.'

'Can I come?' asked Stella, who was clinging to Debbie's hand.

'No, sweetheart,' said Fiona. 'You stay and help Mummy with the little ones. Daddy won't be all that long, and you'll see Debbie again quite soon. She's going to college, like I told you; a school for grown-up people. But she'll come and spend a weekend with us before very long.'

Fiona and Stella waved as Simon backed the car out of the drive and turned into the lane that led to Aberthwaite town centre. The little market town was not very busy at ten o'clock on the Monday morning. They drove along the high street and around the cobbled market square with its stone cross, then took the road which led over the Yorkshire moors to the more industrial part of Yorkshire in the West Riding.

'Fiona's feeling a little low again this morning,' Simon commented. 'That's why she's so upset at you leaving. She's trying to put on a brave face, but I can tell. I've insisted she must go to the doctor again, though she seems to think it's something shameful to feel depressed. I hope she'll improve when we get her some permanent help with the babies. We have to make sure that we get the right person; somebody competent and with a nice manner with the children. And somebody that Fiona likes and can work with, although she gets on with most people, almost everybody I would say. There were a few who disapproved of her when we first got married. I suppose it was because she was so pretty and modern in her outlook; not how they thought the rector's wife should be. But they all love her now. Paula was ideal with the children, and she's made the right decision, to train as a nanny.'

'I'm sure someone will turn up,' said Debbie. 'But she's got friends to help in the meantime, hasn't she?'

'Yes, Fiona's not short of friends. As I said, she's very popular in the parish. It was a very lucky day for me, Debbie, when I met Fiona. Although I prefer to think of it as Fate, not luck. I really believe that we were meant to be together.'

'It certainly seems so to me,' agreed Debbie.

Simon smiled. 'Sorry if I go on about Fiona. It's because she means so very much to me, and I can't bear to see her so tired and dispirited.'

'She'll get over it, I'm sure,' said Debbie. 'She's not the sort of person to give in and feel sorry for herself. And you are there to help, aren't you?'

Simon nodded, then concentrated on the road ahead of them. The scenery was gradually changing from the rural setting to a more industrial landscape. They passed lonely outlying farms where sheep grazed, as they had done for centuries, on the Yorkshire moors. Debbie remembered learning at school about the growth of the woollen industry. At one time the wool carding and weaving had been a cottage industry, moving with the invention of machinery to the mills which drew their power from the fast flowing Pennine streams. The soft lime-free water was necessary, too, for the washing, combing and carding of the wool. With the advent of stream power the main woollen centres moved closer to the coalfields, crowding the valleys of the Rivers Colne, Calder and Aire with a myriad of tall mill chimneys.

Many of the woollen mills had closed in recent years with the coming of synthetic fibres and fabrics. But there were still a sizeable number of mill chimneys on the horizon as they drew near to the city of Leeds.

They drove past the railway station, around City Square with the statue of the Black Prince on his horse, then up the road which led out of the city centre towards the university buildings. Many students had lodgings in that area, and this was the district in which Debbie's digs were to be found. She had the address, of course, but that didn't mean a great deal to her, nor to Simon. Accommodation for the students who required it was arranged by the college authorities, and this would be the first time she had seen it.

There was a maze of streets with old Victorian houses in the hinterland near the university. They found it after asking for directions a couple of times; number fourteen, Blenheim Street, one of a terrace of three-storied houses with a small patch of ground in front of them that could not by any stretch of the imagination be called a garden. Debbie had been informed by letter that the keys for the apartment could be collected on arrival at the house next door, number twelve. This property was identical in structure to its neighbour, but there was a little more sign of life. There were net curtains at these windows – which were cleaner windows than the ones next door – and the paint on the front door was glossy. The paintwork on the neighbouring house was cracked and blistering.

'I'll go and find out,' said Debbie, a little apprehensively.

'Do you want me to go?' said Simon. 'I don't mind.'

'No, it's alright, thanks. I shall have to get used to doing things for myself.' She opened the creaking iron gate of number twelve, walked up the short path and rang the bell.

A woman opened the door almost at once. Debbie guessed she was in her forties. She had frizzy ginger hair of a shade that was assuredly not her own, piercing blue eyes in a heavily made up face, and was dressed in a short skirt and a tight fitting red sweater. Her feet were clad in carpet slippers. She did, however, smile in quite a pleasant manner.

'Hello, luv. You must be one of the students from the garden place. You're the first to arrive; I'm expecting four of you. What's your name, luv?'

'I'm Debbie Hargreaves,' she replied. 'I'm from

Whitesands Bay.'

'In Northumberland,' she added, as the woman looked curiously at her. 'But I've been staying with friends, so I've not travelled very far today. Shall I ... shall we bring my luggage in?'

'Aye, we'll get you sorted out, luv. Step in a minute, and I'll get t' keys.'

Debbie stepped into the hallway of number twelve, turning to give a thumbs-up sign to Simon, although she could feel her stomach turning somersaults. She was dazzled by the multi-coloured carpet, the boldly patterned wallpaper and the doors leading off the hallway, each painted a different colour. It all looked clean, though, which was a good sign if this person was the landlady of the property next door.

The woman disappeared into the room with the blue door. She didn't invite Debbie inside, but appeared a few moments later with a brown envelope.

'Here's yer keys,' she said. 'Two of 'em, one for t' front door, and t'other for yer flat. I've put you in t' first floor flat next door. Alf – that's me husband – and me, we own both properties. We've had it all converted, like. There's two bedrooms, so you'll have to sort out who you're going to share with when t'others come. An' a bathroom and lav, living room and kitchen, so you should have all you need. If you need owt else, give us a shout. I'm Rhoda, by the way, Rhoda Perkins. And there's directions in here, from t' college, telling you how to get there, what number buses an' all that. You start tomorrow, don't you?'

'Yes, that's right,' answered Debbie, feeling

bemused by the woman's chatter.

'There's three young fellers in t' downstairs flat. They came yesterday, but they've gone out today. They're at Stanborough College an' all, same as you. Now, d'you want a hand with yer cases?'

'It's OK; my friend will help,' said Debbie. But Rhoda Perkins followed her out to the car.

She smiled a little fatuously when she set eyes on Simon. 'Hello there...' She held out her hand. 'I'm Rhoda; pleased to meet you.' There was a slight emphasis on the 'you'.

Debbie smiled to herself. Simon was a handsome man, and he was not wearing his dog collar that day; he usually left it off when he was not on church business.

'How do you do?' he replied. 'I'm Simon Norwood. My wife and I are family friends, and Debbie's been staying with us, I wanted to make sure she arrived safely.' He lifted the luggage out of the boot, then he carried one case and Rhoda the other, whilst Debbie carried one of the large boxes.

Rhoda opened the door of number fourteen and they went inside. The interior, as well as the outside, was vastly different from number twelve. The wallpaper was a dull fawn colour, the paintwork dark brown, and the carpet a cheap rubberbacked fabric. Drab-looking but clean, at least, was Debbie's first reaction.

'Here we are then,' said Rhoda when they had mounted the steep stairs. She opened the door to the apartment. It led into the main room, the living room. It was a fair size but again the impression was one of drabness. There was a settee and an easy chair in tan-coloured moquette, which had seen better days, a drop-leaf table, and four fold-up chairs stacked against the wall, a set of empty bookshelves, dark green curtains at the windows, and a carpet of an indiscriminate pattern, worn in places, on the floor.

There was a cubbyhole of a kitchen in a recess opening off the room. 'There's yer cooker,' said Rhoda. 'It's a gas oven, a bit temperamental, like, but you'll get used to it, an' a fridge an' all. You're lucky; it's not every flat that has a fridge included.' It was a minuscule one, but better than none at all, a small wall cupboard, and a porcelain sink and draining board.

'You've not got a washing machine,' Rhoda told Debbie as Simon went down to get the rest of the luggage. 'You can do yer undies in t' sink and take the rest to t' launderette. That's what t'other students have done. We provide you with sheets and towels, but you're responsible for changing 'em and washing 'em. That OK?'

'Er ... yes, of course,' said Debbie, who really had no idea about what was usual. She had noticed a radiator beneath the window, so if there was central heating that was certainly a plus factor.

'And we're centrally heated an' all,' added Rhoda, as if she had read her mind, 'so you don't have to mess with fires and cleaning out grates and suchlike. Alf and me, we had it put in our house at the same time. It's t' best thing ever invented in my book. I remember when I were a nipper, waking up to ice all over t' window. Jack Frost has been, they used to tell us, but it were murder getting washed and dressed in t' freezing cold.

'Course we knew no different then. You'll not remember that, lass?'

'Yes, I do, before my parents had the heating installed,' said Debbie. She was bewildered by the woman's chatter, jumping from one thing to another, but at least she was a friendly soul.

'And here's the bedrooms.' She flung open a door that opened off the room. 'There's nowt much to choose between 'em. One looks over t' front and the other over t' back. You take yer pick, seeing as you're t' first to arrive.'

'I'll have this one then,' said Debbie, 'the front one.'

'OK...' Rhoda plonked a suitcase down on one of the single beds, and Simon, who had re-appeared, brought in the other one and the rest of the luggage. There were twin beds with light oak headboards, covered with candlewick bedspreads in a dusky pink shade, and pink curtains of a thin fabric at the window. The large wardrobe, dressing table and chest of drawers were of a cheap utility design, considered suitable for rooms to let, such as this.

'And the bathroom and lav are along the passage at the top o' t' stairs,' said Rhoda. 'We had to leave 'em there; it were easier wi' all this messing about. There'll be plenty of hot water, well, twice a day anyroad. My hubby sees to the heating and all that... So I'll leave you to sort yerself out. Come and give us a knock next door if you want owt. Bye for now then. Goodbye, Mr ... er ... Simon. Nice to meet you.' She flashed a beaming smile at him

63

as she went out of the room.

Simon grinned at Debbie. 'She's quite a character, isn't she? Good-hearted, though. I'm sure you'll be fine here, Debbie; you could have done a lot worse with digs on spec. Now, do you want me to stay a while and help you to unpack?'

She knew he would be anxious to get back to Fiona and the children; and she must get used to looking after herself. 'No, thanks all the same, Simon,' she said. 'You've got me here safely, and I'll be alright now.'

'OK, if you're sure... I'd better pay a visit to your bathroom, though, before I set off.'

'We'll go and find it together, shall we?' said Debbie.

It was, as Rhoda said, along the passage at the top of the stairs; a room that had obviously not been brought up to date. There was a huge bath with brass taps and claw feet, an oversized wash basin and a toilet with a high cistern and the sort of chain that you had to pull and hold on to. The china knob at the end of the chain said 'Pull', as if you could do anything else! There was a hand towel on the side of the bath, but Debbie had noticed a pile of towels on the bed as well.

'All mod cons!' laughed Simon as Debbie left him.

He came back to the flat a few moments later. He gave her a brotherly hug and kissed her cheek. 'Take care of yourself, and let us know how you go on.'

'Thanks for everything, Simon. Bye for now. Love to Fiona and the children...' She could feel tears starting to prick at her eyelids and was glad he didn't prolong the goodbye. She didn't go down to the car, but stood at the bedroom window, watching and waving as he drove away.

Five

Debbie sat on the bed feeling, suddenly, very lost and alone. The tears that had been threatening began to seep out of her eyes and run down her cheeks. She blinked and gave a loud sniff. 'Don't start crying, you idiot!' she chided herself, taking a tissue from the pocket of her jeans and drying her eyes.

She realized, though, that she did have an incipient headache; this often happened when she found herself in a stressful situation. She was also quite hungry. What would her mum do? Make a cup of tea, of course. Would there be any tea bags, though, or milk?

This was not the sort of lodgings where the landlady provided meals. Debbie knew they would have to make their own breakfasts – which should not be too much of a problem – and a meal at the end of the day. She hoped that her flatmates might prove to be rather more skilled in the kitchen than she was. There was a canteen at the college where they could have lunch: a snack or something more substantial.

Fiona had made a packed lunch for her. She took the plastic bag containing the film-wrapped sandwiches out of her holdall. Chicken on wholemeal bread with lettuce and a touch of mayonnaise; they looked delicious. There was a packet of crisps, a Kit-Kat, and an apple and a banana. And – thank goodness – there was also a small bottle of milk. Fiona was such a thoughtful person.

Debbie carried the items into the kitchen and opened the wall cupboard, hoping to find some crockery. Yes; there were four mugs, heavy ones – certainly not bone china – with pictures of comical animals on them, a selection of plates and dishes, and some assorted cutlery in a tin box. She opened a tin which depicted the Queen's coronation of 1953, and was pleased to find that it held tea bags; only a few, possibly left by the previous occupants. And there was a jar containing an inch or so of Nescafe' coffee granules. There didn't seem to be any sugar, but beggars couldn't be choosers. She would have to drink it without sugar for once. They would need to go shopping for necessities, another thing she was not accustomed to doing. All household chores had been left to her mum. Debbie liked to think she had helped but she was realizing now that she had been rather spoilt.

There was – wonder of wonders! – an electric kettle; an old one, but functional, she hoped. She took off the lid to find that the element was covered in a sort of fur. She knew it wasn't harmful but it had to be removed every so often to make it work efficiently. She knew her dad used some sort of powder, but she didn't know what it was. Anyway, it might work in its present state. She half filled it and switched it on. The red light indicated that it was working.

She popped a tea bag in a beaker with a picture of a grinning pig, and waited for the kettle to boil. Whilst she was putting the sandwiches on a plate, ready for her solitary picnic lunch, she heard a shout.

'Hello, Debbie; I'm here again...' She recognized Rhoda's voice. 'And here's one of yer flatmates. Two down, two to go.'

Rhoda entered the room carrying a large suitcase, followed by a middle-aged man carrying another one, and a girl with a large box in her arms. She was pale with wispy fairish hair, and Debbie thought she looked frightened to death.

'Hello...' Debbie stepped out from the kitchen alcove. 'I'm Debbie,' she announced cheerfully. 'I'm just making some tea. Would you like a cup? Well, it's a mug actually, and there's no sugar, but it won't be too bad.'

'There you are you see, Lisa,' said the man who was most probably her father. 'You've made a friend already. Didn't I say you'd be alright? Now cheer up, there's a good girl, and this nice lass'll look after you, won't you, Debbie?'

'Yes, of course I will. I've not been here long myself though, only half an hour or so.' She turned to Lisa. 'I was feeling a bit down in the dumps, so we can cheer one another up, can't we?'

The girl smiled, looking a little happier. 'Yes ... thank you. That'll be nice.'

Debbie spoke to the man. 'Would you like some tea, Mr ... er, sorry I don't know your name?'

'I'm Mr Dobson... Sam, and I'm Lisa's dad as you probably guessed. No, I won't have any tea, thanks, luv. I'll be getting back now I've seen

67

Lisa's OK. I've left my chief assistant in charge so everything'll be alright, but I said I'd get back as soon as poss. We've a market garden on t' wolds, near to Beverley. Lisa'll tell you about it. Now lass, I'll be on my way.' He hugged his daughter and she clung to him for a moment.

'Ring us when you can, and yer mam'll write to you. Take care of yerself now, luv, and you an' all, Debbie. Keep yer pecker up...' He departed with a cheery wave. Rhoda had already gone.

Lisa looked at Debbie and smiled shyly. 'I would like some tea,' she said. 'I think my mum's packed some sugar lumps, and there's a packet of tea bags. She tried to think of everything I'd need.'

'Yes, so did my mum,' said Debbie, 'but we seemed to overlook tea bags. Do you want it now, or shall we unpack first? I haven't even done that yet.'

'Tea first, I think,' said Lisa, 'if that's OK with you? My mum's packed some sandwiches, so we can share them if you like.'

Debbie laughed. 'I've got some as well. My ... friend made them for me. I've been staying there for the weekend, 'cause I live quite a long way away.'

'Yes ... I think you're a Geordie, aren't you?' said Lisa. 'If you don't mind me saying so? I recognized the accent.'

'Yes; unmistakable, isn't it,' laughed Debbie. 'But I don't mind; why should I? You should hear my dad! He's a real "Why aye, man!" So you're from the south of Yorkshire?'

'Yes, like my dad said; we have a market garden

between Beverley and Hornsea. That's why I've come here, to learn about the more technical side of things, you know? He wants me to be in charge of the greenhouses eventually... Anyway, we'd better get on with our lunch, hadn't we?'

Lisa looked much more relaxed now. 'I'm so glad you were here when we arrived,' she said as they tucked into their impromptu meal of Debbie's chicken and Lisa's roast ham sandwiches. 'I was feeling really scared and ready to burst into tears. I've never been away from home before; well, to live away, I mean.'

'Neither have I,' said Debbie. 'But I think we'll all be in the same boat. There are two more to come yet. I told Mrs Perkins – Rhoda – that I'd have the front bedroom. D'you want to share with me, seeing that we've already met one another?'

'Yes, thank you; I'd like that,' said Lisa. 'That lady, Mrs Perkins, she seems a good sort, doesn't she?'

'Yes, and it all looks quite clean; we'll have to look after ourselves, cooking and cleaning and everything.'

The view from the front bedroom was not a very inspiring one; a row of similar houses across the road. It was just as uninteresting from the back bedroom – they had a peep – consisting of back yards and the backs of the houses in the next street. The room was furnished in much the same way, but the bedspreads were blue instead of pink.

They had dined with their plates on their knees, sitting on the settee. No doubt when there were four of them they would use the table. They rinsed the plates and mugs under the tap, then found some rather worn pot towels in a corner cupboard near to the kitchen alcove. There were some wooden table mats there, too, and an iron. But where was the ironing board? They located it in the back bedroom propped up against the wardrobe.

'Which bed do you want?' asked Debbie.

'I don't mind,' said Lisa. 'You choose; you were here first.' She seemed almost too eager to please, and not to assert herself. She would need to change, thought Debbie, or she might get put upon.

'You have the one near the window then,' said Debbie, 'although there's not much of a view.'

There were, however, two bedside cupboards in the same utility design as the other furniture, and lamps with parchment shades. They were, in fact, very well provided for. Debbie guessed it was the lap of luxury compared with some grotty bedsits she'd heard about. The wardrobe, though, was not likely to be adequate for two of them. They unpacked more or less in silence, taking out their skirts and jumpers, tee shirts and trousers and putting them on the wire hangers.

'Gosh! We've nearly filled it,' said Debbie. 'We'd best shove them up a bit.' There was a peg on the back of the door, though, for coats, and another row of pegs over the chest of drawers. There were four large drawers, so Lisa had the two top ones and Debbie the bottom two for their underwear and tights and odds and ends.

After they had emptied the cases they started

on the boxes.

'Oh, you've got one of those new cassette players,' Lisa exclaimed. 'How super!'

'Yes; it was my special present when I was eighteen,' said Debbie. 'I've not got many tapes, though, yet. But we'll all be able to listen to it, won't we? It doesn't look as though there's a telly.'

'I don't watch the TV very much,' replied Lisa. 'My parents are rather fussy about what they watch. It was ages before they got one at all. They said it was a modern craze and that they weren't going along with it just because everyone else did. But in the end they had to give in. My dad said they wanted it for the news and the current affairs programmes, and the nature films; he likes David Attenborough. They watch *Dad's Army* though, and *Morecambe and Wise*. They try to pretend it's not really their thing, but I've seen them laughing at it.'

'Yes, my parents watch those as well,' said Debbie, 'and Steptoe and Son.'

'Oh, they won't watch that at any price!' said Lisa. '"We draw the line at vulgarity" my dad says.'

Debbie was quickly forming an opinion about her new friend's upbringing, and the influence of her parents. She had noticed that the clothes that Lisa took out of her case were rather old-fashioned: home-made jumpers and cardigans, and skirts that looked to be knee-length, certainly not minis. She was wearing trousers, though, and a turtleneck sweater, which were the standard gear of most teenagers.

'My parents are Methodists, you see,' she told

Debbie, 'No drinking or gambling and all that. My dad's a local preacher, quite well known in our area. He's a good sort though ... well, you've met him, haven't you? Always very friendly and ready to help anybody. It was Dad who encouraged me to come here, though Mum wasn't all that keen at first. I haven't mixed very much with other people, only those at the chapel that we attend, and he thought it was time that I did. And he wants me to get this diploma. It'll be a good advert for the business, you see.'

'But you'll be able to find a position anywhere you like, won't you? In the future, I mean.'

'Oh, they'll expect me to stick around for a while ... but who can tell what the future holds? D'you know, I was really dreading coming here.' Lisa's face broke into a broad smile as she looked at Debbie. 'I nearly cried off at the last minute, but I feel much better now. I'm so glad I've met you, Debbie.'

'Well, that's good,' replied Debbie. 'So am I.' She was looking forward to meeting the other two girls, though, whoever they might be. She was pleased to have helped Lisa to settle in, but she wanted to make other friends as well. She was relieved, really, that it would not be just the two of them sharing the flat.

'Let's have a look at your tapes then,' said Lisa. 'Oh, Cliff Richard; yes, I like him. My parents approve of him, too, because he's a Christian! Adam Faith, Cilla Black ... yes, I've seen them on *Juke Box Jury* occasionally. I watch it when my dad's not there. The Beatles ... yes, I like them as well.'

'I'm not all that way out in my tastes,' said Debbie. 'I've never cared for the Rolling Stones. I like Herman's Hermits, and Simon and Garfunkel; they're my favourites. D'you mind if I put this poster of them up?'

'No, I don't mind; it'll brighten the place up. I haven't any posters, but I could bring a few ornaments back when I go home... Oh, you've got some brass band tapes, too. That's all my dad ever listens to on our gramophone, with him being a Yorkshireman, you see; and Handel's *Messiah*.'

Their conversation came to an end as the door to the flat was flung open, and there was Rhoda again. 'Here they are, yer last two flatmates,' she called. 'I met 'em on t' doorstep with all their luggage. You can come and give us a hand if you like.'

Two young women followed Rhoda into the room, one tall and one much shorter. The taller of the two put down her case and held out her hand.

'How do you do?' she said, in a voice that Debbie immediately labelled 'posh'. 'I'm Francesca, but I'm usually called Fran; Fran Rutherford.'

'How do you do?' replied Debbie, a little overawed. The young woman seemed so very self-assured. 'I'm Debbie Hargreaves, and this is Lisa Dobson. We've only just met, about an hour ago. We were wondering when you'd turn up.'

'How do you do?' mumbled Lisa, as she shook the newcomer's hand. 'Pleased to meet you...'

'And I'm Karen,' said the other girl smiling broadly. 'Karen Stubbs. Hi there, you two.' She had short ginger hair and a freckled face. She didn't bother to shake hands. She looked jolly and friendly; just as self-confident as the other girl but in a different way. Debbie thought that Francesca's name suited her; she looked very much a Francesca rather than a Fran. She was what Debbie thought of as statuesque, with long blonde hair swept back in a chignon.

'We've just met on t' doorstep,' said Karen. 'I got a taxi from t' station. I've had a right carry-on, I can tell you, with all that luggage. Anyroad, we're here now. But we could do with a hand with the luggage, like Rhoda said, if you don't mind.'

'Of course we'll help,' said Debbie. 'We're just about sorted out now, aren't we, Lisa?'

'Yes, we'll come and help you,' replied Lisa, looking rather in awe at the two newcomers.

Debbie smiled to herself. Chalk and cheese, those two new arrivals. All four of them, in fact, seemed to be very different sorts of personalities, no doubt from widely diverse backgrounds. It should all make for an interesting year.

'My fiancé brought me,' said Fran, 'but he couldn't stay. He had another appointment in Leeds. We've driven up from Cheshire; we had lunch before we set off.'

'And I came on t' train from Doncaster,' said Karen. 'I ate me sandwiches, so I'm OK for a while. I'm always hungry, though! P'raps we could have a cup of tea and a biscuit when we're sorted out? Anyway, come on girls; let's get cracking.'

'I'll leave you to it then,' said Rhoda. 'Give us a call if you need to know owt. Cheerio for now...'

Between them they carried up the remainder of

the cases, bags and boxes, and a television set that Francesca had brought along. 'Just a small black and white one,' she said. 'I expect you're used to colour now, as I am, but it will suffice.'

The others didn't reply to that. Debbie guessed that colour television was still pretty well unknown to them.

'Will you two be OK in the back bedroom?' asked Debbie. 'There's very little difference and ... well ... we chose the other one.'

'That's fine,' said Karen. 'First come, first served.'

'Yes, that suits me, too,' said Fran. 'One can't expect home comforts, but it all seems quite adequate. But where's the bathroom?'

'A trek along the corridor outside the flat,' Debbie told her. 'Hot water twice a day, so Rhoda told us. I think we'll have to make a rota for our morning wash, and for baths, or else we'll be queuing up.'

'I usually have a shower,' said Fran. 'But I don't suppose there's one here? That would be too much to ask for.'

'No, I didn't notice one,' replied Debbie. They didn't have such a thing as a shower at home. She had been brought up as a child with the 'Friday night is bath night' routine, until she had convinced her mother that it was not unusual to have a bath more often than that: every day, in fact.

'Depends on who's up with the lark,' said Karen. 'I don't mind having an early turn 'cause I'm used to it. There are five of us at home, as well as me mam and dad, at least there was until me sister moved out a month ago. I reckon we'll manage OK.'

'You two unpack, and I'll make some more tea,' said Debbie. 'Then maybe we could find a shop and get some bread and milk, and whatever else we need.'

'Do you want to be our housekeeper, then?' suggested Karen. 'You know, in charge of food supplies an' all that?'

'No, not really,' laughed Debbie. 'I'm not used to running a house any more than anyone else; probably not as much.' She guessed that Karen, from a large family, would have had to do her share. And Fran; did she have her own place?

They learnt more about each other later when the packing was done and they sat nursing mugs of tea and munching chocolate digestive biscuits that Fran had brought.

Fran lived with her parents near Macclesfield. They had converted the upstairs rooms so that she had her own self-contained flat. She implied, however, that she spent a good deal of time at her fiancé's flat. He was part-owner of a firm of landscape gardeners. She would be working for them as a designer when she had completed her landscaping course. Until recently she had worked in a florist's shop. She was twenty years of age, some two years older than the rest of the girls.

Karen had been working at a garden centre for the past two years, since she left school at the age of sixteen. Unlike Debbie's though, hers had been a full-time job. She had shown such promise that her employer had suggested she should go on a course to learn more about horticulture in general. The government grants were quite generous, but there were additional expenses which some parents could not afford. Karen admitted, unashamedly, that her parents could not do so, and that her boss was giving her a generous allowance.

'He must think a lot of you,' said Debbie.

'Oh, he does that!' said Karen. 'Charlie's a grand bloke...' She smiled, as though he meant a lot to her. 'And I've a job to go back to an' all. I shall be in charge of all the greenhouses. We grow plants and flowers all through the year, in and out of season, and send 'em all over the country.'

At present she lived at home on a large housing estate near Doncaster. The garden centre was a couple of miles away – just a bike ride – but she intended to find a place to live nearer to her work when she returned. And Debbie knew that Lisa had a job to return to in her father's market garden. So she, Debbie, was the only one who would need to find employment when she had finished her course. She knew that Mr Hill, her previous employer, would be pleased to have her back, although he had been the one who had advised her to use her talent for design, and consider a career in landscape gardening. Who could tell, though, what the future might bring? As yet she hadn't even started her course.

Between them they had brought enough provisions to see them easily through the next few weeks. The kitchen cupboard was now filled with tinned goods; salmon, fruit, corned beef, spam, baked beans and spaghetti, as well as biscuits, tea bags and instant coffee. It was the perishable, day to day items, that were missing.

They decided, as Debbie had suggested, to go shopping. They found that the nearest super-market was a Tesco, not all that far away. Debbie and Lisa carried the wire baskets, and they browsed around the shelves stocking up with long-life milk, butter, low fat spread – requested by Fran – eggs, bacon, cornflakes, and bread, both sliced and unsliced.

'I'll pay,' offered Fran, 'then you can settle up with me later.'

Armed with a plastic carrier bag each, they walked back to their new home. They divided the bill into four, and decided they should do that every time they went shopping.

'Now, who's going to volunteer to cook a meal?' said Fran. The others stared at her as though it hadn't occurred to them.

'Well, we do need to eat, don't we?' she went on. 'I'm starving! I'm supposed to be slimming, but I'm going to forget that for today. Come along, girls; don't all speak at once!'

'Couldn't we all do it?' suggested Debbie, not wanting to admit that she was no great shakes in the kitchen.

'There's not enough room in that cubbyhole,' said Karen. 'I don't mind; I'm used to taking my turn at home. You won't get owt fancy, though. How about bacon and eggs? And we've got some baked beans. Are there any pans, though?'

'Oh crumbs! We never thought about that,' said Debbie. 'There must be some, somewhere.'

They found them right at the back of the cup-board behind the iron and the plates and dishes;

a rather wobbly frying pan and two saucepans which looked as thought they might be non-stick.

'Let's be civilized and set the table, shall we?' said Fran. 'Start as we mean to go on.' She was the one who would be least likely to want to rough it, although Debbie was deciding that she liked her. Maybe she was not as posh and self-important as she had seemed to be at first.

They had found a checked tablecloth and some table mats, so whilst Karen and Fran started to prepare their first meal, Debbie and Lisa set the table.

'There's no salt or pepper,' said Debbie, 'at least I can't see any. Oh dear! We'll have to make a list of things we need and get them next time we go shopping.'

In the kitchen the two cooks had discovered that there was no lard or cooking fat, but why should there be? They were supposed to be catering for themselves. They made do with margarine to fry the eggs, and they grilled the bacon.

'We must remember the more pans we use, the more there are to wash up,' said Fran, looking aghast at the mountain of pans already piled up in the small sink. 'We'll have to choose something simpler in future.'

'Bread and jam,' laughed Karen. 'That's a standby in our house.'

'We might manage cheese on toast, or sardines, or spaghetti,' said Fran. 'Oh damn! We've forgotten to warm the plates. One thing I can't stand is cold plates.'

'Ne'er mind; we'll do better next time,' said

Karen. 'Grub up, you two!' she called to the others. 'Come and get it.'

Despite the inadequacies of the meal they all tucked in and thoroughly enjoyed it. They had found a large brown earthenware teapot, so there was plenty of tea, and bread and butter. They finished off the meal with slices of the fruitcake that Fiona had packed for Debbie.

They found out more about each other as they dined. Fran, as they already knew, was engaged – she was wearing a diamond and sapphire ring – and she said that she would most likely spend some of her weekends in Cheshire, if her fiancé, Ralph, was able to come and collect her.

Debbie told them that she had a boyfriend – of sorts – but that it wasn't anything serious. Karen was rather coy about her love life. Yes, she said; there was someone, but it was complicated. Debbie wondered, reading between the lines, if it was her boss, Charlie, whom she had said was so good to her, paying for her expenses on the course and promising her a promotion when she returned. Why, though, was it complicated? Could he possibly be married? If so she was courting disaster, but Debbie decided it wasn't any of her business.

Lisa admitted that there was no one special in her life. She had attended an all-girls grammar school and sixth form and had never had much contact with the opposite sex. Debbie concluded that her parents had been somewhat over-protective of her, their only child. She, Debbie, had been an only child too, and had known what it was like to be cherished and worried over. She had rebelled though, kicking over the traces from time to time, something she could not imagine Lisa doing. She felt sure that Lisa would meet someone who would be attracted by her fair prettiness and her air of fragility.

'What about a visit to the pub tonight?' suggested Karen, when they had cleared away what seemed to be a mountain of washing up. (They had already decided on beans on toast for tomorrow.)

'Great idea!' said Fran. 'Ralph and I noticed one on the main road, not very far from here. It's probably one of the places where the students hang out.'

Debbie saw a look of apprehension, almost horror, on Lisa's face. 'What's the matter?' she whispered. 'Don't you like the idea?'

She shook her head. 'I've never been inside a public house. I know my parents wouldn't approve. I don't know what to do.'

Karen had overheard her. 'Your mam and dad aren't here, are they?' she said, not unkindly. 'There's nowt wrong in going to a pub, and you can drink lemonade or orange juice if you like. We're not going to lead you astray, luv. I don't suppose any of us are what you'd call drinkers. Can't afford it, can we?'

'I like a gin and tonic or a dry Martini,' said Fran, 'but it's the ambience of the place that's important. We won't know what it's like until we've tried it. Don't worry, Lisa, dear; we'll take care of you. Are we all agreed then? We'll get on our way when everyone's ready.'

Debbie had decided that Fran was a kind person. She appeared a bit toffee-nosed at first, but 'her heart was in the right place' as her mother, Vera, might say.

They locked the door of the flat and went downstairs, Fran offering to take charge of the key. As they reached the bottom, the door of the downstairs flat opened and three young men came out. They all stopped and looked at one another, then there was a chorus of hellos and jumbled conversations.

'You must be our new neighbours...'

'We only arrived today...'

'We've been here since yesterday, haven't we, chaps?'

'What do you think of it then?'

'Not so bad; could be a lot worse...'

The young men introduced themselves as Alistair, Ben and Neil.

'We're off to the pub,' said Alistair, the tallest of the three, and the one who seemed to be the chief spokesman. 'Would you like to come with us?'

'Great! That's just where we're going,' said Fran.

So they all set off together to the Red Lion, a popular meeting place situated on the main road leading out of the city.

Six

The students were granted a long weekend at the beginning of November, a half-term break mid-way between September and Christmas. They could, if they wished, go home each weekend, but some students had lectures on a Saturday morning, and it was not worthwhile for others who lived a good distance away.

Debbie had not yet spent any weekends away from Leeds. On Saturday mornings she was busy, with the rest of her group, gaining practical experience in the college garden. Her parents understood that she would not be going up to Northumberland until Christmas when they had a fortnight's break. She had been invited to Aberthwaite for the half-term weekend to stay with Fiona and Simon. It was actually Simon who had invited her. He had told her that Fiona's depression had not improved, even though they now had someone helping with the children on a permanent basis. Speaking with him on the phone, Debbie thought he sounded tense and worried. He assured her that she would not be adding to Fiona's problems by staying with them; rather, he hoped that her company would do Fiona a world of good. She had agreed to travel to Aberthwaite on the Thursday afternoon after lectures finished, and return on the Monday ready to start her studies on the Tuesday. There was a service bus from Leeds to the northern dales, so she would not need to trouble Simon to collect her.

By the beginning of November they had been at college for two months, and the four young women had settled down nicely together. Debbie found that she had become the recipient of confidences from her flatmates. Not so much from Fran, who spent most weekends away from Leeds, with her fiancé, Ralph.

Karen, though, had confided in Debbie about the significant person in her life. As Debbie had guessed, it was Charlie, her boss, the owner of the garden centre where she worked. She had also guessed correctly – or almost so – about the complication in the relationship.

'One problem is that Charlie is quite a lot older than me,' Karen told her one Saturday evening as they chatted together over their supper drink of hot chocolate; Fran was away for the weekend and Lisa had retired to bed early with a slight cold. 'Well, p'raps not an awful lot; depends on how you look at it. He's thirty; twelve years older than me. That's not really the main problem, though...'

She hesitated, looking at Debbie so anxiously that she had no qualms about asking, 'What is it, Karen? He's not married, is he?'

'Well ... he has been married,' Karen answered. 'He's divorced now, and he's got a three-year-old son. Little Alfie; he's a real smashing kid. Charlie has to bring him into work sometimes when his mam – Charlie's mam, I mean – can't look after him.'

'So ... you're saying that the little boy isn't with

84

his own mother?' asked Debbie. 'That Charlie has custody of him?'

'Yes, he's got custody of him. His wife ran off and left him with Alfie when he was only a year old. A right flibbertigibbet she was, that Daphne! I never could stand her. Anyroad, Charlie had no trouble getting a divorce, and the judge didn't hesitate about letting him have the kid. His mam looks after Alfie most of the time. She lives nearby, but there's the odd time she can't manage it. Then Charlie leaves him with me; he helps me wi' t' plants, an' he has his own little watering can, bless him!'

'So you and Charlie got friendly then, did you, after the divorce?' asked Debbie. She was thinking that the girl would be taking a lot on: a divorced man with a young child. All the same, she had come to the conclusion that Karen was a very capable girl.

'Yeah ... we got friendly,' said Karen, smiling and blushing slightly. 'He took me out for a posh meal, to say thank you for looking after Alfie. He said he didn't know what he'd do without me. And ... well ... we got quite close, if you know what I mean. Nowt wrong; I don't mean that we've done ... that. He's a decent sort of a bloke, is Charlie. But I think I know what he's got in mind. That's why he insisted I should do this course, then I'd be qualified to help him to run the place, and then ... who knows?'

'He's young, isn't he, to own a garden centre?' enquired Debbie.

'His father retired, and Charlie took it over. He's their only son, you see, and his father's quite

85

elderly, a lot older than his mother. They bought a little bungalow, not far away, and Charlie lives on the premises with Alfie.'

'So you'll be looking forward to seeing him next weekend,' said Debbie. 'Will you be staying with him?'

'Oh no; there's nowt like that; not yet, like I told you. I'll be staying with me mam and dad, but Charlie says he's missed me, and he's longing to see me again.'

Karen certainly looked starry-eyed; a girl who was very much in love. Or, Debbie wondered, was it just the idea of being in love that made her look like that? 'Falling in love with love...' as the words of an old song went.

She, Debbie, was no longer sure that she had been in love. She had imagined that Kevin was the one for her. But she had been only fifteen years old when she first met him. She wondered now, with all the wisdom of her eighteen years, how she could have been such a crazy kid. And now ... well ... already there were two more young men for whom she was feeling rather mixed emotions.

That first evening in the Red Lion had been a happy time when the girls from the upstairs flat became acquainted with their neighbours from the ground floor. There were three girls and four young men. Not that there had been any idea of pairing off. They all got to know one another, talking about the various courses they would be doing and their future plans.

Debbie and Alistair, who was the oldest and most talkative member of the trio, had discovered

86

that they were both studying landscape gardening and would be attending some of the same lectures. Debbie had felt an immediate attraction to him, but then who wouldn't? He was the stereotypical 'tall, dark and handsome' man with a sparkle in his eye and a roguish grin. She had learnt that his father was a partner in a firm of landscape gardeners and that he would be joining them as a junior partner after he had finished the course. He had already been employed there since he left school, starting from the bottom as a labourer and learning the various skills attached to the work.

Debbie had got to know him better and to like him more as they attended the study groups together. She had been wary of him at first, wondering if he might be too handsome for his own good. He seemed to be friendly with everyone, treating all the girls he met in the same cheerful, light-hearted way. There were, understandably, more men than women on many of the courses. With the men as well, he was the same friendly and good-natured bloke.

Debbie told herself that she must face up to it; Alistair Kenyon was not interested in her as anything more than a fellow student. If he had been he would have made a move before now. Anyway, she shouldn't be thinking about him at all. She had resumed her friendship – one that had never really got under way – with Graham Challinor. He had sought her out when she had been in Leeds for a couple of weeks. By that time the girls had filled in the card next to their door bell with their names, so that visitors would know which bell to push.

It was just after seven thirty on a Tuesday evening when they heard the sound of the doorbell, an unusual enough occurrence to make Debbie exclaim, 'Now, whoever can that be?'

They didn't get many visitors. Fran's fiancé sometimes called unexpectedly, or, in the morning the postman might ring if he had a parcel to deliver; Debbie's mum had sent a parcel a couple of times, containing a home-made fruitcake or gingerbread. The lads from downstairs came up now and again, usually if they ran short of something in the kitchen, but they didn't need to ring the bell; they just ran up the stairs and knocked on the door.

'We won't know unless we go and see, will we?' said Karen. 'Shall I go? Or do you think it might be your Ralph giving you a surprise, Fran?'

'No; I only saw him on Sunday,' replied Fran. 'Actually, we had a bit of a tiff and we parted on not very good terms. I'd be very surprised if he came to apologize, knowing Ralph.'

'You don't sound very upset,' Karen remarked.

'I'm not. It's happened before and it always blows over. We're too much alike, Ralph and I.' Fran shrugged. 'I'm not losing any sleep over it.'

It was the first time she had mentioned the argument. Fran played her cards very close to her chest and, unlike the others, didn't confide much about her personal life.

'Well, whoever it is, they've been waiting long enough whilst we're wasting time wondering,' said Debbie. 'I'll go and see...'

The young man on the doorstep was raising his

hand to ring again when Debbie opened the door. It took her a moment – only a few seconds, though – to realize who it was, although the possibility of him coming had been on her mind since she arrived in Leeds.

'Don't you know me?' he said, laughing at her surprised face.

'Of course I do,' she replied, recognizing the tall, dark-haired young man with the longish nose and strong features: a good-looking fellow in a rugged and rangy sort of way. 'Graham! How lovely to see you!'

She had not seen him, in fact, since the occasion of the triplets' christening when the two of them, along with his brother, Greg, had been godparents to the babies. And before that they had met only once, on that momentous weekend when Fiona had given birth, so unexpectedly, to the triplets. It was not surprising, therefore, that he should appear a little different in her eyes: slightly older and with longer hair. He leaned forward, kissing her gently on the cheek.

'I thought I'd come and look you up – Simon rang to tell me where you were – to see if you'd like to go for a drink and a chat?'

'I'd love to,' she replied. 'Come up and meet the others...'

She had discovered on first meeting him that Graham was not so extrovert as his half-brother, Greg. However, he chatted quite easily with the other three girls. Lisa did not say very much, just smiled pleasantly and answered when a remark was addressed to her. She had come out of her shell quite a lot, however, since embarking on her life away from home, although she was still a little shy of someone new.

Karen was the one with the most to say. 'Excuse the mess, won't you, Graham?' she said, although the room was not really too untidy. Debbie realized that the others had had a bit of a scramble round picking up the debris – unwashed mugs, papers and books and items of clothing – from the floor and straightening the cushions before she had reappeared with Graham. 'Four women living together; well, you can imagine, can't you? Although Francesca here tries to keep us in order, don't you, Fran?'

Graham smiled. 'Looks OK to me. You should see the state of my place sometimes, and there are only two of us. I'm sharing a flat with a friend I met at uni. We don't work together – he's an accountant – but we rub along all right together, and it saves on the expense. We're only renting, of course, but I shall try to save up and get a place of my own ... Now, Debbie; shall we go and catch up with all the news. It's been nice meeting you all. See you again sometime...'

Debbie had enjoyed herself immensely that evening. She found that the liking and the attraction she had felt for Graham when she first met him was still there. They had walked further along the main road towards Headingley. Graham's flat was not far away, but he did not invite her there that evening. They found a little pub, one that was not overflowing with students, and talked easily together over his pint of lager and a shandy for Debbie, renewing what had started a couple of years ago as a tentative friendship.

Graham was twenty-one, three years older than Debbie. He was enjoying his work as the junior member of a firm of architects near to the Leeds city centre. They had a significant interest in common, in that Graham's forte was for house design, and Debbie was discovering that her talent, with regard to landscape gardening, lay more with the designing than the more practical side.

He walked her home that first night, and kissed her gently on the lips as they said goodnight. He had invited her to go with him to a brass band concert that was being held at Leeds Town Hall in two weeks' time. That, also, had been an enjoyable time for the two of them. Graham had learnt to play the French horn whilst at school, and had played in a band at university. He was now on the lookout for an amateur band that he could join.

They met just once more before Debbie was due to go to Aberthwaite; a visit to the cinema in Leeds to see a re-run of *Butch Cassidy and the Sundance Kid*, a film they had both enjoyed previously. They ended the evening with a visit to one of the many pubs in the city, then Graham walked her home. She did not invite him up to the flat, neither had he made any move so far to invite her to his place. Once more he kissed her goodnight, a little more ardently this time, and she felt herself responding to him. But it seemed to be a question of so far and no further.

'Give my regards to Fiona and Simon,' he said, knowing she would be visiting them the following weekend. 'I hope Fiona's feeling better by now; Greg says she's not been feeling too well. Not surprising, though, with three – no, four – young children. And give little Mark a special hug from me!'

Mark, the youngest by some ten minutes of the two boy triplets, was the one that Graham had held, rather gingerly, at the christening. Debbie, Greg and Graham, though, were officially god-parents to all three children.

'Will do,' said Debbie. She stood on tiptoe and kissed him once more, very casually, on the cheek. 'Bye then, Graham,' she said in a light-hearted way. 'Thanks for a lovely evening. See you when I come back, maybe?'

'Yes ... sure,' he replied. 'Thank you, too, Debbie. I've really enjoyed it. Er ... next time, perhaps you could come and have a meal with me at my place ... if you would like to? I'm getting to be quite an expert at this cooking lark. I think I can promise you rather more than beans on toast.'

'Thanks; that'll be great,' she said, trying not to sound as though it was what she had been waiting for. But it was certainly a move in the right direction.

She was not sure what the state of play was with Graham. Was she 'going out' with him – to use the common parlance – or not? She guessed there was no one else of significance in his life; he was not the sort of fellow to have a string of girl-friends. He was obviously the sort of young man who preferred to take things nice and slowly. And there was no harm in that. She had decided all too quickly that she was in love with Kevin, but her possessiveness had only served to annoy him. She would tell Fiona and Simon that she had seen Graham and would pass on his good wishes, without giving any suggestion that they might be 'a couple'.

All four of the flatmates would be away for the long weekend. Fran would be in Macclesfield, although she had not said whether she would be staying with Ralph or at her own place. She, of all of them, was the most secretive about her personal affairs.

Karen was excited about the thought of going home to Doncaster and seeing Charlie again. She seemed to be very hopeful about the outcome of this weekend. And Lisa had confided to Debbie that she had mixed feelings about going home to Beverley to see her parents again.

'Don't get me wrong,' she said to Debbie, one evening when the two of them were alone in the flat. 'Of course I'm looking forward to seeing them again. Mum says it seems like ages since she saw me. We've never been apart for so long before, and I have missed them both... But not as much as I thought I would,' she added, with a shy smile.

'Do you mean because of Neil?' asked Debbie, smiling at her understandingly.

'Yes,' said Lisa softly. 'I really do like him a lot, Debbie.' Her pale cheeks turned pink, and her blue eyes glowed with happiness. 'And I think I'll have to tell Mum and Dad about him. They know me so well you see, and if I don't say anything they'll know I'm hiding something from them. I'm not very good at – what's the word? – dissembling. I'm afraid I'm an open book, and I know they'll start quizzing me. "What's the matter, Lisa? There's something you're not telling us, isn't there?" I can just imagine it...'

'Do you mean because Neil's a Catholic?' asked Debbie. 'I don't see that it matters. He does go to church, doesn't he? And that's what your parents think is important. It's more than a lot of young men do. And we're all ... well, we all worship the same God, don't we, no matter which church we go to?'

Debbie, in fact, had not been to church since coming to Leeds, although she had attended the local church at home, when she had not been working at the garden centre. She still believed in God. How could she not do so when she was continually surrounded by the works of His creation? Each day she learnt more and more, in her studies, about nature and God's wonderful world, although God, of course, was never mentioned at the college lectures. She didn't see, though, why there had to be such an issue made about it all. What did it matter which church you attended, or whether you went to one at all?

Lisa was such a good girl. She, of the four of them, was the only one who had kept up the Sunday tradition. She had sought out the nearest Methodist church and had gone there for either the morning or the evening service: not every Sunday but often enough, Debbie imagined, to appease her parents.

'Try telling my parents that,' said Lisa, in answer to Debbie's remark. 'They worship the Methodist God, and they believe that's the only one! They tolerate the Church of England, provided it's not too "high", and other nonconformist churches. But Roman Catholics – I'm afraid they're taboo!'

94

'Yes... I suppose I see your problem,' said Debbie, although she didn't, not really. Simon was a perfect example of a tolerant vicar. She knew he had friends and acquaintances amongst both the Methodist and the Roman Catholic clergy, and was open-minded about the beliefs of others whilst defending the line of churchmanship that he followed.

That first evening, when the girls had gone to the pub with the young men from downstairs, Lisa had met Neil O'Brien. They were both inclined to be shy and not very talkative. That was why, when they did begin talking together, they found they had a lot in common. Thy discovered that they would be attending several of the same lectures on such subjects as greenhouse maintenance, fruit and vegetable growing, and flower and bulb production. Neil, like Lisa, had worked in a market garden and had come on the course to further his knowledge. Their friendship had started slowly; it was not until a few weeks had passed and they knew one another better, that Neil had asked Lisa to go out with him.

It was clear to the other girls, seeing the new sparkle in her eyes and the radiance on her face – she looked so much prettier now – that Lisa was captivated by Neil. Debbie knew that Lisa had confided in her, more than the other two, about her budding relationship with him. Debbie was flattered that it was so, although she was no great expert on affairs of the heart.

'I've never had a boyfriend before,' Lisa told her. 'I hardly knew any boys at all. I used to hear the girls at school talking about all the boys they'd been out with. I felt a bit silly because I didn't have one. My best friend in the sixth form, Lindsay – she's gone away to training college now – she was just the same as me. She hadn't been out with any boys either. We used to hear them talking, and we felt they were showing off sometimes about ... well, about how far they'd gone; you know what I mean?' Lisa had gone pink and was almost whispering.

'Yes, I do know,' said Debbie, nodding. She laughed. 'They were just the same at my school; it was a co-ed school, so there might have been some truth in it; I don't know. I had a boyfriend – I told you about Kevin – but there was nothing like that with him and me. My friend Shirley and me, we thought they were just showing off, trying to go one better than one another.'

She was surprised that Lisa had mentioned the subject. She had wondered whether her new friend might be naive about such matters, but apparently she did know a thing or two.

'I do know a bit about ... sex.' Lisa spoke the word in a hushed tone. 'About what goes on and all that. But not from my mother! I think she'd run a mile rather than mention it. She told me about periods and everything, but I could tell she was embarrassed. I just found out the rest for myself; talking about it with Lindsay, and then there were the things that they show on the telly ... although my mum turns it off if there's anything too suggestive.'

'It seems as though mothers are all the same,' said Debbie. 'My mother didn't tell me much either; although she's been more outspoken since

I met Fiona.' Debbie had told the girls about her birth mother – her other family – when she had felt she knew them well enough. 'I know Mum worries about me, though – Vera, I mean; she's the one I call Mum. I suppose all mothers worry about that. But Fiona told me what happened to her, how I was conceived and how easily it happened; and I shall try to be aware of that. I haven't – you know – done that. Some girls seem to think it's a sign of being grown-up, an achievement, a milestone ... you know what I mean, but I'm sure I'd be too scared.'

'I didn't even know what it was like to kiss somebody; kiss them properly, I mean, till I met Neil.' She blushed hotly as she said it. 'But ... well, it's nice, isn't it?'

'Very nice, yes!' Debbie laughed. Lisa was such a sweet and innocent girl. 'I'm glad you're getting on so well with Neil. You two are very well suited.'

Neil O'Brien was the quiet one of the three young men; not tall or handsome, but pleasant-looking with fairish floppy hair and serious grey eyes behind tortoiseshell rimmed glasses that he wore a lot of the time.

'Yes, we do get on well together,' agreed Lisa. 'He doesn't seem to think it matters about the religious thing. His father's Irish, as you can tell from the name. The family moved to England ages ago – at the time of the potato famine, I think – and settled near York. They were farming people, and Neil's dad has carried on the tradition. He has his own market garden near to Malton. Strange, isn't it? Just like my dad. Neil's the only son, so he'll follow his father into the business. His mother wasn't a Catholic. She "turned", as they say, when they got married, but from what Neil says, she doesn't go along with it all. He was brought up as a Catholic because they have to promise they'll bring the children up that way. So I suppose she'll understand what it's like and be more tolerant than my parents... Neil's invited me to go and meet them sometime; but I'll have to see how it goes with my mum and dad.'

Lisa loved talking about him. She was never so vociferous as when she was talking about Neil; but it was Debbie she talked with, more than the other two. Debbie hoped that all would go well for her. He was her first boyfriend, but it did seem to be a 'match made in heaven', as the saying went. Depending on which heaven, of course. She hoped that all the people concerned would come to realize that there was only one.

'I think you should pluck up courage to tell your parents about Neil,' Debbie advised her, just before they were due to go home for the long weekend. 'You never know; they might be perfectly all right about it. Anyone can see how much happier you are now. You're quite a different girl from the one you were when you came here. Surely they'll be pleased that you've met a nice young man?'

'Pigs might fly!' replied Lisa.

Seven

Debbie's lectures finished by mid-afternoon on the Thursday, so she was able to catch a service bus at the bus station in Leeds for the comparatively short journey to Aberthwaite; it took less than two hours.

She had been invited to stay for four nights with Fiona and Simon and their family. She had tried to argue that it was too long; not that she didn't wish to stay so long, but she was afraid to overstay her welcome. She got the impression, though, that Fiona wanted her there.

Her parents had made no objection to her spending the long weekend in Aberthwaite rather than Whitesands Bay. She would have had to spend the best part of two days travelling, and lectures started again early on the Tuesday morning. Besides, her mother had said that she and 'Daddy' were going on a coach tour to the Scottish Highlands at the end of October and would be arriving back just as Debbie started her midterm break. Debbie was pleased that her parents had started to make a life of their own since she went away. It would be the first time they had spent a holiday without her. They had always insisted on her accompanying them on their visits to other seaside resorts, such as Scarborough, Whitby or Filey. So this would be a real change of scenery for them. It was good that they were not centring their lives around her as they had done in the past. And she, too, was relieved to have broken away from the apron strings.

It was Simon, on his own, who met her at the bus station at the far end of Aberthwaite. Dusk was falling rapidly by that time. He was waiting when she alighted from the bus, and it was good to see his smiling face. She hoped it meant that he was not as anxious as he had seemed the last time she had spoken to him on the phone.

'Hello, Debbie; great to see you again.' He gave her a friendly hug and kissed her cheek. 'Here, let me take your bag.' She didn't have much luggage; only underwear and a change of clothing, and presents for all the family, including birthday presents for the triplets.

Simon hadn't brought the car as it was only about ten minutes' walk to the rectory, through the town centre and the market square, all closed down now as it was six thirty in the evening.

'How is Fiona?' asked Debbie, her very first question. 'I hope she's feeling better now. I couldn't tell when I spoke to her on the phone. She said she had someone to help her with the children now, so that will be better for her, won't it?' Actually, Debbie had thought that Fiona had not sounded too happy about the arrangement, but she didn't say so now to Simon.

It was a few moments before he replied. 'Yes ... indeed it should be better for her. Glenda's a great help, from what I can see, although I'm not there all the time, of course. But ... Fiona doesn't seem to have taken to her, for some reason.'

'Is she young, like Paula was?' asked Debbie.

'She and Fiona got on so well together, didn't they?'

'Yes, so they did, and I know that Fiona misses her a lot... No; Glenda's an older woman. Well, not really old,' he added with a smile. 'A year or two younger than me. We've got a new curate now,' he went on. 'He's an older man – mid-forties – but new to the ministry. This is his first placement, and he seems to be settling in very well. So does his wife. Gilbert and Norma Henderson; that's what they're called. They have two children, both away at university. And Glenda is Norma's sister.'

'Oh, I see,' said Debbie, sensing some sort of mystery. 'So, is she a full-time helper, living with you? Or is she with her sister?'

'Oh no; she doesn't live in with us. She's living with Gilbert and Norma at the moment, but she's looking out for a flat of her own. They're not supposed to have lodgers at the curate's house, although she is family, of course. We'll have to see how things work out.'

Debbie realized that it might be as well to let this subject drop. It did seem to be a pretty emotive one. Fiona would be able to put her more clearly in the picture, that was if she felt like talking about it. She decided to change the subject.

'And how are the triplets?' she asked. 'Are they looking forward to their birthday? Although I suppose they're rather too young to understand much about it, aren't they?'

Simon laughed. 'I think Stella is the one who's the most excited. She keeps telling them, "You'll

be two years old on Tuesday; it's your birthday!"
Matthew and Michelle ... well, I don't suppose
they really understand, but they've got hold of
the word "birthday" and they keep saying it.
Mark just smiles. He's not as forward as the other
two; he never has been. I know Fiona worries
about it a lot, but I keep telling her that children
don't all progress at the same rate, even though
they're born at the same time. Mark's a happy
little boy, though, and he's certainly not as much
trouble as Matthew. He's a little terror, that one!
He's certainly more than one body's work.' He
made no further comment, however, about the
new helper.

After a moment he went on to say, 'We're having
the children's party on Saturday instead of Tuesday, so that you can be there with us, Debbie.'

'Oh, how lovely!' she said. 'I'm glad about that.'
It was the same weekend, of course, the one that
was usually the half-term break, as it had been
two years ago when she had been in the sixth
form. The three babies had been born on the
Sunday.

'Not a big party,' he explained. 'Just one or two
friends of ours, and a special friend of Stella's from
her nursery school. Saturday's a good day; Sunday
would be too hectic, and Tuesday's an ordinary
working day for most folk. We were pleased when
we realized your break would coincide again. It's a
pity the other two can't be with us; Greg and
Graham, I mean.'

'I've seen Graham a couple of times,' said
Debbie, not wanting to make too much of their
budding friendship. 'He looked me up at the flat;

102

he said you'd given him my address.'

'Yes, so we did. It's nice to see a familiar face when you move to somewhere new. I expect you've settled down nicely, though, by now, haven't you?'

'Yes, we're having a great time, the four of us. We're all different but we get along really well together. It's much better than I thought it would be, and I'm enjoying the course. I feel I've made the right decision, although I don't know yet what I'll be doing when I finish. Some of the others already have jobs to go to.'

'I'm sure something will turn up,' said Simon. 'I'm glad it's working out well for you. So ... here we are.'

They turned in at the gate of the rectory. The rowan tree still held clusters of red berries; the leaves had turned golden brown, raining down on to the path. A few late roses, the last roses of summer, bloomed on the bushes that bordered the path. Debbie experienced again the feeling that she was coming home. And there was Fiona opening the door to greet them with Stella, as usual, at her side.

'Hello, Debbie,' said Stella. 'Mummy says I can stay up late tonight 'cause you're here. An' I'm going to have my tea with you 'stead of with the little ones.'

'Well, that's lovely,' said Debbie, bending down to kiss the little girl. Then she put an arm round Fiona and kissed her cheek. 'Good to see you again, Fiona,' she said. She decided not to ask her how she was feeling. Fiona looked well enough; she had not lost any weight and she was smiling as

103

though she was pleased to see her visitor.

'Good see you too,' she replied. 'I've been looking forward to you coming – you don't know how much!' she added in an undertone. 'Anyway, come and sit down and talk to Stella for a few minutes, while I finish off the meal. Simon, would you take Debbie's coat and bag upstairs, please?'

'Of course,' he said. 'Make yourself at home, Debbie.'

There was an appetizing smell coming from the kitchen. Debbie thought it would be best not to say that she had eaten before she set off. She had just made a quick sandwich, not knowing whether or not her hosts would already have eaten. But it smelled so good she was feeling hungry again.

'It's chicken,' said Stella, as they went into the sitting room. 'Mummy says it's one of your favourite things, and I like it, too. And there's apple pie and cream for after. Mummy bought that, though, from the baker's in town. I went with her this afternoon.'

Debbie laughed. 'You're giving away secrets, young lady! Mummy doesn't have as much time to bake as she used to, with looking after the babies. Well, they're not really babies any more, are they?'

'No, they'll be two on Tuesday, and we're having a party on Saturday. My friend, Susan is coming.'

'Yes, your daddy was telling me about it. Are they in bed now, your little brothers and sister?'

'Yes; you'll be able to see them in the morning. Aunty Glenda helped Mummy to bath them, then she went home.'

'That's the lady who comes to help Mummy,

isn't it?'

'Yes, she comes in the morning, then she goes home when she's helped Mummy to bath the little ones and put them to bed. She comes to see to the little ones, really, but she sometimes takes me to nursery school and picks me up at dinner time, 'pending on what Mummy wants her to do.'

'Oh, I see. And do you like her, your ... Aunty Glenda?' Debbie asked tentatively.

Stella wrinkled her nose. 'Yes, she's alright. I liked Paula best though. She's gone to college to learn to be a proper nanny. I know Mummy wishes she was still here.'

'Yes, I expect she does,' said Debbie, sensing again that something was not quite right. 'That chicken smells good, doesn't it, Stella? I'm just popping up to the bathroom to have a wash before we have our tea.'

'And to go to the toilet,' added Stella, nodding wisely.

'Yes, that as well,' said Debbie, laughing. She stroked the little girl's blonde hair. 'You're a little treasure, aren't you? Your mummy and daddy must be so proud of you.' Whatever Fiona's problem was, Debbie was sure that Stella must bring her a lot of comfort and happiness.

They talked during the meal mainly about family and parish matters and, of course, Fiona and Simon were eager to hear how Debbie was getting on at college.

'It's great!' she told them. 'Really interesting. All sorts of lectures about ... well, everything to do with gardening. Recognition of flowers and plants, and all their Latin names; and planting and pest control and hedge growing and topiary. There's practical work as well. We're designing a garden and doing a lot of the building and construction work; rockeries and water features and all that sort of thing.'

'Isn't it rather strenuous for the girls?' asked Fiona.

'Well, they're mostly men in the group, but we girls have to pull our weight. The fact that you're a woman isn't supposed to make any difference. And we're learning about the famous gardeners in history; I really enjoy those lectures. All about Lancelot Capability Brown.'

'I've heard of him,' said Fiona. 'He designed the garden at Chatsworth House, didn't he? I went there once, on a coach trip, when I lived in Leeds.'

'Yes, so he did,' replied Debbie, 'and Blenheim as well. They're talking about arranging a trip to see some of the famous gardens, next year, in the spring. So I'll be looking forward to that.'

Debbie told them that her parents were well and sent their love, and that she had seen Graham a couple of times. Fiona and Simon told her about the new curate, and the fund raising, and the scheme that was still going strong; providing 'high tea' for groups of visitors from other churches who came on coach trips. She noticed that Fiona's new helper was not mentioned at all.

'Now, I'm going to wash up tonight, all by myself,' said Simon, when they had finished the meal and had all helped to clear the pots from the table. 'And, what is more, I shall make coffee, and leave you girls to have a good old natter.'

'Thank you, Simon,' said Fiona, although she didn't sound overenthusiastic about his offer. 'It's Stella's bedtime first, though. Just a quick wash tonight, love. We won't bother with a bath till tomorrow.'

'And then, can Debbie read me a story?' asked the little girl. 'Will you, please, Debbie?'

'Of course I will,' she replied. 'Is it *Milly Molly Mandy?*'

'No; we've been reading Teddy Robinson, haven't we, Mummy? He belongs to a little girl called Deborah – like you – and he does all sorts of funny things.'

'I shall look forward to meeting him,' said Debbie.

It was always one of the highlights of Debbie's visits to the rectory, to spend some time alone with the little girl with whom she had bonded so well on their first acquaintance, her little half-sister, and now there were two more little half-brothers and a half-sister. As Debbie's mother, Vera, had remarked, it was a very complicated state of affairs, especially when you included Greg, Simon's first born son. Nevertheless, it was a situation that had given a great deal of pleasure, rather than confusion, to the people concerned.

Debbie had decided she would broach the subject of Fiona's new helper, Glenda, when they were alone together. If Fiona wanted to tell her about it, all well and good; but if she didn't want to talk, then Debbie knew she must not pry.

She waited until they were settled with their cups of coffee, and had chatted a little about

Stella and how she was growing and developing into a sensible and helpful little girl.

'Is it easier for you now you've got this new lady to help?' asked Debbie. 'I'm sure she must have made a difference?'

'She's done that all right!' said Fiona, meaningfully. She paused, looking annoyed for a moment, before going on in a more normal voice. 'Yes, she's very helpful, of course. She does take a lot of the weight off my shoulders. I thought it would be marvellous to have some help again, but I'm afraid that it's not really working out all that well. You see—' she stopped, looking intently at Debbie, her lovely blue eyes troubled and her lip trembling a little – 'I think she's got designs on Simon.'

Debbie was shocked. She didn't know whether to laugh or to take it seriously. Fiona certainly seemed to be serious about it. 'Oh ... I see,' she began. 'Well, it's only to be expected, I suppose. Your Simon is a very charismatic man,' she went on, trying to make light of it. 'I'm sure a lot of the women in the church must have taken a fancy to him.'

'But I mean it,' said Fiona. 'I'm not joking. It's no laughing matter, believe me. I think she really wants him.'

'Well, she can't have him!' replied Debbie. 'And he won't want her. How could he? He's got you, and all his lovely children. And you're so happy together, you and Simon. Everybody knows that. Does he ... do you think he knows?'

'He must do,' said Fiona. 'She makes it so obvious. And I've seen them talking and laughing together. He doesn't ignore her or brush her off. They seem ... so friendly.'

'I'm sure he's not interested, though said Debbie, staunchly. 'He's just being polite to her, surely? Simon's such a friendly man; he wouldn't want to hurt anyone. If she doesn't get any encouragement she'll back off ... won't she?'

'I certainly hope so, but there's no sign of it at the moment. It's as though she's trying to impress him, show him how helpful she is. Not only with the triplets – that's what she was employed for, to look after them – but she does little jobs that I usually do. Like making him a cup of coffee in the middle of the morning and ... oh, I don't know! Just generally making a fuss of him.'

'Yes, I see,' said Debbie, although she didn't really understand how it could be happening with someone like Simon. 'How long has she been here?' she asked. 'Simon said she was the new curate's sister-in-law. Did she move here with them when he started his ... curacy? Is that what they call it?'

Fiona smiled. 'I think so... No, she came here a couple of weeks later. Gilbert and Norma Henderson are great people. He's just the sort of helper that Simon needed. He's new to the ministry. He'd been a lay preacher before that, then he decided to go to college when he was turned forty, to take that final step, as he said. He's not – what shall I say? – as unconventional as the last curate we had. You remember Josh, of course?'

'Yes; he was a real character, wasn't he?'

'He raised a few eyebrows at first, but he proved his worth; and most people grew to like

109

him. Anyway, he's moved on; he's gone to a parish in Oldham, on the other side of the Pennines. Gilbert's a good deal older, of course, and far more conventional. He's a good preacher, as he's had years of practice as a lay reader. And Norma's very willing to help with work in the parish. Their children are away at university, and she has no job outside of the home. So she takes a Sunday School class – something I had to give up – and she helps with the Mothers' Union. That was never exactly my forte; that was why I started the Young Wives group. I still do that; the women in the group have become real friends. They're a great solace to me. Clergymen's wives can sometimes feel quite lonely, you know. Sometimes people are a bit wary of us.'

'And Glenda?' Debbie prompted her. 'How did she come into the picture?'

'They're from South Yorkshire, near Sheffield. Glenda worked as a nursery assistant – she's fully qualified – but the nursery closed down and, as it happened, she was looking out for another post. Norma knew how I was fixed with the triplets, so she said she'd ask her sister and see if she was interested in coming here to look after the babies. Of course, I jumped at the idea. I thought she'd be ideal if she was anything like her sister.'

'But she isn't...'

'No, not at all. They look rather alike; small and dark and quite attractive. There's only a couple of years between them. Norma's in her mid-forties, like her husband, and I think Glenda's two years older.'

'Is she married, or single? No; I don't suppose

she can be married, can she, from what you've told me?'

'She has been,' Fiona remarked drily. 'She's divorced, not that I'm holding that against her. Norma said that her husband left her and went off with a younger woman; there were no children. Glenda was still living in the house – the matrimonial home, as they call it – and he doesn't seem bothered about that. So, she came up here a fortnight later; that's about a month ago. For a trial period, supposedly, to see how it works out for her, and for me.'

'So, if it's just a trial period, can't you tell her that you don't think it's working? That you'd prefer somebody ... younger, maybe?'

'It's not as easy as that. It would be regarded as ageist to say that. Besides, she's very good at her job. The children like her. She's very nice and gentle with them, but she doesn't stand for any nonsense with Matthew. It's just this personal thing, with Simon.'

'Maybe he thinks she's just being nice and helpful,' said Debbie. 'And perhaps she is. Could you have mistaken her intentions? And maybe Simon's rather naive about it all.'

Fiona gave a bitter laugh. 'Whatever else Simon may be, he's not naive! I know he's a "man of the cloth" as they say, but he hasn't always been a vicar. He's lived in the world, and there were others before he met me. Well, Greg's evidence of that, isn't he? I believe his time in the RAF taught him a thing or two.'

'But he's got you now,' insisted Debbie. 'And I'm sure – quite certain – that he won't want any-

111

one else.'

Fiona was quiet for a moment before she answered. 'I haven't told anyone else about this, Debbie; she began, 'but I feel I can tell you. Since you came into my life, I've felt that I've got a close friend. I know you're really my daughter, and there are some things that a mother would never confide to her daughter. But it's different with you and me. You see, this thing with Glenda, it seems to be affecting ... the more intimate side of our marriage.'

Debbie felt a shade embarrassed. She knew very little about such matters, but she knew to what she was referring.

'You mean ... making love and all that?'

Fiona nodded. 'It was always a very great joy to both of us. But now, it hasn't happened for several weeks. Hardly ever ... since Glenda appeared on the scene. And that's why I'm worried.'

Debbie shook her head emphatically. 'No, he wouldn't! I know he wouldn't, not Simon. You're wrong, Fiona. He's ... well, he's a clergyman!'

Fiona actually laughed. 'He's a man, though, isn't he? And aren't they all alike, deep down? Susceptible to a bit of flattery. I hope I'm wrong. I keep telling myself that I am, but there's still this doubt, niggling away at me.'

'Have you told anyone else about this?' asked Debbie. 'Not about ... what you've just told me; about this woman fancying Simon?'

'I've told my friend Joan,' said Fiona. 'She says she's aware that Glenda fusses around him, but she tells me I've nothing to worry about, as you said. Anyway, you'll see her for yourself tomorrow. She comes at nine o'clock, and we get the children ready for the day; breakfast and washes and toilet and all that. Mark's still in nappies, I'm afraid. That's another worry for me; Mark's progress, or lack of it.'

'He's not quite two yet,' said Debbie. 'Isn't it rather soon to worry about it?'

'I don't know,' said Fiona. 'Maybe it is, but it's the way I am at the moment. Things get on my mind, and possibly seem worse than they are. Anyway, with regard to Glenda; her hours are flexible, depending on what I want her to do. So she can have most of tomorrow off, and we'll manage the kiddies between us. What do you think about that, Debbie?'

'I think it's a great idea,' said Debbie. 'I'm dying to see them all again.'

Simon joined them in a little while and they watched the ten o'clock news together. Debbie felt very conscious of what Fiona had told her, but she didn't notice any difference in the way the two of them behaved towards one another. She retired to bed first, with a drink of hot chocolate to take up, which Simon had insisted on making for her. She couldn't help believing what she had always thought; that Simon was a wonderful husband who thought the world of his wife.

Debbie breakfasted early the next morning with Fiona and Simon. Stella was up and dressed, but the triplets were left in their cots, to be washed, dressed and fed when Glenda arrived. Debbie was eager to see what the woman was like. She arrived promptly at nine o'clock, just as Fiona and Debbie

113

were washing up, and Simon had disappeared into his study. Was he keeping out of the way? she wondered. Glenda fitted Fiona's description: small, dark, and quite attractive, but 'nothing to write home about', as Debbie's mother, Vera, might say.

'Hello, Fiona,' she said cheerily. They were obviously on first name terms. 'Hello, Stella.' The little girl looked up and smiled briefly. 'Hello, Aunty Glenda.'

'The little uns still in bed, are they?' asked Glenda. She looked around as if she might also be looking for Simon, but she didn't ask where he was.

'Yes, that's right,' said Fiona. 'We like to have five minutes' peace in a morning, don't we, Stella?'

Glenda was looking curiously at Debbie. It seemed to Debbie as though Fiona was playing some sort of game, not willing to divulge who the stranger in the midst might be. Then she spoke up.

'This is Debbie... She's here for the weekend, and for the birthday party, of course. She's a godmother to the three of them, most especially to Michelle.'

Fiona didn't elucidate any further. Debbie guessed that Glenda's curiosity would soon be satisfied. Most of the folk in the congregation knew who Debbie was by now and had accepted her into their midst on her occasional visits. If Glenda wanted to know anything further there would be plenty of people to put her in the picture.

'How do you do?' said Glenda politely, holding

114

out her hand, and Debbie returned the greeting.

'I arrived last night after the children were in bed,' she said, 'so I haven't seen them yet. I expect they'll have grown a lot since the last time I saw them.'

'Which was ... when?' asked Glenda, rather inquisitively, Debbie thought.

'Oh, it was just before I started at college, wasn't it, Fiona? I'm at an agricultural college near Leeds,' she explained. 'It's our half-term break, so I'm here till Monday.'

'Yes; Debbie's going to help me this weekend,' said Fiona. 'She wants to spend some time with the kiddies, of course; so ... you can take the rest of the day off, Glenda, when we've seen to the washing and feeding and everything. OK with you?' It sounded as though Fiona would brook no argument.

'Fine,' replied Glenda, a little curtly. 'I've all sorts of jobs to catch up with. You'll want me tomorrow, though, I take it?'

'Yes, for a little while in the morning, if that's all right? And you'll be coming to the party, of course, with Norma and Gilbert.'

'Of course,' said Glenda. 'Would you like me to come early to help to prepare the buffet, or whatever you're planning?'

'No ... thank you,' said Fiona. 'Debbie will be here to help me ... and Simon,' she added, rather pointedly. 'You're a guest tomorrow, Glenda.' Fiona smiled sweetly at the woman as though butter wouldn't melt. 'Come on now; let's go and see to the terrible triplets, shall we?'

The three of them were in their individual cots.

Matthew was standing up, clinging to the bars and shouting at the top of his voice when he saw the three adults and Stella.

'Deb! Deb!' he cried. He was the most advanced of the three and was always the first to recognize her.

'Hello, big boy,' she said, ruffling his hair. 'My goodness! You've grown, haven't you?'

'Yes! Big boy; two on Tuesday,' he shouted, jumping up and down in delight.

The other two were less demonstrative, but they looked keenly at Debbie, and she felt that Michelle's happy smile showed that the child had remembered her. Mark, as usual, took a little longer to realize who she was.

Between them, the three women washed and dressed the children. They were still wearing nappies at night, just as a precaution. Glenda saw to Mark's daytime one when the other two were out of the way, which Debbie thought was tactful and considerate of her. Matthew had been known to taunt his brother, according to Fiona, calling him a baby because he still needed a daytime nappy. Glenda clearly did have her good points. It was obvious that the children liked her; she was good with them, kind but firm.

They breakfasted on porridge, followed by scrambled egg and bread and butter. Mark needed more help than the other two. He seemed happy for Debbie to assist him, opening his mouth like a baby bird for the next mouthful.

'He'll never learn, so long as there's somebody to wait on him,' Fiona observed, a little anxiously. 'But we'll let him off today, while Debbie's here.'

'He's still only a baby really,' countered Glenda. 'He'll learn to do it in his own time. It doesn't do to force the issue.'

Fiona didn't answer, no doubt seeing it as a mild rebuke. Debbie sensed the slight animosity between the two of them, unless it was because she was looking out for it. They were polite to one another, but didn't have any sort of conversation apart from what centred around the children.

Fiona had arranged for Stella to attend nursery school a little later that day. She had explained that they had a visitor whom she didn't see very often. 'I think that's all for today,' she said, when the washing up was done. 'You go and have some time to yourself, Glenda. Perhaps you could drop Stella off at the nursery school, though, if you don't mind? It's on your way home, isn't it?'

'Certainly,' agreed Glenda, with more enthusiasm than was required. 'You'll collect her, though?'

'Of course,' said Fiona. 'Goodbye, sweetheart; see you in a little while.'

'Bye, Mummy; bye, Debbie,' said the little girl, trotting off happily with Glenda.

'So that's her gone,' said Fiona, seeming to breathe a heartfelt sigh. Debbie knew she was referring to Glenda and not to Stella. She decided to make no comment; and Fiona did not ask her what she thought about the woman.

'I thought I'd do some baking today,' said Fiona, 'ready for the party. Just iced buns and flapjack; things that the children like. And I can prepare the trifle; that's for the grown-ups. The

117

children prefer jelly and ice-cream, red jelly, of course! Would you like to look after the three terrors? There's a programme on the TV they like to watch at eleven o'clock. Then we'll go and meet Stella at twelve, and we'll all have a sandwich lunch. And this afternoon we'll walk into town. It's not market day but I've some shopping to do for tomorrow. Then we could let the kiddies have some time in the playground. I'm always wary of swings and slides if I'm on my own. It can be quite a dangerous place; you have to have eyes in the back of your head. It's far better if there's two of us...'

And that was more or less how the rest of the day worked out. Debbie enjoyed looking after the triplets, although she could see how wearing they might be, day in, day out. It was little wonder that Fiona needed help. For her, Debbie, it was just a novelty. They were as good as gold watching the antics of the teddy bears and dolls on the TV, and they smiled at the lady announcer with the oh-so-friendly – but somewhat patronizing – voice as though she really was a friend. Television certainly had its benefits; a boon for busy mothers, but Debbie couldn't help but think it might also be a cop-out for lazy ones.

Simon joined them for a sandwich lunch. 'Is Glenda not with us today?' he asked in a casual – almost disinterested voice. Or was that an act? Debbie knew she was being extra alert about her hosts' chance remarks. Stop it! she told herself. She knew she could not, deep down, believe that Simon would do anything to jeopardize his marriage.

'No,' Fiona answered briefly. Then after a few seconds, she added, 'I told her I didn't need her for the rest of the day while Debbie's here. She doesn't always stay for lunch anyway. It depends on what I want her to do.' He nodded and the moment of tension passed.

Debbie understood what Fiona meant about the children's playground. Matthew raced around like a mad thing, whooping with delight as he whizzed down the slide. It was only a short one, for young children, but the other two were far more cautious. Stella, their grown-up big sister, helped them up the steps and slid down with Mark in front of her to keep him safe. It was the same with the swings; they were closed-in ones for toddlers so that they couldn't fall off.

'Push, push, higher!' Matthew cried to Debbie, whilst the other two liked a gentler ride. Stella didn't do much sliding or swinging on her own, preferring to stay close to her mum and Debbie, keeping a careful eye on her little brothers and sister.

The *Magic Roundabout* was another treat before the little ones went to bed. Debbie, too, was enthralled by Zebedee and Brian, the snail, and it was so much better in colour! Simon and Fiona had succumbed to pressure from Stella, but Debbie knew that the two of them loved to spend a relaxing evening together in front of the box when Simon was not out on other commitments.

The birthday party on the Saturday was a happy occasion. Debbie was interested to see who had been invited. There was only one other

119

child, a little girl, who was about the same age as the triplets. Her mother was a new member of the Young Wives group, and Fiona had invited them in order to get to know them better. Dawn, the mother, was a shy young woman who didn't mix easily. Debbie noticed how quickly Fiona made her feel at ease. Stella's special friend, Susan, had been invited along with her mother, another of the Young Wives. The husbands, sensibly, had stopped at home.

There were just a few grown-ups; Joan Tweedale, a good friend of Fiona who had supported her when she had first married Simon, and her husband, Henry, who was the church organist; and the new curate, Gilbert Henderson, his wife, Norma and, of course, Glenda.

Debbie took to Norma at once; she was a friendly outgoing person who, she was sure, was an admirable clergy wife. Gilbert was not so chatty as his wife – Simon had said that his talents lay in his preaching and organizational skills – but they seemed a well suited couple. Glenda spent most of the time with her three charges. She was clearly very fond of them whether or not she had an ulterior motive. Debbie was inclined to give her the benefit of the doubt until, at a quiet moment during the meal, she saw Glenda level at Fiona across the tea table a glance of extreme dislike, almost hatred. The moment passed and Debbie believed that no one else had noticed. But it had given her a nasty jolt, and she felt a strange premonition of trouble to come.

Debbie knew that Fiona had spoken to Joan about her fears, but there was no chance during the party for Debbie to have a word with her. The following day, however, Debbie sat next to Joan in the church pew. Stella was with the Sunday School children at the front, the triplets were being looked after in the crèche, and Debbie was pleased to see that Fiona had returned to her former place in the choir stalls. She had told Debbie that the music had helped to soothe her and, for a short time at least, to calm her fears. To see her joyful face as she sang the anthem and hymns with the rest of the choir it seemed as though she hadn't a care in the world.

In a quiet moment before the service started Debbie whispered to Joan, 'I'm rather worried about Fiona; I know she's told you, hasn't she, about Glenda and her fears that she's getting too friendly with Simon?'

Joan nodded. 'Try not to worry, Debbie, love. I'm keeping my eye on the situation. I've noticed myself that she makes a fuss of him, but you know as well as I do how much Simon cares for Fiona. I've never known a happier couple. Glenda is pushy and flirtatious, but if it's any consolation, she's acts like that with some of the other men as well. And you know that Fiona hasn't been at all well for quite a while. She may have let her worries get out of proportion.'

'She's been happy, though, this weekend,' said Debbie. 'She enjoyed the party, and all the company.'

'And especially having you there, Debbie.' Joan smiled at her. 'She thinks a great deal of you.'

'And I do of her,' replied Debbie. 'It's worked out so well, Joan, for all of us.'

'Then try not to worry, dear,' said Joan. 'I've always felt a responsibility for Fiona. There are not many people she feels she can confide in, and I'm glad that I'm one of them.'

It wasn't until the Monday morning when Debbie was leaving the rectory that she had a chance to speak to Fiona again about the matter of Glenda. Fiona had asked her to come later that day as the family would be busy saying goodbye to Debbie. There was a flurry of hugs and kisses, and a few tears as well, as she took her leave of Stella and the triplets, and Simon and Fiona.

Simon was busy getting the car out, and she took the opportunity to have a quiet word with Fiona. 'I'm sure you've nothing to worry about,' she whispered as she gave her a last hug. 'It'll be all right; you'll see...'

'I hope so; that's what I keep trying to tell myself,' answered Fiona; she did seem to be a little calmer now. 'Take care, Debbie. It's been lovely seeing you again.' She waved cheerily as Simon drove Debbie away to catch her bus back to Leeds.

Eight

Simon had made no further reference to Fiona and her state of mind as they drove to the bus station; so Debbie tried not to dwell on the matter as she made the journey back to Leeds.

It would be the second half-term of her course; and how much happier and secure she felt about everything now; the flat and her companions there, and her studies at the college – the various lectures and the projects in which she was involved.

The four of them had worked out a routine – albeit an haphazard one – for the care of the flat: the cleaning and cooking and shopping. As far as the cooking was concerned, they found it easier to have a substantial midday meal each day at the college cafeteria. There was a wide selection of dishes with chips as an accompaniment, also hotpots and casseroles, lasagne and pizzas, beans or eggs on toast, as well as various kinds of sandwiches. Not everything was on offer each day but there was always a good selection to choose from. Tarts and puddings and fruit, too, if they felt like afters.

They worked in pairs to do the cooking at the flat, change and change about. Sometimes Debbie would be paired with Fran, sometimes Karen, sometimes Lisa. Karen, who came from a large family, was the one who was the most competent. Fran, who had lived on her own for a while, liked to try something a little more out of the ordinary, and Lisa, like Debbie, had not really done very much at home. Both of them, as only children, had been rather indulged.

They all coped, though, as they had decided on quick and easily prepared dishes for their evening meal. Spaghetti, baked beans, soups, sardines – there was always a wide variety of tins in their cupboard – and eggs were a good standby. On

Sundays, depending on who was in the flat and not out elsewhere, they sometimes tried a typical roast dinner.

They had worked out a rota for the shopping, too, to be done in pairs, if possible. They decided each morning if there was anything they needed – bread, tea bags, milk: things that they ran out of more quickly – and two of them would do the shopping at Tesco's when they got off the bus. There was a convenient bus service to the college. Firstly, a bus from the stop on the main road, not far from their flat, to City Square. Then another bus, which involved a longer journey, to Stanborough College, which was midway between Leeds and the city of York. The ten-mile journey took about half an hour as there were various stops on the way. They had to make sure they were out of the house by eight o'clock each morning to catch the bus to town. There was an understanding that they shouldn't wait for anyone; if one of the four had 'slept in', maybe suffering from the effects of the night before, then it would be her hard luck. Fortunately this had not happened, so far. They didn't always catch the same bus home as it depended on what time the various lectures ended. But they were usually all home by six o'clock; and after their meal the rest of the evening was their own to do as they wished.

The cleaning got done if and when they felt inclined! They had a good dust and tidy round if a guest was expected; but they had all agreed that the bathroom and toilet had to be kept clean at all times. The bath must be rinsed out after every use, and the toilet kept spotless with Domestos. They were all very fastidious young women.

Rhoda had told them that the washing was their responsibility. Their 'smalls' were done in the sink, so there was always an array of knickers, bras and tights festooned on radiators and on a clothes maiden they had found tucked away in a corner, quickly removed if a visitor should call. They paired up every fortnight or so to wash the sheets and towels at the launderette.

Debbie realized she was looking forward to returning to college. She had thought that she knew a good deal about gardening when she started on the course, but each day she was learning something new. She didn't know, yet, where she would find a position when the course came to an end, but she was confident there would be a place for her somewhere.

She was surprised to feel that she was also looking forward to the return to the flat and to her friends. Only two months ago it had been a step into the unknown. But now, as she turned her key in the lock and went inside it felt almost like coming home. Comfortably warm, too, on what was quite a chilly autumn day. Alf Perkins saw to the central heating, and he didn't stint on it either. All the girls knew that this was a bonus for a student flat.

The living room had a much more cheerful aspect than when they had first moved in. Fran, who had been home several times, had brought back some bright scatter cushions in a bold design of yellow and black to liven up the rather dilapidated settee and armchair. Their selection of books with brightly coloured dust jackets filled the bookshelves, giving a lived-in look to the place, as books always did. It was Fran, too, who had supplied the posters of paintings by Degas and Monet that adorned the empty walls. There was the small television in one corner, and Debbie's cassette recorder and tape deck.

Debbie was the first of the four to arrive back, and she felt glad to have the place to herself for a while. When she had visited the bathroom and unpacked her few belongings she made herself a spot of lunch; it was still only early afternoon. She had told Fiona that she didn't need any sandwiches, but she had insisted on her taking some bread, cut from a farmhouse loaf, and a small bottle of milk, 'just in case'. 'You won't have time to shop,' she had said, 'and you'll be ready for a cup of tea.' Ever thoughtful Fiona, always concerned about the welfare of others. Debbie felt sure that some of her flatmates would bring back a few provisions.

She made a mug of tea, toasted some of the bread and opened a small tin of beans. There was still some fruit loaf in the cake tin that Debbie's mother had sent the previous week, so she finished off her solitary meal with a slice of that, lavishly buttered.

She was just clearing away the pots when the door opened. She turned round from the kitchen alcove and saw that it was Karen.

'Hi, there,' called Debbie. 'Good to see you again.' So it was, although it had been only four days. 'Have you had a nice weekend?'

She had not noticed at first that Karen looked

far from happy. The girl flung her travel bag on the floor, then collapsed on to the settee with her head in her hands and burst into tears.

Debbie hurried across and sat down, putting an arm round her. 'Karen, what is it? What's wrong?'

'Charlie ... that's what's wrong,' Karen managed to say between her sobs. 'Charlie... He's dumped me!'

'Oh ... oh dear!' A futile remark, but Debbie couldn't think of anything else to say. 'Do you want to tell me what's happened?' Charlie, Karen's boss, on whom she had centred such high hopes; Debbie had wondered if it was all too good to be true.

'I'll make you a mug of tea,' she said. 'A lot of sugar in it, then perhaps you'll feel a little calmer.'

By the time Debbie had returned with the tea Karen had taken off her coat and appeared a little more in control of herself. She seemed to want to talk, and as the story poured out of her Debbie realized that Karen had been living in a fool's paradise, as she, Debbie, had suspected. It wasn't so much that she had been dumped, as that Charlie had never been hers in the first place.

'I've been no end of a bloody fool,' she wailed. 'He was never interested in me, not in that way. However could I have misread the signals? Because they were there; I was sure they were.'

'That's men for you,' said Debbie, trying to sound philosophical, although she hadn't had much experience herself. 'You did tell me, though, didn't you, that he had kissed you? I know you said that there had been nothing else, but you're not to

127

be blamed for thinking he was interested, are you?'

'I must have read too much into it,' said Karen, 'because it was what I wanted to believe. Perhaps he was just grateful to me for looking after Alfie. It was awful, Debbie, the way he told me, as though I'd be pleased for him. I don't know how I managed to keep myself together.

'I called to see him at the garden centre, and he was as cheerful as anything. He actually kissed me – only a peck on the cheek – but he seemed really pleased to see me. Then he said, 'I've got a surprise for you, Karen. I'm getting married!'

'Oh, how dreadful!' said Debbie. 'Whatever did you say?'

'I just stared at him. I thought for one moment that he meant him and me. Then I realized... "No, you bloody fool!" I says to meself "It's not you; he's been having you on." Then I managed to say, "Congratulations! Who is it?" I'd no idea there was anyone else. I'm sure I must have gone dead white; I thought I was going to pass out... Anyway, she's called Stephanie, and he said he'd known her for ages, even before he married Daphne.'

Apparently the young woman had moved away to another part of Yorkshire, but Charlie had got in touch with her and had started seeing her again. 'And so it's Bob's yer flippin' uncle!' said Karen. 'He's been bloomin' secretive about it.'

'So how does it affect you with your job and everything?' asked Debbie. 'Do you still want to go back and work there? He's promised you a promotion, hasn't he?'

Karen nodded. 'So he has, and he's coughed up

for this course an' all. So it looks as though I've no choice. I reckon I'll just have to grin and bear it.' She stared moodily into space.

'He was too old for you, though, wasn't he?' Debbie was trying to find something consoling to say. 'And there was his little boy; Alfie, isn't it? I thought you'd be taking a lot on with the child as well.'

'Alfie's a little love,' said Karen, 'and I enjoyed looking after him. I must admit, though, that Charlie made use of me when it suited him. Anyway, they're getting married next spring. No doubt he'll expect me to be there in me best frock and a fancy hat. Happen I'll have got over it by then.'

'Of course you will,' said Debbie, giving her a hug. 'You're sounding more cheerful already. There are better fish in the sea than ever came out of it. That's one of my mother's sayings. There'll be somebody else for you, quite soon I should think.' Karen was not beautiful, but she was very attractive. Her fresh complexion with a light scattering of freckles needed very little make-up. Her ginger hair had a natural curl, and her wide beaming smile lit up her face.

She smiled now, though her brown eyes still looked a little troubled. 'I shall be wary in future, I can tell you. I must admit, though, I've hardly looked at the fellers at college. I was so sure that Charlie was the one. Well, you live and learn...'

'Have you told your parents about it?' asked Debbie.

'No. They've never bothered much about what I get up to. Mam's always busy with the younger ones, and Dad's off to the pub or his darts' match. It was nice seeing 'em both again, and the kids, and they seemed pleased to see me. I caught up with an old school friend – a girlfriend, I mean. We went out for a drink; well, a lot more than one as it turned out. I spent Saturday night at her place. I don't think Mam and Dad even missed me. So, here we are again. I wonder what the next half term'll hold for us? An' I've forgotten to ask you, Debbie – selfish cow that I am! – did you have a good weekend?'

'Lovely, thanks,' replied Debbie. 'It was good to see the kiddies again, and Fiona and Simon. I'm concerned about Fiona, though. She's still tired and not coping all that well.' She didn't intend to elaborate on the situation.

'I'm not surprised, with triplets,' said Karen. 'Rather her than me! I 'spect you'll be seeing Graham again soon, won't you? Lucky you! He seems a nice bloke; quite a catch, I should think, eh?'

Debbie smiled. 'I'm not sure. I can't quite make him out, to be honest. He's invited me round to his flat, but we haven't fixed a date yet. I dare say he'll be in touch soon.' She thought to herself that perhaps she should take heed of Karen's situation. It would be better not to have high hopes of Graham and his intentions. Maybe he just liked having her as a friend. Only time would tell…

Fran was the next one to arrive back, mid-afternoon. She looked her usual elegant self as she came through the door, not at all travel-stained or weary. She was not one for duffel coats or

130

anoraks. Her bright red trouser suit was the height of fashion, with its hip-length jacket and flared trousers. With it she wore a baker's boy style cap in herringbone tweed and brown suede boots. She put down her brown leather holdall and smiled at them.

'Hello, girls. It's good to be back. I never thought I'd say that, but it is.'

'That's what we said as well,' agreed Debbie. 'Has Ralph brought you back?'

'No,' Fran answered, rather curtly. 'I came on the train, and took a taxi from the station.' She shrugged her shoulders in a casual manner. 'It's all over with Ralph and I,' she said. Debbie and Karen couldn't help but exchange a smile.

Fran gave them haughty a glance. 'Have I said something amusing?'

'No ... sorry,' muttered Debbie, feeling somewhat abashed.

'Join the club!' retorted Karen. 'It's all over with Charlie and me an' all; not that it was ever on, really. I've just been saying to Debbie what a bloody fool I've been! Sorry; we weren't laughing at you, Fran, honest!'

'Oh, I see,' said Fran, sitting down in the armchair and crossing her long legs with a languid air. 'Actually, it's not been going well for quite some time. It was a mutual decision, and I've given him his ring back.' She glanced down at her slender tapering fingers. She was still wearing a ring, a large dress ring of three garnets, on her middle finger. 'I shan't be losing any sleep over it, I can assure you.'

Debbie knew that Fran, like Karen, had had a

131

position lined up for her on leaving college, as a designer in Ralph's firm of landscape gardeners. She was not the sort of person, though, that you could quiz about her future plans. It would be better to leave it until she volunteered any information herself.

'I'm ready for a cup of tea,' Fran remarked now. 'I had a sandwich on the journey that Mum had made for me, and I was brave enough to try a cup of British Rail tea; but it was like dish water! What about you two? Shall I make you one?'

They were both agreeing to the suggestion when the fourth member of the quartet arrived back. Lisa looked troubled as she came through the door. They thought her father would be following closely behind her. He seldom seemed to let her out of his sight, and carried her bags for her.

'Hi, Lisa,' said Karen cheerily. 'Come and join the happy gang; we're all here now. Where's your dad?'

'He's not with me,' replied Lisa, looking very close to tears. 'I came back on the train and I've just come in a taxi from the station.'

'The taxi firms are doing well out of us today,' Karen remarked. 'Is your dad working?'

'No... Well, he is working actually,' said Lisa. 'But we've had words and he said I had to find my own way back. Mum was cross with him; she said he should take me, but he can be real obstinate when he's that way. Mum tried to talk him round, to persuade him to bring me back at least ... but they're both very upset, you see.' She gave a loud sniff and took out her handkerchief, but she was unable to stop the tears from starting to flow. She dabbed ineffectually at her eyes.

Karen was the one who dashed over and put an arm round her. 'You have a damn good cry if you want to,' she said. 'Don't worry about us. I've just had a weep meself, haven't I, Debbie? Come and sit down; we're all going to have a cup of tea.'

Lisa gave a feeble smile. 'Sorry,' she said, shrugging off her coat and sitting down on the settee.

'I'll go and see to the tea,' said Fran quietly. The other two sat down, one on either side of Lisa.

'Do you want to tell us what's the matter?' said Debbie, taking hold of her hand. 'Or ... can we guess?'

'I expect you can,' replied Lisa. 'Yes... I plucked up courage and I told them – only last night – about Neil. I said that I'd met this nice young man – I stressed that he was a really nice lad – and that I'd started going out with him. Well, I knew they were a bit taken aback, even at that. Mum looked so worried, as though ... well, you know ... as though I was about to tell them I was pregnant, or getting married! Anyway, I decided I'd better tell them the truth. But when I said he was a Catholic my dad nearly hit the roof! He went on and on about them being infidels and papists. I'd heard it all before of course. He's so bigoted about anybody who's not a Methodist; well, not a nonconformist, I should say. I've never argued with him before, even though I didn't agree with him. But this time I was really annoyed. I answered him back, the first time I've ever dared to!'

'Good for you!' said Karen. 'Let's hope it'll do

133

him good.'

'He told me I was an ungrateful girl, and he didn't want any more to do with me until I saw the error of my ways. And then Mum started crying...'

'Oh dear!' Debbie felt really concerned for her friend. 'Your dad seemed so nice when we met him.'

'He can be, when everything's going his way,' said Lisa. 'I'm realizing, now, what Mum has had to put up with. His word is law in our house. Anyway, he stormed off to work this morning without speaking to me. Mum went with me to the station; we got a taxi, then she saw me on to the train.'

'So at least you've made it up with her, have you?' asked Debbie.

'I'm not sure,' answered Lisa. 'I suppose she thinks I'll change my mind about Neil, for my dad's sake. But I shan't! I told Mum that if she met Neil she'd like him. But she just shook her head, all sorrowful like, as though it was the end of the world.'

'Religion can cause such trouble,' said Fran, who had heard the last of the conversation as she came back with the mugs of tea. 'That's why I have very little to do with it. Come on now; let's drink our tea. Things are never as black as they seem.'

'I must say we're a lot of weary Willies, aren't we?' observed Karen. 'What with me and Charlie, Fran and Ralph, and now Lisa and her dad. There's only Debbie who hasn't got any man problems! I've got an idea, girls! Why don't we go out for a meal tonight to cheer ourselves up? I don't suppose any of us feel like cooking, do we?' They all agreed that they didn't.

'What about the Red Lion then?' suggested Debbie. 'We know they serve good meals, and they're not too expensive. And we can drown our sorrows as well. You three can anyway, and I'll join you!'

They all agreed that it was a great idea.

Nine

The Red Lion was quieter than they had ever seen it when they went in just before seven o'clock. They were all ravenous after their make-shift lunches and, in Lisa's case, hardly anything at all. She had been too upset by the family crisis to eat.

The menu was what might be called cheap and cheerful, but well cooked and the portions were a satisfying size. Debbie, Karen and Lisa decided on scampi and chips, but Fran, always the one to be different, chose a vegetarian lasagne. With the meal they polished off their first bottle of wine, a Chardonnay which was a little dry for Debbie's taste; but as Fran had said it was her treat and as she had chosen it the rest of them didn't argue. They took their time with the meal, then decided to push the boat out and have a pudding; lemon meringue pie for all of them with fresh cream poured over it.

When they returned to the bar lounge and found a table in a corner, Fran and Karen seemed to have put their troubles behind them and were enjoying a good old laugh together. Debbie always thought that those two were chalk and cheese, but they appeared to get along together surprisingly well. They shared a room, of course, as did she and Lisa, so it was important that they should learn to live amicably with one another.

'Are you feeling better now?' asked Debbie, as she and Lisa sat together on the bench seat with their backs to the wall.

'Yes, a bit better, thanks,' said Lisa. Debbie felt that she understood Lisa's problems more than the other two would. As an only child, Debbie, also, had been brought up by parents who had no one else to think about. Because of that she had, on the one hand, been overprotected and indulged; on the other hand they had kept her on a tight rein, watching her every move. In Debbie's case, her mother more so than her father. They had been more lenient as she reached her late teens, not wanting an out and out rebellion on their hands, because Debbie had kicked against the restraints on occasions. She guessed that Lisa had never done so until now. In her case it was obviously her father who ruled the roost in that household and who would brook no arguments.

'My dad's word is law,' she said now. 'I've not crossed him before, though I've often felt like it. Funnily enough, it was Dad who persuaded me to come on this course.'

'Yes, so it was,' said Debbie. 'I remember you saying that he thought it would do you good to mix with other people.'

'Yes, and now I have done it's wrong! They have to be people that he approves of. He would like Neil, though, if he met him, wouldn't he, Debbie? How could anybody not like him? And he can't help being a Catholic. It's the way he's been brought up, same as I've been told I have to be a Methodist ... like it or not!' she added, with more than a touch of resentment.

'Yes, I think that Neil's a very pleasant young man,' agreed Debbie, 'and I can see why you like him so much.' She felt that he might be rather quiet for her liking and – possibly ... a little boring? But he and Lisa seemed well suited.

She could see as the next half hour went by that Lisa's eyes kept straying to the door. She was no doubt hoping that Neil might appear, although she hadn't said that she would be meeting him. Sure enough, at about half past eight the three young men from the downstairs flat came in. They made a beeline for the girls in the corner, who budged up to make room for them. Debbie moved to let Neil sit next to Lisa. The two of them smiled shyly at one another.

'I'll get the drinks in,' said Alistair. 'The usual, pints all round, is it, lads? And what about you girls? Can I get you anything?'

'I'm OK thanks,' said Lisa, putting her hand guardedly round her glass of shandy. That was unusual to start with, as she normally drank orange juice. Debbie guessed that she was being rebellious that evening.

'I'm OK too, thanks all the same,' said Debbie. 'Maybe later.'

Fran and Karen both said that they would like a drink. 'Gin and It for me, please, Alistair,' said Fran.

'An' I'll have the same, please,' said Karen. 'I'll go all posh tonight, eh? I feel like a change.' She usually drank beer or lager, like the lads.

Debbie was aware that Karen was the one who was 'knocking it back' rather too much that night. But who was she to be a spoilsport and tell her she had had enough? She knew that she, too, was drinking more than she had used to do at home. Sixth formers could not afford very much, and she had not wanted to go home smelling of drink. She was slightly more affluent, now, thanks to her grant and a small allowance from her parents, but she tried to keep it to a reasonable limit.

She had been very green about such matters when she first came to Leeds, but she was getting more used to the terms they used now. She knew that 'gin and It', Fran's favourite drink, was made up of gin and Italian vermouth, hence the 'It'. Whisky and 'dry' referred to the dry ginger; Bacardi was a sort of white rum – holidaymakers brought it back from Spain – which was drunk with Coca-Cola. And a snowball was that nice yellow advocaat with lemonade. Debbie thought it was a very pleasant drink. It reminded her, rather, of a milkshake, but with more kick with it. She thought she might have one later.

'I'll come and help you carry them, Alistair,' Fran called, getting up and going over to the bar.

It became clear as the evening went on that Fran had decided to concentrate her attention on Alistair. The two of them, and Debbie as well, were in the same study group for design, and were all involved, too, in the project work on a Saturday morning, designing and constructing a landscaped garden. Alistair had never paid particular attention to Fran, but it seemed now that she was determined that he should do so. Whether she was really interested in him – or he in her – only time would tell. Maybe she was just on the rebound from her broken engagement, and he happened to be there. At all events, they appeared to be getting on well, chatting and laughing with their heads close together.

Debbie was content to be an onlooker and watch the proceedings. When she had first met him, Alistair had set her heart fluttering – just a little – but she had got over that since her friendship with Graham had got under way. She hoped he would get in touch with her soon.

She couldn't hear what Lisa and Neil were saying. She had purposely moved away a little so that she could not eavesdrop. The general noise all around as the lounge filled up made it difficult to hear anyway. They were deep in conversation, though, with Neil's arm around Lisa's shoulders.

They were an interesting trio: Alistair, Neil and Ben. Totally different in appearance, and probably in personality as well, but they seemed to get along fine together, as did the girls. Alistair was the handsome one, and the one who always had the most to say. Neil was a pleasant young man, much quieter and more serious. His glasses gave him a studious air, but he had a nice smile which Lisa, more than anyone, managed to evoke. Ben was something of an enigma. He was tall and thin-featured, good-looking in a gaunt sort of way, and he wore his dark hair much longer than that of his friends. Hair was generally worn longer now by a lot of men, young and older. Ben's was shoulder length, sometimes tied back in a pony tail but tonight it was loose. He was friendly and easy to talk to, but Debbie felt it was difficult to get to the core of him, to find out what 'made him tick'.

It seemed, however, that Karen was trying hard to do so now. Maybe she thought it was worth a try; what had she to lose? Debbie feared she was hurting a lot about Charlie although she was putting on a brave face and pretending that she didn't care. Fran got up and went to the ladies' room, and Alistair took the opportunity to move closer to Debbie.

'You're quiet tonight,' he said. 'Are you OK? Nothing worrying you?'

'No, not at all,' she answered. 'I'm just sitting here and enjoying the company, even though I'm not saying much. I'm just taking in the whole ambience of the surroundings.'

'My goodness! Listen to you ... ambience!' he teased. 'That's a posh word!'

She laughed. 'D'you think I don't know any grown-up words? I got a grade A in English Language! You know what I mean. It's always nice and friendly in here. Congenial company, good atmosphere... I was thinking how lucky we've been, the four of us in our flat, to get on so well together.'

'It's the same with the three of us,' Alistair agreed. 'We've all settled down well together, strangely enough.'

'Why is it strange?'

'Well, we're all so different. But it seems to work. I'm afraid Neil and I tend to leave most of the domestic chores to Ben. He cooks and tidies up after us and I must admit we let him. Lazy blighters, aren't we?'

'I suppose it's OK if he doesn't mind,' said Debbie. 'We try to share out the jobs, and take it in turn to cook. Fran and Karen are the best in the kitchen.' She gave a nod in Karen's direction. 'She's from a large family and she's had to do her share.' At the other side of the table Karen was deep in conversation with Ben.

'And the fair Francesca cooks as well, does she?' commented Alistair. 'Surprise, surprise, eh? I'm discovering she's a girl of many talents.'

As you seem to be finding out tonight, Debbie thought but did not say. 'Aren't we all,' she said, 'in our different ways? Karen and Ben seem to be getting on well, don't they?' she added in a low voice. They were not listening, though, seemingly engrossed in each other, although it was difficult to hear anyone's conversation except for one's own.

Alistair laughed. 'It won't do her much good, I'm afraid.'

'What do you mean?' asked Debbie.

'Well, Ben bats for the other side, doesn't he?' Alistair gave a meaningful smile, but it didn't convey much to Debbie.

'Oh ... you mean he plays cricket?' said Debbie. 'I didn't know.' And why should it matter? she wondered.

Alistair threw back his head and laughed, so much so that the rest of the crowd stared at him for a moment, then looked away. 'Oh, Debbie, you're priceless!' he said. 'What a naive little girl you are!'

Debbie was annoyed, and her face showed it. She didn't like being laughed at, and she didn't like being called a little girl. Fran came back at that moment and sat down on the other side of Alistair.

'What's going on?' she enquired, noting the slight tension and Debbie's cross face. 'Am I missing something?'

'Nothing much,' said Alistair. He patted Debbie's hand. 'Sorry, Debbie, I shouldn't have laughed at you, but I thought you'd get my meaning.' He turned to Fran. 'I was trying to explain to Debbie ... about Ben. She hadn't realized.'

'Oh yes, I see,' said Fran, who obviously knew what he was on about. Curiouser and curiouser, thought Debbie.

It was Fran who explained to her. 'Ben's gay,' she said in a whisper. She didn't glance at him, and he was quite unaware that they were talking about him. 'Hadn't you guessed?'

'Gay?' said Debbie. 'Do you mean ... queer?' That was the word she had usually heard, although she didn't know much about it at all.

'Yes, if you like,' said Fran. 'Gay's a nicer word, though. Good as you, I believe it means. And they are, aren't they? Just as good as the rest of us. Different, that's all.'

'Yes ... I suppose so,' replied Debbie, quite mystified. She had heard about them, of course – sixth form gossip – but as far as she knew she had never met anyone who was that way inclined. Until now. And Ben was such a nice likeable chap.

'How did you know?' she said quietly to Alistair. 'I'd no idea, honestly.'

'We just realized, Neil and I,' he replied. 'We haven't talked about it, and he hasn't come on to us, or anything like that. But I think he knows that we know. Anyway, as I said, we get along together all right. He's the one who has the single room, which is perhaps as well! And Neil and I share.'

'You didn't say anything about Ben being ... like that,' Debbie whispered to Fran, quite indignantly.

'Why should I?' Fran shrugged. She had lit a cigarette, and she nonchalantly blew a puff of smoke into the air. 'I thought it was obvious, anyway; and it's not something to gossip about, like a crowd of silly schoolgirls.'

Debbie felt annoyed again. Was that remark levelled at her? If so then it was best ignored. Yes; she supposed she had been a naive schoolgirl when she first came to Leeds. But she was learning. She was having her eyes opened to a lot of things she hadn't known about before. She smiled to herself. She was quite sure that Lisa was totally ignorant about such matters, even more so than she was. And maybe Karen, too, despite seeming so streetwise, had not realized either. She had certainly jumped to the wrong conclusion about Charlie.

They didn't stay until closing time. It was Fran who called a halt at ten thirty. 'It's time we weren't here, girls,' she called. 'Early start in the morning.'

'So you'd best sup up,' added Karen, draining the last of her pint of lager. She was the one who had had 'one over the eight', as Debbie's father might say. No, maybe not as many as eight, but she had been mixing her drinks, and Debbie knew that that was not good.

Karen staggered to her feet, laughing hysterically. Debbie and Ben, one each side of her, walked her back home. 'Naughty girl, aren't I?' she giggled. 'Shan't do that again!'

'No, I should hope not,' said Debbie, reprovingly. It was the first time that any of them had got into that state, and she didn't like it.

Lisa and Neil walked home hand in hand, and Fran and Alistair walked together, her arm linked through his. They didn't linger, though, when they arrived back at the house as did Lisa and Neil. The others dispersed and left the two love birds to say goodnight.

Karen stood on tiptoe and kissed Ben on the cheek. 'G'night, Ben,' she said. 'Thanks for looking after me.'

'It's a pleasure,' he replied politely, but he didn't sound as though he meant it. 'Hope you'll be OK in the morning.'

Debbie helped her to climb the stairs and guided her into her bedroom. She collapsed on the bed. 'I'm a bloody fool, aren't I?' she giggled. 'First Charlie, and now Ben. It was no go with him – he's gay!'

Fran helped her to undress and get into bed, then she made coffee for herself and the other two. 'It'll be a miracle if she's ready for college in the morning,' she commented. 'Still, she probably needed to get Charlie out of her system ... poor girl!' she added with an unusual show of empathy. 'She's not as blasé as I am about men, but she'll get over him in time. I think with Ben it was a question of any port in a storm. But she's got her answer there, hasn't she?'

Lisa didn't understand at all about Ben, and still seemed mystified when both Fran and Debbie tried to explain to her. 'Never mind, love,' said Debbie, as Lisa shook her head in bewilderment. 'We're finding out about all sorts of things, you and me, aren't we? What about Neil? Did you tell him about your dad?' One thing was obvious; Lisa had no intention of ending her friendship with him.

'Yes, I told him,' she said, with a smile. 'And he said I mustn't worry. He said my dad will come round in time, and I think he might be right. Do you know ... I think I'm in love with him...' She sounded like a little girl with a wonderful secret.

Debbie knew that it was partly the drink that was loosening her tongue; Lisa had drunk more than her usual limit that night. But it was obvious that she really did love Neil.

Fran was right about Karen. She didn't stir when the alarm clock went off in the morning, and didn't respond when Fran shook her, except to say, 'Go away and leave me alone.'

She did come round eventually whilst the other three were having breakfast, but it was clear she was in a sorry state as she staggered into the living room. She was pale and her eyes were bloodshot.

'My head's thumping,' she said. 'It's like a herd of elephants doing a clog dance. Don't tell me! I know I'm a complete idiot,' she said. 'But never again! Never ever again, do you hear me? I'll stick to lemonade in future.'

Debbie was quite sure she wouldn't, but at least the good intention was there. They plied her with black coffee and aspirins, but she was in no fit state to travel with them on the bus.

'You go,' she said. 'You know what we agreed; we don't wait around for sluggards like me. I'll go in later if I feel up to it. I've only one lecture this morning. I might make it this afternoon for the greenhouse one; I don't want to miss that... Oh, to hell with that Charlie! And Ben flippin' Robson an' all!' She buried her head in her hands, rocking to and fro. 'They're not worth it, any of 'em.'

'Do you think we should leave her?' Lisa asked anxiously. 'She seems in a bad way to me.'

Karen heard her remark and she looked up and gave a weak smile. 'Take no notice of me, luv. It's my own bloomin' fault. I'll be OK. I won't do anything stupid, if that's what you're worried about. Off you go now. See you later...'

Lisa sat next to Debbie on the journey to college, with Fran behind them. Lisa was quiet, so much so that Debbie asked what was worrying her. Was she still concerned about her father and the situation with Neil? She had seemed much easier about it the previous night.

'Well, of course it's partly that,' replied Lisa, 'but to be honest' – she was speaking in a whisper now – 'I was really worried about Karen getting into that awful state last night. I've never been used to it, you see. I'd never been in a pub at all till I came here, as I told you. And I've always had a fear, sort of, of people who are drunk. It upset me to see Karen like that. I know my parents would be horrified if they thought I was getting into what they call bad company. That sounds awful, doesn't it? Really prim and prudish. Because I like Karen. I think she's a smashing girl and ... well ... it worried me, that's all.'

'I should think she's learnt her lesson,' said Debbie. 'And I do understand how you feel, you know. I guess we've been brought up rather differently from the others, you and me. I don't think my parents are as strict as yours about drinking, but they're the sort who bring out a bottle of sherry only on very special occasions; like Christmas, or when I got my O-level results; I remember us having a drink to celebrate, then. And my dad's never been one to go off to the pub like a lot of fellows do. He spends most of his time with my mum.'

'I don't think either of my parents have ever set foot inside a pub,' said Lisa. 'My dad told me that he "signed the pledge", as they call it, when he was about thirteen years old, vowing that he'd never touch alcohol, and so did my mother. And they never have done.'

'Good for them if they can keep to it, I suppose,' said Debbie, 'but where's the harm if you just have an odd drink, to be social, like?'

'Oh, that's the thin end of the wedge, according to them. And an odd drink can lead to another. They believe they have to set a good example and not lead others astray. I've had dozens of lectures about the evils of drink, I can tell you!'

'So where do they think you go for a night out? Surely they must realize, now you're at college, that you might go to ... pubs!' Debbie whispered the last word. 'You haven't signed this ... pledge, have you?'

'Oh no; I don't know whether they still do it or not. Probably not. Some Methodists are much more broad-minded now, but not my father. Strange, isn't it? I plucked up courage to tell them about Neil, but I haven't told them that I've been inside a pub! They probably think we go to coffee bars.'

'Well, you're not likely to overstep the mark, are you, Lisa? I know you have very high standards, and I admire you for it. Don't worry about Karen. As you say, she's a great girl, and I should imagine she's feeling quite ashamed of herself now. I remember the time when I had far too much to drink—'

'Did you?' Lisa looked at her in amazement.

'Not only that; I did something else that was very stupid. I was at a party that one of the girls in our form had. We'd just finished our O levels and we were celebrating. And an older lad, from the sixth form, offered me a joint...'

Lisa gasped. 'Do you mean ... cannabis?'

'Well, I suppose it was. Anyway, I had a few puffs, and I was well away. I was friendly with Kevin at the time, and he was really annoyed. What with that and the drink I was sick all over the place. He had to take me home, and my parents were furious.'

'Gosh! I think my dad would have killed me!'

'No, he wouldn't. They love us, you know, and they just feel ashamed. I pretended it was just the drink, and they believed me. And I learnt my lesson, believe me! I never touched anything like that again, and I never will. I was just a silly kid, but you learn by your mistakes. I sound like my mother now; she says things like that, but it's true, isn't it? Anyway, we're here now,' she said as the bus pulled up near to the college gates. 'Time to start work again.'

Ten

Debbie, Fran and Lisa walked up the path between the lawns and flower beds, bare now apart from late blooming rose bushes, towards the college buildings. The main building, which held the administrative offices and most of the lecture rooms, was an old Victorian mansion that had fallen into disrepair following the Second World War. It had been renovated and brought up to date to fit the requirements of a college.

As well as the offices and lecture rooms there was a comfortable common room where the students could relax during their breaks, and a refectory; a new building at the back of the college, adjoining the large kitchen, where meals and snacks were served.

Beyond the college were acres of land for vegetable and flower gardens, shrubberies and greenhouses, where the practical work took place. There was also the area where those students studying landscaping, including Debbie and Fran, were working out their own ideas of garden planning.

The three friends separated once inside the building, making their way to the lecture rooms. Debbie and Fran were bound for the same place to listen to the next lecture in the series dealing with the development of the English garden.

Debbie enjoyed all the lectures, no matter what they were about, from the propagation of plants to pest control, trees and shrubs, maintenance of lawns or the art of topiary. She was ready to absorb it all, as a sponge absorbs water. Her chief interest, though, was in the study of landscape gardening.

Today they were learning how English garden design had been influenced by gardens in other countries. They were shown colourful slides of gardens of the ancient Near East; the hanging gardens of Babylon, paradise gardens in Persia, gardens in Rome and Egypt. Debbie wondered if she would ever be able to see such faraway places. She had not even been abroad. Her parents had never had any desire to venture so far, being more than content with the British Isles, and she had been obliged to follow their lead. She had, in fact, not been any further south than Blackpool! Apart, that is, from a three-day visit to London on a school trip, when she was fourteen. Her parents had taken a good deal of persuading that she would be perfectly safe; and as her friend, Shirley, was going, they had finally agreed. As it happened they had been watched over continually by hawk-eyed teachers, both in the hostel and outside. Debbie had been somewhat homesick on her first time away on her own, although she had enjoyed seeing all the sights of London.

She had no fears now about being away from home. She was determined to take any opportunity that came her way to see more of the world; well, if not the world then certainly more of the British Isles. The trip that was being planned for next spring to visit some of the well-known gardens would be a good start.

She noticed that Fran and Alistair were sitting together during the lecture, and they went off at the morning break chatting in a friendly way. She found Lisa in the common room. She was, of course, accompanied by Neil, and she joined them for coffee. They served themselves from a machine which offered a choice of black or white coffee, tea, hot chocolate or orange juice. The coffee was just about palatable, better than the tea at any rate, which always tasted stewed and smelled like the wood from sharpened pencils! Debbie had not noticed this until Lisa had pointed it out to her. Now it always took her back to her days in the Infant classroom.

When it was lunch time, Karen joined her in the refectory queue, rather to Debbie's surprise.

'Here I am, my jolly old self again ... or nearly,' she quipped. 'Those aspirins and black coffee did the trick. I tell you what though, Debs; I'm off men, no kidding! I shan't touch any of 'em with a barge pole from now on.'

Debbie grinned. 'Good for you,' she replied,

though wondering how long it would last.

'I made a real bloody fool of meself with Ben, didn't I?' Karen raised her eyebrows in horror. 'I had no idea. I couldn't believe I'd been so naive.'

'If it's any consolation I hadn't twigged it either,' said Debbie. 'Fran and Alistair had a good laugh at my expense. I felt a real idiot! But I'd never come across any – what do they call 'em? – any "gays" before. At least not as far as I know. How did you find out about Ben?'

'Oh, I suddenly realized there was summat not quite right. He was, sort of, backing away from me, and it came to me in a flash. I didn't say anything, of course. I'd had too much to drink anyroad, and everything was getting rather fuzzy and unreal. I've learnt my lesson about the booze, an' all. I bet little Lisa was horrified, wasn't she?'

'She was a bit taken aback Debbie admitted. 'But she's getting more accustomed to the ways of the big wide world now. Like I am. I'm learning a thing or two as well ... right now; what are we going to have today?' She looked at the array of dishes keeping warm by the hotplates. There was a good choice, and they had found that the food was always well cooked. She decided on a piece of cheese and onion quiche, with salad and a few chips on the side, with a strawberry yogurt to follow. Karen was still a little unsettled after her excesses of the night before, so she had just a bowl of chicken soup and a roll.

She had recovered, though, by the end of the day, when they all sat down to enjoy beans on toast, followed by ice cream, one of their favourite meals, quick and easy to prepare.

'Alistair has asked me to go out with him on Saturday,' said Fran, in quite a casual manner; it was not her way to enthuse and show too much excitement. It was obvious, though, that she was pleased; she was unable to disguise the slight smile that played round her lips.

'Nice work if you can get it!' remarked Karen. 'That didn't take long, did it? Off with the old and on with the new, eh? I shall be a bit more wary meself. Like I said to Debs, I'm off men; you can't trust any of 'em.'

'We're only going out for a meal,' Fran replied. 'It's no big deal, is it? I'm not making anything of it. I've known Alistair for quite a while... Yes, I know it's only a couple of months, but it's the same length of time as I've known you girls, and I've seen him nearly every day. We've always got on quite well together. He noticed my engagement ring, though, didn't he? It shows that he's high-principled, or else he might have asked me out before now.'

Debbie was pondering on Fran's words. It was, indeed, only a couple of months since the four flatmates had met one another; but it felt as though they had known one another for years. And she wouldn't have described Alistair Kenyon as high-principled. She suspected that he might have a roving eye, but she made no comment.

'Neil and I are going out on Saturday as well,' said Lisa, 'to the pictures, and then we'll probably go for a bag o' chips. My mum thinks it's common to eat in the street, and I never did till I came here. It's Neil who's taught me to enjoy chips with lashings of salt and vinegar. Yummy!'

Her blue eyes lit up with delight.

'Watch out! He's leading you astray!' laughed Karen. 'So that leaves just thee and me, Debbie. What shall we do? Stay in and do our knitting? Or do you fancy a night on the town? Happen a disco and a few bevvies?'

'Steady on,' said Debbie. 'You're supposed to be off the booze as well as men, aren't you?'

'Whoops! I forgot,' said Karen. 'We couldn't afford it anyroad, could we? Never mind; we can always go to bed with a cup of hot chocolate.'

Debbie was hoping, though, that Graham might contact her soon; there was the promised visit to his flat pending. She was not to be disappointed. Graham called at the flat the following evening, just as they were finishing their meal.

'Cup of tea, Graham?' asked Karen. 'We're just going to have one; well, a mug of tea to be more correct. You don't mind a mug, do you?'

'No, of course not,' he replied. 'Good old northern custom, isn't it? A cup of tea at the end of every meal. That's the way I was brought up.'

'Like the rest of us I reckon,' said Karen. 'There's nowt like a nice cup of tea.'

Debbie noticed Fran's raised eyebrows and slightly contemptuous glance in Karen's direction, although she made no comment. Fran, coming from Cheshire, liked to show that she was not used to such working-class customs. She was also aware that Karen, so far, was doing most of the talking.

'How do you like your tea then?' Karen asked now, picking up the large brown earthenware pot.

'Oh hot and strong, please,' said Graham.

'Just like you, eh?' retorted Karen, just as

154

Debbie might have expected her to do.

Graham smiled weakly, looking a shade embarrassed as he took the large-sized mug, adorned with a fierce-looking tabby cat, from Karen.

'And two sugars, please, if you don't mind,' he said.

Debbie offered him the sugar bowl. 'So ... what brings you here?' she asked. 'We're pleased to see you, of course.' He hadn't, yet, said why he was there. It had been Lisa who had answered the ring at the doorbell.

'I've come to invite you for a meal at my flat on Saturday,' he said to Debbie. 'Nothing special, you know, but I thought it would be ... rather nice,' he finished lamely.

'Ooh, that sounds good!' said the irrepressible Karen. 'Can we all come? Only joking,' she added at Graham's startled expression. She winked at him. 'Two's company, but three, four, five, would be a crowd.'

'We haven't room anyway,' Graham commented. 'Mark – he's my flatmate – he and I don't do much entertaining, Not that he'll be there on Friday. We have an arrangement that the other one goes out if one of us wants to entertain ... depending on who it is, of course,' he added.

'Of course,' said Karen, smiling. 'Sounds like a good idea. 'Like I said, three's a crowd.'

Debbie threw a 'shut up, can't you?' sort of glance in her direction before turning to Graham. 'I shall look forward to it,' she said.

'I can't stay long now,' he told her. 'I'll go when I've finished my tea and leave you girls to your washing up. I'm meeting a chap at a pub in

155

Leeds. I answered an advert saying that members were wanted for a newly formed brass band, so I'm going to find out about it tonight.'

'Oh, how nice! What do you play?' It was Lisa, surprisingly, who asked the question. 'My dad likes brass band music,' she added, 'being a Yorkshireman; and so do I.'

'I play the French horn,' he replied. 'I was in a band at school, and at uni as well; so I've been looking for another opening.'

'French horn; that's a round curly thing, isn't it, with lots of twiddly bits?' said Karen.

Graham laughed. 'Not a bad description,' he said. 'It has a lovely tone, if it's played well, of course. I'm a bit out of practice. I don't like to play when Mark's around, and I'm worried about disturbing the neighbours. We've got the upstairs flat, and there's a couple with a baby downstairs.'

'So I'll be all on my owny-own on Saturday,' said Karen, after Graham had gone. She gave a mock sniff and pretended to wipe her eyes.

'Sorry about that,' said Debbie, although there was nothing unusual about one of them being alone in the flat. They had all agreed that they must each 'do their own thing'. They were not tied to one another in any way. Debbie knew, though, that Karen might be feeling rather vulnerable, being the only one at the moment without a male companion, despite her vow to give men a wide berth.

Debbie had said goodbye to Graham downstairs, away from the rest of the girls, especially from the outspoken remarks that Karen was apt to make. Graham always seemed rather embarrassed

156

and wary with Karen, although Debbie knew that what she said was only meant to be in fun. They had agreed that Debbie should find her own way to Graham's flat in Headingley. He had offered to come and collect her, but she assured him she was a big girl now, quite capable of getting a bus for the few stops, then walking the short distance to the flat. He said it was quite easy to find, situated on the corner of a road that led up to Beckett's Park.

'It will give you plenty of time to prepare a sumptuous meal,' she told him. 'I'm expecting great things, you know, Graham.'

He laughed. 'Then I hope you won't be disappointed! I must admit I'd never done a damn thing in the kitchen before I left home. My mum spoiled me rotten. I learned to fend for myself a bit at uni, so I'm rather more experienced now. Not cordon bleu, though, by any means.'

'It was just the same with me,' Debbie assured him. 'I was spoiled as well by my doting mum. But I'm learning! Fran and Karen are pretty good in the kitchen, but they insist on Lisa and me taking our turns.'

'Is there anything you specially like?' he asked her. 'Chicken, beef steak, salmon...'

'Oh, I like most things,' she told him. 'Surprise me, Graham! I'm sure it'll be great, whatever it is. I'm looking forward to it already.'

'That's good!' He grinned at her, then he leaned forward and kissed her cheek. 'I'm looking forward to it as well, just you and me. Bye for now, Debbie.'

Eleven

Debbie wondered whether this evening with the two of them alone together in the flat would be the time when their relationship took a step forward. Graham had made a point of telling her that his flatmate would be out for the whole of the evening.

She deliberated about what she should wear. Nothing too dressy; it wasn't as if they were going to a posh restaurant in town. All the same, Debbie wanted to look her very best. She knew which colours and styles suited her, and always tried to make the most of herself. She was reasonably satisfied with her looks – her dark brown hair that had a natural curl, her warm brown eyes and her rosy complexion – without being too vain. Her figure was not too bad either: a trim waist and quite adequate bust measurement, and her legs looked OK in a miniskirt.

A few weeks ago, in the Leeds Marks and Spencer's store, she had treated herself to a black and white checked pinafore dress – short length, but not too short – and a cherry red sweater made from a soft acrylic fibre, much easier to wash than the conventional wool. She had worn them only once, during her weekend with Fiona and Simon, at the triplets' birthday party. Fiona and her friend, Joan, had commented that the colour suited her perfectly. For this Saturday evening date she complemented them with red floral earrings from the John Lewis store, and sheer tights in the shade called barely black.

The evening was chilly, and she was glad of her long tweed coat, almost ankle length, to cover her legs. Her mother always laughed at the modern juxtaposition of miniskirts and extra long coats, but it made good sense when you thought about it. Like most modern girls, though, she seldom wore anything on her head, however cold it might be. Neither did she wear a vest, something that her mother could never understand!

She found the house easily from Graham's directions, and he answered promptly to her ring at the doorbell. He greeted her affectionately, kissing her cheek and remarking that it felt cold.

'You'll soon warm up in here though,' he told her. 'The central heating's on and we've a gas fire as well.'

He led her up the floral carpeted stairs to his flat. She could tell at once that this flat was far superior to the one where she lodged. The rent would he higher, of course, but then Graham and his friend were both earning a satisfactory salary, even though they were just starting out in their careers.

He led her through a small vestibule into the living room. It was spacious, and warm, too, as Graham had said, and was comfortably furnished; far more luxurious surroundings than Debbie was accustomed to, if somewhat old-fashioned. There was a large settee and two armchairs in brown velour, far less worn than the ones in her own flat, a sideboard with a mirror at the back, which she thought must be Victorian, and a table surrounded by four chairs with carved backs. The table was covered with a white cloth, and already set for two with shining cutlery, table mats with pictures of hunting scenes, and two different sorts of glasses, one for water and one for wine.

'Very nice,' Debbie commented. She looked admiringly round the room, taking in the floor-length green damask curtains, matching the green leaves in the floral carpet. 'And warm, too, like you said.'

The gas fire, unlike the rest of the fittings in the room, was a modern one with imitation coals, but in a conventional tiled fireplace. 'Quite luxurious,' she added. 'I'm very impressed. You've done well here, Graham.'

'Yes, I must admit that I have. The furniture's a bit antiquated for my liking. The flat was fully furnished, so there's not much we could do about that. Still, it's OK for a rented place. The rent's not too bad with two of us sharing. It'll give me a chance to save up and get a place of my own ... one of these days!

'The bedroom's more up-to-date, though.' He opened a door leading off the main room. 'Let me take your coat, Debbie, and if you want the bathroom, it's through there, opening off the bedroom.'

'Thanks, I will,' she murmured. 'I'll just ... wash my hands.'

The bedroom was at the front of the house. It seemed that Graham and Mark shared, as there were two twin beds in the room, and utility-type furniture such as was in the girls' flat. The bathroom was modern, too, with a fitted bath, wash basin and toilet in pale green, and half-tiled walls. On the top of a small cupboard there was the shaving equipment of the two men, toothbrushes, soap, and Old Spice aftershave and talcum powder.

She made use of the facilities and dried her hands on a matching green towel. It seemed as though Graham and Mark were remarkably clean and fastidious, unless there had been a tidy-up for her benefit. She thought not, though; Graham was a tidy person, in appearance and in his mind and manners.

She went back to the large sitting-cum-dining room. 'Mark and I usually dine in the kitchen,' Graham told her, turning round from the window where he had been adjusting the curtains. 'It's a fair-sized kitchen, you see...' He opened a door at the back of the room, and an appetizing aroma wafted on the air. Chicken, thought Debbie; possibly in a casserole. A sensible choice in that nothing much could go wrong.

She looked through the kitchen door. 'Gosh! That's terrific!' she exclaimed. 'Not a poky little cubbyhole like ours.'

The kitchen was far larger than the one where the girls cooked. There was a Formica breakfast bar – no doubt used for most of their meals – an electric cooker and a fridge, built-in cupboards, and still enough space to walk around.

'And something smells good as well, Graham,' she told him.

'Let's hope it tastes as good,' he said, laughing.

'I've got everything ready, so we'll have a drink first, shall we? Come and sit down, Debbie.'

She sat on the settee with her knees pressed together demurely. Miniskirts were apt to reveal too much if you weren't careful. Graham opened the sideboard cupboard. 'Now, Martini with a dash of lemonade? That's what you like, isn't it, Debbie?'

'Yes; lovely, thank you,' she answered politely. He handed her the drink in a nice crystal glass, then poured himself a tot of whisky, adding a small amount of dry ginger. He sat down next to her on the settee.

'Cheers,' he said, and they clinked their glasses. 'Here's to a happy evening. It's so nice to see you on your own, Debbie, and not in a crowded bar.'

She smiled and nodded, suddenly feeling a little shy and ill at ease. 'Mm ... lovely,' she said again, sipping at her drink. 'Posh glasses, Graham! Are they part of the fittings?'

'Oh no; I brought them from home,' he replied. 'Mum had an abundance of glasses, of all kinds, so she gave me a nice selection; crockery as well and knives and forks. She's had two lots of wedding presents, of course, and Charles had been married before – then widowed, like Mum – so they ended up with two of everything!'

'How is your mother?' she asked, as a matter of course.

Graham replied that she was well and happy with her new husband. 'We all like Charles,' he said, 'and we're pleased that she's not on her own now that we've all fled the nest You've never met my mum, have you?' It was a rhetorical question, and he went on to say, 'We must arrange a meeting, quite soon, if possible. She's heard a lot about you.'

'Yes, that would be nice,' said Debbie. She had not met Yvonne, but she knew the story, of course, one more facet of the complicated family – or families – to which she and Graham belonged.

She had learnt that Simon, whilst serving in the RAF during the Second World War, had met Yvonne, a WAAF stationed at the same camp. Their friendship had developed, heightened by the danger that Simon experienced as a navigator and the traumas he had faced. When Yvonne had suspected that she was pregnant she had asked for a transfer to another camp whilst Simon was at home on leave. He had not known that he had fathered a son until Gregory Challinor had arrived on his doorstep some twenty-two years later.

Graham was Greg's younger brother – half-brother, to be exact – and there was also a sister, Wendy, who was a schoolteacher. Yvonne's husband, Keith, had been a doctor, several years her senior. He had died in 1967, and that was when Greg had decided to find the man, who, unknown to him until then, was his real father. Yvonne had now remarried and, as Graham had said, was happy again.

The situation had become more complicated when Debbie had turned up on the rectory doorstep the following year, seeking the woman who was her real mother. It could have caused trouble a-plenty, but Debbie's adoptive parents, Vera and Stanley, had been very understanding.

Debbie found the family relationships – who

163

was related to who, and how – very complicated to fathom. She had worked out that Greg was her stepbrother – sort of! – but no blood relation. And Graham, his younger brother, was her boyfriend – sort of! – but he was proving to be something of an enigma. The two of them were now sitting primly side by side on the settee as though they had only just met.

'I spent a few days with Simon and Fiona last week,' she told him, 'and the triplets, of course, and little Stella. It was the babies' second birthday party.'

'Oh yes; so it was,' said Graham. 'I sent cards and a postal order so that Fiona could buy them something... How are they all?'

'Quite well, on the whole,' Debbie answered. 'Fiona has another lady to help her now, so I'm hoping she will improve. She's been very tired and down in the dumps as well.'

She did not elaborate on the story of the new helper, Glenda. It was too involved and personal to talk about. Fiona had been very much in her thoughts. She did so hope that her fears were groundless, but she had sensed that things were by no means right in that household.

'I'm not surprised that things get her down, with four small children,' Graham observed. 'And how is my special little godson, Mark?'

'He's doing well,' replied Debbie. 'Starting to talk and be more alert. He's a well-behaved little boy, compared with Matthew.' She didn't tell him that it was feared, particularly by Fiona, that Mark was not progressing as well as he might; that he was possibly a little retarded in his development. It was just one more thing to worry Fiona, and better not to be talked about.

'I must pay them a visit soon,' said Graham. 'Perhaps we could both go?'

'Perhaps,' said Debbie.

Graham clasped his hands decidedly and stood up. 'Now ... let's eat, shall we, Debbie?'

'A good idea,' she replied. She was glad to bring the chit-chit to an end, and she was quite hungry.

Graham pulled out a chair for her in a gentlemanly way, and she sat down. 'I'm afraid one thing I don't have is posh napkins and rings,' said Graham. 'I'm afraid we'll have to make do with paper serviettes.' The green ones which matched the decor were, however, artistically folded and placed in the water glasses.

Debbie laughed. 'I'm afraid we don't often use serviettes at all... This is all very nice and civilized, Graham.'

He disappeared into the kitchen and came back with the 'starter'; prawn cocktail in small glass bowls with dainty triangles of bread and butter at the side. A popular dish to be found on most menus of the time, and one of Debbie's favourites.

They ate in comparative silence at first. Graham took her dish away, refusing her offer of help to bring in the main course, It was, as she had guessed, a chicken casserole; succulent breast portions with onions, mushrooms, celery and diced carrots in a creamy sauce. He placed a piping hot helping in front of her, and dishes of fluffy mashed potatoes and broccoli in the centre of the table.

'This looks lovely,' she said, wishing she could think of a more original comment. But it did look appetizing, and it tasted so as well.

'Delicious!' she enthused again. 'You're a good cook, Graham.'

'I'm afraid the sauce came out of a tin,' he confessed, 'and I just followed the directions.'

'Don't we all?' she said, 'But it still has to be cooked properly, and this is perfect.'

'Oh!' He jumped up again. 'I almost forgot the wine.' He poured out a German Riesling. 'I hope this is to your taste, madam!'

'I'm learning to like all white wines,' she said, 'so long as they're not too dry.' He poured out glasses of water as well, which was very acceptable as the chicken sauce was a little spicy.

Conversation flowed a little more easily as the meal progressed, Graham talking about his work, and Debbie about the courses she was enjoying. They finished off the meal with a lemon meringue pie, which Graham admitted he had bought from a local bakery.

'And why not?' said Debbie. 'They're usually made from a packet anyway, and this is just as good as any home-made one.' Lemon meringue pie was another very popular dish of the time, but most housewives relied on the easy packet variety.

Graham did accept her offer to help to clear the pots, but not to wash up. 'I'll leave them till morning,' he said, stacking them all neatly at the side of the sink and putting the casserole dish to soak. Debbie reflected again that he was a very tidy-minded young man. 'Mark and I usually have a lazy Sunday morning with the papers, after we've had our bacon and eggs, our weekly treat.'

'You'll have a mountain of washing up,' Debbie observed, but he was determined to leave it.

'All the more time to spend with you,' he said, smiling at her. Debbie wondered what he had in mind. 'Coffee?' he asked. 'It's only instant, but I'll make some if you like?'

'No, thank you,' she replied. 'I really couldn't manage another thing to eat or drink. Perhaps ... later.'

'Later then,' he agreed. 'Come and sit down, Debbie, and make yourself at home.'

They sat side by side on the settee as before. Graham drummed his fingers on his knee as if unsure what to do next. Then, 'Shall we listen to some music?' he asked.

She had noticed there was some up-to-date stereo equipment at the side of the fireplace. 'Yes, I'd like that,' she replied. 'Is that yours?' She pointed to the box and the twin speakers, far more complicated than anything she had seen before; a far cry from her old Dansette gramophone or even her more modern cassette player.

'Yes, it's mine,' he answered with some pride. 'It was the first thing I bought after I'd started earning. It plays records and tapes as well. Er ... shall we listen to some band music first?'

She laughed. 'Of course! What else?'

He put in a cassette of the famous Brighouse and Raistrick band playing a selection of well-known favourites: traditional marches, opera, ballet and Gilbert and Sullivan. Graham hummed and tapped his foot in time to the music, to the catchy rhythms of 'Blaze Away' and 'Marching Through Georgia'. After a few moments he

167

glanced sideways at Debbie and put his arm round her. She, daringly, snuggled closer towards him, resting her head on his shoulder. He turned to look at her for a moment, then he kissed her, gently at first, then more eagerly as she responded to him. They exchanged a few ardent kisses and embraces, then he drew away from her, sitting back and listening intently to the music.

'This is one of my favourites,' he remarked as they listened to Sullivan's overture to *Iolanthe*.

'Yes, that's my favourite of all their operas,' she agreed. They sat hand in hand enjoying the melodies. In a few moments he put his arm around her, holding her closely. They began to kiss as the band played on... Debbie recognized some ballet music – *Dance of the Hours*, she thought – then a couple of operatic arias, just the melodies, of course.

It was the first time that he had kissed her like this. She felt herself warming to his embraces, feeling roused in a way she had not experienced before with Graham. Then, once again, he drew apart from her. The band was playing a melody that sounded familiar, although she couldn't put a name to it. She glanced at Graham. He was smiling beatifically, but she realized that it was at the music, and not at her.

'This is the duet from *The Pearl Fishers* by Bizet,' he told her. 'A haunting melody, isn't it?'

'Yes ... so it is,' she agreed. 'Very ... very lovely music. I've heard it before but I didn't know what it was.' She was bemused, not knowing what to make of Graham, or of his feelings towards her. She had thought that the music might have been intended as a background to … what? To their relationship taking a step further, to Graham making more intimate moves? She had been starting to feel that she was ready, even willing for this, but he seemed to have other things on his mind as well. She could not help but feel a little amused, but somewhat affronted as well.

'I'm learning to play this piece on my French horn,' he told her, the enthusiasm showing in his voice. 'It lends itself well to the rich tones of the French horn.'

'Yes,' she nodded. 'I can imagine that … it would.' It seemed that his cautious lovemaking, if that was what you could call it, had come to an end for the moment.

She remembered about his intention to join a newly formed brass band in the area, and she asked him about it. He was only too eager to tell her how he had gone along on Thursday evening to the meeting in a church hall in Leeds; how he had been warmly welcomed as they had only one more French horn player so far. He was well into his stride now…

'The French horn is the link, you see, between the woodwind and the brass instruments. It has a mellow tone and it can blend with all kinds of instruments. It's good as a backing for the rhythm sections as well. Yes … I enjoyed my first session with them, very much indeed.'

'So you'll be going again next week?'

'Rather! I'm looking forward to it. They seem like a good crowd of blokes, very friendly, and it's so nice to meet other people with the same interest.'

'All men, are they?' asked Debbie.

'Well, there are a couple of girls, actually. One of them plays the French horn, like me, and the other plays the clarinet. It used to be an all-male province, you know, the brass band; but nowadays they're starting to include women.'

Debbie smiled. 'Women's rights!'

'Yes, of course. And the bands are no longer attached solely to collieries and mills as they used to be. That's good, because they're attracting people from all walks of life.'

'And has your band got a name?' asked Debbie.

'Not yet; we're trying to think of something suitable. Have you any ideas?'

'Me? No! It's not really down to me, is it?' She found the idea of him consulting her rather amusing.

'No, maybe not. But I thought you might be interested, Debbie. You'll come to our first concert, won't you?'

'I'd love to,' she answered. 'I shall look forward to hearing you play.'

'I could play for you now,' he suggested. 'Would you like to hear me, Debbie?' He sounded like a little boy, dying to play his party piece. 'Like I said, I'm just learning *The Pearl Fishers'* duet. I could do with some practice.'

Debbie tried to keep a straight face. 'That would be lovely, Graham,' she told him, smiling at him, but trying to stem the laughter bubbling up inside her.

He opened his instrument case and took out the French horn. He put up a music stand and placed a copy of music on it. Then he gave the instrument a quick polish, and blew one or two experimental notes. When he began to play she realized that he was quite proficient, at least as far as she could tell. It was a lilting melody, and sounded well suited to the mellow tones of the French horn. He fluffed one or two notes, but on the whole it sounded good. When he stopped playing he looked at her expectantly.

She applauded. 'Well done!' she said. 'You don't sound like a learner to me.'

'The trill was a bit wobbly,' he replied, 'but I'll get it right in time. Now ... shall I put on another tape, or a record. Your choice this time. What would you like?'

'Oh ... have you got Simon and Garfunkel?' she asked. She had heard enough of brass bands for the moment.

'Indeed I have.' He put on a long-playing record, then sat down beside her again.

He put his arm round her and kissed her several times whilst the duo sang about the bridge over troubled waters. He got up and turned the volume lower. When he sat down again he took hold of her hand. 'Debbie,' he began, 'I would like to go on seeing you, and I hope you want to continue with our friendship?'

'Yes, of course I do,' she replied, feeling a little bewildered.

'What I mean is ... I don't want to rush things,' he said. 'I like you very much; I'm growing very fond of you, but I want us to take things slowly. I want to be very sure, you see ... and I want you to feel sure as well.'

'Yes, I understand, Graham,' she replied, not

altogether sure whether she did or not. She had realized that he was a very serious young man, certainly not one to throw caution to the winds. That suited her fine, for the moment; at least she thought it did. She didn't want to rush into a mad frenzy of lovemaking; but was Graham being altogether too circumspect? She liked him, though, and enjoyed his company. 'Yes, that's OK,' she said. 'I enjoy being with you, and we seem to get on quite well, don't we? Let's just see how things go, shall we?'

'That suits me.' He smiled at her, then kissed her cheek. 'I'll go and make us some coffee, then I'll see you safely home.'

She told him there was no need. It was not too late and she could easily get a bus back. But when they had drunk their coffee he insisted on going with her. It was a fine, clear night so they walked the mile or so back to Debbie's flat.

'It's been a lovely evening, Graham,' she said when they reached her gate. 'Thank you very much for inviting me; for the meal ... and everything.'

'The pleasure is all mine,' he replied. 'Thank you for coming, Debbie. It's been great.' He kissed her on the lips, holding her close for a moment. 'Goodnight, Debbie. See you soon,' he whispered. Then he turned and walked away quickly.

Karen was still up watching the television. 'Hello,' she said, sounding surprised. 'You're back early. It's only just turned eleven. The others aren't back yet.'

'Oh, I think it's quite late enough for Graham,' said Debbie with a wry smile.

Karen got up and turned off the TV. 'I've seen enough of that,' she said, putting an end to the late-night chat show. 'It's a load of waffle. Now–' she patted the seat next to her – 'how did it go? Tell me all...'

Debbie took off her coat and flung it over a chair back. She sat down, then she started to laugh. 'There's nothing to tell,' she said, shaking her head. She wiped tears from her eyes, but they were tears of merriment, not of sorrow.

'What d'you mean?' Karen was all agog. 'He didn't ... try anything? You're just the same as you were when you went out?' Trust Karen to get to the nitty gritty!

'Absolutely,' replied Debbie. 'You might say that I played second fiddle to the French horn, if you forgive the pun!'

'What?' Karen frowned. 'What the heck are you talking about?'

'He played the French horn for me,' said Debbie, collapsing into another fit of giggles. 'Honestly! That's what we did all the evening. Listened to music, than he played his bloody French horn!' Debbie very rarely swore, but it just came out. It seemed so funny now when she looked back on it.

They were still laughing a few moments later when Fran and Lisa returned, both of them coming in at the same time.

'What are you two laughing at?' enquired Fran.

'Oh ... nothing much,' replied Debbie. She glanced at Karen, frowning a little and shaking her head to warn her not to say anything. She didn't feel like telling the other two – not at the moment

173

at any rate – about her evening with Graham. It seemed unkind, somehow, to be laughing so much at his expense. He was, after all, a very nice young man, kind and considerate, if a little staid and overcautious. 'We were just having a giddy five minutes, weren't we, Karen?' she added in explanation.

'That's right,' Karen said nodding. 'What about you two? Have you had a good time?'

'Oh yes; it was lovely,' answered Lisa, starry-eyed as she always was after an evening with Neil.

'Enjoyed your bag of chips, did you?' asked Debbie, smiling at her friend. Lisa was such a love that you felt you wanted to mother her. She did hope that things would work out all right for her and Neil despite her father's opposition.

'Oh yes. We decided we were both feeling hungry, so we went and had haddock and chips – and mushy peas as well! – at that big chip shop near to City Square.'

'Wow! Talk about living it up!' remarked Karen. 'What about you, Fran?'

Fran was smiling a little complacently. Debbie guessed that she and Alistair would not have partaken of such a plebeian meal.

'We went to that new Italian place on the Headrow,' said Fran. 'They have a wide-ranging menu there, not just Italian food, but when in Rome, you know... It's quite expensive, of course, but Alistair is something of a gourmet; he likes to try new places.'

'It all met with your approval then?' asked Debbie, trying not to smile.

'Very much so. He's good company as well,'

replied Fran.

'You'll be seeing him again then?' asked Karen. 'Apart from at college, I mean?'

'I hope so... Yes I expect I will,' said Fran, guardedly. 'Well, I'm off to bed now; I don't know about the rest of you...'

The others followed suit, each of them wrapped up in their own thoughts.

Twelve

'I did warn you that you might be asking for trouble,' Gilbert Henderson, the curate of St Peter's, remarked to his wife, 'when you suggested that Glenda should come and look after the children at the rectory. And it looks as though I was quite right to be concerned.'

'But I thought she'd learnt her lesson, really I did,' replied Norma. 'It's ages since that unfortunate episode. How long is it now? It must be seven or eight years ago.'

'You did a good job of trying to convince me that your sister had changed her ways. But it seems that a leopard doesn't change its spots, as the saying goes.' Gilbert had raised his voice and he sounded quite cross. 'I was willing to give her the benefit of the doubt – I agree that she's good at her job – but she's getting herself talked about. You must know that as well as I do, Norma.'

This conversation was taking place on a Sunday in late November, following the morning service, whilst the Hendersons were having their lunch. Norma knew that her husband was right. She was sorry now that she had been so insistent that Glenda would be the ideal person to help Fiona Norwood with her children. She had done an excellent job at the nursery where she had been employed for several years, and her references when the place closed down had been impeccable. No one there, of course, had known anything of her reputation with the opposite sex. It would have had no bearing on her ability to do her job anyway. And Norma had really believed that her sister had changed.

'I'm sorry, Gilbert,' she said now. He was usually so even-tempered, and she hated him to be upset, especially if her actions had been the cause of it. 'Maybe I should have thought more about what I was suggesting. I do realize, of course, that Simon is a very charismatic sort of man. I dare say he's already had a few female hearts fluttering in the parish if we knew it all. But he's got a lovely wife. Fiona's not only lovely to look at; she's such a nice person as well. And it's obvious that she and Simon think the world of one another.'

'I've noticed a bit of tension between them lately,' remarked Gilbert. 'And Fiona looks very tired and fed up sometimes.'

'It's not to be wondered at with those triplets,' replied Norma. 'They're more than one body's work. Glenda says they're quite a handful, especially Matthew. He's a little tearaway! And Mark, bless him, he's not coming on quite as well as he might. I don't wonder that Fiona looks exhausted.'

'But she shouldn't, should she?' retorted Gilbert. 'Not now she's got Glenda helping her. But it seems that my dear sister-in-law has done more harm than good in that family. It's noticeable that the two of them – Fiona and Glenda – don't hit it off all that well, and it's not surprising if Glenda's trying to pinch her husband!'

'Oh, surely not, Gilbert! She wouldn't go so far, would she? I know she can be flirtatious. She likes the company of men – although I really did think she'd calmed down – but she'd draw the line at the rector, surely?'

'You should have seen her today, fussing around him after the service. She came into the vestry when he was disrobing – taking off his surplice, I mean, nothing else!' He did manage a grin. 'Although I bet she wouldn't mind if it was more than his surplice!'

'He wouldn't! Not Simon. He should tell her if he thinks she's getting too friendly. He must have noticed if other people have.'

'So you are admitting it, Norma? You are aware of it, aren't you? Has anybody said anything to you?'

'Well, as a matter of fact they have,' said Norma. She had not wanted to admit that she might have made a big mistake in inviting her sister to come to Aberthwaite. 'Joan Tweedale – she's a very good friend to Fiona – she mentioned that Fiona was getting worried about the friendship between her husband and Glenda. But Joan has tried to tell her that Simon is just being nice and friendly – as he always is with everyone – and that there's no need to worry. And apparently Fiona had confided in

Debbie when she came a few weeks ago. It seems that Fiona and her daughter are very close; more like sisters or friends. Anyway, Joan says that Debbie told her that Fiona was worried and very unhappy about it all.'

'Then it has to be nipped in the bud before it goes any further,' said Gilbert, banging his hand on the table so that the cutlery and plates jingled. 'Think of the scandal if it got into the papers! The rector and his children's nanny!'

'You're overreacting, Gilbert,' said his wife. 'Simon's got his head screwed on the right way. He's not going to jeopardize his career, or his marriage. But I have to agree that people are starting to talk about it. What do you intend to do?'

'It's down to you, isn't it, Norma? She's your sister ... and it was your idea to ask her to come here. Can't you have a quiet word with her?'

'I suppose I could ... but I don't want to. You remember what happened the last time? She was furious with me; told me to mind my own business, and we were at loggerheads for ages afterwards.'

'At least it brought it all to a head, didn't it? Her sorry little affair came to an end, as it had to do, of course. And she got over it in time.'

The situation to which Gilbert was referring had happened some eight years ago when they – Gilbert and Norma and their children, and Glenda and her then-husband, Clive – had lived in Sheffield and attended a parish church there. Glenda and Clive had been married for several years but no children had arrived on the scene, much to their disappointment, Glenda's in particular. One of her good points was that she was very fond of children. She had worked as a nursery assistant and eventually had charge of a day nursery.

But Glenda liked men. She enjoyed their company and became quite a different person – flirtatious and, indeed, quite bold at times if one should take particular notice of her. She had sung in the church choir and, somewhat bored with her marriage and the status quo, had turned her attention to the organist and choirmaster, a man called Basil Jones. She had a good voice; she was one of the leading sopranos and sometimes she was asked to sing a solo at a special service or a church concert. This led to private rehearsals with Basil; and so the two of them became friendly, rather too friendly. It was not entirely Glenda's fault, although it was clear that she had encouraged him. Probably the man had just wanted a fling, but Glenda had wanted more than that. She had believed herself to be in love with him – and he with her, or so she thought – and she tried to persuade him to leave his wife and family.

It was at this point that Norma had stepped in and warned her that she was heading for serious trouble. It had to stop or she, Norma, would tell the vicar about the relationship. The sisters quarrelled bitterly. Norma was determined to carry out her threat although a part of her was loath to betray her sister.

As it happened, though, it was Basil's wife, Helen, who became aware of the goings-on, and she it was who told the vicar. He was an unworldly man, as 'men of the cloth' should be, of course; but he was a genuinely virtuous man who always tried to believe the best of people rather than condemn them. He was shocked and disturbed at the revelations. He had not noticed anything of the developing friendship, but he knew it was his duty to have a quiet word with his organist.

Basil Jones had admitted readily, and with a sense of relief, to his affair with Glenda Forbes. He was realizing what a fool he had been to get friendly with her in the first place. He explained how 'one thing had led to another' and now he was more deeply involved than he had intended. The vicar wanted to make as little of the matter as was possible. A less tolerant vicar would have asked Basil to resign from his post, but the clergyman decided it was only fair to give him a second chance. Besides, he was a very good organist. Basil promised to bring the affair to an end right away. He told Glenda that it was all over between them. And his loving wife, seeing it for what it was – a sort of mid-life crisis – forgave him.

Glenda believed, and continued to do so, that it was Norma who had betrayed her. She left the church and she and her husband moved to another part of town. Their marriage, though, had been damaged, and the affection and trust they had once shared had gone. A year later Clive left her and went to live with a young secretary from the council office where they both worked.

Glenda had got over it all in time. She had concentrated on her work as a nursery assistant;

she was well thought of by the mothers, and the children loved her. She had had a couple of gentlemen friends but neither had lasted. The sisters had become friendly again; and so it was that Norma, believing that Glenda had changed for the better, had invited her to come to Aberthwaite.

'Very well then; I will have a word with Simon,' Gilbert said eventually, relenting from his previous insistence that it was up to his wife to act. 'He may not realize that people are talking. Then it will be up to him to tell her to keep her distance. I'll go and see him at the rectory tomorrow morning. We'll have a man to man chat. I don't want to detain him after the evening service. I know he likes to get home to his family. Yes ... that's what I'll do. I'll pay a visit to the rectory in the morning.'

On that same Sunday, after the evening service, Joan Tweedale was surprised when Ethel Bayliss stopped her as she was leaving the church.

'Could I have a quiet word with you, Joan?' she asked. She was glancing round to make sure that no one else on the church path was near enough to hear.

'Of course,' said Joan, agreeably. She had not always seen eye to eye with Ethel Bayliss; she was the woman in charge of the Mothers' Union, officially known as the 'enrolling member', a position she was determined not to let go. When the rector's new wife, Fiona, had arrived on the scene Ethel had been fearful for her position – one that was traditionally held by the vicar's, or rector's,

181

wife – but Fiona had had no such aspirations.

Nevertheless, Ethel Bayliss, a determined and dogmatic lady – who was now well into her seventies – had taken a dislike to the newcomer, considering her to be most unsuitable to be the wife of a clergyman, with her short skirts and make-up and her generally modern outlook. When it had become known that little Stella was not Fiona's first child – and that the first one had been born out of wedlock! – Ethel and her minions had tried to make trouble for the young wife of the rector. But it was all to no avail. Simon had stepped in and 'read the riot act', in a tactful, though forceful, way, and the gossip had come to an end.

Over the intervening years the once indomitable Mrs Bayliss had, seemingly, undergone a personality change – to some degree, at least – and Fiona, now could do no wrong in her eyes. Ethel admired the way she cared for her children, and was always ready to spring to her defence. Joan, at one time, had regarded her as ... not quite an enemy, but certainly as an adversary. But she smiled at her pleasantly now.

'What is it, Mrs Bayliss?' she asked. She had never got round to calling the much older woman by her first name.

'It's that Glenda Forbes,' replied Ethel. 'Didn't you see her? She's gone into the vestry – again! – to talk to Simon. She did the same thing this morning. Arthur has noticed, of course, but he says it's not really up to him to say anything to the rector; he thinks it would be interfering.' Arthur Bayliss was Ethel's husband and one of the two

182

churchwardens. 'He says that Simon surely must be aware of it, and that he would say something to her if he thought she was getting too friendly. But that's typical of Arthur, always wanting to take the line of least resistance! So I've decided that I must do something myself.' Ethel's mouth was set in a grim line like an angry bulldog.

'You know what men are like, and maybe Simon's not much different. Can't help themselves if a pretty woman takes notice of 'em. It's Fiona I'm bothered about, the poor lass! He couldn't have a nicer wife or a better mother to those kiddies. She looks real unhappy sometimes. Well, you must know; you're a good friend of hers, aren't you?'

'Yes ... I am,' agreed Joan. 'And I must admit I'm rather worried about the situation.' Unwilling though she was to gossip with Mrs Bayliss, she knew that what the woman was saying was not just gossip but the plain truth. And maybe they had all been somewhat dilatory having noticed what was happening and not doing anything about it.

'Fiona is unhappy about it,' she went on, 'but she won't say anything to Simon. She keeps trying to tell herself that Glenda's just being friendly and that she's imagining things. She's never really got on with Glenda, right from the start, although she can't say why. So she thinks she might be prejudiced without any real reason. I don't think there's any impropriety about their behaviour,' Joan hastened to add. 'Simon wouldn't. We all know that ... don't we?'

'I'm sure she would, though,' said Ethel, grimly,

183

'and I'm not taking any chances. I'm going to strike while the iron's hot. She's coming now so let's tackle her; there's no time like the present... Come along, Joan; I need your support.'

Glenda Forbes was coming towards them on the church path, a contented smile on her face. She looked attractive, as she always did, in a bright blue coat with a fur collar and a little black fur hat perched on top of her dark curls. Ethel stepped forward to stop her in her tracks. 'Could we have a word with you, Mrs Forbes?'

'Yes ... I suppose so,' the woman answered, the smile disappearing from her face at the sight of Ethel's formidable countenance. 'What do you want?'

'We want you to leave our rector alone,' said Ethel Bayliss. Joan felt that she could have approached the subject more tactfully, but that was not Ethel's way of doing things.

'I beg your pardon?' said Glenda, although she had, of course, heard the remark perfectly well. She looked haughtily at the pair of them. 'I don't know what you mean. Anyway, what business is it of yours if I talk to Simon? I'm looking after his children, and he's very glad of my help. So would you kindly mind your own business!'

'It is our business when you're causing trouble between a man and his wife,' said Ethel. 'Fiona is very unhappy. You are supposed to be looking after the children, not flirting with our rector.'

'I've done no such thing!' retorted Glenda. 'I admit I get on well with Simon,' she added, although she was clearly determined not to back down. 'He likes to talk to me ... about the children. And Fiona hasn't complained. Anyway, from what I've heard she's no better than she ought to be, is she?' Her eyes blazed with anger, and defiance, too, as she made the remark, one that Joan had always thought to be a silly meaningless one.

'How dare you speak like that about our lovely Fiona!' said Ethel, her face turning red with fury. Joan smiled to herself. Ethel had certainly done a complete 'volte-face' about Fiona since her early days as the rector's wife. 'She made a mistake when she was a young girl,' Ethel continued. 'Have you never made any mistakes? We all know about it and think no worse of her. Her daughter, Debbie, is a grand girl... Anyway, that's not what we're on about. I'm warning you, Mrs Forbes, just you leave our rector alone, or I shall make it my business to take this matter further. My husband is the churchwarden, and he could take steps to have you removed from here.'

Joan knew that Ethel Bayliss was bluffing. Arthur was a mild sort of man who would not want any trouble. But there was a flicker of unease, now, in Glenda's eyes. She turned to Joan.

'You're very quiet, Mrs Tweedale,' she said. 'Have you nothing to say about all this ... nonsense?'

'I agree with Mrs Bayliss that people have noticed your friendship with the rector,' answered Joan. 'Maybe you meant no harm,' she added. 'Simon is a very charming man, and friendly with everyone. We all know that. And Fiona is a loving and loyal wife; we've always regarded them as an ideal couple. They've done so much good together in the parish. But Fiona is far from happy at the moment. She hasn't been well; she has never really got her strength back since the triplets were born, and she certainly doesn't need all this added worry, even if there is no real cause for it, which is what you are telling us.' Joan looked steadily and unsmilingly at Glenda, hoping that the woman would take heed of the warning in her glance.

Glenda shook her head. 'You've got it all wrong,' she said, giving a nervous little laugh. 'I admit we're friendly, Simon and me, but I wouldn't dream of...' She didn't complete the remark, and there was a hint of wariness, almost guilt, in her eyes. She turned abruptly and marched away down the path to the gate.

'Well, I think she's got the message all right,' said Ethel. 'There was guilt written all over her face, though she tried to deny it. Thank you for supporting me, Joan. Let's hope she realizes that we won't put up with her philandering any longer. It would be best for all of us if she decided to clear off... Ah, here's my husband, at last. You've been a long time,' she said, turning to Arthur as he joined them on the path.

'Sorry, my dear,' he said. 'As a matter of fact, I've just been having a word with Gilbert about ... er, well ... about that little matter that you mentioned to me. He says he'd already decided to go round to the rectory in the morning to have a quiet word with Simon, and he's asked me to go with him.'

'Well now, fancy that!' said Ethel, with a triumphant smile. 'You've seen sense at last, Arthur. And I've got news for you an' all. Just wait till I

186

tell you!' She turned to Joan. 'Goodnight, Mrs Tweedale. 'We'll just wait and see now, won't we?'

'Yes ... so we will. Goodnight, Mrs Bayliss; goodnight, Arthur,' said Joan. Her own husband, Henry, was just leaving the church; he was always one of the last to leave after tidying up the music and putting the organ 'to bed'. She smiled at him. 'Yes, I'm still here. I've been chatting.' She was usually home by now to make him a cup of tea. 'Come along; let's go and get the kettle on.'

When Simon answered the knock on his door at ten o'clock on Monday morning he found his curate and one of the churchwardens standing there.

'Ah, a deputation, is it?' he commented, smiling enquiringly at them. 'Come along in, Gilbert, Arthur ... we'll go into the study. Actually, it's pandemonium here this morning. Our helper, Glenda Forbes, hasn't turned up, and she hasn't sent any message either. I've been looking after the triplets whilst Fiona took Stella to nursery school. And now she's got all three of them in the sitting room, playing a game, and I expect they'll be watching something on the TV soon.'

He saw the two men exchange a knowing sort of glance as he ushered them into his study. 'Why? Do you know anything about Glenda?' he asked. She was living with Gilbert and Norma, so surely his curate would know something about her unexplained absence.

'No ... I don't know where she is,' replied Gilbert, looking mystified. 'She left the house at the usual time, as though she was coming here. As a matter of fact, Simon, that's the reason that we've come here, Arthur and I, to talk to you about Glenda.'

Simon sat down, not behind his desk, which he felt would look too formal, but in one of the extra chairs that were there for visitors. Arthur sat in the only armchair, the other two men regarding it as his privilege as the senior one.

'Glenda ... yes; I think I can guess what you're going to say,' Simon began, steepling his fingers and looking down at them thoughtfully. 'I've been concerned myself but I didn't really know what to do about it.'

'You mean about her overfriendliness?' Gilbert ventured. 'Arthur and I, we thought it was time we said something about the way she tries to monopolize you; because people are starting to notice and talk about it.'

'Quite so,' replied Simon. 'It's getting embarrassing to me, and it's causing friction with Fiona, although she's never broached the subject with me. And I haven't mentioned it to her – to Fiona, I mean – because I didn't want to make an issue of it. I try to tell myself that it is an occupational hazard.' He smiled. 'You know how some women like to fuss around those of us who wear our collars back to front. It happened to me before, when my first wife died. Then I met Fiona...' He looked steadily at the other two men.

'Fiona is a wonderful woman, and I love her just as much now as I ever did. She means all the world to me, and I would never look at anyone else. Actually, it was getting to the stage when I

188

knew I would have to say something to Glenda, but I had no idea how to go about it.'

'She hasn't ... er ... propositioned you, Simon, has she?' asked Arthur Bayliss, a little tentatively.

Simon smiled. 'No, she hasn't, not directly. She's commented on how well we get on together, and how nice it is to have someone to talk to. That's all. So, where do you think she is now? Could it have something to do with ... all this?'

'More than likely,' said Gilbert. 'You see, Simon, Norma and I had decided it was time to do something. I told Norma at first that it was up to her – Glenda's her sister – but she didn't want an out and out row with her. Glenda has a fearsome temper when she's roused. To be honest with you, she has done this sort of thing before. At the church we all attended in Sheffield, she took a fancy to the organist; in fact they were having an affair until his wife found out.'

'And you have waited till now to tell me?' Simon was more bewildered than annoyed. 'It might have helped if I had known about her fondness for men! To be forewarned is to be forearmed, so to speak.'

'Yes, I know. I'm really sorry now, Simon. But Norma and I really thought she had changed and learnt her lesson. There was a dreadful row, and the organist went back to his wife. Well, he'd never left her; he was just led astray, I suppose. We never dreamt she'd try the same thing here. Anyway, I told Norma I'd come and see you myself. I asked Arthur last night if he would come with me.'

'And I said that I would.' Arthur took up the story now. 'Then, when we came out of church we found that my wife and Joan Tweedale had been having a confab together,' he chuckled. 'And it turned out that Ethel had already tackled Glenda and given her a piece of her mind.'

'As only your good lady can do,' observed Simon with a chuckle.

'Aye, my missus can pack a mighty punch,' said Arthur, 'metaphorically speaking, of course. So maybe Glenda's got the message. Ethel said she was all hoity-toity about it, denying it all; but maybe she's thought better about it and decided to call it a day.'

'But we don't know where she is, do we?' said Gilbert. 'She didn't say anything to Norma and me. Like I said, she left the house at the same time. I'd better get back and see if Norma has heard anything from her.'

'Yes, and I'll get along as well,' said Arthur. 'I'm sorry about all this trouble. It must have been a real nightmare for you, Simon. Of course we know that you're not to be blamed at all ... except, perhaps, that you're too kindly disposed towards people, always trying to see their good side and not the worst. But that's what you're supposed to do, isn't it? To set an example to us all.'

'This time I've been very naive,' admitted Simon. 'I saw the signs – too late – and I did nothing about it.'

'It might be as well if she's done a runner,' said Gilbert. 'But she didn't take any luggage with her, not as far as we could see. She's a crafty one, though, is Glenda. I'll get back home, and let you know if there have been any developments.'

'I'm sorry if your wife has been let down with

regard to the children,' said Arthur. 'We're all very fond of Fiona, you know. I'm sure we'll be able to sort out some help for her, if Glenda has ... well ... decided to leave.'

'I think Fiona will be relieved,' said Simon. 'I'll have a talk to her and put her in the picture about what's been happening. It's been a "no-go" area between the two of us, so it's about time we cleared the air.'

When the two men had gone Simon breathed a sigh of relief, not at their absence, but at Glenda's. He closed his eyes and said a quick prayer asking for guidance when he talked to his wife. He knew he had been a fool. He had enjoyed Glenda's company at first, finding her friendly and amusing and easy to get along with, although he had never been attracted to her as anything but a friend. When he had realized that Glenda might have other ideas he had been nonplussed and had not known how to act. Poor Fiona! She had been aloof and preoccupied of late and he had felt unable to approach her, either physically or mentally. He had put it down to her tiredness and depression that had never really left her since the birth of the babies. Only lately had he become aware that she might be worrying about something else. Whatever had been going through her mind? He had to put things right between them at once.

'No, Glenda's not come back here,' said Norma when Gilbert arrived back home. 'What are you telling me? That she didn't turn up at the rectory? And you think she might have got the message and

191

cleared off?'

Gilbert explained to her how Ethel Bayliss had had words with Glenda.

Norma laughed. 'Trust Mrs Bayliss! I bet she didn't mince her words. Fiona has told me that she used to be far more of a battleaxe than she is now and that she'd calmed down a lot. But she's still a force to be reckoned with. So ... where is Glenda now? What the dickens is she up to?'

Gilbert shook his head. 'I don't know. Having a quiet think somewhere, maybe. It's Fiona that I'm bothered about. She really does need help with those children. She's not at all well. Simon says she has never got her strength back since the birth of the triplets.'

'I shall go round there straight away,' said Norma, 'and see if there's anything I can do. I'm not an expert with children, like Glenda is, but I've brought up two of my own. I know little Stella will have to be picked up from nursery school. And those triplets! Well, I know they're adorable, of course, but they're jolly hard work.'

'I have some parish visits to do,' said Gilbert, 'and there's old Mrs Bates to see in the hospital so I'll be gone a couple of hours or so. I'll run you round to the rectory, then you can see what sort of help Fiona would like. We'll have a late lunch when we get home. And maybe Glenda will have reappeared by then...'

They drove off in their Morris Minor, Gilbert dropping off his wife at the rectory gate.

Thirteen

Simon opened the door of the lounge to find Fiona sitting on the settee with Mark on her lap and Matthew and Michelle one each side of her. They were engrossed in a television programme where teddy bears were prancing across the screen. Fiona looked up and smiled at him in a vague, almost disinterested, manner. It was a long time, he realized, since he had seen her face light up with a radiant smile on seeing him, as it had used to do.

'Hello,' she said. 'You've had visitors, have you? I thought I heard Gilbert's voice.'

'Yes, it was Gilbert, and Arthur Bayliss as well.'

'Oh... I see. Did Gilbert have any news about ... Glenda?' She seemed loath to speak the woman's name.

'Yes, he did, sort of... He doesn't know why she hasn't turned up here, not exactly, but–' he stopped, looking at her pleadingly – 'Fiona ... darling, I need to talk to you. Can you leave the children for a little while? They'll be all right, won't they, watching their programme?'

'Yes, they should be; it's got another fifteen minutes to run,' Fiona replied in the flat unemotional voice she had used of late. 'Michelle–' she turned to the little girl – 'will you be a big help to Mummy and look after your brothers for a little while? And if Matthew starts being a nuisance, come and tell me.' She sounded brighter now when she was speaking to the child.

Michelle nodded. 'Yes, Mummy,' she replied, hardly taking her eyes off the screen.

'Let's go in here and have a chat,' said Simon, opening the door of their living-cum-dining room at the back of the house. It was a large room and as well as the dining table and four chairs there was room for two small armchairs. Simon sat down in one, and Fiona in the other, looking enquiringly at him.

As he looked across at his wife his heart surged with his love for her. It had never lessened despite the constraint that had existed between them recently. He felt at a loss now as to how to begin. He leaned forward, regarding her intently. 'Fiona ... whatever has gone wrong between us, it's going to be put right now, this very minute.'

She stared back at him steadily, not speaking for several seconds. Then she said, rather coolly, 'Do you have something to tell me about ... Glenda?'

'We won't be seeing her again,' he answered. 'That's why Gilbert and Arthur came to see me. Oh, Fiona, my darling, I know you've been unhappy, but I didn't realize at first why it was. I know now, and I'm sorry, so very sorry.'

'Why are you sorry, Simon?' she asked, the coolness still there in her voice. 'Is it because you regret what has been going on between you and Glenda?'

'There's been nothing going on,' he replied, his voice sounding louder than he intended. He moderated his tone. 'Nothing at all, my darling. I

194

admit I found her friendly and easy to talk to, but I didn't realize – honestly I didn't – that you were reading more into it than was really there... You were, weren't you?'

Fiona nodded. 'I thought you were having an affair,' she answered quietly, 'or ... leading up to one, at any rate.'

'Fiona...' He got up from his chair and went over to her, kneeling on the floor and putting his arms around her. 'How could you possibly think that? You are the only woman for me; you have been ever since I first set eyes on you. Oh, Fiona, darling, I'm so sorry you've been upset and hurt.'

'You must admit she's attractive,' she replied. 'Glenda; she's lively and ... well, she has sex appeal, I suppose. Something that I know has been lacking in me recently. I can't help it, Simon. I've felt so weary, and I've not been able to shake off this depression. And we haven't ... you haven't come near me, Simon, not for ages, not properly. And that was what made me suspicious.'

He shook his head sorrowfully, and unbelievingly too. 'Oh no, you couldn't have thought that? I wouldn't; you know I wouldn't.'

She smiled grimly. 'Yes, I know you're a clergyman, but I don't suppose you would be the first one to stray from the straight and narrow.'

'No, probably not. But I didn't, and I wouldn't. Not because I'm a rector, but because there's no one else for me but you. Yes, I can see that Glenda's an attractive woman, looking at her objectively. But I wouldn't care if it were ... Sophia Loren! I would never look at anyone else. I know we haven't made love as we used to, because I know how tired and dispirited you've been feeling. And besides, my love for you means far more than just that. I love you in every possible way, Fiona. Please, darling, forgive me for whatever I might have done; for making you feel insecure and causing you to have doubts about me. Yes, I can see it now...'

He was staring at her intently, and she leaned forward and kissed him gently on the cheek. 'Yes ... and I can see that I might have been silly and jumped to the wrong conclusion. Of course I should have trusted you. But other people in the church have noticed you and Glenda, you know, although I can see now that she was doing all the running. Where is she, anyway? What were you going to tell me about Gilbert and Arthur?'

Simon explained the reason for their visit, how they were anxious about Glenda's behaviour, and that people were noticing the way she was monopolizing him. Fiona actually laughed when he told her that Ethel Bayliss had tackled the woman and, seemingly, might have scared her off. 'It appears you've got a good ally there now, darling,' he said. 'Ethel's enough to scare anyone when she's on the warpath.' He told her, though, that Gilbert had not known that Glenda had not turned up at the rectory that morning, and that she appeared to have left the house with the intention of coming there.

'We'll just have to wait and see,' he said. 'Gilbert and Norma will let us know if there are any developments.'

At that moment the doorbell rang. 'I'll go and see who it is,' said Simon, giving Fiona a quick kiss as he rose from his knees. 'Now, stop worrying, darling. Everything's going to be fine.'

It was Norma at the door. 'I've come to see if I can help Fiona,' she said. 'Gilbert's told me that Glenda hasn't turned up. Perhaps just as well, though. Honestly, that sister of mine! I'm sorry she's causing so much trouble. I invited her here in good faith. I'd no idea she would get up to her old tricks Oh, hello, Fiona,' she said as the lady appeared. 'I've come to help–'

She was interrupted by Michelle dashing out of the lounge. 'Mummy, Mummy; Matthew's being naughty! The telly's finished, and he's twiddling the knobs, and you said he's not to...'

Fiona laughed. 'It seems you're just in time, Norma. Yes, I could do with a helping hand. If you could entertain these little terrors for a while, and then collect Stella from nursery school? I haven't even washed up the breakfast pots yet, it's been so chaotic; and Simon's been busy with Gilbert and Arthur.'

'Calm down, love,' said Norma. 'Everything's going to be OK,' she told her, just as Simon had done.

'Yes, we've been having a chat about ... things,' said Simon. 'I've been an idiot, I admit, not realizing the way it was going. But it's going to be different from now on with Fiona and me.'

'You've been naive, Simon, that's all,' said Norma, 'and I blame myself for being the cause of it, in a way. Anyhow, I'm here to make amends... Oh, hello there, Mark, and teddy as well.' The little boy had appeared clutching his beloved bear. 'What is he called?'

'Billy,' said Mark, pushing the bear towards Norma, who politely shook his hand. 'How do you do, Billy?'

Mark laughed, and Fiona breathed a sigh of relief. She felt that things were getting better already.

Norma amused the children, then collected Stella from the nursery school before starting back home at half past twelve. She arrived at the house to find that Glenda had returned. She was in the process of loading suitcases and boxes into the back of her red mini car. It had been parked on the driveway for most of the time she had been staying there, as most places she wanted to visit were within easy walking distance.

'I'm leaving,' she announced, looking angrily at her sister. 'I won't stay where I'm not wanted, and I'm not going to be spoken to the way I was by that old witch, Mrs Nosey-parker Bayliss. Of course, I can guess who put her up to it; it was either you or him.' She gestured towards the house with her thumb, and Norma gathered that Gilbert must be already back home.

'You're wrong, Glenda,' said Norma, quite calmly. 'Mrs Bayliss is her own person. She acts according to her convictions. I know she sometimes gets it wrong, but not in this case. We invited you here because we knew that you needed a job, and we thought you would be an ideal help at the rectory. But you have let us down. We are ashamed and embarrassed at your behaviour.'

'So what am I supposed to have done,' demanded Glenda. 'I've tried to be friendly, that's all. Simon didn't seem to mind. We've had many a good laugh together. And that's more than he's been having with that wife of his just lately. I felt sorry for him. He's had a miserable time with her moping around the place. Suffering from depression, indeed! She should be thankful she has four lovely children and such a good husband instead of sitting around feeling sorry for herself.'

'Be careful what you are saying about Fiona,' Norma warned her. 'Everybody in the church loves Fiona, and they won't hear a wrong word about her. She has been ill, and you were supposed to be helping her, not trying to seduce her husband.'

'I've done no such thing!' retorted Glenda, her face turning pink with indignation. 'How dare you? As if I would! If that is what people are suggesting, then they've got nasty minds, that's all I can say.'

'People are concerned,' said Norma, 'and it seems they've had good reason to be. If they had known what Gilbert and I know about you they would have been even more worried. We believed you had learnt your lesson, though.'

'Oh yes; I might have known you would drag all that up again,' said Glenda. 'I'm surprised you haven't broadcast it all over the parish.'

'Well, we haven't,' replied Norma. 'We haven't told anyone. I thought it was all in the past, Glenda.' Despite her anger and disappointment with her, Norma was beginning to feel a little sorry for her sister. They had always been good friends as well as sisters and had hardly ever fallen out, except about the incident with the church

199

organist. She could see that Glenda was really quite close to tears. She knew her well and could see the signs. She went over to her and put a hand on her arm.

'Don't let's fall out, Glenda,' she said. 'I think I can understand how you feel.' Glenda looked at her, and her eyes showed a trace of sorrow as well as defiance. A tear glistened in the corner and she shook her head, trying to brush it away.

'Simon's an attractive man,' Norma continued. 'If you fancied you were a little bit in love with him ... well, from what I've heard, you weren't the first one. You did ... like him a lot, didn't you?'

'Of course I did,' said Glenda. 'I couldn't help myself. I knew it was no use. He didn't look at me in that way, but I suppose I had my fantasies. I'm a bloody fool, aren't I? He would never have strayed from the straight and narrow. I don't suppose I would have done either, for that matter. I'm not quite so lacking in morals.'

'No, of course you're not,' said Norma, putting an arm round her. 'I don't really want you to go, Glenda. It's been good having you here, but I suppose it might be for the best if you leave ... without saying any goodbyes. They might prove rather embarrassing.'

'I've left them in the lurch, haven't I, Fiona and the children?' said Glenda. She looked sorry and a shade guilty. 'I loved those kiddies, really I did. I never took to Fiona ... I was jealous of her, I suppose,' she said, with a touch of real honesty, 'and I do know she's been having a bad time.'

'People will rally round and help,' said Norma.

'I went there this morning when I knew that you hadn't turned up, and I looked after the triplets for a while. I think Simon and Fiona had been having a heart to heart talk, so I'd leave them alone if I were you.'

Glenda nodded. 'I suppose that would be the best thing to do. I would like to have said goodbye to the children. As I said, I'm very fond of them. But I'm under no illusions. They'll forget all about me in a day or two.' She shrugged. 'That's what kiddies do. So long as they're being cared for, that's all they're bothered about. Their needs come first; they're very self-centred at that age. It will be off with the old and on with the new.'

She looked regretful, and Norma felt sorry for her. 'How will you go on when you get back to Sheffield?' she asked. 'Your house is let at the moment, isn't it? You won't be able to move back in, will you?'

'It's a short-term lease,' replied Glenda. 'It has only a few more weeks to run. I've plenty of friends there,' she added, with a show of nonchalance. 'As a matter of fact, I rang a very good friend of mine this morning, and she says I can stay there until my house is vacant again. And I'll be able to find another job. Childminders are much in demand these days with more and more women deciding to go back to work. So you won't need to worry about me...'

'But we are concerned, Gilbert and I,' said Norma. 'We're not as heartless as we may seem. We just didn't want you making too much of a fool of yourself and upsetting people.'

'Yes, they're very protective of their rector ... and his wife, aren't they? Neither of them can do any wrong. I didn't mean any harm, you know.' She sounded a shade bitter but Norma decided to ignore it. She supposed she had reason to be so.

'Stay and have some lunch with us before you dash off,' she suggested. 'It'll be pot luck today, I'm afraid. Scrambled eggs, or something equally quick and simple.'

'OK, thanks,' said Glenda following her into the house.

Norma levelled a warning glance at her husband who, she was pleased to see, was already working in the kitchen. 'Glenda's staying for lunch,' she said, nodding meaningfully. They understood one another very well, and he knew that he mustn't dwell on the emotive matter any longer. All that needed to be said had already been covered.

'I've found some bacon and sausages in the fridge,' said Gilbert, 'so I'm doing a fry-up. So if you two girls set the table and make a cuppa, I'll get on with the cooking. OK?'

'Very much so,' said Norma. 'Thanks, Gilbert.' She was relieved that the parting was going to be an amicable one.

'You and I need to get away for a few days, just the two of us,' Simon said to Fiona that evening. The children were all in bed and they were sitting together on the settee. His arm was around her in the loving and companionable way that she had missed so much of late.

'What about the children?' she asked. 'We've

never left them before, not overnight. It's Mark I'm most worried about. I wouldn't want him to fret.'

'They've all been happy enough today, haven't they?' Simon reminded her. Their friends had rallied round to help Fiona and promised that they would continue to do so until she was able to get some more permanent help. 'They know Norma and Joan very well, and you have a lot of friends amongst the Young Wives group. I'm sure we could arrange for someone to stay here with them for a night or two. I don't mean that we should be away over the weekend. Maybe a few days in the middle of the week?'

'It's winter, though,' said Fiona, although the idea was beginning to sound very tempting. 'Most places will be closed down, and it's bound to be cold.'

Simon laughed. 'So when have we been bothered about the cold? We're used to it, living in Yorkshire. And there will be several hotels still open in Scarborough. How do you fancy that?'

'Scarborough,' she repeated, her eyes lighting up at the thought of the popular seaside resort. It was a place they both loved very much. They had spent their honeymoon there, and they had so many happy memories. 'Yes ... yes, Simon,' she answered. 'That's a wonderful idea! Oh, thank you, darling! You're right. It's just what we both need.'

Fourteen

'Phone call for you, Debbie,' shouted Rhoda Perkins, knocking at the door of the girls' flat one evening in early December.

The telephone was in the house where Rhoda and Alf lived but the lodgers in the house next door were allowed to make personal calls there and receive calls as well. Rhoda didn't seem to mind acting as messenger. The girls had guessed that she liked to know what was going on – in fact she was nosy, but in a nice sort of way – and she often recognized the voice of the person who was on the phone.

'I think it might be that friend of yours, the one that's married to that nice vicar up in the Dales,' she said as Debbie opened the door.

'Oh, thank you, Rhoda,' said Debbie, smiling to herself. She recalled how Rhoda had taken a fancy to Simon when he had brought her to Leeds that first day. He hadn't been wearing his clerical collar then, and Rhoda had been astounded to hear, later, that he was a clergyman. She did not know, however, about Debbie's kinship with Fiona and Simon, as did the girls in the flat. She still thought that they were close family friends, and Debbie had decided that it was better to keep it that way.

She followed Rhoda into the hallway of the house next door and picked up the phone. 'Hello,

Fiona,' she began. 'So how are things with you?'

'Much better,' answered Fiona. 'It's ages since I felt as well as I do now.'

Debbie could tell from the tone of her voice that Fiona was, indeed, much happier. 'You sound fine,' she said. 'Positively bubbling over. I take it that things have improved, with regard to–' She didn't even get out the name Glenda, before Fiona interrupted her.

'Yes ... she's gone! Glenda's gone,' she replied. 'And jolly good riddance to bad rubbish, as we used to say when I was at school. I know that's not the sort of thing that a clergy wife should say but... oh, Debbie! You can't imagine how relieved I am. And Simon and I ... we're alright again. Just as we were before; well ... nearly.'

'That's wonderful,' said Debbie. 'So ... what happened?' She was agog with curiosity.

'It's a long story,' said Fiona. 'I'll tell you more when I see you. But, in a nutshell, certain folk in the church had a word with Glenda and told her they didn't like the way she was behaving with Simon. As a matter of fact, it was my old adversary, Ethel Bayliss.'

Debbie laughed. 'Well, fancy that! Good old Ethel! I bet she didn't half tell her where to get off. And it did the trick, did it?'

'There was a bit more to it than that. Gilbert and Norma spoke to her as well. And then Gilbert and Arthur – that's Ethel's husband – came to talk to Simon. It was quite a carryon, I can tell you! Anyway, the long and the short of it is that Glenda realized she wasn't getting anywhere with Simon, and she decided to leave as discreetly as

205

she could. She didn't say goodbye to anyone; she just went back to Sheffield.'

'So what you were imagining – between Simon and Glenda – it wasn't so, was it? I never really thought it could be.'

'No ... I'd let my imagination run away with me. I told Simon what I'd feared, and he re-assured me that there was never anything like that. I know now that it was silly of me. But he did admit that he enjoyed talking to her at first – and of course I was being a bit of a misery, wasn't I? Not that Simon said so, but I know it's true. Anyway, he realized that she was trying to get too friendly. And Simon being as he is – not wanting to give offence – he didn't know what to do about it. But it's all over now, thank God! Simon and I are going away for a few days next week, just the two of us. We're going to Scarborough.'

'Oh, that's nice! A second honeymoon, eh?' said Debbie, laughing.

'Well, I'm hoping so,' said Fiona coyly. Debbie could imagine her cheeks turning pink. 'We're going to the same hotel – just a small one – on the north bay, where we went the last time; just Monday to Friday, so that Simon doesn't miss any services.'

'What about the children?' asked Debbie. 'Have you found a replacement for Glenda?'

'No, not yet. But my friends at the Young Wives group have been very good. They've been taking turns to come and help. And Joan Tweedale has offered to come and stay at the rectory while we're away. She has the shop to look after, of course, but there's no shortage of volunteers to help out here. The three little ones seem very happy with the arrangement: all these nice ladies making a fuss of them. And Stella is in her element. As you can imagine, organizing the triplets, and showing the ladies where to find everything. She's a little treasure, really she is... I'm very blessed, you know, Debbie,' Fiona added. 'I'm realizing that all over again.'

Debbie could hear the emotion, a sort of sob in her voice. She felt almost moved to tears herself, knowing that things were working out so well for Fiona after all her anxiety and depression.

'So you are feeling better in health as well, are you?' she asked.

'Tons better! I still get tired, of course – the children are hard work – but I'm not depressed or worried now. And there's a lady in the congregation who's granddaughter has done a course in child care, and she's looking for a job. If she's suitable she might be able to start with us after Christmas. Till then we'll manage with all the extra helpers ... anyway, that's quite enough about me. How are things with you, Debbie? You're still enjoying your course and everything? I'm sure you'll be glad to go home for Christmas though, won't you?'

Debbie agreed that she would. It was ages since she had seen her mum and dad. Three months ... maybe not so long really, but sometimes when she thought about her home in Whitesands Bay – remembering it all with a feeling of nostalgia – it seemed much longer. At other times, though, it seemed that the days flew by: she was enjoying college life so much.

Fiona asked if she had seen anything of Graham. She told her that she had gone round to his flat, not long ago, and he had cooked a meal for her. 'And he played his French horn for me,' she told her with a chuckle.

Fiona laughed too. 'Goodness me! Serenading you, was he? Well, that's one way of doing your courting, I suppose!'

Debbie hastened to tell her that they were just good friends, and that she was quite content for it to stay that way.

'Maybe it's good to start off by being friends,' said Fiona, 'rather than falling in love with the wrong person. Graham's a nice lad, steady and reliable... But you're young, Debbie. Better to leave your options open; make sure before you commit yourself.'

'I intend to,' said Debbie. 'I'm enjoying myself, as well as concentrating on my course. We have lots of fun together, the four of us in the flat. It's amazing how well we get along together. We're all different, but we just seem to gel, if you know what I mean.'

'That's good,' said Fiona. 'It takes all sorts to make a world, as they say, and we've all got our good points as well as a few bad ones. I've learnt that myself, living in such a close community. It's great when you can learn to live together peaceably.' She laughed. 'Listen to me, sermonizing! That's what comes of being married to a rector.'

They passed on their respective love and good wishes to Simon and the children, and to Debbie's parents. Debbie promised that she would pay a visit to Aberthwaite after the Christmas break, possibly in January or February if it could be arranged.

Debbie felt happy and relieved at Fiona's news. She had been worried about her and Simon, but now it seemed that all was well again. She thought about Fiona's remark that Graham was steady and reliable. So he was; but that was not what she wanted at the moment. She liked him well enough, but he was not ... exciting.

She had agreed to go out with him again the following week. There was a new film, a remake of *David Copperfield*, showing at a cinema in Leeds, and Graham was eager to see it. Debbie was not really into Dickens in a big way – she would have preferred something more light-hearted – but she had said she would go.

Her flatmates would all be out that same evening. Fran would be going out for an evening meal – again – with Alistair. That friendship seemed to be blossoming, although Fran remained tight-lipped about it. Debbie thought about it now a trifle ruefully; she had thought at one time that Alistair was interested in her, not Francesca. Now, Alistair was an exciting young man! She could still see his appeal, although she guessed he might not be entirely trustworthy. But she had lost her chance there...

Lisa and Neil were still inseparable despite the continuing opposition from her parents. Her mother still wrote to her, although she was not happy about the situation; but Lisa's father was proving intransigent. Neil, most certainly, was steady and reliable. To Debbie's mind he was rather dull and humourless, but he seemed to be just what Lisa wanted and needed. She was able to awaken in him a spark of animation that made such a difference to his personality. They were so obviously in tune with one another. And from the hints that Lisa had dropped to Debbie, blushing and smiling coyly, it was clear that it was by no means solely a platonic friendship. They were both very young, but Debbie had the feeling that they would make a go of it and stay together, come what may. She only hoped that, in the end, they would have the blessing of both of Lisa's parents.

And as for Karen, despite her vow that she was finished with men, there was now a new one on the scene.

Ben Robson, the flatmate of Alistair and Neil, with whom Karen had tried, to her embarrassment, to strike up a friendship, had now left the flat in Blenheim Street. He had gone to lodge with a young man he had met when he was out for the evening with a group of friends. The young man in question, whose name was Lionel, was also at the pub with a group of second-year students from the university. It turned out that one of the uni students was acquainted with one of the men at the agricultural college – they had been in the same year at school – and so the two groups had joined forces and ended up having a good time together.

Ben and Lionel soon discovered that they had a great deal in common... So, after a couple of meetings, Lionel asked Ben if he would like to share his flat. His former flatmate had decided his university course was not to his liking and had gone back home to rethink.

Alistair and Neil did not have to search long for a replacement lodger. There was always someone who wanted a change or wanted to make a break from living with parents. Such a one was Adam Fletcher, a student at Stanborough College who had not mixed a great deal with his peer group as he was still living with his parents. He had soon realized that he was missing out on the social side of things. When the other lads – and girls – were going back to their lodgings to cook a meal and to make plans for the evening, Adam was returning to his parental home in York.

It had seemed a good idea at first; it was far cheaper than living in digs, and there was a bus that ran from near his home to the college and back. Most of the students, though, were living with the new friends they had made. Adam, too, had made friends with a few of the men, in particular with Neil O'Brien. They sat together for lectures and found that they liked one another's company. He envied the freedom that Neil had, sharing a flat and fending for himself. He had a very nice girlfriend, too. (Adam had recently split up with his girlfriend from schooldays.) And so it seemed to be the answer to his problem when Neil told him of the vacancy at the flat and asked if he might be interested. He had agreed at once, and after persuading his parents that it was the best idea, and that he would still come and visit them, he moved in with Neil and Alistair.

Very soon he met the girls from the upstairs

flat; Lisa, Debbie, Fran and Karen. He had met Lisa already and he knew the others by sight, in the way that all the students recognized one another. On knowing more about them he decided that Fran was a trifle snooty; Lisa, he knew, was shy, but apparently not so with Neil; Debbie seemed a nice friendly girl; and Karen, he guessed, was the devil-may-care one. She appealed to him at once, though he wasn't sure why, when they all met together for a welcoming drink in the girls' flat. He thought she was like a little leprechaun, dressed as she was in an emerald green sweater and tight-fitting black trousers. She had a mop of bright ginger hair, a prettily freckled face and dancing green eyes.

This first encounter had soon led to an evening out for all of them at their usual venue, the Red Lion pub. Lisa and Neil, and Fran and Alistair were couples, but they didn't isolate themselves. There were times, though, when Adam found himself between Debbie and Karen. He learnt, as he had guessed on first hearing her speak, that Debbie came from 'way up north', and when he found out that she had a boyfriend – of sorts, as she put it – who lived and worked in Leeds, he didn't feel so bad about trying to get to know Karen a little better. Karen had noticed Adam around the college, sometimes with Neil, but she hadn't spoken to him until he came to join the other lads in the flat. He was a pleasant-looking young man with dark hair that he wore long, but not excessively so, and candid blue eyes that looked straight into your own when he spoke, and lit up with a merry glint when he laughed.

That was the first thing she had noticed about him – his eyes. She was determined, though, not to fall beneath their spell, though she had had an idea, right from the start, that he would like to get to know her better.

But Karen was still holding fast to her vow that she was finished with men; well, for the time being at any rate. Her promise to herself was to last less than a month. Her determination to avoid Adam when they all went for an evening out, and to leave the talking to Debbie, did not work out as planned. Debbie moved away to chat to someone she knew at the other side of the room – Karen felt sure she had done it on purpose – leaving the field wide open for Adam.

'You're a Yorkshire lass, same as me, aren't you?' Adam said to her. 'Well, I'm not a lass, but you know what I mean. Yorkshire born and bred, eh?'

'Aye, thass reight, lad!' she replied, broadening her already distinctive accent. Recently, though, she had been trying to temper the more un-refined sound of her speech. It sounded, even to her own ears, incongruous when compared with Fran's posh tones, or the more homely and gentle accent of Lisa. Not that she was ashamed of her Yorkshire roots, far from it, but there were times when she thought it was expedient to give a good impression of herself. Likewise, she was trying to curb her tendency to swear. She knew that Lisa found it rather disturbing, and she was very fond and protective of little Lisa, as they all were.

She told Adam that she was from the south of

Yorkshire, near Doncaster, and had worked in a garden centre before starting the college course. Adam, like many of the students, had worked in his father's market garden near York, but wanted to gain more experience before rejoining the family firm, or, alternatively, starting out on his own.

By the end of the evening she had decided that, yes, she did like him. When he asked if he could see her later in the week she agreed, not too eagerly, but not unwillingly either. She was playing it down with the other girls, who were smiling knowingly. She didn't like to admit that her pledge to avoid men had been of such short duration. In fact she was hoping, now, that he would ask her out again. And so he did, for the following Saturday; they would choose a film that they would both like to see.

Karen was glad for another reason. The other three girls would be out that night, and she was tired of evenings in on her own with only the telly for company. Fran and Alistair would be going for another sumptuous meal; Lisa and Neil would enjoy their usual bag of chips and one another's company, no matter what they were doing, and Debbie and Graham were off to the cinema to see *David Copperfield.*

On the Thursday, however, Lisa started to suffer with a debilitating cold. Her throat was sore, her nose was running continually, and her eyes were red and streaming. She did not go to college, and when she was no better on the Friday the other girls suggested that they should call a doctor in case it was something more serious. Lisa refused, insisting that it was only a cold, though a particularly virulent one. If she rested and dosed herself with Beecham's powders and hot drinks she would get better.

The girls did not like leaving her on her own in the flat on Saturday night. She was unable to go out with Neil, of course, and she had told him, regretfully, to keep away from her. She did not want him succumbing to the same germ, whatever it was.

She felt miserable and sorry for herself when the others had gone out. She was missing Neil and was tempted to go down and see him – he, too was home alone – but common sense prevailed. It wouldn't be long before she was well again. What was it they said about a cold? Two days coming, two days there, and two days going; well, something like that. She decided to get undressed early and watch the TV.

It was then she decided that she felt a bit hungry. The girls had insisted she should have a little of the scrambled egg on toast at teatime but she had only picked at it. Now she felt that she might enjoy a bowl of soup. Heinz tomato soup was so comforting with its rich red colour and creamy taste. She opened a small can and poured it into a saucepan. The first gas ring she tried wouldn't light, so she tried the second one which lit straight away. She poured the warmed soup into a bowl, then sat on the settee, clad only in her nightdress and dressing gown, to enjoy it. It tasted delicious and soothing to her dry throat.

She turned on the television, but found that she was soon bored with the variety show. She didn't feel in the mood for the noise and laughter and her head was too achy for her to read. She was feeling a little woozy, so she decided that a really early night might be the best plan. She swallowed a Beecham's powder with a drink of water, and after nipping along to the bathroom she climbed thankfully into bed, snuggling beneath the covers. She was not aware of the faint smell of gas.

She fell asleep quickly, but awoke an hour or so later, disturbed by the sound of loud voices in the street below the window. There was something wrong, too. Her head felt worse than before and her throat was tight. She did not know what made her get out of bed, but she did so, putting on her dressing gown and feeling around with her feet for her slippers by the side of the bed.

She sniffed. Even though her nose was blocked and her sense of smell had diminished, she could sense, just faintly, an odd smell. She sniffed again. It was gas! Oh, whatever had happened? They knew that the gas stove was a little temperamental, but they had always managed alright. Only half conscious, she staggered through the living room to the kitchen alcove, managing to switch on the small light in there. Suddenly, though, her legs felt wobbly and her head was spinning. She tried to grab hold of the edge of the sink as her knees buckled and everything went black. She fell to the floor, banging her head on the corner of the fridge as she landed in a lifeless heap.

Neil put down the book he was reading. It was

not holding him, even though it was an adventure story by Wilbur Smith, an author he usually enjoyed. He hadn't felt like watching TV and had thought it might be a pleasant change to read a book without any interruptions. Alistair and Adam were out for the evening with the girls from upstairs, which was where he and Lisa should have been. It had made good sense, though, for them both to stay in tonight, separately. He would have preferred to keep her company in either her flat or his, but Lisa had convinced him it would be foolish. She really had a shocking cold, the poor love. He knew she must be feeling absolutely wretched. It wasn't like her to miss lectures and, as she said, he wouldn't want to catch it when they could avoid that by staying apart. It would only be for a day or two.

But he was missing her so much and was worried about her, too. She looked such a frail little thing, although he knew she had hidden reserves of strength. Look at the way she was facing up to her parents about their opposition to her friendship with him. He glanced at his watch. It was just turned ten o'clock. Although she had told him not to do so, Neil decided he would pay her a visit and see how she was feeling. She may well have gone to bed. If so he would not disturb her. But if she was sitting on her own he could stay with her for a little while, keeping his distance, of course.

He went up the stairs hoping that Lisa had not locked the outer door of the flat. She hadn't; it was closed but not locked. As soon as he entered the room he was aware of the strong smell of gas.

He switched on the light and hurried through to the tiny kitchen. Then he stopped dead in his tracks. Lisa, his lovely Lisa was lying on the floor, clearly unconscious, with her head perilously near to the gas stove. Surely she couldn't have tried...? No, she wouldn't have done that. Lisa hadn't been depressed, just feeling miserable and ill with the cold. The smell was very strong in here and there was an unmistakable hissing sound. He gasped in horror as he realized that one of the gas taps had been turned on and not lit. He quickly turned it off, then knelt down and put his arms around Lisa, trying to rouse her. There was a bruise on her forehead, her eyes were closed and her breathing was very shallow. He left her, just for a moment, while he went to the window. He drew back the curtains, then opened all the windows to let in as much air as possible. Then he hurried back to her, feeling frantically for the pulse in her wrist. He must ring for an ambulance at once, but he didn't want to leave her. He knew he mustn't try to move her, but he grabbed a cushion from the settee and placed it beneath her head.

'I shall have to leave you for a minute, Lisa, love,' he whispered to her, although she couldn't hear him, 'while I ring for an ambulance.'

Just as he was crossing the room he heard the sound of voices on the stairs. The door opened and Debbie and Graham came in.

'Oh ... hello there, Neil,' said Debbie. 'I thought you weren't seeing Lisa tonight...' She stopped at the look of consternation on his face. 'What's the matter? Is she worse?'

218

'She's had an accident,' he shouted back as he rushed towards the stairs. 'Gas ... in the kitchen. Look after her, will you, while I ring for an ambulance?'

'Oh goodness! Poor Lisa!' Debbie crouched on the floor by her friend. 'Lisa ... Lisa, it's me, Debbie. Can you hear me?' But the girl made no response.

She turned frantically to Graham. 'You don't think she's ... gone, do you? We should never have left her on her own.'

Graham knelt down as well. He took hold of Lisa's limp wrist and felt for a pulse. 'She's alright ... just; she's still with us, but it's very faint. Try not to worry too much, Debbie. She'll be in good hands very soon.'

'I wonder what happened? She's usually so very careful.' Debbie looked around the small kitchen. 'It looks as though she had a tin of soup. Oh dear! We should have made her something, but she said she wasn't hungry.'

'I should imagine she left a gas ring on,' said Graham. 'Easily done, I suppose, if you're not feeling well.'

Neil returned at that moment. 'Yes, that is what happened,' he said. 'This one was full on and not lit. It's a good job I came up when I did, although you were not far behind me, were you?'

'The film finished quite early,' said Debbie, 'so we came back instead of going for a drink. Everywhere was crowded... Oh, I feel so helpless. I hope the ambulance won't be long.'

'I'll go downstairs and wait for it,' said Graham. 'If I stand outside they'll know just where to stop.'

'Mr Perkins is already waiting,' said Neil. 'I told him what had happened.'

'I'll go and wait with him,' said Graham. 'One feels so inadequate, but all we can do is wait.'

'I love Lisa very much,' Neil said quietly to Debbie as they knelt together at her side. 'I haven't known her very long, but I know she's the right girl for me.'

'And she feels the same way about you, Neil,' said Debbie.

'I hope things work out alright for you, with her parents.'

'It will... It must,' said Neil.

There was a sound on the stairs, not the ambulance men, though; it was Karen and Adam returning, with Alistair and Fran close on their heels.

'We've just heard,' said Fran. 'Poor Lisa!'

'Oh please, God, let her be alright...' It was Karen, surprisingly, who uttered the unspoken prayer of them all. Then they waited in silence.

It wasn't long, although it seemed much longer to them, before the ambulance arrived. Two men came up the stairs and got on efficiently with their task. They lifted Lisa on to the stretcher, covered her with a blanket and placed an oxygen mask over her face.

'We'll do our best,' one of them said. 'Try not to worry too much. Perhaps one of you would come with her to the hospital? Are any of you relations?'

'No, just good friends,' replied Debbie.

'I'm her boyfriend,' said Neil, a little diffidently. 'I'd like to be with her, if that's alright?' They all agreed that it was the best idea.

'Righty-ho then, young feller,' said the ambulance man. 'You come along with us.'

They all went downstairs and watched as their friend was lifted into the ambulance. It drove off swiftly, with the blaring noise of the siren, to the hospital near the city centre.

The six of them sat looking at one another disconsolately for a few moments, not speaking. Then Karen said, 'I'll go and make some tea, shall I?' The others all nodded assent. She laughed a little shakily. 'It's what we always do in a crisis, isn't it?'

'I suppose it gives us something to do while we're waiting,' said Fran. 'I wonder when we'll know about Lisa? Do you think we should ring up soon and see how she is?'

'I think we ought to let her parents know,' said Debbie. 'I mean – we hope she's going to be alright – but if ... well, if something was to happen to her – God forbid – it would be a dreadful shock for them if they didn't even know she'd gone into hospital.'

'You're right,' said Fran. 'Of course you are. Drink your tea first, Debbie,' she told her, as Karen returned with the teapot and mugs on a tray, 'and then go next door and ring. Unless you'd like me to do it? I don't mind, but you're the one who knows her best, I would say, with sharing a room, and she confides in you, doesn't she?'

Debbie nodded. 'Poor Lisa! She's such a dear little girl, isn't she? Well, she's not a little girl any longer, but I'm sure that's how her parents still think of her. And she does bring out our protective instincts, doesn't she? Oh ... we must find their telephone number – Lisa's mum and dad – mustn't we?'

'It'll be in her address book,' said Karen. 'I know she's got one 'cause she writes a lot of letters to friends. I'll see if I can find it.'

She came back in a few moments with a little red book which she handed to Debbie. 'You look for it; D for Dobson.'

'Yes, I do know that...' Debbie half smiled. 'Here it is; a Sheffield number. Lucky she's put the code as well. I'll go right now.'

Rhoda Perkins waited with her as she dialled the number, and Debbie was glad of that. The woman gave her moral support; it was such a difficult message to give to Lisa's parents. It was Mr Dobson who answered.

'Hello, who is that?' he asked, a trifle gruffly. It was rather late in the evening.

'Hello, Mr Dobson; it's Debbie Hargreaves she replied. 'I'm afraid Lisa has had a slight accident.' She heard his sharp intake of breath.

'What? What is it? Is she alright? Where is she?'

'She had a bad cold, and we think she left a gas tap on by mistake,' Debbie tried to explain. 'She was ... well, she'd fainted, you see, and when we found her we sent for an ambulance straight away. She's in the hospital in Leeds. We thought you ought to know'

'If there someone with her? You didn't let her go on her own, did you?'

'No, of course not. Her friend's with her ... Neil. He wanted to go with her, and the rest of us are waiting in the flat.'

'Oh yes ... I see.' Debbie heard a muffled conversation and realized that his wife had come to the phone. 'It's our Lisa. She's had a little accident, and she's in hospital ... yes, in Leeds. Now try not to upset yerself, love. We'll go and find out what's happening. Yes, we'll go right now... We're coming now,' he said in a louder voice to Debbie. 'We were just going to bed, but we'll set off in the car straight away. Which hospital did you say? Where is it?'

Debbie told him as accurately as she could the way to Leeds City Hospital.

'Thank you, Debbie, for letting us know,' he said as he rang off.

Alistair and Adam had made no move to go back to the downstairs flat, nor Graham to make his way home. When Debbie returned they decided there was nothing they could do and it was pointless to hang about any longer.

'Let's hope there's some good news by morning,' said Debbie as they all said their goodbyes. She reflected that at least it would put an end to the friction between Lisa and her parents.

Once again it was Karen who uttered the thought that was in all their minds. 'God moves in a mysterious way, doesn't He?' she said, as the girls made their way to bed.

Fifteen

Debbie slept fitfully, waking up every hour or so with the happenings of the evening before being played over and over in her mind. The time she had spent with Graham, though, had been overshadowed by the later events.

She had felt quite contented and at ease with him as they had walked back home after the visit to the cinema. She had enjoyed the film despite her misgivings, and as far as Graham was concerned she had decided to let matters take their course. She didn't feel like making any commitments yet with regard to settling down to a steady relationship, either with Graham or with anyone else. She felt, though, that he might be making a tentative move towards a more permanent friendship, inasmuch as he had invited her to visit his home – that was the home of his mother and stepfather – in Manchester during the Christmas period. They had not arranged a definite date, but one suggestion was that she could travel to Manchester for the weekend just before the college term started. It would mean curtailing her stay with her parents whom she had not seen since September, and she was not too happy about that. But she had not liked to turn down Graham's invitation. All thoughts of this and everything else had vanished, however, on finding Lisa unconscious on the kitchen floor.

Debbie was wide awake at half past seven. She knocked on Fran and Karen's bedroom door, and on entering she found that they, too, were awake and talking, of course, about Lisa.

'Do you think it's too early to ring and find out how she is?' said Debbie. 'I won't be able to eat any breakfast or do anything until we know.'

'I'll go and ring now,' said Karen, jumping out of bed. 'I'll just put my dressing gown on seeing as it's only next door. I dare say Rhoda and Alf'll be up. Put the kettle on, you two. I've got a feeling that Lisa's going to be OK.'

'I hope to goodness she's right,' murmured Fran as the two of them waited for Karen to return. It's incredible, isn't it? The four of us have only known one another a short while. I know it seems longer but it's less than three months. And yet we care so much, don't we, about one another? I've had girlfriends before, but it's never been like this. I'd always thought of myself as a rather blasé sort of person. It just goes to show...'

She didn't say exactly what it showed, but Debbie understood her meaning. She felt touched by Fran's words. Francesca gave the impression at times that she was uncaring and somewhat self-centred, but now she was as concerned about Lisa as any of them. 'It's with us living together,' Debbie replied. 'We've become responsible for one another ... and I think it's wonderful.'

She glanced at Fran now as she sat smoking a cigarette in a seemingly nonchalant manner, but things were not always as they appeared to be. Debbie was wearing her old fleecy red dressing gown with the cord tied round the waist, the one she had had since she was fourteen or so. Fran's gown – or housecoat, as she called it – was rather more exotic; midnight blue velvet with a pink rose motif on the collar and pockets, and her feet were shod in wedge-heeled mules adorned with satin bows.

They didn't have to wait long, and when Karen returned they knew at once that the news was good, or at least promising. 'Lisa's OK,' she shouted even before she entered the room. 'They don't give much away, but I was put through to the ward, and the sister – or whoever – said that Miss Dobson was conscious and as well as could be expected.'

'Oh ... thank God for that!' breathed Debbie. 'When can we go and see her? Did you ask?'

'Yes; visiting time is two till four, then again in the evening. Only two at a time, so if we all go we'll have to take it in turns.'

'Of course we'll all go,' said Fran. 'I wonder if Neil's still there? Maybe not, as she's come round. And Lisa's parents...'

Right on cue there was a knock at the door, then Neil popped his head round. 'Oh, sorry,' he said, noting their night time apparel. 'Just wanted to tell you that Lisa's awake. She's a bit woozy, but it seems that she's going to be alright, thank God.'

'It's OK, Neil. Come right in,' said Karen. 'We're all quite decent! I've just rung up and heard the news meself. We're having a cuppa; d'you want one?'

'No thanks; I'm going to get some shut-eye,' said Neil. 'They let me wait in the lounge, and

226

there's a comfy chair so I nodded off once or twice. Not for long, though, as you can imagine. I'm so relieved now...' He shook his head dazedly. 'You can't imagine how much... Lisa's parents arrived in the early hours. So we met, didn't we?' He gave a rueful smile.

'Oh ... I see. So how did it go?' asked Debbie.

'Quite well... Yes, I think it's going to be OK.' His face lit up with a satisfied smile. 'Anyway, I must go. See you later, girls.'

Karen grinned. 'What did I say?' She cast her eyes heavenwards. 'He moves in mysterious ways, doesn't He?' The three girls took a bus to the city and arrived at the hospital soon after two o'clock. On arriving at the ward they were told that Lisa already had a visitor, a young man, whom they guessed would be Neil.

'You go in first, Debbie,' the other two told her, 'and we'll wait.'

'P'raps we shouldn't all have come,' Karen said to the nurse in charge, 'but we've been real worried about our friend.'

'Well ... I dare say we could stretch a point and allow three,' said the nurse. 'But the young man hasn't been here long.'

'It's OK,' said Karen. 'We'll sit and read your magazines, won't we, Fran?' She flopped down in a chair in the waiting area and picked up a three-month-old copy of Vogue.

Lisa was sitting up in bed with Neil close beside her, holding her hand. She looked pale and tired but her eyes shone with pleasure when she saw her friend. Debbie hugged her and kissed her cheek.

'You gave us such a fright,' she said. 'Thank

goodness you're alright.'

'Thanks to you, and to Neil,' said Lisa, smiling lovingly at him. 'I'm a chump, aren't I? I can't remember what happened, only feeling dizzy, then I woke up in here, and I saw Neil standing there.'

'Fran and Karen are outside,' said Debbie. 'We have to take turns to see you. Anyway, here are some treats for you.' They had called in a small shop that opened on Sundays before catching the bus. 'Here's some grapes – that's a must, isn't it, when you're poorly? And your favourite jelly babies, and a Mars bar, and a Crunchie. And this week's *Woman's Own*.'

'Gosh! You're spoiling me,' said Lisa. 'I'm coming home soon, though.'

'We hope so,' said Neil. 'She's staying in another night, aren't you, love? Then if all's well they'll let her come home.'

'Home ... to the flat,' added Lisa. 'My mum and dad want me to go back with them, but I don't really want to do that. I know the three of you will look after me. Anyway, I want to go back to college as soon as I can.'

'You'll need to take it easy for a few days,' said Neil concernedly, taking hold of her hand again. 'You were ... well ... let's say it was a good job we found you when we did.'

They all turned as two more people entered the private room, accompanied by the nurse. 'Here are your mum and dad, Lisa,' she said. 'My goodness, you're popular this afternoon! We're breaking the rules ... so use your discretion, won't you?' She smiled understandingly as she left them.

Debbie noticed that Neil quickly let go of Lisa's

228

hand, getting up to offer his chair to Mrs Dobson. Debbie had met Mr Dobson before, but not his wife. Connie Dobson was an older version of Lisa, small and fair and with a worried expression which, at the moment, was understandable. Debbie guessed, though, that Sam Dobson was the dominant partner and that his wife tried her utmost to please him. Mrs Dobson hugged and kissed her daughter, then sat at her side, looking at her tenderly.

'Mum, this is my friend, Debbie,' said Lisa. 'You've heard me talk about her, haven't you?'

'Indeed I have,' said the lady, smiling at Debbie. 'And we've just met your other two friends outside. They're waiting to see you, so I said that Daddy and I wouldn't stay too long.' Debbie smiled to herself; she was reminded of how her own mother still referred to her father as 'Daddy'.

She shook hands with Mrs Dobson. 'I'm pleased to meet you at last,' she said. 'What I mean is ... I'm not pleased at the circumstances, but Lisa's recovering well, isn't she, thank goodness. Yes, we're very good friends, all four of us in the flat, and I promise you we'll take good care of Lisa when she comes home.'

Neil had stepped back, a little self-consciously, when Lisa's parents entered the room. Mr Dobson went over to him now, grasping his shoulder in a comradely manner. 'And we're so very grateful to this young man for looking after our Lisa. We can't bear to think what might have happened if he hadn't found her when he did. It was touch and go, I believe, touch and go. Thanks a million, young man ... er, Neil.'

'Debbie arrived almost as soon as I did,' said Neil, rather awkwardly, 'and she rang to tell you, didn't she? Anyway, all's well that ends well, as they say.' He grinned, looking a little embarrassed. 'I think I'd better go now,' he said, 'and make room for the others. Shall I come again tonight, or...' He looked at Lisa uncertainly.

'You come by all means, Neil,' said Mrs Dobson, looking at her husband for support, and he nodded. 'Yes, of course.'

'We'll be here as well,' said Mrs Dobson. 'We're staying another night at the hotel, then we'll take Lisa back to the flat – seeing that it's where she wants to be – before we head back home.'

Neil went over to Lisa, touching her hand gently as he said goodbye. Debbie noted that he didn't make any attempt to kiss her, as he assuredly would have done had her parents not been there. Probably a wise decision, she thought, for him not to be too demonstrative at the moment. It was a great step in the right direction, anyway, that Lisa's parents had met Neil; and how could they fail to like him?

'Aye, I must admit, he seems a decent young fellow,' Mr Dobson said, nodding his head thoughtfully when Neil was out of earshot. 'And thank God he came along when he did, and you too, Debbie. We've heard all about it, and we're just so thankful that our Lisa's going to be alright, aren't we, Connie?' His voice was hoarse with emotion and his eyes looked a little moist. Clearly there was a much softer side to him, a contrast to his brusqueness and his determination not to compromise. It seemed that he was already making the first move towards seeing a different point of view, something that Debbie guessed he did not find easy to do.

'Yes, of course we're thankful, Sam,' said his wife, putting an arm around her daughter. 'And we're so pleased that our Lisa's got so many lovely friends. Neil seems a nice young man … a very nice young man indeed,' she added, almost defiantly.

'Yes, well, I reckon we'll have to wait and see how things go on there,' said Sam Dobson with a touch of his former doggedness. 'Our Lisa's very young when all's said and done. She's not had a boyfriend before, and I dare say she'll meet a lot of young chaps before she makes up her mind. Anyroad, it's too soon to be thinking about stuff like that.'

Debbie was aware that he was talking about Lisa as though she wasn't there. The girl just sat there looking mystified.

'Just leave it, Sam, can't you?' said Mrs Dobson, a trifle sharply. Debbie guessed she didn't often stick up to her husband in that way. At the same time she looked across at Debbie, raising her eyebrows in a meaningful way. 'I just happen to think that Neil is a grand lad,' she went on, 'and we want our Lisa to be happy.' She smiled at her daughter, gently stroking her soft blonde hair.

'Yes … well; I was only saying, wasn't I?' Mr Dobson blustered, taking out his handkerchief and making a show of blowing his nose. 'She's leaving hospital tomorrow, and that's the main thing just now.'

'I think I'd better go now,' said Debbie tactfully, 'and let Fran and Karen come in.' She went over to Lisa and kissed her cheek. 'We'll look forward to seeing you home again tomorrow, Lisa. Don't worry, Mrs Dobson. We'll look after her, and it won't be long before we're all going home for Christmas, will it?'

The woman smiled and nodded. 'It's been lovely meeting you, Debbie. And you'll always be welcome at our house, you know, just like all of our Lisa's friends are.' She cast an almost defiant glance in her husband's direction but he wasn't looking at her.

'Bye, Debbie,' said Lisa, holding on to her friend's hand. 'See you soon. And thanks ... for everything.'

'Bye, Debbie love,' said Mr Dobson. 'I know our Lisa'll be alright with you lasses. Take care of yerself now...'

Karen and Fran spent just a few moments with their friend, then the three girls made their way back to the flat leaving Lisa with her parents.

'Gosh! They're a bit much, aren't they, Lisa's mam and dad?' Karen remarked when they arrived back at their lodgings. 'Talk about suffocating the girl! Poor Lisa must feel smothered Thank goodness my parents don't behave like that,' she added. Debbie thought, though, that she sounded just a little regretful that they didn't.

'There's too many of us for my mam and dad to fuss like that,' she went on. 'That's not to say that they don't care about us. I'm sure they do, really, in their own way.'

232

'My parents are not like that either,' said Fran. 'They've always tended to treat my sister and me more like adults, even when we were only quite young. That's why I'm so independent. I've had to stand on my own two feet for ages. Of course, they've always been so wrapped up in one another that Laura and I have made our own way in life. Luckily Ted and Maureen don't try to interfere with our decisions. That's my mum and dad, Ted and Maureen; they've always encouraged us to call them by their Christian names.'

Debbie thought again, but more acutely than ever now, how different the four of them were, and no wonder, considering the disparity in their upbringings. She commented on it to the other two. 'I'm sure all our parents care about us; but they all have different ways of showing it. I experienced some of the over-protectiveness that Lisa does at one time, but I was never as docile as our little friend. I suppose it was only to be expected, with me being adopted. They'd waited a long time before I came along, so I must have seemed like a little miracle to them.' She laughed. 'I was a damn nuisance at times, though.'

'You've not changed much then, have you?' quipped Karen, and they all laughed.

Debbie knew that Karen was joking, as usual. She, Debbie, had changed a good deal – for the better she hoped – and that was because of the tolerance of her parents and the added bonus of finding her birth mother. Something which might have proved disastrous, but had turned out to be a good thing for all concerned.

'Lisa's parents are possessive, certainly,' she

233

said, returning to the subject of their friend. 'With her father it seems that he wants to dominate both of them, to prove that he's the one in charge. He does seem to be giving way a little, though, with this business with Neil. And you can tell that Lisa's mother is only too glad that her daughter's none the worse for her accident. I think Mrs Dobson would agree to anything now that Lisa's all right.'

Lisa left hospital the next afternoon. The three girls went to college as usual, and on arriving home they found that Lisa was there with her parents in attendance.

'We thought we'd wait until you came back,' said Mrs Dobson, 'so that we can hand her over into your safe keeping. The doctor says she must take it easy for another day, then she can go back to college on Wednesday if she feels able.'

'I feel well enough now, Mum,' argued Lisa. 'What will I do all on my own, kicking my heels here?'

'You can enjoy being a lady of leisure,' said Karen. 'Make the most of it, kid. We'll bring you your breakfast in bed, then you can read and watch telly to your heart's content.'

'OK,' said Lisa grinning. 'Mum's bought us some nice pork chops for our tea, and a home-made apple pie and cream from that little bakery we like.'

'A special treat for you all,' beamed Mrs Dobson. 'You've been so good to our Lisa. I think we'd better be going now, Daddy,' she said, turning to her husband. 'Come along, Sam. It's time to say goodbye to these lovely girls...'

The couple shook hands all round, then Lisa went downstairs with them to see them into their car and say goodbye before they set off for home. When she came back some ten minutes later she was smiling a little embarrassedly.

'Honestly! They don't half fuss! I should be used to it by now, but they make me feel so silly in front of my friends. Sorry, you lot. But at least Mum bought us some nice things for our tea.'

'Don't worry about them,' Lisa said Debbie. 'We were saying yesterday – weren't we, girls? – that it shows how much they care about you. And about how all parents are different. I know they can all be an embarrassment to us at times, in one way or another, just as we are to them sometimes. Now, who's going to cook those pork chops? I must say I'm looking forward to them.'

'Then how about you volunteering, Debbie Hargreaves, for a change, eh?' teased Karen.

'Oh, I don't know about that.' Debbie smiled disarmingly. 'You can do it so much better than me. Anyway, aren't we supposed to have a rota? Whose turn is it?'

'I think that's gone by the board with all the excitement,' said Fran. 'Never mind about that. You and I will do the cooking, won't we, Karen. After all, we're the best cooks, aren't we?' She smiled across at Karen and winked. 'And we want to do justice to them. You're let off all the chores today, Lisa; and perhaps you could lay the table, Debbie?'

'Oh, I'll do that,' offered Lisa. 'I must do something. I can't let you all wait on me.'

'And I'll peel some spuds to make chips,' said Debbie. 'I think I can manage that!'

'I persuaded Mum to get some mushrooms as well, to go with the pork,' said Lisa. 'I convinced her that we all like them. We don't have them at home, would you believe? She says they're just fungus.'

'Exactly what my mum used to say,' laughed Debbie, 'until I persuaded her to try them. Parents, honestly!'

'Are we going to grill them or fry them?' asked Karen.

'Oh, we'll grill them,' replied Fran. 'I can see they're the best quality. We can fry the mushrooms, and how about a few onion rings to go with them?'

'A banquet fit for the Queen!' observed Karen when they all sat to dine half an hour or so later. 'I bet she and Philip don't dine any better than this.'

'Hold on a minute,' said Fran. She opened a cupboard door, then, 'Tah-dah!' she cried, waving a bottle in the air. 'This is to celebrate your homecoming, Lisa. I bought it at Tesco on the way home, but I didn't have it on display whilst your parents were here. It's only Liebfrau, but I think you've become rather partial to that since meeting us lot, haven't you, Lisa?'

'I'll say I have,' grinned Lisa, 'but not a word to my dad!'

Fran poured the white wine into their four Woolies' glasses. 'Here's to us, girls,' she said. 'To the four of us and our ongoing friendship. And especially to our Lisa, safe and well again.'

'Cheers...' they all said, clinking their glasses and sipping the wine, before tucking into their sumptuous meal.

Sixteen

It would soon be Christmas and all the girls were looking forward, in varying degrees, to going home for the holiday period. It would be the first time that Debbie had been home since the term started in September. None of them, except Debbie, had made arrangements to see their various boyfriends during the vacation.

Graham had insisted that she should come and stay with his family in Manchester the weekend before the college term began; that would be the second weekend in January. He, of course, would be back at work in Leeds by then, but he had decided to spend that weekend with his family, 'so that they can all meet you and get to know you,' he had said.

The college break was a long one – three weeks in all – so Debbie hoped that her parents would not mind her returning a little earlier. She had not broken the news to them yet, not wanting them to read more into her relationship with Graham than was actually there.

Karen was still seeing Adam, and clearly liked him very much. It seemed that her feelings for Charlie were now a thing of the past. She said she was looking forward to thumbing her nose at him, although it was doubtful that she would do so literally. After all, he was still her boss and employer, and she was expected to return there to work for him when the course came to an end.

Alistair and Fran had no plans, as yet, to meet one another's families. Fran remained guarded about the friendship. Of the four of them, she was the one who gave the least away about her personal affairs.

Debbie guessed that Lisa and Neil would miss one another very much during the three-week break; but at least the ice had been broken now. Lisa had said that she hoped her parents would be willing to talk about him now and accept that he was an important part of their daughter's life. Their feelings for one another had developed very quickly, but it seemed already that they were deep and would prove to be lasting. Lisa had shown Debbie Neil's Christmas present to her. He had insisted that she should open it and start wearing it straight away; it was a silver pendant in the shape of a heart. There was a parcel for her to open on Christmas Day as well.

'I love surprises, don't you?' she said to Debbie, 'although I think I can guess what it is. I know it's a book.' Her eyes lit up with anticipation. 'I'm collecting the leather-bound editions of Jane Austen. I've only got one so far – *Pride and Prejudice* – so I expect it'll be one of the others. I've bought him some onyx cufflinks,' she confided, 'and a book as well. It's an omnibus edition of C.S. Forester; you know, the Hornblower series.'

Debbie and Graham, also, had exchanged gifts at their last meeting before the holiday. She too had opted for books, not wanting to give him anything too personal at this stage. She had found a couple of first editions of the novels of Dorothy L. Sayers, knowing that he was keen on vintage murder mysteries. From the feel of it, his gift to her was two or three tapes. Would they be brass band music? she wondered.

She had been pleased to receive a phone call from Fiona one evening not long before she was due to leave for home. She had been wondering how Fiona and Simon had enjoyed their holiday in Scarborough, and hoped that all was well with them now. She could tell from the elation in Fiona's voice that it had been wonderful and just what they had both needed to put their marriage to rights. Not that it had ever really been in danger. Fiona had admitted that most of the problems had existed only in her own mind. She was thinking straight again now.

'When are you coming to see us again?' she asked. 'Stella keeps asking about you and saying when will we see you. I know you won't want to give up any of the time you'll be spending with your parents. They must be looking forward so much to you going home.'

'Yes, so they are,' said Debbie. 'Actually, though, I've said I'll spend the last weekend of the holiday in Manchester with Graham and his family, but I've not told Mum and Dad yet. Graham was so insistent, and I didn't like to refuse.'

She heard Fiona chuckle. 'Oh, I see. That's a good sign if you're meeting his family.'

'Not for me, it isn't,' Debbie answered a little

curtly. She realized she might have sounded abrupt so she went on to say, 'I do like him, Fiona, but ... well, it's too soon to be making any decisions.'

'Quite right,' agreed Fiona. 'Give my love to Vera and Stanley, won't you? And have a lovely Christmas...'

They decided, provisionally, that Debbie would visit Aberthwaite sometime in February. 'Give my love to Simon and the children,' she said as she rang off. 'And I'm so pleased that all is well with you both again.'

Fiona reflected on Debbie's words when they had said goodbye. Yes, everything was good again, thank the Lord, at least between herself and Simon. Whilst they were in Scarborough they had recaptured all the tender feelings and the deep love for one another that they had known previously.

It had been a cold week but only what they could expect in early December. It was frosty rather than rainy and they wrapped up well against the chilly east wind blowing from the sea. They loved the long walk around the headland, from the north to the south bay: the ruined castle perched on the hilltop, the seagulls wheeling and screeching around the cliffs, and the waves dashing against the sea wall. At night they stood for a while on the spa bridge as they made their way back to the hotel, looking at the vista of the Grand Hotel, the now famous landmark on the promontory; the twinkling lights, like a string of jewels shining out round the harbour and the sweep of the bay; and the vast stretch of the midnight blue ocean.

'Are you happy, darling?' Simon had asked her several times. And she had answered that she was, immeasurably so.

They were pleased to get back home to the children, though, at the end of the five days, no matter how much they had appreciated their time alone together. Joan was there, in charge of the four of them, when they arrived back on the Friday afternoon. There were hugs and kisses all round, all the children shouting excitedly about what they had been doing with the ladies who had looked after them. They had been to the park, and the playground, had some nice things to eat, watched the telly – inevitably, and Stella had spent an afternoon 'helping' at Aunty Joan's shop.

Fiona noticed that Matthew seemed a little subdued, not chattering as much as the others. Mark could not say very much, but he joined in with the laughter and the general excitement and appeared to understand all that was going on. It was unusual, though, for Matthew to be so quiet.

It was Simon who remarked on it. 'Are you OK, Matty?' he asked, using a little pet name as he did sometimes, referring to the boys as Matty and Marky, although Fiona preferred to use their proper names. 'Is that tongue of yours still there? Let me have a look. It's not wagging as much as usual.'

Matthew put out his tongue, grinning a little sheepishly.

'Oh, there it is! I'm glad about that,' said Simon.

'It's a bit bewildering, isn't it? You'll soon get used to Mummy and Daddy being here again.'

Stella pulled at Fiona's skirt. 'Mummy,' she said, whispering confidingly, 'Matthew's been a bit naughty this week.'

'Oh dear!' said Fiona. 'Has he really? That must be why he's quiet. But we won't talk about it any more just now. I expect Aunty Joan will tell me all about it.'

Joan had been shopping to get the necessary items to make a quick sandwich meal and was staying for tea to help Fiona to get back into the routine. When they were preparing the makeshift meal in the kitchen, and Simon was looking after the children, she told Fiona about Matthew's behaviour.

'He's been playing up a little bit in your absence, I'm afraid,' she said. 'He loves to tease Mark and really tries to wind him up about ... oh, you know ... spilling his food, and wearing a nappy, and so on. The poor little lad hasn't got the words to retaliate, and he gets so frustrated and cross. It's ended in a fight – well a scuffle, you know – a couple of times; once when I was in charge, but I managed to separate them. And Hilary has had a bit of trouble with the two of them as well. I don't like telling tales, but I thought you ought to know.'

'Oh, my goodness! I'm so sorry,' said Fiona, 'but you were quite right to tell me. Simon and I could tell there was something wrong by the look on Matthew's face, the little rascal! If we'd known they'd be so much trouble we wouldn't have gone and left them. We'll have to have words with

Matthew; we can't have him behaving like that. And you can't really blame Mark for trying to stick up for himself, though I don't like them fighting.'

'All brothers do,' answered Joan. 'Don't be too cross with him. I had a talk to him, and he did seem a little ashamed of himself. But they're only babies yet, aren't they, all of them? Apart from Stella, of course. She's been a grand little help. You've got a little treasure there, Fiona.'

'Yes, I know,' smiled Fiona. 'The triplets have to learn how to behave, though, young as they are. We worry quite a lot about Mark being rather slow, at least I do. Simon seems to be more complacent about it.'

She and Simon discussed the problem later that evening when the children had gone to bed.

'I really am concerned about Mark,' said Fiona. 'He doesn't appear to be making much progress at all. Do you think he's going to be backward, Simon? Really backward, I mean? Unable to learn like other children? Sometimes they have to go to a special school.'

'No; I don't really think so,' replied Simon. 'He's just slower than the other two. But they're only two years old when all's said and done. And as long as Stella is there to speak for Mark, and Michelle tries as well, in her own way, maybe he thinks he doesn't need to talk. Some children can be rather lazy. I don't really know though, do I, darling? I can't see into his little mind. Nor Matthew's ... but we must try to stop him from teasing his brother. He does have rather a cruel streak – well, naughty and wilful really, rather

243

than downright cruel – and we must teach him that it's wrong to upset his brother. But … just supposing that Mark did turn out to be slow to learn, would we love him any the less? Of course we wouldn't!'

'No, of course not,' echoed Fiona. 'I realize all that, Simon. I just want the very best for all of them.'

'They call it "learning difficulties" now, I believe,' said Simon. 'Children are not talked about as being backward. They have special classes, and all sorts of ways of helping them. Anyway, we'll cross that bridge when we come to it, shall we? The next thing we must do is to make arrangements for the young lady who's coming to help out in January. Until then you've got a team of willing helpers, haven't you?'

'Yes, indeed I have. But I'm feeling so much better and stronger since our holiday, Simon. It's done me a world of good, and I'm much more able to cope with things now.'

'That's good to hear, darling. And with Christmas approaching we'll both need to be on top of things, won't we? Only three weeks to go...'

Seventeen

Debbie was happy to be going home. She hadn't realized just how happy she was until the train was approaching Whitesands Bay on the last lap of the journey from Leeds. She had smiled contentedly as she watched the landscape unfolding, the green hills and dales of North Yorkshire changing gradually to the chimneys and slag heaps, the dockyards and tenement buildings of the industrial north-east. It was when she caught her first glimpse of the sea that she felt the tears welling up in her eyes. Yes, it was good to be home. But she hastily brushed any trace of tears away, even though they were tears of joy. She knew that any sign of emotion would set her mother off, and she wanted it to be a joyful reunion.

Both her parents were there to meet her, waving from the barrier as she made her way along the platform with her large suitcase and a couple of bulging carrier bags. They looked just the same, which was hardly surprising as it was only three months since she had seen them, although in some ways it seemed much longer. Mum was wearing her best coat, the tweed one with the fur collar; Debbie remembered her buying it from C&A on a shopping trip to Newcastle, more than two years ago. Dad was dressed in his 'Sunday best' – he must have taken an hour or two off work – namely his overcoat and the trilby hat he wore when he was going anywhere special.

Mum opened her arms wide as she rushed towards Debbie. They hugged and kissed and there was no sign of tears on her beaming face.

'Eeh, it's been a long time, pet,' she said in the familiar Geordie accent that Debbie realized she had missed hearing so much.

'Aye, it's real champion to see you again, lass,' said her father, kissing her cheek and giving her a less demonstrative hug. As she looked at him more closely Debbie thought he looked a little older, his face rather drawn with dark shadows under his eyes. She didn't say so, of course. She just said how lovely it was to be home again, for almost three weeks.

'Come on then, pet,' said Stanley, picking up her suitcase and marching off towards the station exit. He was managing the heavy case quite easily; he had a wiry strength that belied his somewhat small stature. 'We're going home in style, aren't we, Vera? There's a taxi waiting outside.'

They all piled into the black cab. Debbie looked out at the familiar streets as though she was seeing them for the first time. They were familiar, but appeared smaller, somehow, than she had remembered them. It was already dusk at four o' clock in the afternoon, and the shops were ablaze with lights illuminating their Christmassy windows, several of them displaying Santas and reindeer and snowy scenes. In the small town square a Christmas tree – a real one, but not overlarge – shone out bravely, its twinkling lights changing from blue to red to yellow.

'That's new this year,' said Vera, with a touch of pride. 'It's a canny sight, isn't it, pet?'

Debbie agreed that it was. The one outside the Leeds town hall was massive by comparison, but this one thrilled her far more. Eeh! It was grand to be home!

The house felt warm and welcoming as they entered, and there was a lovely smell of cooking. 'I've left a casserole in the oven on a low light,' said Vera. 'I guessed you'd be hungry, pet.'

'So I am,' said Debbie. 'It smells delicious.'

She was glad her parents had had central heating installed; she would have missed it after being so warm in the 'digs' and in the college rooms. Her parents had taken the plunge just before she had started her college course. It was still something of a luxury to ordinary folk, especially to those like Vera and Stanley who were usually cautious about spending their 'brass'. It was Debbie who had persuaded them that they would never regret it. Nor had they, although Vera had lit a small coal fire in the living room as she often did, to make it look more cheerful.

Debbie unpacked, then went to chat to her mother in the kitchen whilst she prepared their tea. 'I made the casserole and got it in the oven earlier,' said Vera. 'It's braised lamb chops, with the potatoes browned on the top, the way you like them. It'll be ready soon, then there's a custard tart to follow.'

'Lovely!' said Debbie. 'It seems ages since I had a proper home-cooked meal.' She remembered, fleetingly, the chicken dinner that Graham had prepared for her, but decided not to mention it. 'None of us are great shakes at cooking. I would say that Karen's probably the best.'

'Karen; that's the lass from Doncaster, isn't it?' said her mother. 'The one from a large family?'

'Yes, that's right.'

'You're lucky that you've made such nice friends, aren't you, pet? It's grand that you all get on so well... That reminds me; I saw Kevin the other day. I just happened to bump into him in town; he was doing a bit of Christmas shopping, he said. Anyway, he asked about you, and of course I said you were coming home on Friday, today, I mean. He said he'd phone you. It'll be nice for you to see him again, won't it?'

'Yes...' said Debbie. 'Yes, it will.' Actually she was feeling a little guilty. She had hardly given Kevin a thought recently. She had said she would write to him, and she had done so, a time or two, and he had replied, although he wasn't the best letter writer in the world. The correspondence had lapsed, then she had been seeing Graham, and Kevin had taken rather a back seat in her mind. Now, though, she realized it would be good to see him again.

'I always liked Kevin,' said her mother. 'I thought you were too young at the time, mind, to have a steady boyfriend. You're old enough now, but I know you're concentrating on your studies at the moment, aren't you, pet?'

'Yes, that's right, Mum,' she replied.

It would have been a good opportunity then to tell her mother about going back a little earlier to visit Graham's home, but she did not do so. To get away from talking about boyfriends she offered to set the table.

The braised lamb with the browned potatoes, carrots and onions tasted just as good as it smelled, and the custard tart, too, was enjoyed by them all, although her mother apologized because it was not home-made. They had their usual cup of tea to end the meal.

'We've a little job to do tonight,' said Vera as she and Debbie cleared the table. 'I said to Daddy that we'd wait until you came home because I know it's something you enjoy doing.' She beamed at Debbie. 'We're going to decorate the tree!' she said excitedly. 'Daddy got it down from the loft, and all the trimmings and the lights – I hope they still work.'

'Oh yes, I'll enjoy that,' said Debbie. It was the seasonal ritual, but when she had been going through her awkward phase, a couple of years ago, she had affected to show contempt for it. Now, though, she felt quite nostalgic, and the thought of it did bring back happy childhood memories.

They washed the pots, Debbie helping more willingly than she had used to do, whilst Stanley read the paper and smoked his pipe.

'Now, Daddy ... er, Stanley,' said Vera, when they had finished, 'are you going to fetch the tree?'

It was the one they had had since Debbie was a little girl; not a bad tree compared with some artificial ones, although it had lost some of its needles now and a couple of the branches were rather wonky. It would stand on a table in the window of the front room, as Vera called it: the lounge that was only used on 'high days and holidays'. It was used more now, though, than it had used to be. Debbie remembered its cold clamminess and the musty smell from disuse, but the central heating, thankfully, had put an end to that.

Stanley fixed the lights – fortunately they were all still working – then Debbie and Vera started to take the decorations out of their cardboard box. They were fragile baubles of shiny coloured glass, and every year they found that another one

249

or two had shattered. There was still a goodly number left, though, with some silver and gold tinsel and the fairy for the top. One of her wings and her wand were bent, but they didn't look too bad when they were straightened. She had lost a little of her blonde hair and her white dress was a shade off-white. But they wouldn't dream of replacing her.

'There!' said Vera with satisfaction when Debbie placed the fairy on the topmost branch. 'Doesn't it look grand? Switch on the lights, Stanley. We'll draw the curtains back then we can see what it looks like from outside.'

They all trooped out to view their handiwork from the garden path, and pronounced it a job well done.

Christmas Day fell on a Friday that year. On the previous Monday Debbie had a phone call from Kevin.

'Hi there, Debbie,' he began. 'How are things with you?'

'Fine, thanks, Kevin. It's good to be home.'

'Yes; your mum said you'd be home for three weeks. I thought we could meet up again. What do you think about it?'

'I'd like that very much,' she replied. 'It'd be great to see you again.' How nice it was to hear his voice again, the familiar sound of the north-east – though his accent was nowhere near as broad as that of his father, nor of her own dad – and his husky way of speaking.

He suggested that he could call for her the following evening. 'What time?' she asked, wondering what he had in mind; a meal out, or the pictures, or maybe just a drink and a chat.

'Oh, about half past seven,' he replied. 'After tea.' So that settled that problem. 'We could drive out into the country and have a quiet drink. I've got my own car now, you know.'

'Yes, you told me in one of your letters.'

'So I did. Sorry I've been so lax about writing.'

'It doesn't matter... I'll look forward to seeing you, Kevin.'

It was good to see him on the doorstep on Tuesday evening, his strong-featured face beaming with pleasure at seeing her again. His wide grin revealed rather uneven teeth with a small gap between the front ones. Not that it spoiled Kevin's rugged good looks; it was, on the contrary, a very attractive feature. His dark blond hair, usually tousled, appeared a little more under control. He was wearing a country-style tweed jacket and a bright blue shirt that enhanced the colour of his eyes. Debbie felt her heart skip a beat as she greeted him; she hadn't realized just how much she had missed him.

'Hello, Debbie.' He leaned forward to kiss her cheek. 'You haven't changed, but then why should you?' He laughed, then he greeted Vera who was not far behind her daughter. 'Hello, Mrs Hargreaves. Nice to see you again, too. You're looking well,' he remarked as he kissed her cheek.

'Yes, I'm not so bad, Kevin. All the better for having our Debbie home, of course.'

'I'm sure you are,' he answered. 'Don't worry; I'll take good care of her. We'll just have a run out

251

into the country; we won't be late back.'

'Oh, she's a big girl now,' said Vera, 'and I can't be worrying all the time about what she's doing while she's away, can I? I know she'll be safe with you.'

'I'm ready, Kevin,' said Debbie, a little impatiently. 'Let's go, shall we?'

'Certainly; your carriage awaits, ma'am. Bye, Mrs Hargreaves...'

Kevin's new car – well, a new one to him but actually four years old – was a shiny green Morris Minor.

'Very posh,' said Debbie approvingly as he started it up and zoomed off down the road. 'You're pleased with it, are you?'

'For the moment,' he replied, 'until I can afford something else. At least I'm independent now; I don't need to borrow my father's car.'

'Actually, my dad's thinking of buying a car,' said Debbie. 'I was quite surprised when he said so. He's so cautious about spending money as a rule, and he's always said he didn't need one.'

'So ... why has he changed his mind?'

'Well, I think he's feeling tired, though he doesn't always admit it. Mum says it takes it out of him cycling to work and back, then the manual work he does all day. I thought he looked tired when I saw him again; older and slower, too, but I didn't say so.'

'So he would have to learn to drive?'

'Oh, he can drive already. He learned when we moved here to Whitesands, when I was a little girl. He drives the work's van sometimes, but another chap is in charge of it. Anyway, we'll see.'

'How is college?' asked Kevin. 'Your mam said she doesn't know what you get up to while you're away. So ... have you anything to tell me, Debbie?'

What was he asking? she wondered. If she had met someone else? She and Kevin had had no sort of understanding when she went away to college. They had fallen out at one stage, and had stopped seeing one another. Then their friendship had resumed, but with no promise that it might lead to anything else.

'I can tell you that I'm working hard and enjoying the course,' she said, in answer to his question. 'I've made some good friends. The four of us in the flat are all very different, but we get on really well. And in the downstairs flat there are three lads; well, not really lads – young men who are at the college. As it happens they have all paired off with my three friends.'

'Oh dear!' said Kevin, with a wry smile. 'So where does that leave you?'

'I'm not complaining. I go out quite a lot and enjoy myself. All work and no play, you know...' She decided she had better be straight with him. 'I've seen Graham a time or two. He's a junior architect now, working in Leeds.'

'Graham? Who's he?'

'It's rather complicated; I'm sure I've mentioned him before, though. You know my birth mother, Fiona? Well, her husband, Simon – the rector – he has a son called Greg, and Graham is his brother; well, half-brother. So when he found out I was at college and lodging in Leeds he looked me up. I've had a meal at his flat, and he

253

played his French horn for me! It was a laugh, Kevin, honestly! And we've been out together a couple of times. That's all.' She decided not to tell him about the plan to see Graham at the end of the holiday.

'I see...' He nodded, not looking away from the steering wheel.

'What about you? Don't tell me you've been staying in, night after night?'

'No ... I haven't.' He turned to grin at her. 'But I'm with you now, Debbie, and that suits me just fine.'

They had been driving through a maze of country lanes. Northumberland had its share of rural landscape, green and pleasant, with quaint villages and isolated farms, when you got away from the collieries and mills. There was the beginning of a change now, though, in the north-east. The old industrial scars were disappearing with the challenge of modern industry. There were new housing estates and bright modern factories where once there had been soot and grime.

Kevin pulled off the road when they came to a pub called the Fox and Grapes. He drove round to the back of the squat greystone building to the car park. 'It should be fairly quiet in here,' he said. 'It's well off the beaten track, and there's a nice atmosphere to the place.'

It was an olde worlde pub which didn't need any gimmicks to make it seem so as it was genuinely old; pre-Victorian, Debbie guessed. She hadn't been there before, nor did she remember ever seeing it from the road. Part of the floor was stone-flagged, but there was a bright patterned carpet in the lounge bar and a log fire at one end in an inglenook fireplace. A decorated Christmas tree stood at the other side of the bar, the scent of the pine needles adding to the welcoming atmosphere. Toby jugs, copper lustre jugs and pewter tankards stood on the delft rack, and pictures of hunting scenes, and portraits of Victorian bewhiskered gentlemen and apple-cheeked old ladies adorned the walls.

They found seats at a small round table in a corner. Debbie took off her cherry red coat as the room was comfortably warm. She had dressed with care, but in her usual casual style: black and white miniskirt with a polo-necked white sweater and shiny black boots with silver heels.

'What are you drinking?' asked Kevin. She could see him looking at her admiringly but he made no comment.

'I'd like a sweet Martini with lemonade, please, Kevin,' she replied.

'And I'll have a pint of bitter,' he said. 'I'll always allow myself one and no more when I'm driving.'

'Very sensible,' said Debbie.

'Anything to eat? They do very nice ham sandwiches.'

'Oh no, thanks. I've just had my tea. Mum's insisting on feeding me up now I'm home.'

'Packet of crisps, then?'

'Oh, go on ... cheese and onion, please.'

He came back with the drinks and two packets of crisps. 'It's great seeing you again, Debbie,' he said, as he sat beside her on the red plush bench. 'I've missed you, you know.'

'That's good to hear.' She smiled at him. 'Not too much though, I hope? I'm sure you've not been sitting at home all the time, watching the telly?' She was feeling rather guilty. She had missed Kevin, whenever she had thought of him, but it certainly hadn't been every day.

'Not all the time, no.' He grinned at her. 'As a matter of fact, I've been going to night school classes. I know now that I should have worked harder at school and got more O levels than I did; but I was eager to leave and go into the business with Dad. I decided I could be a great deal more help to him than I am, so I'm taking a class in bookkeeping and finance, and another in horticulture. I thought I knew it all, but it seems that I don't! I can't have you showing me up with all your knowledge.'

'Good for you, Kevin,' she said, rather surprised at what he had told her.

He had always been a happy-go-lucky sort of lad, taking life easily, just as it came. He had not seemed concerned about his lack of book learning, although he had sometimes made remarks, jokingly, about her being brainier than he was. And had she, maybe, been a teeny bit proud of her scholastic achievements? she pondered now, to her shame. Had she, deep down, thought she was rather too good for him even though she had fancied herself in love with him?

Kevin was certainly much more mature now and had developed a more serious and responsible manner. She felt her previous attraction towards him coming back more strongly than before. When she was fifteen she had been flat-

256

tered because a lad two years older than herself had taken notice of her. He had been her first boyfriend and she had imagined he was the love of her life. It had been Kevin who had ended their friendship. She knew now that it was because she had been silly and irresponsible, a bit of a pain, to be honest!

'Your father must be pleased about your studies,' she said. 'Have you taken over the office work now?'

'I will, quite soon,' he replied. 'Mum and Dad have been doing it between them, but it's too much for them really. Dad has enough to do running the practical side of the business, and Mum likes to concentrate on her flower arranging. She's been especially busy this Christmas... My parents would like to see you again, Debbie. Mum said would you like to come for tea, one day after Christmas? My sister and her husband and children are coming for Christmas, but they'll be going back after the weekend.'

'Yes, that would be very nice,' she answered. 'I'd love to see them again.'

They decided on the following Tuesday, which was exactly a week away. They chatted easily together for the rest of the evening. The time flew by as they talked reminiscently about friends they remembered and their days at Kelder Bank School – although they had not known one another then – and about Kevin's plans for the garden centre and Debbie's college course.

Debbie had another drink, a lemonade shandy, while Kevin had lemonade on its own because he was driving. 'I must take special care of you, now

I've met up with you again,' he told her.

She felt very contented and at ease with him as they drove home. When he stopped the car outside her house he put his arms around her and kissed her, gently at first, then again, more ardently as he felt her responding to him. He let go of her reluctantly.

'Goodnight, Debbie,' he said. 'It's been a lovely evening. I'll look forward to seeing you next week. I'll come and pick you up, but I'll ring you before then. Have a happy Christmas with your parents ... and open this on Christmas morning.' He reached under the dashboard and gave her a small parcel wrapped in silver paper.

'Oh ... thank you,' she said, rather taken aback. 'I'm afraid I haven't–'

He grinned. 'You didn't get anything for me? No, why should you? Our friendship had lapsed somewhat, hadn't it? But who knows what next year will bring?'

He went round to open the passenger door for her. 'Bye, Debbie,' he said fondly as he kissed her cheek.

She was pleased that her parents had gone to bed, partly because they no longer insisted on waiting up for her, and partly because she was filled with a quiet happiness that she didn't want to share with anyone just at that moment.

It was a very happy Christmas for Debbie, Vera and Stanley; just the three of them on their own for a good deal of the time, but Debbie didn't mind that.

She was delighted when she opened her present

from Kevin. It was a pair of dainty earrings in a silver filigree design. She had had her ears pierced when she was sixteen, which had caused a heated argument with her mother at the time. But now that was a thing of the past, and Vera said how pretty they were.

'Oh ... so you and Kevin are seeing one another again, are you?' she asked.

'Well, yes; I'm seeing him, Mum, obviously,' she said with a smile, 'I'll be seeing him on Tuesday when I go for tea, but as for "seeing him" in the sense that you mean ... let's just wait and see, shall we?'

It was good to see Mr and Mrs Hill again; Debbie had enjoyed working for them, and it had given her the incentive to pursue a career in horticulture, particularly in planning and design. She had worked with Mrs Hill on the floral arrangements she had sold in the shop, and this had furthered her interest in garden design. This would be on a much larger scale, of course, but she was finding as she pursued her college course that she had an eye for what looked right and would work in a particular setting.

'I reckon you'll go a long way with yer gardening career,' Mr Hill told her. 'You were right to go and learn more about it. An' I'm pleased our Kevin has decided to do a bit more studying an' all. I've learnt it all as I've gone along, but I can see there's a lot more to it these days. I often get asked about ideas for gardening – designs an' layouts an' all that sort o' thing. We've got some Californian bricks in stock now – they seem to be all the rage at the moment – and urns and trellis and garden ornaments. None of yer hideous gnomes, though! There seem to be a lot of "do it yerself" enthusiasts around. We're thinking we might expand and do a bit more in that line. Anyroad, that's something to be thinking about for the future...'

She saw Kevin a few more times during the holiday. He visited their house for Sunday tea, as Vera thought she ought to return the hospitality. He chatted easily with her parents, as he had always done.

They went to the pictures twice, to see reruns of *Midnight Cowboy* and the musical, *Oliver*; it would be a while before the more up-to-the-minute films would be shown in Whitesands Bay.

The night before she was due to go back they walked along the promenade, hand in hand, stopping now and again to look over the railings at the dark grey sea. Kevin kissed her tenderly and lingeringly, as he had done many times that week.

'I shall miss you,' he whispered, 'much more this time. I know you can't make any promises about ... well, about the future. But you'll write to me, won't you?'

'Yes, I will,' she promised, 'more regularly than I did before.'

'And ring me if you can. If you give me the number of that phone next door, I'll ring you. When will you be home again?'

'I'm not sure. It's a long way to come for the half-term break, but I'll see. Otherwise it will be Easter.'

'That's more than three months,' he said, a little gloomily.

'Never mind. It'll soon pass,' said Debbie, trying to sound light-hearted. 'I'll be busy, and so will you. Come on; I'd better get home now. I'm off tomorrow, so I don't want to be late.'

They didn't linger long over their goodbyes at Debbie's gate. They had said all that there was to say, and they were both feeling a little down in the dumps.

'It's been lovely seeing you again, Debbie,' Kevin said, as he had said so many times. 'Like you say, it might not seem so long if we are both busy. Write to me ... and enjoy your weekend.' One last kiss and then he was gone.

Debbie felt dreadful because she had had to lie to Kevin about the weekend. She had told him that she was going to stay with Fiona and her family before she returned to college. How could she possibly tell him the truth, that she would be spending the weekend with another young man and his family, after the happy times she and Kevin had shared over the past few weeks? On the other hand, how could she contact Graham and tell him that she had changed her mind and would not be coming? That would be very impolite when his mother had, no doubt, made all the arrangements. She would have to go along with it, but make it clear to Graham that she was there just as a friend. Not that he had made any definite moves towards her being anything else, and that was fine with her. And as far as Kevin was concerned... As he had said, who could tell what the next year might bring?

261

They were already into 1971. Debbie had spent New Year's Eve with her parents, which she felt was only right. They had gone to the Midnight Service at the church they attended; then they had had a glass of sherry at home to welcome in the New Year.

Vera had not been upset or annoyed that Debbie was going back early to spend the weekend with Graham: rather surprised, that was all. She had looked a little mystified.

'But you've been seeing Kevin all this holiday, haven't you, pet? Does he know about Graham?'

'No, not really... Well, not that I'm going to stay there,' Debbie prevaricated. 'Look, Mum; they're just friends, both of them. Like you're always telling me, I'm still young, aren't I?'

'Very well, pet, if you say so,' her mother answered with a knowing smile. 'Just make up your mind, though, before it gets too complicated. That would be best...'

Eighteen

Graham was waiting for her at the station barrier when she arrived in Manchester on Saturday afternoon. She could see him looking anxiously at the crowd streaming along the platform as she hurried towards him with her heavy suitcase. He smiled and waved when he caught sight of her; he looked genuinely pleased to see her. Debbie smiled back, determined to enjoy the two days as much as she could and put thoughts of Kevin to one side. Not entirely, though; she had rediscovered the special place that had been there for him in her heart and mind, but it was better not to think of that too much now.

Graham hugged her and kissed her cheek. 'You're looking well. Had a good Christmas?'

'Yes, very nice,' she answered. 'It was good to see Mum and Dad again. How about you?'

'Yes, we've had a good time together, all the family, and Greg's fiancée, Marcia, was with us as well. They're getting married in the spring.'

'Oh, that's nice. Will they be here this weekend?'

'No, they're both back at work, and so am I, of course. I've come this weekend so that you could meet everyone. My sister, Wendy, is there as well; she wanted to meet you. Anyway, let's get going.' He picked up her suitcase. 'I've borrowed Charles's car; it's in the car park.'

It was a fairly new blue Triumph car that Graham handled very well. He told her he was hoping to have a car of his own very soon, although it was not really necessary in Leeds where the transport was good, but the parking facilities were not.

'What have you been doing these last few weeks?' he asked her as they drove along.

She told him she had spent a good deal of time with her parents, which was true; and that she had had a girls' night out with her former best friend, Shirley, who was home from training college, and two other girls they had known in the sixth form.

'And I went for tea with my former boss and his family,' she said. 'You know, Mr and Mrs Hill at the garden centre, Sunnyhill, where I used to work.' True again, but with a slight omission; she did not mention their son.

They pulled up outside a semi-detached house in a wide tree-lined avenue in Didsbury. Debbie had heard that this was one of the more affluent suburbs of Manchester. although it was a semi the house had an imposing frontage, with a gabled roof, large bay windows, a well tended lawn with a hedge of copper beech, and a wide path leading to a double garage.

Debbie knew at once that it was Yvonne who opened the door to greet them. She was very much as Debbie had imagined her: pretty and plumpish with dark curly hair and smiling blue eyes. She was older than Fiona, roughly the same age as Simon, in her early fifties.

'How do you do?' she said, shaking Debbie's hand. She kissed her cheek. 'I'm so pleased to meet you at last.'

'Yes, so am I,' agreed Debbie. 'Thank you for inviting me.'

'It's a pleasure,' said Yvonne. 'We've heard a lot about you, haven't we, Charles?' the remark was addressed to the man who had joined them in the hallway. 'This is my husband, Charles.'

He was a tall distinguished-looking man with a moustache and greying hair, a good few years older than Yvonne, Debbie guessed. He was Yvonne's second husband, not the father of Wendy and Graham. They had married only a couple of years ago.

He smiled pleasantly as he shook her hand. 'Delighted to meet you, my dear.'

Yvonne led the way into the spacious lounge, an elegant room with a baby grand piano standing near the bay window. Debbie's eyes flew to it at once. A young woman got up from the settee.

'So you're Debbie,' she said cheerfully. 'Pleased to meet you. I'm Wendy.'

Graham's sister was a younger version of her mother, dark and pretty, though not as plump. 'Pleased to meet you, too,' replied Debbie.

'Sit down and make yourself at home,' said Yvonne. 'Graham, would you take Debbie's case and coat up to her room, please?'

Debbie sat down on the easy chair opposite Wendy. 'Do you come home most weekends?' she asked.

'No, it's rather too far, although I've got a car now, a mini. Much to my brother's annoyance!' Wendy laughed. 'I've got one before he has. The school I teach at is a few miles from where I'm lodging. It's a village school; I did a teaching practice there, then I was fortunate enough to get a post there. I've got digs in Bingley; that's where I went to college.'

'Do you like teaching?' asked Debbie.

'Yes ... most of the time! The village children are pretty well behaved. I've got the infant class, but there are only two classes; the headmistress has the Juniors. We're wondering how long the school will stay open, with the falling numbers. Anyway, we'll see.'

'My mother wanted me to be a teacher,' Debbie told her, 'but I knew it was not for me.' She glanced at the piano. 'Do you play?' she asked.

'After a fashion,' said Wendy. 'I had lessons but I'm not very good. I have to play nursery rhymes and hymns at school, though. I can just about manage that!' She grinned. 'The piano really belongs to Charles; he's a good pianist and he plays quite a lot, and Graham plays the French horn, of course. Have you heard him?'

'Yes, I have,' said Debbie, trying not to smile. 'He's good, isn't he?'

'Not so bad, I suppose. He and Charles play duets sometimes, so we all have to suffer!' She grimaced. 'No, I don't really mean that,' she added with a laugh. 'But Graham's getting quite carried away with this new band he's in, and everything.'

Charles and Graham joined them at that moment, then Yvonne appeared with a tray holding glasses and a bottle of sherry. 'Let's have a drink before dinner,' she said. 'It's almost ready.'

Charles poured out the pale cream sherry and handed it round. 'To our new friend,' he said as they lifted their glasses. 'You are most welcome, Debbie.'

She noticed that Yvonne called the early evening meal 'dinner' and not 'tea'. It was a delicious, well-cooked meal: leg of lamb with mint sauce and a selection of vegetables; and an Eve's pudding to follow. They drank Chardonnay from crystal glasses.

Conversation flowed easily enough, about work and college and teaching. Yvonne said that she was retiring soon from her office job. Charles was the managing director now of the insurance firm – that was where they had met – but they had decided it was time now for her to stay at home.

'I shall be a lady of leisure,' she smiled, 'but I've got our newest family member to look after, haven't I?' A chocolate Labrador puppy lay asleep in a basket near the fireplace. Debbie had met him earlier and he had pawed her excitedly and tried to lick her. 'I think Ollie might be quite a handful in a while,' Yvonne went on, 'and it's not fair to leave him on his own all day.'

'What are you youngsters doing tonight?' asked Charles. 'Have you any plans?'

'I think we'll just go for a drink,' said Graham. 'We can't talk if we go to the pictures. Is that OK with you girls?'

They both agreed that it was. Debbie was rather surprised that Wendy would be accompanying her and Graham; on the other hand she was quite pleased about it. Graham had made it clear, more than once, that he didn't want to rush things. It seemed as though he was still of the same mind. She wondered, then, why he had been so keen for her to meet his family, unless it was that they had been curious about the girl that Fiona had given birth to before she knew Simon?

'I'll drive us somewhere tonight,' offered Wendy. 'Maybe we could try The Blue Boar. What do you think, Graham?'

'Good idea,' he said. 'I know you're showing off, though, because you're the one with the set of wheels! Never mind; my turn will come.' They piled into Wendy's little blue mini car, Graham sitting at the back where he had more room to stretch his long legs. The Blue Boar was a cosy little pub a few miles away, not exactly in the country but away from the built-up surroundings of Manchester. When they were settled with their drinks – Wendy was sticking cautiously to bitter lemon whilst Debbie and Graham opted for shandies – the conversation drifted to their complicated family relationships. The subject had not been mentioned earlier with Yvonne and Charles.

'Yes, it's certainly a muddle,' said Debbie. 'My mother – Vera, I mean, not Fiona – found it all really confusing at first, Simon and Fiona both having had a child before, out of wedlock, as they used to say.'

'Your mum doesn't mind you seeing Fiona and her family then?' asked Wendy.

'No, not at all. I was rather naughty, though, doing what I did...' She explained how she had ferreted away at the issue until she had discovered enough to go looking for her birth mother. 'It could have been disastrous, but it's all worked out well. I know Mum and Dad must have been hurt at first, understandably, but it's all fine, now.'

'We had a shock, too,' said Wendy, 'when we found out that our dad, Keith, wasn't Greg's dad as well, didn't we, Graham? It was only after he died that Mum told us about it he was a wonderful father to us all. He loved us all just the same.'

'We knew that Greg didn't look much like either of us,' said Graham, 'but there's nothing strange about that; he has Mum's dark hair and her brown eyes. When I met Simon, though, I saw how much Greg resembled him.'

'I haven't met Simon yet,' said Wendy, 'or Fiona.

I hope I will sometime.'

'You'll meet them at Greg and Marcia's wedding,' said Graham. 'Don't say you've forgotten! And there'll be an invitation for you as well, Debbie.'

'Oh, thank you,' she replied, wondering what her relationship with Graham would be by then. 'Where is it, and when?'

'The end of May, at the church that Marcia's family attend. And they've booked the reception at a nearby hotel.'

'I'm to be a bridesmaid, along with Marcia's sister,' said Wendy. 'What is it they say? Three times a bridesmaid and never a bride? This'll be the second time for me, so I hope nobody else asks me!'

'No suitors on the horizon then?' asked her brother.

Wendy looked coy for a moment. 'Well...' she began. 'I've got friendly with the father of a little girl in my class. We met at an Open Evening and we seemed to hit it off straight away. He's a widower,' she added. 'Quite a bit older than me... I haven't said anything to Mum yet.'

'That wouldn't worry her,' said Graham. 'Both her husbands have been older than her, haven't they?'

'And Simon's thirteen years older than Fiona,' said Debbie, 'and they are perfect together.'

'Yes, so they are,' agreed Graham. 'Simon's one of the best; he's a great guy. And Fiona's a smasher! That's where Debbie gets her good looks from.'

'Thank you!' She laughed 'But I'm quite a lot

like Mum as well, perhaps not in looks – although we both have dark hair – but I have the same mannerism and tone of voice and all sorts of little things. I talk like my parents, of course,' she laughed. 'Our accent is one on its own, isn't it? It's seems that your upbringing plays just as large a part as hereditary in forming your personality. Nature as against nurture, they call it, don't they?'

'Whatever it is, I reckon you've turned out very well,' said Graham. 'I remember meeting your parents at the triplets' christening. Perhaps I'll meet them again, sometime?'

'Perhaps...' agreed Debbie. She was not sure about that. It would depend on ... quite a lot of things.

They spent a companionable couple of hours at The Blue Boar before Wendy drove them home. When they got back she said goodnight to them, disappearing upstairs with her book and a drink of chocolate.

'I shall read till I'm tired,' she said, 'like I do every night, and let you two have some time on your own.' Debbie noticed that she winked slyly at her brother. 'See you in the morning.'

Yvonne and Charles had retired to bed as well, so Debbie and Graham were left alone for the first time since she had arrived. They sat together on the settee drinking the hot chocolate that Wendy had made for them. Debbie wondered if Graham had another session of brass band music in mind, but she soon discovered that he just wanted to talk. As his sister had said he was very wrapped up in the new band he had joined.

'We had our first concert just before Christmas,' he told her. 'I'm sorry you couldn't be there, Debbie, but it was after you'd gone home for the holiday. It was quite an informal affair at a church hall in Leeds. Everyone seemed to enjoy it, and we hope it will lead to bigger things. I hope you'll be able to come to our next concert?' He looked at her eagerly.

'I hope so too,' she answered, trying to sound enthusiastic. 'When is it?'

'We're not sure yet. Possibly in March, if we can find a suitable venue.'

'I shall be there,' she said, smiling brightly at him.

'It's lovely having you here, Debbie,' he said. He put his arms round her and kissed her, but did not prolong the embrace. 'They all wanted to meet you; they'd heard such a lot about you.'

'That's nice,' she replied, wondering what he had told them. His body language seemed to indicate that he was ready to retire for the night. He carried their beakers into the kitchen, and she followed him there and then up the stairs.

'Sleep well,' he said, as they paused on the landing. He kissed her again, but made no move to follow her into her room. She was relieved about that, although she hadn't thought for one moment that he would do so.

She slept well; she never had much difficulty in sleeping, wherever she was. After a hearty breakfast of bacon and eggs Graham suggested that they should take Ollie, the puppy, for a walk. This time it was just the two of them who set off for the nearby park. Ollie was delighted to be out in the fresh air and ran ahead excitedly, pulling on his long lead.

'Are you going to let him off on his own for a while?' asked Debbie.

'Oh no; I daren't do that; he might run away. He's not fully trained yet, so we'd better play safe.' They sat on a park bench, and the little dog sat obediently at the side. They chatted easily together, but it was more as friends than as a couple who were going out together. He asked about her friends. How was Lisa, and was she still seeing Neil? And Karen; how was it going with her new boyfriend, Adam?

'I don't know for certain,' replied Debbie. 'I feel pretty sure that Lisa and Neil will stay together whatever her father says. As for Karen, she might be going out with Adam on the rebound from her disappointment over Charlie. Anyway, I'll be able to find out soon, won't I?' She realized how much she was looking forward to seeing her flatmates again.

After another delicious meal cooked by Yvonne – roast pork this time – it was time for the young people to be on their way. They all wanted to be home before darkness fell, and it was work – or college – for all of them the next day. Wendy had offering to run Debbie and Graham to the station before making her way to Bingley.

Yvonne hugged Debbie and said how lovely it had been to meet her, and she hoped she would come again. Charles shook her hand and said they had enjoyed having her. Debbie smiled and thanked them again, making no remark, though, about hoping to see them again.

There was little opportunity to talk on the journey to Leeds as the train was quite full and they were seated at a table with two people opposite them. They took a taxi from City Square as Debbie had a heavy case, and it was the simplest way to get them both home to their respective lodgings. When they arrived at Debbie's digs Graham asked the taxi driver to wait while he carried Debbie's case up the stairs for her. Their goodbye, therefore, was short and unemotional.

'I'll ring you soon, Debbie,' he said as he kissed her cheek and gave her a brief hug. 'Thanks for coming to meet my family. It's been great; see you soon...'

She felt a sense of relief as she opened the door to the flat. She was glad to be back despite the sadness that she had felt on parting from her parents ... and from Kevin. She was relieved, though, that the weekend with Graham's family was over. She had enjoyed it, although she had felt guilty about lying to Kevin; but her friendship with Graham was still a mystery to her. She had an idea that it might be Yvonne who was keen for her son to have a steady girlfriend. She had certainly made her very welcome and genuinely seemed to like her, just as Debbie liked Yvonne and the rest of the family. But she was ambivalent about her feelings for Graham.

The four flatmates soon settled down again to their domestic routine and to their college courses. Lisa was overjoyed to be reunited with Neil. Karen and Adam were still friendly as were Fran and Alistair, although Debbie sensed that

273

sparks flew now and again between the latter pair.

It was almost two weeks before Graham contacted her again. They went into town to see a film, during which he held her hand. They walked the mile or so to her flat, then he kissed her goodnight and said he would see her again soon.

In the meantime she had received two letters from Kevin, which was quite an achievement as he confessed he was not a good or an enthusiastic letter writer. He said how much he missed her and was looking forward to seeing her again, soon, he hoped. She wrote to him in the same vein.

She was pleased when Fiona rang and invited her to Aberthwaite for a weekend in mid-February. She would try to put her complicated relations with the opposite sex to one side for a couple of days.

Nineteen

Debbie travelled to Aberthwaite early on the Friday evening, after lectures had finished. Simon met her at the bus station, and she could see at once that all was well with his world.

'Fiona's fine,' he said in answer to her question. 'She's completely over her depression, or whatever she was suffering from. A lot of it is thanks to our new helper; she's a sort of nanny, I suppose, but she's really a general help to Fiona in all

274

sorts of ways. She's called Tracey; I'm sure you'll like her as much as we do.'

Debbie soon found herself drawn into the happy, busy and noisy household. All the triplets recognized her and greeted her with smiles and hugs; even Mark was less shy this time. Stella, of course, was delighted to see her again. She was full of stories about her nursery school, and how she was looking forward to going to 'proper school' – which would be in September – and about Tracey, the new lady who had come to help Mummy.

Debbie soon realized that Tracey Moffat was a very welcome and much needed addition to the rectory family. She was seventeen years old, a sturdy, healthy girl who was well able to cope with her small charges. She had a pleasant manner; she was friendly and not at all shy, but respectful to Fiona and Simon. She was firm with the children but loving and caring as well. Fiona said that she could not be more pleased with her.

They had needed to review their sleeping arrangements as Tracey was living in with the family. The fourth bedroom which had formerly been the guest room was now Tracey's room. This weekend, however, she was sharing with Stella so that Debbie could have her usual room. Debbie suggested that it was unfair, but Fiona insisted that it was the way it must be. Tracey didn't mind at all. She was a most accommodating girl, and Debbie took to her straight away.

The two of them took all the children to the playground on Saturday morning. Mark and Michelle seated in one pushchair and Matthew on his own in the other one, with Stella helping to push first one and then the other.

'This is the best way of keeping the boys apart,' said Tracey. 'Matthew loves to torment Mark; he pokes and pushes him to make him cry, then he laughs and says he's a crybaby.'

'Yes, I'm afraid Matthew does have rather an unkind streak,' said Debbie. 'But he's bigger and stronger than the other two, and I suppose he likes to show off and make out he's the boss.'

'And yet he can be so lovable as well,' said Tracey. 'He loves to cuddle up to me when I read a story; you wouldn't believe it was the same child. They're all adorable, though. I really love them. Michelle is the most placid; I think she'll be the sensible one. They're so different, considering they're triplets.'

'You really love your job, don't you,' said Debbie, really impressed by the girl's comments.

'Yeah, I do. I wanted to be a teacher but I'm not brainy enough, so they suggested at school that I should go in for child care, and I'm glad I did. I couldn't have a nicer place to work for my first job. It's worked out very well because my gran lives in Aberthwaite and goes to St Peter's Church – that's how I got the job, really – so I'm able to see her. And my parents aren't far away; they live in Richmond.'

'I can see you're doing a grand job,' said Debbie. 'How's Mark going on? He seems a little more advanced than when I last saw him, though he still doesn't say very much.'

'Yes, he's coming on gradually,' replied Tracey. 'Fiona told me she was worried about his progress, but I've seen children like him before – not that I'm all that experienced – but I've come across kids like Mark. I don't think there's anything wrong with his brain, which was what Fiona was worried about. He's maybe a bit slower than the other two, but so what? I'm not exactly the brain of Britain!'

'That's not everything,' said Debbie. 'I think you're doing fine.'

The children played happily in the playground and, for once, there were no scuffles between the boys. Debbie noticed that Mark tried to keep his distance from his brother, and Stella, who was clearly aware of the situation, took special care of Mark, helping him on the slide and pushing him gently on the swing. She didn't seem to want to have a go on anything herself, preferring to act as nursemaid along with the two grown-ups.

The weather changed suddenly. It had been cold but sunny; now black clouds were appearing and it started to rain quite hard. 'Home time, I think,' said Tracey, 'or we're going to get very wet.'

They were, indeed, drenched when they arrived back at the rectory. Tracey took charge of the children, changing them into the dry clothes that Fiona found and drying their hair. Then she took charge of them whilst Debbie helped Fiona in the kitchen.

'Just a quick lunch today,' she said. 'Soup and sandwiches. I'll cook a meal tonight for the four of us; well, perhaps five. I expect Stella will want to stay up while you're here.'

'Tracey's a grand girl, isn't she?' said Debbie. 'I'm very impressed with the way she deals with

277

the children. And she's a sensible girl ... a great improvement on your last helper,' she added with a smile.

'I'll say,' agreed Fiona. 'I don't think she'll have designs on my husband! Although I can tell she admires him, like a father figure, you know. Anyway, let's hope we have a peaceful time from now on, as peaceful as it can be with four children.'

The weather showed no signs of improving after lunch; in fact the rain was now pouring down in torrents. Tracey agreed to keep all the children busy playing games, reading stories or watching the TV whilst Fiona and Debbie spent some time together and Simon put the finishing touches to his sermon for the following day.

Debbie was telling Fiona about her complicated love life – if that was what it was – whilst they prepared the vegetables for the roast dinner that Fiona was planning. One or the other of them popped into the lounge now and again to see that all was well.

'All's well in there,' said Fiona. 'Tracey's going to read a story to them. Now, what were you telling me about Kevin? It seems to me that things are going well there...'

A few moments later Stella came rushing into the kitchen. 'Mummy, Mummy, come quick! The boys have been fighting again, and Matthew pushed Mark and he pushed him back, and now he's lying on the floor and he won't get up.'

'Oh goodness, not again!' muttered Fiona. 'Matthew's done this before, and Mark pretends it's worse than it really is.'

They followed Stella into the room. 'Come on now, boys; what's going on?' Fiona began, before she stopped and gave a gasp of shocked surprise. It was not Mark who was lying on the floor, but Matthew. Mark was whimpering and looked scared as he stared at his brother lying motionless on the hearth with Tracey kneeling at his side. His eyes were closed and it was clear that he wasn't bluffing.

'I'm sorry,' said Tracey in a whisper, her face white with shock. 'They had a fight; they both wanted to sit next to me – it was something and nothing really. I got them apart and I thought it was alright, then Mark flew at Matthew and knocked him down, and he banged his head on the edge of the fireplace...'

Fiona knelt down at Matthew's side. 'Come on, Matty,' she whispered. 'Wake up; come along, love.' But he didn't stir.

'I'm sorry, I'm so sorry,' Tracey was muttering. 'It all happened so quickly. I've never seen Mark in such a temper; he really flew at him.'

'I know it's not your fault,' said Fiona, 'but we'll have to get some help. Go and tell Simon; he's in his study.'

Everything happened quickly after that. Simon rang for an ambulance which came in less than ten minutes, although it seemed ages to the anxious group of people who were waiting.

There was a huge lump the size of an egg on Matthew's forehead. Fiona was trying to believe it was a good sign if the bruise was coming out. She had heard people say that, but none of them really knew. Tracey had learnt a certain amount of first aid on her course, but as Matthew was unconscious they knew they mustn't move him.

Simon and Fiona both went in the ambulance with Matthew, leaving the two girls to look after the children. 'I don't know how long we'll be,' said Fiona. 'We'll ring and let you know what's happening.' She hugged Tracey. 'Now, none of this is your fault; you mustn't worry about that. We must just hope and pray that Matthew isn't badly hurt. I'm sure he'll be OK. He's a strong, sturdy lad.' But she spoke with more conviction than she was feeling.

All the children were subdued. 'Matty hurt, Matty hurt,' Mark kept saying, almost to himself.

Both the girls knew that they must not be cross or blame the little boy in any way. Tracey turned the television on – it had its uses at times – and the children settled down, though much more quietly than usual, to watch the antics of Tom and Jerry.

'Let's make a cup of tea,' said Debbie, and the two of them went into the kitchen.

'I'm really scared,' Tracey confessed. 'Matthew went down with such a bang. There was a real loud crack when he knocked his head on the hearth. I daren't tell Fiona that. He was taken unawares, you see, by Mark lungeing at him, and he wasn't ready to retaliate. Oh Debbie...' She burst into tears. 'He will be alright, won't he?'

Debbie put her arms round the girl. 'I should think so,' she answered, not wanting to say that she was sure he would come round with no ill effects. She, too was scared, but didn't want to admit it. 'The same thing happened to my friend,

Lisa,' she said, wanting to offer some degree of comfort. 'She fell in the kitchen and banged her head. She was inhaling gas as well because she didn't realize she'd left a gas tap on. She was on her own, you see, because we'd all gone out, and it was ages before we found her. But she was OK; she came round in hospital after a few hours, and she's been fine ever since. So try not to worry too much about Matthew. Let's just wait and see, eh?'

The best thing to do, for the two of them and for the children's sake, was to keep busy. They decided to make tea for everyone. When he was asked what he wanted to eat, Mark replied promptly that he would like 'sojers'.

'Soldiers,' interpreted Tracey. 'He likes fingers of toast dipped in a boiled egg. They all like them.'

Debbie smiled. 'Don't we all? That's what my mum used to call them.'

They made what the children thought was a lovely tea with the boiled eggs and buttered soldiers, a red jelly they found in the fridge to which they added a tin of fruit cocktail, and iced buns that Fiona had made the day before. Debbie and Tracey dined with them, guessing that the roast dinner planned for the evening would have to be put off until another day. They put the half prepared vegetables in the fridge with the leg of lamb that, fortunately, Fiona had not started to cook.

They were waiting anxiously for the phone to ring although neither of them mentioned it. They were just starting to get Mark and Michelle ready for their nightly bath when Simon returned. They could tell from his face that the news was not good – he looked serious and there was none of the usual warmth in his eyes – but at least it was not all that bad.

'There's no change,' he said. 'Matthew's still unconscious, but as far as they can tell there should be no lasting damage. He's suffering from concussion, poor little lad, and they obviously don't know how long it will last. He's having oxygen to help his breathing and he appears to be breathing normally, but how can I tell?' He hastily wiped away a stray tear from the corner of his eye.

'Fiona insisted I should come home and she'll let me know if there's any change. She's staying overnight at the hospital. They are so good there; I know they'll do all they possibly can...' He gave as bright a smile as he was able. 'Now, what can I do? Bath time is it?'

'We'll see to them, Simon,' said Debbie. 'I'm sure you must be ready for something to eat. We've had our tea with the children; and we've put the lamb back in the fridge. It'll keep for a day or two.'

'That's the least of our worries,' said Simon. 'You carry on with the little 'uns, and Stella can come and talk to me while I rustle up something to eat. OK, Stella?'

The little girl had been listening intently to all that was said. She nodded gravely. 'I'll come and help, Daddy. I've had a lovely tea, though. There's some jelly and fruit left, and some of Mummy's special buns.'

'Splendid!' he enthused. 'And I think there's some cold chicken, so I'll make some sandwiches.'

They were all trying to act as normally as they could. Simon went up to read a bedtime story to Mark and Michelle, then Debbie read to Stella about *The Folk of the Faraway Tree*.

'She's just discovered Enid Blyton,' Tracey told her, 'and it's her nightly treat. But she told me that Debbie would read to her tonight. You two get along famously, don't you?'

Debbie agreed that they did. The bond between her and her little half-sister grew stronger every time they met. Simon came in after the story to say goodnight to Stella. Debbie left them alone; she was sure they would be saying a little prayer for Matthew to get well again.

Simon joined the two girls in a short while. There was the usual variety show on the television, but when Simon looked at it with a slight frown Debbie got up and turned it off.

'I don't think we're watching this, are we Tracey?' she asked.

Tracey shook her head. None of them felt like settling down to a normal evening watching TV.

'I've been having a little chat with Stella,' Simon told them. 'She really is a most sensible child. Fiona and I have been so blessed with her; and with all our children, of course, but the triplets have given us more cause for worry. Stella said that we hadn't to be cross with Mark because she's sure he didn't mean to hurt his brother.' He smiled. 'I suppose you could say that Matthew had it coming to him. He's teased his brother once too often, but no one could foresee this happening. Of course little Marky didn't mean it.'

He turned to speak just to Debbie. 'We were looking forward so much to you coming this weekend. But it's turning out to be a miserable time for you, isn't it? I'm really sorry, Debbie. The children kept talking about you coming; well Stella did, and she kept telling the little ones that Debbie was coming soon.'

'It's OK, Simon,' replied Debbie. 'I'm glad I'm here. I'm shocked about Matthew's accident, but it's a good job I'm here to keep Tracey company. I think I've managed to convince her that she wasn't to blame.'

'Nobody is,' said Simon. 'It was just an unfortunate accident. You always seem to be here when there's an emergency, don't you, Debbie?'

She smiled. 'It seems like it. I've been here for happy times as well, though.'

Simon nodded. 'If you girls don't mind I'll leave you on your own for a while. I must ring Gilbert about tomorrow's services. I'm supposed to be preaching in the morning and Gilbert in the evening, but I doubt that I'll feel much like it. I shall have to see how Matthew is and relieve Fiona at the hospital. I dare say Gilbert will have an extra sermon tucked away that he can rehash. I'll see you later.'

Debbie guessed that he needed some time on his own: a time of quiet prayer and meditation as well as sorting out the plans for the next day. She told Tracey how she had been at the rectory when Fiona had given birth, unexpectedly, to the triplets.

'They were several weeks early,' she told her,

'and until they arrived everyone had thought they would be twins. Not even the doctor knew. Fiona had a bad time at the birth. She lost a lot of blood, but fortunately I was there to help.'

'What do you mean?' asked Tracey.

'Fiona has an unusual blood group, and I have the same one. So I gave some blood...' She smiled a little embarrassedly. 'You know I'm Fiona's daughter, don't you?'

'Yes, she told me. She said it isn't a secret any more, and how pleased she was that you came to find her.'

'It's opened up a whole new chapter for all of us,' said Debbie. 'I've made new friends ... that's how I met Graham, the young man I'm seeing in Leeds. He and Greg were here that weekend as well; that's how we came to be godparents to the triplets.'

'Yes, I know about Greg, too,' smiled Tracey. 'He came here with his fiancée a few weeks ago. So you're going out with his brother, are you?'

'Sort of,' said Debbie. She told Tracey a little about the quandary she was in with Graham and Kevin. It helped both of them to take their minds off the much greater problem.

'Lucky you!' said Tracey. 'Two boyfriends, and I haven't even got one!'

'You're only seventeen,' said Debbie, with the wisdom of her nearly nineteen years. 'I'm sure you'll meet someone soon.'

Tracey was what one might describe as a hefty girl with a bonny round face and dark curly hair.

'I need to lose some weight,' she said ruefully. 'Who'd look twice at me?'

'Lots of lads would,' said Debbie. 'Don't be so hard on yourself. You're very attractive.'

'The trouble is I went to an all-girls' school,' Tracey replied, 'and then the job I decided to do isn't for men; it's only girls who go in for child care. I'm quite happy, though; I'm not fretting about it.'

They chatted for a while about their homes and family life, and found that they got on well together. Simon joined them at about nine thirty. They had heard the telephone ring and wondered if there was any news.

'There's no change,' he told them, 'but perhaps that's good in one way. He's fairly comfortable, as they say, but he's still unconscious. Fiona's staying the night.' He looked sad and weary. Debbie had never seen him like this with the strain showing in his eyes. Even when he had been concerned about Fiona there had still been the vestige of a sparkle there. She made a supper time drink for them all, and they retired to bed early, glad to end the day and hoping that tomorrow would bring better news.

Fiona returned as they were having breakfast the next morning. She was trying to put on a brave face.

'Matthew's eyes were fluttering a little bit,' she told them, 'and I thought he was going to wake up ... but he didn't. I'm sure he will soon, though. I'm going to stay at home and cook us all a dinner – there's the lamb to use, isn't there? – and Simon can take my place at the hospital. There must be one of us there when he comes round.' She smiled with a false brightness, trying to act as normally as possible for the children's sake.

Simon didn't look as wretched now that his wife was there with him. Debbie knew that whatever they had to face they had their love for one another to sustain them. Fiona chose to stay at home whilst Debbie and Tracey attended church, leaving Mark and Michelle in the crèche, whilst Stella attended her Sunday School class.

As the congregation listened to Gilbert's announcement about Matthew's accident, Debbie sensed how much they all cared about the family at the rectory. Prayers were said for the little boy, and the girls were overwhelmed by the good wishes and promises of help and of prayers as they left the church.

It was time for Debbie to leave when they had finished the roast dinner, postponed from the previous evening. Fiona had worked hard making a delicious meal, never forgetting for one moment that Matthew was still lying in hospital in what appeared to be a comatose condition; but she knew that keeping busy was far better than sitting around brooding.

She put Simon's meal to keep warm in the oven while she drove Debbie to the bus station. 'I'll go and change places with him at the hospital when I get back,' she said. 'I was hoping there might be some good news before you left Debbie...'

The phone rang at that moment and she dashed to answer it. It was Simon, but there was no change in Matthew's condition. All the doctor could say was that he was stable. Debbie could see Fiona biting her lip in an effort to keep back the tears of disappointment, and she felt exactly the same.

'Come along now, all of you,' said Fiona cheerfully, but with a slight wobble to her voice. 'Let's all go and see Debbie off, shall we? The washing up can wait till we get back.'

It was not a great distance to the bus station but too far for Debbie to walk with a heavy case. She sat at the front of the car with Fiona whilst the three children piled into the back with Tracey. There were car seats for the little ones, and Stella sat on Tracey's knee. It was a tight squeeze but it provided a much-needed moment of light relief.

Debbie was glad that the bus was waiting and there was only a short time until her departure. She hugged all the children. Stella looked unusually sombre as she kissed her grown-up half-sister and whispered to her that she must 'say a little prayer for Matthew'.

'It's been great meeting you,' Debbie told Tracey. 'Let's hope all is well when we meet again.'

She hugged Fiona and told her to be brave. 'But he'll be OK, I'm sure,' she added. 'They don't come much tougher than little Matthew.'

'I'll let you know the minute there's any news,' promised Fiona. Debbie hurried on to the bus before they both gave way to tears.

The children waved as the bus drove away, and Debbie tried to settle down for the hour's journey to Leeds. It had not been a happy weekend, but she was glad to have been there. It had strengthened the ties she already had with the family at the rectory.

Twenty

It was difficult for Debbie to settle down to her college work. The thought of Matthew still lying in his hospital bed was with her all the time. Her flatmates were sympathetic, and every time Rhoda knocked on the door they were hoping it would be a phone call for Debbie, and that it would be good news.

Plans were going ahead for the visit of the landscape gardening group to some of the outstanding gardens in England. Derby had been chosen as the centre where they would stay. Derbyshire was not too far away from Leeds, and there were three houses with gardens that were worthy of a visit, in the vicinity. The largest and the most well known of them was Chatsworth House, the long-time home of the Dukes of Devonshire, with expensive gardens and parkland. There was also Haddon Hall, and Kedleston Hall, both smaller but with a good deal to offer.

They had been fortunate in booking accommodation at a sports college on the outskirts of Derby. Easter that year fell during the second week of April. The students at Stanborough were due to return to college the third week in April, but as the sports students had a week longer vacation the college was available for visiting groups to use. The little group of ten from Leeds would travel to Derby on the Tuesday morning and return on the Friday. There would be leisure time as well as the time spent visiting and in study. As the young people were no longer at school and – supposedly – able to be trusted to behave themselves, they would not be under such close supervision.

Debbie and Fran were both going, as was Alistair. There would be four women and eight men. Debbie had been looking forward to it, but she was unable, now, to join in the discussions about the forthcoming visit with much enthusiasm.

Her parents had been sorry to hear about Matthew; she had phoned them as soon as she arrived back from Aberthwaite. Debbie's news certainly took the edge off theirs.

'Daddy has bought a car,' Vera informed her. It was a Ford Anglia, though not a new one, in Vera's favourite colour of pale blue. 'Plenty big enough for the two of us,' she said, 'and for you, of course, when you come home. Daddy will be able to pick you up at the station, and take you there when you're going back.'

She said how Stanley had got used to driving again, and they were now enjoying little jaunts out into the countryside and along the coast. Debbie was pleased for them. They seemed to be getting far more out of life since she had moved away, which was good for all of them.

It was, in fact, only four days later that Fiona rang with news about Matthew, but to Debbie, who had been waiting anxiously, it seemed much longer. She hurried to the phone when Rhoda came with the message early on Thursday evening.

'It's that friend of yours,' she said, 'the one that's married to that vicar up in t'dales. She sounds cheerful, so I hope it's good news. I know you've been worried sick about the little lad.'

It was, indeed, good news. 'Matthew's awake!' Fiona almost shouted down the phone.

'Oh ... thank God for that!' gasped Debbie, feeling tears of relief springing to her eyes. 'You must be over the moon. And he's OK, is he? No ill effects? No ... signs of anything wrong?'

'Not as far as they can tell,' said Fiona. 'I was there this afternoon when he came round. He opened his eyes and looked at me; it seemed like a miracle. He hasn't spoken much; he seems very subdued, which is not like Matthew.' She laughed. 'They say he may not be able to remember the accident at all. Anyway, they're letting us bring him home tomorrow, so I'll let you know.'

'Thanks, Fiona ... love to the children and Simon, and to Tracey as well. You must be so relieved, all of you. Bye for now.'

All the girls were at home in the flat. They whooped with delight at Debbie's good news. And now she could get back to her studies with renewed enthusiasm ... and give some thought to her complicated matters of the heart.

When Fiona and Simon went to collect Matthew from the hospital he was sitting up in his little bed, staring around as though he was not sure where he was. The minute he saw them, however, his face lit up and he held out his arms. 'Mummy … Daddy…' he shouted as they hurried to his side.

Fiona put her arms round him. 'Hello, darling. Are you feeling better?'

The little boy nodded unsurely, looking as though he didn't understand.

'Hello, old chap,' said Simon, ruffling his hair. 'You've been in the wars, haven't you? Never mind, you're all right again now. Let's get you home, shall we?'

Matthew stared at him uncomprehendingly. Then, 'Go home…' he said.

He was unusually quiet as the nurses made a fuss of him saying goodbye. He waved, though, automatically, saying, 'Bye-bye,' in a dazed sort of way.

'It will take him a little while to get acclimatized again,' said the chief nurse, 'but as far as we can see there's nothing much wrong now. His memory may be affected for a while, but we'll be keeping an eye on him from time to time.'

'At least he knows who we are,' said Simon as they got into the car, with Simon driving and Fiona sitting at the back with Matthew on her knee.

The children were all waiting with Tracey when they arrived home. Stella had been allowed to miss nursery school as this was a special occasion. Mark had not been chastised at all about the accident, and it seemed as though it had gone from his mind. Fiona wondered if Matthew's memory of it would return when he saw his brother, or if Mark would remember what he had done and be afraid of greeting Matthew. She was astounded, therefore, when Mark dashed towards Matthew and gave him a hug.

'Matty home,' he said delightedly. 'You better, Matty?'

Matthew nodded uncertainly, then he, too, put his arms round his brother and hugged him without saying a word.

Fiona and Simon looked at one another, metaphorically crossing their fingers. 'So far, so good,' said Simon quietly.

'I'll make us all some lunch,' said Fiona brightly. 'I'm sure you must be hungry, Matthew.'

Matthew nodded, but it was his brother who answered, 'Me hungry!'

The children stayed with Tracey whilst Simon and Fiona prepared a quick lunch of soup and sandwiches. 'Do you think he's really all right?' asked Fiona. 'He's not like the old Matthew, is he? He's so subdued.'

'I suppose he's bound to be,' said Simon. 'He was unconscious for quite a while. It's sure to have had some effect on him.' He laughed. 'Let's enjoy it while it lasts.'

But Fiona was doubtful. 'I'd rather have my boisterous little boy back,' she said.

'Then let's be thankful that things are no worse,' said Simon, 'and just wait and see.'

As the days went by Matthew started to speak more, but he was no longer as loud or as aggressive in his behaviour. As for Mark, he had started to talk a little more each day. Not as well as Michelle, who had been the first of the triplets to string words together, but his parents felt that a corner had been turned.

And the two little boys now appeared to be the best of friends. They made it clear that they wanted to share the same pushchair, which they did without any pushing or scuffling. Fiona wondered if it was the calm before the storm, but the affinity of the two boys continued.

'God moves in mysterious ways sometimes,' Simon remarked to Fiona one night when all the children were tucked up in bed.

'It seems so,' she replied. 'But you can't mean that God wanted it to happen; the accident and everything?'

'No, of course not,' said Simon. 'What I mean is that good things can come out of bad. You know how often I've quoted that favourite text of mine, that "all things work together for good". Well, this is a wonderful example of it.'

At college the spring term was well under way. It was always a bleak time after Christmas, when the weather was inclement and the snow remained on the ground for ages in places such as Yorkshire. But now, in mid-March, the sun was appearing more and more and signs of spring were to be seen in the countryside and in the college grounds.

Debbie continued to write to Kevin and to see Graham, and she had decided to let matters take their course. She attended the next concert given by Graham's brass band. It was held in a church hall in Leeds and was well attended and well received, too, by the audience. It was still quite a small band of sixteen members, the majority of whom were men. There were two girls, one of whom was a French horn player along with Graham. She was a pretty little blonde girl and he introduced her to Debbie as Felicity, known as Fliss. She thought how much the name suited her.

After the performance some of the band members went along to a nearby pub with their wives – several of them were married – or girlfriends, if they had one. Fliss went along with Hazel, the only other girl member, who played the oboe. Debbie noticed Fliss looking over in their direction a few times, then looking away if Debbie caught her eye. It occurred to Debbie that the girl was more than a little interested in Graham; whether he was aware of it or not was another matter.

It was towards the end of March when Graham surprised Debbie by asking her if she would go out for the day with him on the following Sunday. One of the reasons was that, at long last, he had bought the car he had been wanting, partly to keep up with his brother and sister.

'Jolly good,' she said in answer to his news about the car. 'What sort is it?'

'A Morris Minor, a red one,' he replied, 'just a few years old. I doubt that I shall use it for work – it's easier to go by bus – but it'll be handy for going home to see Mum, and I hope we'll be able to make good use of it, Debbie.'

'And you can drive it alright?' she asked.

'Of course!' He sounded rather indignant. 'I passed my test a while ago, you know. Greg let me drive his mini, and I had a few lessons. I passed the first time!'

'Good for you. So ... where were you thinking of

going on Sunday?' She thought it sounded a nice idea, but she wondered what he had in mind.

'I thought we could have a run over to Ilkley; it's not very far. It's a pretty little town. We could have some lunch there, and there are some pleasant walks on the moors, weather permitting, of course. If it rains we'd have to think again.'

'Nothing too strenuous, I hope. I haven't got any hiking boots.' Fell walking or climbing had never been of interest to Debbie, although she enjoyed a country ramble.

'No; we'll do an easy walk,' he assured her. She knew that Graham had done more difficult walks with friends when he had been at uni, but just lately it seemed that the band had taken over as his all-consuming interest. 'Are you game for it, then?'

'Yes ... yes, I think so.'

'You don't sound too sure.'

'Sorry, Graham,' she replied. 'I was taken by surprise, that's all. Yes, I shall look forward to it.'

'That's great then. I'll pick you up on Sunday morning. Is ten o'clock OK?'

She told him that was fine. 'Bye for now, Graham. And thanks for asking me. See you soon.'

The other girls were interested to hear her news. 'Things are looking good there,' said Karen. 'He's getting keen, kid!'

'But do I want him to?' said Debbie, almost to herself. She had been content with things the way they were, being friendly with both Graham and Kevin. But how long could it go on?

Graham had phoned on the Monday. On Tuesday evening Rhoda came up to say there was another phone call for Debbie. 'Another young man!' she commented with a gleam in her eye. 'You're a popular young lady, aren't you?'

It was Kevin, as Debbie had guessed it might be. He had started phoning her now and again. She guessed it was because he wasn't all that keen on writing, but she was always pleased to hear his cheery voice.

'Hi, Debbie,' he greeted her. 'How are things with you?'

'Fine, thanks,' she answered. 'I'm looking forward to coming home for Easter. It's only a few weeks away now.'

'Ah well, I've got a surprise for you,' he said. 'I thought I might pop over to Leeds this next weekend and see you. I'm missing you, you know, Debbie.' She was silent for a minute as she took in what he was saying. This weekend ... and she was meeting Graham! She began to panic.

'Debbie ... are you still there?'

'Yes ... yes, I'm still here. You surprised me Kevin, that's all. I'd love to see you, but it's only just over two weeks before I come home. And I'll be home for a fortnight.'

'Don't you want to see me?'

'Yes, of course I do, but–'

'I thought I'd come on Saturday. You could find me a B and B near to where you live, couldn't you? We could go to the pictures or something, and go out for the day on Sunday. What do you think?'

'I think it's a great idea, Kevin,' she said 'but–' she was in a real panic now – 'but I'm sorry, I can't, not this weekend. A few of us have arranged to go out on Sunday to Temple Newsam; that's a big house near Leeds, and the grounds were landscaped by Capability Brown. So we thought we ought to see it, those of us who are doing the landscaping course.' It was only a half lie, she told herself. A few of them, including Debbie had, in fact, visited the place a couple of weeks ago. It was fortunate she hadn't told Kevin about the visit. 'I can't back out now ... I'm really sorry.'

She couldn't tell him the truth, that she was planning to spend the day with another young man. She was feeling dreadful because it was the second time she had lied to him, firstly about visiting Graham's home just after Christmas, and now this.

'I'm sorry,' she said again. 'It would have been nice; and I do miss you, Kevin.' She was realizing that she did. 'But I'll see you soon.'

He sounded deflated when he answered. 'Alright then; I suppose it can't be helped if you've got something you'd rather do.'

'No ... it's not that, Kevin.'

'Whatever you say. But I'm disappointed, Debbie. I thought you'd jump at the idea.'

'It's ... it's rather short notice...'

'Yeah, I suppose it is. Well, never mind. I'll see you in – what is it – about three weeks?'

'Yes, two and a half actually. It won't be long now.'

'OK then, see you.' He rang off abruptly.

She didn't get much sympathy from her friends; they seemed highly amused at the situation. Lisa, who was more tender-hearted, seemed to understand more than the other two. 'You must make up your mind, Debbie,' she said. 'You can't play them along like this.'

'But I'm not,' Debbie persisted. 'It isn't as if either of them want to be serious, at least I don't think they do. And as my mum keeps telling me, I'm only young, and I've got my career ahead of me ... though I don't know what I'm going to do yet. Oh, why does it all have to be so complicated?'

Fortunately Sunday turned out to be fine, not too warm but sunny with no threat of rain. Debbie was well prepared in her warm trousers and anorak and a pair of strong shoes. She had tried to put all thoughts of her duplicity to the back of her mind and to enjoy the day.

Ilkley was a charming little spa town near the banks of the River Wharfe. They strolled along the main street looking in the windows of gift shops, antique shops and those selling walking and climbing gear, most of them closed. They found a cosy little café where they had a snack lunch of sandwiches, with the tasty roast ham cut off the bone, followed by Yorkshire curd tart.

'We mustn't eat too much,' said Graham. 'We can't walk on a full stomach. We can have a more substantial meal later before we go back.'

Debbie agreed that it was a good idea. He was certainly going all out to please her today. They walked on the lower slopes of the moor towards the Cow and Calf rocks, so named because of their shape, which you could make out if you looked closely. It was a favourite place for rock climbers. There were a few of them climbing that day. Debbie and Graham sat on the ground near an outcrop of rock, watching the climbers, but ready for rest after their own exertions. Graham produced some Kendal mint cake from the capacious pocket of his anorak, and they munched contentedly. Debbie realized, despite her feeling of self-reproach, that she was having a very enjoyable day.

Graham had to tell her, of course, that the song – or rather the melody – of 'On Ilkley Moor Baht 'at', was in the band's repertoire, as it was the nearest thing to Yorkshire's national anthem. 'Baht 'at means without a hat,' he told her, as if she didn't already know, but she listened politely.

He drew her close to him in the shadow of the rock, and they kissed several times, then they sat, his arm around her, looking across the valley to the little town below. When the afternoon turned chilly they made their way down again. They found a rather grander restaurant where they were already serving early evening meals.

They enjoyed a heartier meal this time; sirloin steak with chips, tomatoes and mushrooms, followed by sherry trifle. They restricted themselves to a small glass of red wine each, as Graham had to drive home.

'It's been a lovely day,' she told him, when they arrived back at her flat. 'Thank you for inviting me, Graham. I've enjoyed it so much.' And so she had, far more than she had thought she would, and maybe more than she deserved to.

'The pleasure is all mine,' he told her, leaning across and kissing her on the lips. 'We'll have some more outings, now I've got my own set of wheels. I'll think of somewhere else to visit when you get back from your Easter break.'

'Yes, that will be nice,' she said, feeling a prick of conscience creeping up again.

'I'll see you before you go home, won't I?'

'Yes ... of course.'

He declined her invitation to come up to the flat for coffee, and promised to ring her later in the week. She was dreading the cross-examination that might follow. What could she say? That she had had a lovely day, but the dilemma in which she found herself was now even worse?

As it happened there was only Lisa at home. She was entertaining Neil, quite circumspectly, whilst the other two were out. Lisa was always discreet, so there were no awkward questions. The three of them drank coffee and chatted together until Lisa and Neil went out together at ten o'clock for a quiet stroll and to say goodnight.

Debbie saw Graham only once more before she went home for the Easter break. He said they were having extra band meetings for a forthcoming concert, and there were two new members who needed their extra help.

'Have a good holiday,' he said when they arrived back at her flat. 'I shall miss you, but it's only two weeks, isn't it?'

'Yes, but then I'm going to Derbyshire,' she reminded him, 'the week after I come back.'

'Oh yes, of course. Well, I'll still be here when you've finished your gadding about.'

'It's an educational visit,' she told him, 'not a jolly holiday.'

'Oh, I expect you'll enjoy it all the same,' he said.

301

'See you sometime, then...' He waved cheerfully as he drove away.

Debbie's parents were overjoyed to have her at home again. Her father was eager to show off his new possession, his Ford Anglia with the odd-shaped back window, which he polished till the paintwork gleamed, every weekend.

'We've had some grand little trips out, haven't we, Vera?' he said. 'I thought we might make a day of it, the three of us, next Saturday. You can decide where we go, Debbie. Happen we could take a picnic if the weather's fine. And you could invite Kevin to come along with us if you like, Debbie. You've not seen him much since you got home, have you?'

'He's busy at work, Dad,' she replied. 'It's Easter, and people are planning their summer gardens. He'll certainly be working on Saturday.'

It was true that she hadn't seen much of Kevin. He had phoned her, not straight away but a couple of days after she returned home. He had called for her that same evening and they drove into town, then had a walk along the promenade. Dusk was falling as they stood by the railings, looking out across the dark sea. The day had been fine and there was a colourful sunset, the clouds edged with gold in a sky shading from orange to crimson, to a deep purply-red.

They had chatted together pleasantly, mainly about the garden centre and Kevin's and his father's ideas for the coming year. Debbie told him about her course and how much she had learnt over the past months. But there was a constraint between them.

'How did you enjoy your day out?' he asked her. 'You were going to see a garden, temple ... something or other?'

'Oh yes ... Temple Newsam... Yes, we enjoyed it very much.'

'What's up, Debbie?' he asked. They were well attuned to one another by now. Debbie was aware that Kevin knew when she was being evasive or keeping something from him.

She had been brought up to be truthful. She had been a troublesome teenager at times, but she had always hated telling lies; even the memory of little fibs had lingered in her mind. And so it was now. She had lied to Kevin about her day out with Graham, and although it might cause trouble between them she knew she had to admit to what she had done.

'I've got something to tell you, Kevin,' she began. 'I did go to Temple Newsam, but it was a couple of weeks before. That day, when you wanted to come to Leeds I'd already said I'd go out for the day ... with Graham.'

She heard Kevin's sharp intake of breath. His face was serious, but more distressed than angry. He looked steadily at her. 'Graham? The fellow who plays the bugle, or something? You're still seeing him?'

'The French horn, actually. Yes, I do see him, but only now and again. Because he lives in Leeds ... and it's somebody to go out with. There's nothing ... like that ... between us.' She didn't explain like what; he would know what she meant. 'We're only friends.' Which was true

303

because Graham hadn't taken things any further. 'It's nothing serious, Kevin. I don't want to get serious yet ... with anybody. I'm still at college, and I don't know what I'm going to do or where I'll be when I finish.'

'That's beside the point,' he replied. 'I'm talking about now, and about you and me. You must know how I feel about you, Debbie. I know we haven't made any promises ... but there's nobody else for me. I'm not seeing anyone else while you're away, and I thought it was the same for you. I feel let down, Debbie. I really thought–'

'Oh, Kevin ... don't get so upset. I won't see Graham again if you don't want me to. But, like I said, we're just friends.'

'But you lied to me, didn't you?'

'Only because I'd said I'd go out with him, and I didn't know what do.'

'Because you didn't want to tell him about me. That's the truth, isn't it?'

'I suppose so. But when we got back together again, you and me, I thought we were just going to see how things worked out for us. We'd fallen out once before–'

'We were only kids then, Debbie. I've grown up now, and I thought you had, too. But maybe you haven't, not enough to know your own mind. I know what I want...' He took hold of her hand, looking unsmilingly into her eyes. 'I want you, Debbie, just you. But unless you feel the same it's no use, is it?' She didn't answer. 'Come along,' he said, 'let's go and have a coffee somewhere, then I'll take you home.'

Debbie was confused. Kevin hadn't said he

loved her, but she thought that was what he meant. Did she love him? Ages ago, when she was a silly schoolgirl, she had thought she did. But now ... she wasn't sure. She enjoyed his company, and their more intimate moments, too; although he had not asked too much of her. But she enjoyed being with Graham as well. She wanted to enjoy the rest of her time at college without making any promises she might not be able to keep.

She saw Kevin a few more times before she returned to Leeds. He did not put any pressure on her, but she knew he was waiting for her to make up her mind.

She spent a good deal of her time with her parents. Stanley took a few days off work and they went further afield in the car: to Hadrian's Wall; to the market town of Alnwick and its castle; and to the Holy Island of Lindisfarne. Looking back on it she felt pleased that she had accompanied them on their outings. She knew they had been delighted that they were together as a family. And Debbie realized afresh just how much they meant to her.

Twenty-One

Debbie made up her mind that she was going to enjoy the visit to Derbyshire, looking upon it as a little holiday, although it was, in truth, an educational visit as part of the course. She tried to put all thoughts of Kevin and of Graham to the back of her mind as she got on the minibus on Tuesday morning with the other members of the group.

She sat with Janet, another of the landscape students. There were only four women in the group. Fran, of course, was sitting with Alistair, although Debbie had an idea that their relationship was going through a rocky patch. The other girl of the four, Stephanie, was sitting with Alan, the young man with who she had become friendly. The rest of the group, it appeared, were fancy-free. It was inevitable that relationships would be formed in a co-ed college; inevitable, too, that some would founder whilst others would last throughout the course and continue afterwards. As would seem to be the case with Lisa and Neil.

They had been provided with a packed lunch which they ate when they stopped at the spa town of Buxton. The weather was fine and they enjoyed a short break in the pleasant gardens near the pavilion.

It was not far, then, to Derby; they arrived there by mid-afternoon. The sports college was an ideal venue for their three-day visit. Each of them had their own room, small but adequate – students could not expect five-star treatment – with shower, wash basin and toilet, single bed and functional furniture consisting of a wardrobe and a dressing table-cum-desk.

All the facilities were available to them as well; swimming pool, tennis courts, gymnasium. There was also a billiards room, a bar, and a common room with comfortable chairs and a television. Debbie had never been a sporty sort of girl, but she could swim reasonably well and had brought her costume along in case she felt inclined to have a dip. The evening meal was served at six thirty, and they queued at the serving hatch to make their choice. During term time, with more than a hundred students to cater for, there would be a wider variety. Tonight, as there were only two small groups staying there, the choice was more limited; soup or melon as a starter, followed by battered fish or steak pie with chips, then a choice of apple pie or cheese and biscuits.

Coffee and tea were available from the machine in the common room, then the twelve students were free to do as they wished. It was rumoured that the two lecturers who were in charge of the group, Mr Hartley and Mrs Bell, were friendlier than maybe they ought to be. They certainly left their charges to their own devices.

The other visiting group consisted of middle-aged ladies – their badges indicated that they were members of the Townswomen's Guild – who were on a cultural visit to the pottery factories and museums that abounded in the area. Debbie and Janet chatted to two ladies who were of a similar age to their own mothers. They were very interested to hear about the landscape gardening course, and said that they, too, would be visiting Chatsworth House later in the week.

It was, however, the gardens, rather than the house itself that the students were bound for the following morning. They had already learned that this had been the home of the Dukes of Devonshire since the seventeenth century. The gardens and grounds, which were of more interest to them than the architecture and treasures of the house, had been designed at a later date during the eighteenth and nineteenth centuries.

The grounds covered a vast area, and it was planned that they would stay there for most of the day. They listened, first of all, to a talk by their own lecturer, Mr Hartley; he outlined the planning of the designers, who had worked along with the dukes of the time to create the ideas they had in mind. They were then free to explore the grounds themselves, following a detailed map. They would, of course, be obliged to take notes and report back to the group as a whole when they returned to the college in the late afternoon. There was so much to see that it would serve no purpose to be shepherded around together like a group of schoolchildren. They were to meet near the terrace at the front of the house for lunch, in a couple of hours' time.

Debbie and Janet paired up with two of the men students, Andy and Bob. They went, first of all to view the work of Lancelot Capability Brown, one designer they had all heard of before starting on the course. It was Brown who had created a more informal aspect to the scene. The formal gardens had been swept away as he embarked upon his extensive tree planting, He had even altered the course of the River Derwent to accommodate his plans.

As they surveyed the vista stretching out all around them, the curve of the river and the strategically placed groups of trees, they marvelled at how he had visualized, in his mind's eye, what the scene would look like a century or more later.

The planners had created parklands that would be enjoyed by future generations rather than their own. They identified the trees that had been introduced by Brown, including American species that had been imported from Philadelphia.

Fortunately the weather stayed fine, although there was a chilly breeze. They were glad of the hot tea and coffee provided by the catering staff of the house, to drink with their sandwiches and pork pies.

As they continued their exploration of the grounds they met other little groups belonging to their party and exchanged points of view and directions as to where to go next. There was so much to see, and a great deal of walking and scrambling was involved, but by the end of the day when they met together in the common room, they had all managed to tick off everything on the list.

Although the name of Capability Brown immediately sprang to mind when speaking of Chatsworth, they had also viewed much of the planning that had been done at a later date by Sir Joseph Paxton. He had worked closely with the sixth duke during the nineteenth century to design the parterre gardens and the flower gardens adjoining the house. Particularly appealing to the students was his water feature named The Strid, after a natural feature of the same name in Wharfedale. The Strid at Chatsworth was a picturesque rocky stream, fringed by trees and crossed by a rustic bridge.

They had talked eagerly about the arboretum

and the pine grove where the oldest species of Douglas fir were to be found. And the dell and ravine, the rugged part of the garden with steep paths and a stream running through a valley. Azaleas and rhododendrons were flowering there; visitors later in the year would miss the full beauty of the colourful blooms.

Some, however, had failed to be impressed by the exhibitionism, the showing off of extreme wealth and influence. Namely, the extravagant cascade and the fountain. The Emperor Fountain had been built for the intended visit of Tsar Nicholas of Russia in 1843. It was planned to be the world's highest fountain with the water rising to a height of 296 feet. However, the tsar had died and the visit did not take place. Neither had the desired height been achieved. The present fountain could reach only a much lower height, due to a limited supply of water and lack of pressure.

Their minds were overbrimming with facts and figures, and full of ideas, though on a far less grand scale, that they could adapt for gardens they might create themselves in the future. After another satisfying meal – with a choice of roast beef or pork – there was a good deal to talk about. They were all enthusiastic about what they had seen that day. Little groups formed and re-formed as they spent a leisurely evening.

Janet, it seemed, had struck up a friendship with Bob who had been part of their splinter group all day. At around nine o'clock Debbie found herself sitting on her own. She didn't mind; they all knew one another quite well by now, and she could easily go and join one or another of the little gatherings.

'Penny for them,' said a voice at her side. It was Alistair, smiling at her in that enigmatic way of his. 'You were miles away, Debbie ... and all on your own. That won't do, will it?'

'I'm quite happy, Alistair,' she answered. 'I'm on my own – at the moment – but not lonely, if you know what I mean. You can't be lonely in a jolly crowd like ours. We're having a great time, aren't we?'

'Yes, I agree. So we are. Mind if I join you?' He didn't wait for an answer, sitting down in the armchair opposite her. 'You were impressed, then, by all that we've seen today?'

'Very much so,' she replied. 'Not quite everything, though. I thought some of the features were way, way out. That fountain, and the cascade ... well, honestly! A case of one-upmanship, isn't it? Moderation in all things, that's what I believe in.'

'Yes...' Alistair gave another of his slow thoughtful smiles. 'That's by way of being your raison d'être, isn't it, Debbie?'

She gave him a quizzical look, feeling somewhat annoyed. She had often felt cross at the comments he made, although she knew he didn't do it just with her. 'I don't know what you mean,' she replied, dismissively.

'Sorry ... sorry,' he added. 'I didn't mean to offend you. Actually, it was meant as a compliment. And I agree with you about the ostentation. Not that we will ever be called upon to create such fantasies for our clients. Have you a job to go to, by the way, when you finish the course?'

311

'No, there's nothing in the pipeline, so far. What about you? Oh yes, I remember,' she added. 'You'll be going back to work for your father, won't you?' Fran had told them that his father owned a landscape gardening business in north Cheshire, not far from Knutsford.

'Working with my father, not for him,' he corrected her. 'I have shares in the firm, and he's promised to make me a partner – which I shall hold him to. I've come on this course to learn all I can and to bring the business into the twentieth century. Sometimes I feel that I'd like to move right away from Cheshire, but it's a good place to live, by and large. Some very wealthy folk in Cheshire who don't mind parting with their brass.'

'Where's Fran?' she asked now. She had also remembered that her friend had mentioned, casually, that there was a possibility that she might go and work with Alistair's firm.

'She's not with me, that's for sure,' he replied. 'She's over there.' He pointed a thumb in the direction of the small bar where Fran was standing with Stephanie, ordering drinks.

'You've had a row?' Debbie asked, carefully.

'Yes; makes a change, doesn't it?' He sounded more than a little sarcastic.

'Never mind; you'll soon make it up,' Debbie told him. She knew that the spats between them happened quite frequently.

'Not this time we won't,' he said. 'No; I think we've come to the parting of the ways. The fair Francesca only took up with me on the rebound, you know, when she broke up with her fiancé;

Ralph, wasn't it?'

Debbie nodded. 'Yes, that's right ... I don't think Fran really knows what she wants. She's a good friend, though. I thought she was a bit stuck-up at first, but she has a really kind and caring side, when you get to know her.'

'Then maybe I don't know her very well,' said Alistair. 'As you so rightly say, she doesn't know what she wants...' He paused. 'But I do.' He leaned forward in his chair, looking at her intently. 'Tell me, Debbie; how are things with you? Are you still seeing the fellow in the band; French horn player, isn't he?'

'Oh, you've heard about that, have you? Fran's been telling you stories?'

'She mentioned it, that's all. You'd been out with him that night when Lisa had her accident, hadn't you?'

'Oh yes, I'd forgotten that you'd met him.' She hadn't heard from Graham since her return to Leeds. She had only been back a couple of days before coming to Derby, but she had expected him to ring her. 'I still see him ... on and off,' she said, not sure why she was wanting to tell Alistair. 'He seems more interested in his band than he is in me.'

'Maybe he isn't sure what he wants, either?'

'No ... maybe not. I seem to be getting myself in a fair old muddle at the moment. there's Kevin at home, you see: I used to work with him at the garden centre. I write to him and I see him when I go home. He found out about Graham, and he wasn't best pleased, but Graham doesn't know about Kevin. So I don't know whether I have two

313

boyfriends or none at all.'

Alistair laughed. 'Oh, what a tangled web we weave...'

'I didn't mean to deceive either of them,' said Debbie. 'It's just – oh, I don't know!'

'I do,' said Alistair. 'Do you know, Debbie, I've wanted to get to know you better ever since we first met. But I knew you had a boyfriend at home; you mentioned him, though you may not remember. Then you seemed to be going steady with the chap in the band, at least that was what I thought. I've had some fun with Fran, even though we're always rowing; maybe we're too much alike, I don't know. But I do know that she's not the girl for me.'

Debbie was, momentarily, at a loss for words. There was no hint of mockery or sarcasm as Alistair smiled at her. He appeared to be sincere in what he was saying. 'I'd like to think you'd give me a chance, Debbie,' he went on. 'To start with we'll have a drink together, shall we? Whatever am I thinking of, us sitting here without a drink! What would you like?'

'Oh ... a sweet Martini, with lemonade,' she replied.

'Coming up right away,' he said, caressing her shoulder as he walked past.

She had already had a couple of drinks earlier in the evening and was feeling in a mellow mood; but she was not so muddleheaded as to trust Alistair entirely. But she was seeing a different side to him. Maybe he was not the playboy she had once thought him to be ... and she knew that she had, deep down, always felt attracted to his good looks and charm.

He was soon back with the drinks. 'Cheers, Debbie,' he said as he raised his glass. 'Here's to us. Would you consider having a night out with me when we get back to Leeds? But to start with ... maybe we could spend some time together tomorrow? We've two visits, haven't we, one in the morning and another in the afternoon?'

'Yes, why not?' she answered. It would do no harm to be friendly.

They talked together comfortably for the next half hour, and when she said it was time she retired, Alistair stood up with her. 'Me too,' he said. 'We've another full day tomorrow.'

As they walked out of the room together he put his arm casually round her waist. The bar had closed and most of the other students had gone, including Fran. They paused outside Debbie's door – Alistair's room was on the floor above – and he put his arms round her. Very gently he kissed her lips, a tender kiss, full of promise. But he did not linger.

'Goodnight, Debbie,' he said. 'It's been a lovely evening. See you tomorrow.'

'Yes, see you, Alistair...' she replied. She went to bed feeling bemused but strangely light-hearted.

The following day, Thursday, as had been pre-dicted, was a busy day. They set off after break-fast for Kedleston Hall; only four miles away from Derby. Debbie sat with Janet on the bus as she had done the day before. Alistair gave her a cheery smile and a nod as he passed to a seat further back.

Kedleston Hall was a grand country house with architecture in the Palladian style. The gardens and the grounds had scarcely been altered in style since they were designed two hundred years ago. There was plenty to see in the two hours they spent there, although the estate was small when compared with that of Chatsworth House.

As they wandered through the grounds in twos and threes rather than in one larger group, Alistair caught up with Debbie, and Janet and Bob encountered one another. Fran was walking round with two of the men; there was, of course, a preponderance of men. She gave a slow smile – a sort of 'Well, fancy that now!' sort of smile – as she walked past Debbie and Alistair and gave a little wave of her fingers. Debbie smiled back feeling a mite self-conscious, but Alistair took no notice. Fran didn't seem annoyed, although Debbie had not expected her to be. She had shown very little emotion when she broke up with Ralph, and she had always given the impression that her relationship with Alistair was a casual one.

The gardens had been designed by Robert Adam. There were several follies to be admired, or to be regarded with amusement: a triumphal arch, an ornate bridge spanning the stream, and a cascade, though not as grand as the one at Chatsworth. There was also a summer house and an orangery, and a Long Walk between tall trees now fully in bloom.

Packed lunch consisted of sandwiches, as it had done the day before. They set off then for their next port of call: Haddon Hall, not far from the pleasant town of Bakewell. They were to spend a couple of hours there before having some free time in the town itself.

Haddon Hall was quite a surprise: a sort of medieval castle with a garden that had been designed in the seventeenth century, one of the few still remaining in England. There was a balustraded terrace and ancient stone steps leading up to the house, and mullioned windows which glinted at oblique angles in the afternoon sunshine. Cameras were at the ready as they strolled round the garden, an English representation of a sixteenth-century Italian garden. Late spring flowers were in full bloom, but they were too early to see the reputed splendour of the rose garden, which was a twentieth-century addition to the grounds.

'That's the end of our educational visits,' said Mr Hartley when they gathered in the minibus once more. 'We'll have the usual meeting when we arrive back this evening, to exchange thoughts and ideas. But we are having two hours in Bakewell so that you can shop or have a cream tea, and don't forget to buy a Bakewell tart!'

'Actually, they call them Bakewell puddings,' Janet told Debbie as the bus set off. 'There's a little shop that sells them. It's their own special recipe and it's a closely guarded secret. I shall buy one to take back.'

Debbie decided that she would do the same. It would be a nice treat for the girls. If Fran had the same idea then they would enjoy a double treat. She discovered as she strolled round the town – Alistair having now come to join her – that there

317

were several shops that claimed to have pudding made to the original recipe. She chose the shop that looked the most authentic, a quaint little place with its window full of the oddly shaped tarts – or puddings. When Debbie's mother made her version of a Bakewell tart it was perfectly symmetrical. These were of irregular rounded shapes with a deep crust filled with a yellowy brown custard mixture sprinkled with nutmeg. Both she and Alistair bought one to treat their flatmates.

Bakewell was a pretty valley town surrounded by wooded hills stretching away to the high moorland of the Peak District. They climbed the steep steps of an old-fashioned little café to the top floor. There they looked out on the busy main street, enjoying freshly baked scones with jam and cream.

Debbie was having a lovely time, and thoughts of Kevin and of Graham did not intrude as she took pleasure in Alistair's company. He was not cynical or flippant, as she had sometimes known him to be. She wondered if that was a guise he liked to assume, and that this was the real Alistair that she was seeing now.

She told him that she intended to visit a gift shop she had noticed further up the street. She wanted to buy a gift for her mother, who loved all kinds of pretty ornaments. She suggested that he should make his own way back to the bus as her errand might not appeal to him, but he insisted on coming to the shop with her.

She was mesmerized by the dazzling display of goods; china tea sets, figurines, cut glass and silverware, most if it out of her price range but lovely to look at. Eventually she settled on a posy bowl with dainty spring flowers crafted from bone china. She had been undecided between that and a cute little china teddy bear. Her mother still treasured an old bear from her own childhood days. Debbie, too, had never parted with her first teddy bear.

'Let me buy that one for you,' said Alistair, picking up the little bear that she had put to one side. It really was cute; golden brown with a bonny face and a blue ribbon round its neck. She decided not to offend him by refusing his offer. Instead she said, 'Oh, how nice of you, Alistair! Thank you...'

At the same time she was seized by a feeling of déjà vu. She had owned a little bear once before, a pink fluffy one that she had called Rosie. She had learnt later that it had been left in her cot by her birth mother, Fiona, when she had been forced to give her up for adoption. Debbie had taken the little pink bear along with her when she had gone to seek out Fiona, and she had given the little bear back to her.

Fiona had told her how she had been given the bear by her boyfriend when they had visited the funfair at Battersea, back in 1951. They had been on a church visit to the Festival of Britain. Fiona had also told her what had happened later that evening, and how, consequently, she had found herself pregnant at the age of seventeen.

'What's the matter?' asked Alistair, noticing that she had suddenly gone quiet.

'Er ... nothing,' she said, smiling at him. 'Noth-

319

ing at all. It's lovely, Alistair.'

But the memory of what Fiona had told her niggled at the back of Debbie's mind, as though her birth mother was warning her to be careful. It had turned out well, though, for Fiona in the end. She, Debbie, was here as a result of that indiscretion. Moreover, she and Fiona had found one another and had become close friends. It was an example of 'things working together for good', a text she had heard Simon bring into his sermons more than once.

The group of students met together in the common room following the evening meal. When they had exchanged ideas and opinions about the gardens they had seen they stayed together as a group for a while, enjoying a last tête-a-tête and a drink to celebrate the three happy days they had spent together. New and closer friendships had been formed. They had all been acquainted with one another beforehand, but spending time in close proximity had cemented a few relationships.

Debbie and Alistair were alone together as the evening drew on. Fran was across the room with the two men, Dave and Barry, who she had been with earlier in the day. Debbie noticed her looking across a time or two, then looking away as Debbie caught her eye. She seemed happy, laughing and joking along with her two companions. Fran had an ease of manner that enabled her to socialize with most people.

Debbie's feeling of a warning voice in her mind receded as the time passed by. She was enjoying Alistair's company so much; he was witty and amusing, and very interested in her and her plans for the future. He even mentioned, tentatively, that there might be a possibility of her finding employment at his place of work, as an assistant in their team of landscape gardeners.

She nodded non-commitedly; she was not thinking of the future, only of the present, the here and now. What did it matter if she had drunk more than she usually did? Alistair kept topping up her glass with the sweet Martini that she liked, and she did not say no. She was starting to feel aroused in a way she had not done before, as she anticipated how the evening might end. They were not talking so much now as they sat close together with Alistair's arm around her.

Thoughts of her three flatmates flickered through her mind. She knew that Fran was experienced when it came to intimate relationships. She had spent several weekends with Ralph, in his flat or hers. And little Lisa had a secret smile and such an air of contentment that made Debbie wonder if she and Neil were not a great deal closer. And as for Karen ... Debbie felt that she was far more sensible and circumspect than she appeared to be, beneath all her bluff and bluster. But Debbie pushed that thought away as she was not feeling at all sensible.

Alistair turned his face towards hers and kissed her. 'I think it's time to call it a day, don't you?' he whispered. 'But there's still the night time ahead of us.'

She nodded silently as they got up and left the room. The few who remained paid no heed to them. She felt a sense of relief that Fran and her

321

friends had gone. They mounted the stairs with their arms around one another. As they paused at Debbie's door he kissed her again.

'I'll join you in a little while, shall I?' he said. He looked at her questioningly. 'You are sure about this, aren't you, Debbie?'

'Yes...' she replied. 'Quite sure.'

She entered the room and switched on the light. The bulb was covered by only a parchment shade and its harsh light shone down on the bed with its candlewick cover in an unappealing shade of olive green, the worn rug at the side of the bed and the cheap utility furniture. But what did they matter? She felt all tingly inside and soon she would forget all her inhibitions when Alistair's arms were around her.

She started to undress, taking off her jumper and skirt. She felt a little wobbly as she stood on one leg to remove her tights. She reached out to grab the side of the dressing table, and her eyes alighted on the little bear that Alistair had bought for her earlier that day. Just as it had that afternoon, the thought of that other little pink bear flashed into her mind ... and the memory of what Fiona had told her. How it could happen so quickly, so easily, especially if your head was in a whirl and you were not fully aware of what you were doing.

Suddenly, Debbie became fully aware of what was happening and what she had come so close to doing. It was as though Fiona was there, watching over her. Debbie knew that she must not go on with this, not because of what might happening as a consequence, but because it was wrong. She did not love Alistair. She doubted that he had any real feelings for her either. She quickly stepped into her skirt again and pulled her jumper over her head.

She sat on the edge of the bed. Her head was beginning to clear a little now as reality dawned upon her. She was feeling ashamed of herself, and stupid as well. What should she do? Tell Alistair that she had changed her mind, of course. And how would he react? She knew how sarcastic and mocking he could be sometimes; but it was not entirely his fault. She had come close to going along with it quite willingly.

There was no time to think about it any more, though. She heard Alistair's knock on the door, then he entered without waiting for her 'come in'. He stared at her.

'What's wrong, Debbie? I thought you'd be all ready and waiting in your sexy nightdress, or without it...'

She looked at him, opening her mouth to speak, when he spoke again. 'Oh, I get it. Changed your mind, have you? Well, I suppose I'm not surprised, really. I might have known – whatever would Mummy and Daddy say?'

She didn't like his mocking tone, but it might have been worse. At least he hadn't sworn at her or turned violent – not that she had really thought he would – or even raised his voice in anger. He was merely being cynical, a side to him that he had hidden so well over the last two days.

'I'm sorry, Alistair,' she began, although she wasn't sorry that she had changed her mind. But what else could she say? 'It's nothing to do with what my parents would think. But I don't love you, do I? And I know you don't love me. It ... it wouldn't be right.'

He gave a bitter laugh. 'What has love got to do with it? Have you never thought of having a bit of fun ... with somebody that you like? Where's the harm in that? Because I did ... I do like you, Debbie, and I thought you liked me.'

She nodded. 'I do like you, but I just can't ... do that.'

'Fair enough.' He gave a shrug and turned towards the door. 'Goodnight, Debbie. Sweet dreams!'

She burst into tears as she heard the door close, tears of relief. She had got out of that quite easily, but it didn't stop her from feeling no end of a fool.

Alistair nodded curtly at her the following morning, and Debbie half smiled at him. The four women in the group sat together for breakfast as they had done before.

Fran spoke quietly to Debbie. 'How are you and Alistair getting along? I couldn't help but notice...'

Debbie shook her head. 'We're not ... seeing one another. It was just ... well, whatever it was it's over now.'

'I'm very glad to hear it,' said Fran. 'I only mentioned it because I was concerned for you, Debbie. I'm not jealous; don't think that. It didn't work out for Alistair and me, and I know he's certainly not the right man for you.'

'Thanks, Fran; I know that myself,' she replied,

aware that her friend was perfectly sincere.

Debbie was glad to get back to college and the routine of lectures and study groups, and practical work in the gardens now that spring was well advanced. She and Alistair spoke to one another only when they needed to do so. And as far as the other two men in her life were concerned, things were very quiet there as well. Two weeks had gone by since the start of the term and she had not heard from Kevin. Neither, strangely, had she heard from Graham. She was beginning to wonder if she had burned her bridges with both of them.

Twenty-Two

'It's a lovely day,' Vera Hargreaves said to Stanley one Saturday afternoon in mid-May. 'Do you feel like a run out into the country, pet? Perhaps we could stop somewhere and have our tea? It'd be a nice little treat for us.'

'Yes, good idea,' he replied. 'I've something else in mind, though, that we could do first. How about a trip to the garden centre? It's time for bedding plants now, and they have a good selection at Sunnyhill. Mr Hill always gave me a discount when Debbie was working there.'

'She's not there now, Stanley.'

'No, but that doesn't matter, does it? He's very reasonable with his prices. And happen we'll be able to have a word with Kevin an' all. Nice lad, isn't he, Kevin Hill? We didn't see him very much, though, when our Debbie was home the last time. I thought they were getting ... you know ... more serious, like?'

'Oh, I don't know, Stanley. I think they might have had a bit of a fall out. Debbie didn't say so, but she was rather quiet about it, and I didn't ask. Anyway, like I keep saying, she's still very young.'

'She'll be nineteen next week...'

'Yes, I hadn't forgotten, Stanley. I must get her card in the post and I'll send a box of treats for them to eat, chocolate cake and biscuits and a couple of tins of salmon. And I've bought her that silver pendant that she liked in the jeweller's window.'

'It won't be long before she's home for good, will it?' Stanley remarked. 'Only two months or so, and she hasn't mentioned a job yet, has she?'

'No, but I dare say something will turn up, Stanley. She's a clever lass. She could've gone to college – proper college, I mean, or university – but she was so set on this gardening idea.'

'So long as she's happy, doing what she wants to do,' said Stanley. 'When she gets a job, though, it might be miles away. Have you thought about that, Vera?'

'Yes, I suppose I have, but it's time enough to worry about that if it happens. Now, we'd better be making a move, hadn't we? You go and start the car and I'll be with you in a jiffy.'

'What sort of flowers do you fancy, pet?' Stanley asked his wife as they drove along the country lanes.

'Oh, you're the expert, Stanley,' she replied. 'I just like a nice splash of colour. Begonias always do well, and Busy Lizzies; and marigolds, those nice big African ones.'

'Aye, and petunias, they make a good display. And how about some fuchsias; I thought I might make a hanging basket with trailing fuchsias–' He stopped talking suddenly, and Vera heard him give a gasp as though he was short of breath.

'What's the matter, Stanley?' she asked. 'Have you got that pain again?' He had complained a few times about indigestion recently, but it had passed off when he had taken a couple of Rennies.

'Aye, just a twinge,' he replied. 'It'll go off. We're nearly there, then we can go and have a cup of tea at that little café they've opened.'

'Stop the car, Stanley, and have a rest.'

'No; it'll be alright, I tell you. We'll be there in a minute or two.' He drove along slowly. Then, 'Oh, Vera ... oh, dear God!' he cried. 'I can't ... I can't breathe... Vera ... help me!'

He bent towards the steering wheel, trying desperately to hold on to it. Vera never knew what had happened. It was thought that his foot had landed on the accelerator pedal instead of the brake as the car sped away out of control, veered across the lane and crashed into the ditch.

Vera was knocked unconscious as she was thrown forwards, hitting her head against the windscreen. The next thing she was aware of was a knocking on the car window and someone opening the door. An anxious voice, a man's voice was saying he would get help, he would phone for an ambulance.

Vera opened her eyes and looked into the face of a complete stranger; a kindly middle-aged face, and his wife was beside him. 'Yes ... please,' Vera managed to gasp. 'My husband. Stanley ... heart attack, I think.' She knew that she was injured as well. She could feel blood running from a cut on her forehead and she was hurting all over. But she managed to get out the words, 'Garden centre ... up the road... Tell Mr Hill ... and Kevin ... friends of ours...' She slumped sideways as the pain became too much to bear.

'Stay here with them,' the man said to his wife. 'I'll drive back to Sunnyhill and phone for an ambulance. That poor chap doesn't look good to me. I hope he's going to make it.'

Mr Hill was surprised to see his last customer back again, and in a very anxious state. 'An accident ... just round the corner,' he began. 'A man and his wife; they're friends of yours, so the woman said. And she said to tell Kevin; he's your son, isn't he? We must get an ambulance, quick as we can.'

'Right away,' said Mr Hill. He dialled 999 and gave the details, then he called to Kevin who was working nearby.

Kevin was distressed when he heard that the car was a Ford Anglia, a blue one, and it was a middle-aged couple who had been injured. 'Most likely a heart attack,' said the man; he was a customer known to Kevin as Mr Armstrong. 'The woman, she said her husband was called Stanley. Then she passed out again, poor lass. They're friends of yours, she said.'

'Yes ... yes, they are,' replied Kevin, almost too

shocked to speak. 'Their daughter, Debbie ... she's my girlfriend.' He shook his head in a state of bewilderment. 'I must phone her, right away.'

It was late afternoon when Rhoda knocked, then poked her head round the door. 'Phone call for you, Debbie. I think it's that young man of yours.'

'Oh, thank you,' said Debbie. She didn't ask which one. Rhoda would find that very amusing, and sometimes she was far too nosy.

Debbie and Karen had just returned from a shopping trip to town and were having a cup of tea. It was Karen who remarked with a grin, 'Now, I wonder which one that'll be?'

'Haven't a clue,' said Debbie, 'but whichever one it is they took their time.'

When she picked up the phone and said a curt 'Hello...' she heard Kevin's voice.

'Hello, Debbie,' he began, sounding subdued, as well he might. But then he went on to say, 'I'm sorry; I have some bad news for you, It's your parents...'

'Why? What is it? What's happened?' She clung to the table for support, then sat down on the chair at the side, feeling her legs turn to jelly.

She listened intently as he told her about the accident. He guessed they were on their way to the garden centre – they were only a quarter of a mile or so away – when the car left the road and landed in the ditch. 'We think your dad must have had a heart attack. I don't know any more at the moment. My dad's gone back with Mr Armstrong – that's the man who came to tell us – to see how they are; and we've phoned for an ambulance. It should arrive very soon.'

'Oh! Oh no ... how awful!' Debbie was trembling and could hardly speak the words. But she knew what she had to do. 'I'll come as soon as I can,' she said. 'I'll get a train and I'll be there ... I don't know when, later tonight I expect.'

'No, Debbie,' said Kevin. 'I'll come and fetch you, right away. I'll find out what I can, then I'll drive down to Leeds. It'll take ... oh, about three hours, maybe more? But I'll be there. Just wait for me, and try not to worry.'

'Oh, Kevin ... thank you, so much!' She didn't try to dissuade him, to say she would be alright on the train, because she was so relieved to hear his familiar friendly voice, and she realized how much he cared about her.

'But you don't know where I am; you've never been,' she said feebly.

'Don't worry about that. I've got the address. I'll find it. You go and pack a case, and it'll be alright, you'll see. You've got me, Debbie, and I'll always be there for you ... bye for now. See you soon.'

Rhoda had disappeared, and Debbie didn't feel like telling her, just then, what had happened. She dashed back upstairs, and it was Karen who listened and comforted her as she broke down, unable to keep back her tears any longer.

It was Saturday evening, a time when most young people were out enjoying themselves, but her friends put aside their own plans and waited with her. It was around nine o'clock when Kevin arrived. Debbie dashed down the stairs when she

330

heard the bell ring. She had never been more pleased to see anyone. There was Kevin, smiling at her with his eyes full of concern. He opened his arms and she fell into them. They stood on the doorstep for a few moments as he held her close to him, then he kissed her gently. She was still fearing the worst, and she had to know.

'My mum and dad?' she said in a whisper. 'They're not...?' She couldn't say the word.

'No, they're alive,' said Kevin. 'I waited until I had some news before I set off. Your father had a heart attack at the wheel. He's still unconscious, but he's having the best possible care. Your mother was quite badly injured, and she's in a state of shock. But she'll pull through. You must believe, Debbie, that they'll both get well again.'

The other girls had not met Kevin before and they made a great fuss of him. Karen put the kettle on and Lisa made him some ham sandwiches. Fran talked to him about his garden centre, all of them trying to bring a feeling of normality to the situation. Debbie wanted to set off to Northumberland straight away, and Kevin would have done so; but the others persuaded her that he needed a rest after driving for such a long time. They would make up a bed for him on the settee, then they could set off in the morning when they had had a night's sleep.

Debbie could not rest, though, until she had rung the hospital in Whitesands Bay. She was informed, as a close family member, that Mr Hargreaves was 'critical but stable', and Mrs Hargreaves was 'fairly comfortable', which was the usual answer; but she was satisfied that the situ-

331

ation had not worsened.

'I don't know when I'll be back,' Debbie told her friends the following morning, as Kevin put her case into the boot of the car. She hugged them all, promising to let them know the news about her parents. 'Tell them at college about what is happening, and I'll write and explain,' she said. She smiled sadly at them as they stood waving as the car drove away.

'They're such lovely friends,' she remarked. 'I've been so lucky with my flatmates.'

'Yes; they're grand girls, all of them,' Kevin agreed.

'I don't think I'll be coming back,' she said. 'It'll be exam time in a few weeks from now, and I doubt that I'll be there.' She gave a deep sigh. 'But what does it matter? My mum and dad are more important than exams or anything. I've got to be with them, Kevin.'

'And you will be, very soon,' he assured her. 'Try to relax, Debbie, and try not to worry. They're in good hands.'

They didn't talk much on the journey up north. Debbie felt safe, and as hopeful as it was possible to be, because Kevin was with her. They broke their journey near Durham, where they had a quick meal of egg and chips at a roadside café. She understood that Kevin needed a break from driving.

'I must learn to drive, sometime,' she said, as they set off again.

'We have all the time in the world, pet,' he told her, reaching over and squeezing her hand. She smiled at him, certain now that Kevin would be an important part of her future.

They drove straight to the hospital. It was visiting time in the afternoon, although they would, no doubt, have been admitted anyway.

The doctor told Debbie that her father had had a heart attack while driving, which had caused the accident but, fortunately, he had no broken limbs. He had not regained consciousness, and was in a private room being closely monitored. She gathered that his heart attack had not been a massive one, which might have killed him. It was rather less severe, but his condition had been worsened with the shock of the crash. However, he was clinging on to life. She had been allowed a glimpse of him, pale and motionless, with an oxygen mask covering the lower part of his face.

Her mother was in a ward with three other women. Her head was bandaged and her arm in a plaster cast. Debbie had been told that she had a broken arm, a few cracked ribs and cuts and bruises. She would need to stay in hospital for a while as she had suffered from concussion at the time of the accident and was still in shock. Her eyes were closed, but she opened them as Debbie came up to the bed and touched her hand.

'Hello, Mum,' she said quietly.

'Oh ... oh, Debbie!' she cried in delight, trying to smile, although her face was badly bruised. 'You're here, and Kevin as well. How lovely!' Her voice was faint, but her eyes were bright despite the dark bruises around them. 'I knew you'd come...' Her smile faded as she went on. 'Your daddy is in a bad way, pet. They won't tell me very much, but I know that he is.'

'He'll be OK, Mum,' Debbie tried to reassure her. 'He looks peaceful, and they're taking great care of him. Just say a little prayer, and trust that he'll get well again.'

They didn't stay long that afternoon. Vera was trying bravely to talk, but her eyes kept closing and it was obvious that she was in pain and very tired.

'I'll come and see you again tomorrow,' said Debbie, kissing her cheek. 'Try not to worry, Mum. Just concentrate on getting better; you're doing fine.'

She was anxious to get home and sort herself out. It would be the first time she had been alone, completely alone, with no one else in the house. As they drove away from the hospital Kevin tried to persuade her to go home with him. 'My parents say that you can stay with us Debbie, until your mum comes out of hospital. They're concerned about you being on your own.'

She shook her head. 'No; I'm a big girl now, Kevin,' she said, trying to sound light-hearted. 'I'm OK, honestly. I must see to things at home, and I know that's where I'll have to stay. Mum will need me there when she comes home. She's not too good, is she, Kevin?' she asked a little fearfully.

'No, not at the moment,' he agreed, 'but she'll be much better in a day or two, you'll see. I shall come and pick you up each day to take you to the hospital. Dad is insistent that I must take as much time off as I need.'

Again, Debbie did not demur. 'Thank you,' she

said quietly, 'and to your parents as well. It was lucky – that's not really the right word, but you know what I mean – fortunate that they were so near to your place when they had the accident. And that your customer came along and found them.'

'Yes; Fate maybe, rather than luck,' said Kevin. 'Whatever it was, things could have turned out much worse.' Kevin's father had told him that it was the speedy attendance and the care of the ambulance men that had saved Stanley, in the nick of time. He had not told Debbie, however, that she had very nearly lost her father.

He carried her case into the hallway. 'Now, are you sure you'll be OK? Shall I stay with you for a while?'

Debbie assured him, despite an empty feeling inside her, that she would be fine.

'I'll call for you tomorrow afternoon, then. Try to keep hopeful and optimistic. They'll let you know at once if there's any change, you can be sure of that.'

He put his arms around her, holding her very close. 'Bye for now, Debbie, love, see you soon.' He kissed her tenderly and with a longing that she, too, felt deep inside her.

The house felt strange and empty. There were signs, though that her parents had expected to be back: her mother's slippers by the hearth, her father's newspaper on the chair where he always sat, and a few pots left draining in the kitchen. She found, to her surprise, that she was hungry, so she made a quick meal before unpacking her case. Her mother's fridge and cupboards were always well stocked. There was boiled ham, lettuce and tomatoes in the fridge, fresh bread in the bin, and her mum's home-made fruitcake and flapjack in the cake tin. She turned on the radio to combat the uncanny silence and heard the sound of a church congregation singing a hymn. Of course, it was Sunday. She had scarcely been aware of what day it was.

She resisted the temptation to ring the hospital. She did, however, ring her flatmates – via Rhoda – to tell them what was happening. She had been seized with the certainty as she unpacked her belongings that she would never be returning to college. Her mother would need her to be there when she came out of hospital; and her broken arm and other injuries would prevent Vera from caring for her husband as fully as she would wish to do.

All thoughts of the college course and the forthcoming exams had receded to the back of her mind. She was back at home now, and Debbie knew that it was where she was meant to be. A ray of hope that shone brightly on the uncertain path that lay ahead was that Kevin would be there with her. Whatever else might happen, she felt sure of that.

She also rang Simon and Fiona. Simon was at church taking the evening service, but Fiona was understandably distressed at her news. Her assurance of their loving thoughts and prayers meant a great deal to Debbie.

By the following afternoon Vera was a little brighter, not quite so tired, and eager to talk although she soon got out of breath. There was no change in Stanley's condition, but at least he was no worse and his heartbeat had steadied.

Vera was still lying down, her head raised on two pillows. Unfortunately, her right arm was in plaster, so it was her left hand that she stretched out towards Debbie as she approached the bed.

'Debbie, how lovely to see you, pet. And Kevin too.' She managed a coy smile. 'You two have made it up then, have you? I thought you'd fallen out.'

'Just a little misunderstanding, Mrs Hargreaves,' said Kevin. He and Debbie grinned at one another. 'But we're back together now, aren't we, Debbie?' The smile they exchanged spoke volumes.

'I'm very glad.' Vera nodded contentedly. 'Come and sit down and tell me what's going on.'

They passed on the good wishes of neighbours and friends, of Fiona and Simon, and Debbie's flatmates.

'And it's your birthday on Thursday, pet,' said Vera. 'I hoped I'd be home by then, but somehow I don't think I will.'

'Don't worry, Mum,' said Debbie. 'We'll have a celebration when you and Dad both get home.'

'I was talking about it to your daddy that day,' said Vera. 'Your card's all ready to be posted in the sideboard drawer, and a little present an' all. I hope you'll like it.'

'I know I will, Mum, but I'll wait till Thursday before I look at it.'

'Eeh, your daddy and me, we were making such plans for the garden. We were on our way to Sunnyhill to get some plants. Petunias, Stanley said, and he was going to make a hanging basket with fuchsias. And I said inlaced begonias and marigolds ... but it'll have to wait, and I doubt that Stanley'll be able to do it.'

Debbie and Kevin looked at one another. She knew that they were both having the same idea about the garden. They would choose the plants and she would put them in the garden. It would be a lovely surprise for them both, and it would give Debbie something to concentrate on in their absence.

'You're coming home with me,' Kevin told her when the visiting time came to an end. 'My parents insist that you come for a meal and stay as long as you like. You've nothing to rush back for, have you?'

Debbie was pleased to be going to Sunnyhill again. She had been happy working there part time when she was still at school, and she had always got on well with Arthur and Alice, Kevin's parents. They were both working, Arthur in one of the greenhouses and Alice at her flower arrangements, but they downed tools to welcome her.

Alice hugged her. 'We're delighted to see you, Debbie. Sorry about your parents. What a shock that was, but we were glad we were so near and able to help.'

Arthur put a friendly arm round her. 'Grand to see you, pet. Like old times, isn't it? Do you fancy giving Alice a hand while you're here. Flower arranging was always your forte, wasn't it?'

Debbie was happy to watch Mrs Hill at work again, and she helped by cutting off the long stems and trimming the superfluous leaves. Kevin's mum had taught her a lot about shape and design, although Debbie worked on much larger projects now.

'We're expanding the garden centre,' Mrs Hill told her. 'Arthur has great plans in mind, but I'll let him tell you about it later. Now, I think that's enough for today. You go and relax while I finish off what I'm doing in the kitchen.'

She refused Debbie's offer of help. 'No, you're a guest – and a very welcome one – and we think we'll be seeing a lot more of you now,' she added with a smile.

Kevin found her in the comfortable sitting room after he had helped his father to close up at the end of the day. 'We have a few more staff now,' he told her, 'which means that Dad isn't so overworked as he used to be. A lot of it was his own fault, mind, but he's learning to delegate some of the work to others... It's great to have you back here, Debbie.' He put his arm around her as they sat on the settee. 'Back at Sunnyhill as well as back with me. That's what started your enthusiasm for gardening, wasn't it?'

'Yes, partly,' she agreed, 'and my dad's influence as well. I used to help him in the garden almost as soon as I could walk and talk.'

She was more than ready for the steak and kidney pie and the sponge pudding that Alice had made. The conversation drifted to Debbie's college course, and the fact that she would miss the final exams.

'Nothing matters, though,' she said, 'so long as Mum and Dad get well again. I can do some more studying later on and get the qualifications I wanted.'

Arthur was looking at her intently. 'Why don't you come and work here?' he said.

She smiled, remembering the time when she had wanted to do just that. It had caused arguments with her parents when she had said that she didn't want to go into the sixth form or to college. She wanted to work at Sunnyhill full time instead of just at weekends and holiday times. Of course, it had been because of her infatuation with Kevin and her desire to be grown up and earn money instead of being a schoolgirl. But common sense had prevailed in the end. She had gone into the sixth form and then to college. Now she was back where she started.

'That's what I wanted to do when I was sixteen,' she said. 'I wanted to leave school. But you persuaded me to go to college, Mr Hill, and I know you were right.'

'That was because I knew you could go much further,' he replied. 'I'm not suggesting that you should come and work as an assistant gardener, or serve in the shop like you used to do. I want you to be in charge of our landscape gardening team.'

'But you haven't...?' she began. 'What do you mean?'

'I mean that we have great plans for the future of Sunnyhill. I mentioned to you a while back, at Christmas, I think it was, that we get asked about landscaping, by "do it yourself" enthusiasts as a rule; and we've been stocking fancy bricks and paving stones, trellis and that sort of stuff. But we

340

haven't got the expertise at the moment. That's where you come in, Debbie. We'd better tell her all about it, Alice.' His wife nodded approvingly, and Kevin smiled at her as though he already knew about it.

'We've been wanting to expand our business for quite some time,' Arthur continued, 'but we didn't have the brass, and we didn't want to take on a huge loan. Anyway, a couple of months ago Alice's old aunty died. It was sad, like; she was a grand old lady, but we weren't heartbroken 'cause she'd had a good innings; she was ninety-five. She left everything she had to Alice; she had no other close relations – Alice's parents have both gone now – and Alice was the one who was good to her, like a daughter, you might say. But we didn't realize just how much she was worth, did we, pet?'

Alice shook her head. 'No; we knew she had her house in Darlington – she'd managed to stay there almost till the end – but we didn't know she had thousands stashed away and invested. We only found out a few weeks ago. So we're going to in-vest it all in the business. What else would I do with it? Arthur said would I like to go on a cruise, but I said no. I think he was only joking anyroad! We might have a holiday somewhere this summer; it's ages since we went away. But we've got great plans for the rest of it.'

'Aye, so we have.' Arthur took up the story. 'We've already got the little café and that's going splendidly. But the main idea is to go in for landscape gardening. There are already a couple of firms in the area, so we decided we must get in

341

there an' all. And we've got our designer all ready and waiting, haven't we?' He looked eagerly at Debbie.

'But I'm not qualified yet,' she said. 'That's what I was saying; I shall miss the exams.'

'You're qualified enough for us, Debbie,' said Arthur, 'and, like you said, you can get the diploma you want in the near future, maybe a night school course. Our Kevin's going to night school, and he'll be in charge of the office work and do his share of gardening now and again. And Alice has the shop and her flower arrangements and vases and suchlike. And as for me, I suppose I'll be the gaffer, but I've never gone to do any studying; I've picked it all up as I've gone along. I thought I knew it all, but Kevin's already shown me that there's a lot more to this gardening business than meets the eye.'

'Yes, I thought I knew quite a lot,' said Debbie, 'but I've widened my experience with these last months at college.' She looked across the table to Arthur. 'What can I say but thank you. I'd love to do what you suggest ... but it isn't because you feel sorry for me, is it? With my parents, and everything?'

'Not at all,' Arthur said decidedly. 'We've had you in mind from the start. We knew you'd finish college in a couple of months and be looking for employment. Unless you'd already been offered a job elsewhere, of course?'

'No; I was waiting for something to turn up ... and now it has.' Was it what she had been waiting for all along? Debbie wondered. She had known, when the accident happened, that she would need to stay up here with her parents. And this was a stroke of good fortune in the midst of all the uncertainty.

'Let's leave the washing up and have a drink to celebrate,' said Alice.

'Here's to the future, and to Sunnyhill,' said Arthur when they were all seated in the lounge with glasses of rich cream sherry. They raised their glasses. 'To the future,' they echoed.

Debbie was feeling mixed emotions. She was happy that her career prospects were hopeful, but the anxiety about her parents was still with her. Arthur had not forgotten.

'And here's to Vera and Stanley,' he said. 'May they soon be back with us again ... please God,' he added.

Cards were already arriving for Debbie's birthday. There was one from each of her flatmates, from Fiona and Simon, a special one from the children, made by Stella, and one from Graham. She had written to tell him what had happened and that she would be staying in Whitesands Bay. He said he was sorry, and hoped he would see her soon. It probably hadn't dawned on him that she would not be returning to Leeds at all.

She was delighted with the silver pendant that her mother had bought for her; an abstract modern design that she had admired in the jeweller's window. How thoughtful of Mum to have remembered.

Kevin arrived on Thursday afternoon to take her to visit her parents. 'Happy birthday, Debbie love.' He hugged and kissed her. 'As happy as it can be, I mean...' Each day they had been waiting for her father to regain consciousness.

He handed her a small box; it was a ring box. 'I can't buy you the proper ring just yet,' he told her, 'if you know what I mean. But you know how I feel about you, and sometime soon, I hope...' There was no need to say any more. It was not the time to be thinking of an engagement and long-term plans; but they both knew what they wanted.

The ring was a wide silver one in a modern design, engraved with tiny hearts and flowers. It fitted exactly on the middle finger of her left hand. 'Thank you; it's just perfect,' she said. She hugged him, and as he held her close she knew that was how it would be for ever.

The best birthday present of all was the news that Stanley had opened his eyes that morning. 'He's still confused,' the nurse told them as they entered his room, 'but he's back with us and we're satisfied that all seems to be well.'

His eyes were closed but he was breathing normally. His face was pale and the few day's growth of beard made him look older. He looked different, somehow; as though he was no longer in another world, apart from them.

Debbie touched his hand. 'Hello, Dad...' she said.

He opened his eyes, staring uncertainly for a moment. Then, 'Debbie!' he cried, his voice husky with lack of use. 'Grand to see you, pet.'

'And you too, Dad,' she replied, although she could scarcely speak as tears of happiness welled up in her eyes. 'You're going to get well again now.'

The nurse had advised them not to stay long.

His eyes were closing as they left him and went off to share the good news with Vera. Further good news was that she would be allowed home in a few days' time.

Epilogue

Debbie did not return to college to complete her course and to take the exams. She was, however, given glowing testimonials from the lecturers and urged to continue with her studies when she was able to do so.

Vera's injuries prevented her from doing much in the home for several months. Her fighting spirit, though, made her determined not to give in, and by the end of the summer she was almost back to her normal self.

Stanley's heart attack had been a severe warning that all was not well. His heart condition prevented him from returning to work, and he realized, sensibly, that he had to do as he was told. He contented himself with his own garden; he was delighted that Debbie and Kevin had planted and nurtured the flowers that he and Vera had intended to buy.

It had come as a shock to Debbie to be suddenly catapulted back to her home life in Whitesands Bay. One moment, it seemed, she had been engrossed in her work at college, and the next minute it had all come to an abrupt end. One of the worst aspects was the ending of the happy times in the flat with Lisa, Fran and Karen. It was amazing how close they had all become in such a short time. She knew, though, that the friendships they had formed would be lasting ones. She was keeping in touch with them all, especially with Lisa, who said she was missing her very much.

She had received a letter from Graham, saying that he valued her friendship, but that he was now friendly with Felicity, the girl who played the French horn with him in the band. Debbie was not surprised to hear the news, and she wrote to wish him well. They would be able to play duets together.

In September she enlisted on the night school courses that would enable her to gain the diploma she wanted. In the meantime, though, she was already working at Sunnyhill as a designer and the supervisor of the team of landscape gardeners. The work there was going on apace. Mr Hill had purchased an adjoining plot of land. A new office was being constructed there, and all the requisites for those who wished to do their own garden designing: bricks and stones of all shapes, colours and sizes; decking; fencing; trellis; water features; urns and containers. For those who needed guidance and help, or someone to do the job for them, there was a team of experts who would plan and undertake the work.

On a sunny day in June 1972, the parish church in Whitesands Bay was half full with guests, and others who wanted to be there to wish them well. Debbie and Kevin had been engaged since last

Christmas, and now it was their wedding day.

They had both decided that they didn't want a lavish wedding with lots of guests, but just a simple affair with those nearest and dearest to them. Nor did Debbie want a large retinue of attendants. As she came down the aisle on her father's arm, wearing a simple dress of ivory satin, with a short veil, she was followed by two bridesmaids dressed in cornflower blue. Her chief bridesmaid was Lisa; she was proudly wearing an engagement ring, but she had promised her parents that she and Neil would not get married until the following year when she was twenty-one.

The other bridesmaid was Stella, now aged five and a half. Debbie could not possibly have resisted her little half-sister's pleas to be a bridesmaid. It would have been nice to have had three-year-old Michelle as well, but both Fiona and Debbie had decided against it. Matthew and Mark, now the best of friends – well, most of the time – would have wanted to be included, and that might have been too much to cope with.

There they all were, though, sitting beside Fiona, turning their heads to look at Debbie as she made her way down the aisle. She smiled at them all, and little Matthew gave a cheeky wave. Simon, at Debbie's request was helping to officiate at the wedding service along with their own vicar.

She acknowledged the wide grins of Fran and Karen sitting together, neither of them with a partner. Debbie had heard that Fran was 'seeing' a rather older man, but there were complications, and Karen was said to be between boyfriends at the moment.

Vera smiled lovingly at her daughter as she passed, looking proud and happy, and elegant in a flowered summer suit with a wide-brimmed hat. Debbie handed her bouquet to Lisa and turned to face Kevin. They exchanged adoring glances as the congregation started to sing... 'Now Thank We All Our God...'

The publishers hope that this book has given you enjoyable reading. Large Print Books are especially designed to be as easy to see and hold as possible. If you wish a complete list of our books please ask at your local library or write directly to:

Magna Large Print Books
Magna House, Long Preston,
Skipton, North Yorkshire.
BD23 4ND

This Large Print Book for the partially sighted, who cannot read normal print, is published under the auspices of

THE ULVERSCROFT FOUNDATION